Core Drift

A Coruscant novel

FX HOLDEN

Copyright © 2021
FX Holden

This novel is an adaptation of an earlier manuscript titled 'Vanirim', edited and updated to the Coruscant universe. All rights reserved. No part of this book may be reproduced in any form, except in the form of brief quotations for review or academic use, without permission in writing from the author/publisher.
This book is a work of fiction. Any references to historical events, real people, or real locales are used fictitiously. Other names, characters, places and incidents are products of the author's imagination and any resemblance to actual events or locales and persons living or dead is entirely coincidental.
Independently published in Birkerød Denmark

All novels in the Coruscant series are stand-alone stories based in the Coruscant universe
Other books in the Coruscant series
Deep Core

Contact the author at
FXHolden@yandex.com

With deepest thanks to Lise, Asta and Kristian who lost me for many hours to the demon of the word.

Contents

1. The First ... 6
2. The Mirror ... 18
3. The Second ... 25
4. The Letter ... 68
5. The Kiss ... 75
6. The Expositor ... 81
7. The Soldier ... 91
8. The Miner ... 97
9. The Third ... 106
10. The Fugitive ... 112
11. The Hunter ... 120
12. The Pickpocket ... 136
14. The Handover ... 146
15. The Law ... 152
16. The Fourth ... 155
17. The Underbelly ... 161
18. The Advocate ... 168
19. The Ghost ... 182
20. The Prosecutor ... 187
21. The Leader ... 199
22. The Protocol ... 222
23. The Code ... 235
24. The Sixth ... 252
26. The Revolutionaries ... 270
COMMONWEALTH OF CORUSCANT PRIMER ... 280
CORE MELT ... 287

1. THE FIRST

The blood of the human is a different color to ours. Bright cherry red. Ours is darker, more ruby red. And human blood flows more freely. There is so much of it after all. It makes streams and rivulets. Ours pools and clots.

Better not say that to the police. What *can* I tell them?

I just walked in and found him here. It was one p.m.

I've worked with this person for about two years. Why did I wait so long to call the police? I don't know. I don't know why I didn't call straight away. I just stood here and looked at it. Have you seen how much blood came out of his body? The way it spills across the floor of the lounge toward the front door, like even his blood was trying to escape?

I didn't know it was possible to kill a person like that. Gut him? *Who* could do that, *what* could do it – except for another human?

I won't tell them what I saw in the mirror.

Let me say, here and now, I was under no illusions that me being the first one at this killing was Not A Good Thing. To be the first cyber on the scene and discover a dead human, gutted? That doesn't make anyone's bucket list.

To make things worse, if that could be possible, the dead citizen was a Sanctioner. A People's Republic of Coruscant official who is responsible for punishing criminals.

It will just be a matter of minutes now until the Police and the Security Service with their Wards arrive. The PRC Security Service, or SS, brags about how all its officers are unarmed, but they don't need to be armed. Everywhere they go, their Wards are with them. Cybers, like me, but patterned on PRC animals, not humans. They are black-scaled, big, the size of maybe a panther or lion, incredibly fast, moving on two legs, with large wings they fold over their backs. Large enough to be imposing, but small enough to be able to enter any house or building. They aren't exactly aggressive, but they are decisive. Using their wings or long, elegant tails and strong hind legs they can trap you, block you, pin you, or in other ways passively prevent you from whatever you are trying to do, with very little risk to themselves. If that fails, they can stun you, with a neural blow like a mental thunderclap. No hangover devised can equate to how you feel after being stunned by a Ward. When you eventually wake up. You can take my word on that.

I'm a domestic violence caseworker, with the Department of Community Services in the PRC capital of New Guangzhou. It's not as exciting as it sounds. (That was a joke. Sorry, jokes aren't my strong point anymore.)

There are two parts to the job, the casework intervention, which is pretty much like it is in any city on any moon in Coruscant, and then the Sanctions. The casework comes to me when a citizen is sentenced for lesser cases of domestic violence and an SS judge sends them home on probation with the threat of prison or a Sanction, and an order to behave and see someone like me once a week/fortnight/month. I make sure they are behaving; I teach them what good behavior looks like. You wouldn't believe how many men still abuse their wives and children, even when they know it contravenes the Law. And yes, it is usually men. In fact, in all these years I saw maybe one woman who used to beat her children, or actually, burn them, when she was off her face on Creep. She was my first Sanction.

The SS is the judicial arm of the post-war government. Think secret police and secret court, rolled into one. The SS administers the Law.

For those who can't or won't learn – the repeat offenders, recidivists, or the just plain dumb – I have the power to request a Sanction. I don't use it often. Only an SS Sanctioner can conduct a Sanction, so when it happens, I meet with the Sanctioner to manage the family liaison side of things. That's what was happening today. Today we had an order to carry out a Sanction at this address.

The order for a Sanction is always issued in secret. There is a lot of fear and misunderstanding still about the process of being Sanctioned, and people will often flee, or fight, to avoid it. That usually only ends in harm to themselves or those around them, so we do it this way: when the case has been judged and the Sanction ordered, first I make a routine appointment with the criminal, and preferably also their family or a close friend, and then when we are all there, I send a signal to the Sanctioner. He or she arrives and then it can get a bit tense. But a Sanctioner arrives in the company of Wards with powers to subdue, immobilize and restrain, so one way or another, it usually goes smoothly.

Family, friends or neighbors can sometimes be a problem though, in which case we would take some police with us, but the family generally welcomes the Sanctioning once I explain it. I mean, these are people living through the hell of domestic violence, and we are offering them a solution. I can usually talk them around.

The criminal gets to choose. This is important. Everyone who has ever been Sanctioned has chosen to be. The choice is a simple one: Sanctioning, or life in prison. And by that, the humans really mean *life, in prison*. If the criminal has family or friends there, they can discuss it with them before they choose. Most families don't want to lose their father or husband to prison. Most criminals don't want to grow old and die in prison either. They almost always choose Sanction. But if they can't decide, the default is prison.

Sanction. That is the PRC name for it. We cybers have a name for it too. We call it 'cauterization'. The way the Sanctioner reaches into your mind and sears away the part of you that can hate, that feels anger. But taking with it the part that loves, too. Afterward, when it is done, the criminal is no longer violent, which is usually a huge relief to partner and family. Of course, at first, it seems like they are no longer themselves either. They are neither too happy, nor too sad. They feel attachment, but not exactly love. They work with resolve, but no longer with passion. But they learn, and they adapt, and gradually some of the person they were returns.

Never fully though, never really. But enough that it is better than the alternative, which is the abuser, the beater, the torturer.

Sanction is the ultimate penalty for the ultimate crimes: crimes of violence against other people, against the environment, and against nature. Only those. You could get caught for stealing a billion credits and you wouldn't face Sanction. Unless you did it at the point of a knife. Or you could just knock down an old lady in the street and steal her purse. First offense, the PRC Security Service would probably give you another chance, a chance to reform, knowing you don't get a second chance. Next time, it would be Sanction or life in prison. *Death* in prison, to be exact.

For 90 percent of people a Sanction is a better choice than dying in prison. PRC is 90 percent red sand desert above subsurface ammonia seas and the prisons are all either surrounded by a sea of sand, or a sea of sand leaking ammonia. The view alone can drive a sane citizen mad, so the prisoners' cells are lined with holo walls showing cityscapes.

But Sanction is still the better option for most, if you ask me. Doctors, Advocates, manual laborers, after they've been Sanctioned they can still go to work, live their lives, stay with their families. Some describe it as a life lived in sepia rather than color. But a life in color, behind bars? That is no life either. Like I said, for most, Sanction is the right choice. For artists and musicians, though, prison is definitely the best. You take passion and emotion away from artists, and their art dies. They and their families usually choose prison, knowing that painters will still be able to paint in jail; musicians will still be allowed to play.

Whether you choose Sanction or prison, as soon as you are judged guilty, you are stripped of your citizenship, your right to vote, to participate in any sort of decision making in normal society. It's just a legal mechanism created to allow the State to withdraw certain freedoms and impose punishments, like Sanction and lifetime imprisonment, which otherwise are not allowed to be applied to PRC or Tatsensui citizens under the Articles of Alignment.

My name is Fan Zhaofeng. I'm nineteen years old and I am the only living cyber who has ever been Sanctioned.

It's not something I put on job applications.

The client, the citizen who was to be Sanctioned this time, is not here. His name was Le Thuyen.

Something went wrong. Obviously. But before the killing, I mean. Like I said, the way it is supposed to work is, I make a routine appointment with the Sanctionee and their family. They don't know there has been a judgment, and a Sanction ordered. Once I'm with them, I hit a button on my holo unit, which calls in the Sanctioner. Then he or she takes over with their SS team, the criminal is subdued, and I facilitate, usually just by getting the family together and talking the whole Sanction thing through. There's a lot of crying, though sometimes it's from relief.

Then the criminal is allowed to speak, discuss with their family or friends, and choose: Sanction or prison.

But I got here today and there was no Le Thuyen and family. There was just one dead Sanctioner. Someone had called him in early, and killed him. So of course they suspect me, even though it's impossible.

My theory, I'm telling the PRC Security Service officer, it was an insider. Someone in the SS. "Who else would have known he was going to be here? Whoever did this was waiting for him."

There are both humans and cybers working with the PRC Security Service, but this SS officer is a cyber, so he is capturing all I say, doesn't write anything down. He's looking at me with a squint.

"Yeah, that's a theory," he says. "Except there was one other person who knew he was going to be here."

"Me? Sure," I tell him. "That's a fair theory too."

"You don't seem too freaked out by that," he says.

I shrug. "I'm a cyber," I tell him. "I can't commit murder." Even though I know I would normally be a prime suspect, I'm both a cyber and a Sanctionee. I can't hide anything. As a Core-chained cyber, every moment of my life is uploaded to the Core for the SS to see. Every protocol in my wetware prohibits me from violence. As a Sanctionee, I am incapable of hate, or rage, or even malign intent. I look down at the dead Sanctioner. "You'd need a heck of a blade."

He bends and looks at the wound. "The skin looks cauterized along the edges. Something hot," he says. "A dark matter lance would do it."

"Oh yeah, just pick up one of those at the local supermarket, I guess."

"Sure, they're hard to come by…" The SS trooper looks up from the bodies. "But not impossible."

As he speaks, a Ward prowls behind him. His, I assume. "A Sanctioner is usually accompanied by SS Wards," I point out. "So, where were his?"

The SS trooper considers this. "He came alone for some reason, it seems."

I'm thinking, oh right, the most hated official in all the SS and he decides to just bowl in for a Sanction on his lonesome?

"Is he…have you heard of anyone else being killed like that?" I ask the trooper straight out. "Sliced open from neck to navel? I mean, that's not just a murder, that's a *statement*."

"Maybe, maybe not," he says enigmatically, stepping with some difficulty around the blood to the front door. "You can wait outside with me."

When the SS Expositor arrives, it's starting to get a bit crowded so she sends her Ward to circle overhead.

I realize I know her. This is another one of those times where I know something, but it's unfortunate, the circumstances of the knowing. A few months ago she came with her cyber partner to an incident where a man shot his wife and was going to shoot his baby and then himself but he couldn't, so he just shot himself. The neighbors heard. The police called the Department of Community Services to come and get the baby, and they sent me. The SS were there because, well, when there is violence, they are always there.

I don't get romantic thoughts anymore. But I still know a good-looking girl when I see one. She was young, that was my first thought. Maybe sixteen, seventeen. OK, that's unusual for an Expositor. Old Earth looking…long dark hair, not too tall, a little chubby, looked both strong and cute. Kind of kick-your-ass cute.

I could see she was affected when I arrived to pick the baby up. She was holding the baby in her arms and rocking it to and fro, this dead man on the floor next to her, and she was beside the table rocking the baby. She looked a couple of years younger than me.

I tapped her shoulder to let her know I was there. She looked at me, then looked around vaguely, but all the other officers were outside. I spoke gently. "Expositor, I can take the baby," I told her, and she looked at me for the first time.

I often think to myself, what did she see that first time? A tall, kind of awkward guy probably. Not thin, but wiry. Trousers a bit loose on his hips, shirt probably worn more than once between washes. Hair, well, call that wiry as well. Dirty blonde and wiry. Blue Core-link diode between my brows, pulsing softly. Tattoo on my forearm of a pre-Alignment flag.

She didn't move to give me the child, just kept rocking it. "I can't reproduce," she said quietly. "But this…mongrel…here," she was talking about the dead guy under the table, "had an angel like this and it wasn't enough for him."

I looked at the dead guy. I could only see his trousers, his feet and a big belly, a couple of pretty hairy arms. "Some people kill themselves because they don't think they can live up to the expectations they see in those little eyes," I told her.

She looked at me coldly, her brown eyes suddenly jet black. "Are you saying that you can understand why someone would do something like this?" Expositors' eyes do that, even though they are human. It's something that happens when they finish training and get Core-paired. SS officers are the only humans with a neural link to the Core. It's not a big fat 'always-on' pipe like mine, they have to drift to make the connection. Their irises change color when they are Core drifting: accessing the Core to retrieve or store data. It's something to do with the surgery they get to hook their visual cortex into a Core feed.

I shrugged. "I understand the how, I don't pretend to understand the why," I told her.

She thought about this for a minute, but then decided it was all too much and piled the baby in my arms. She turned and left, and I took the baby.

It seems she recognizes me today, because she nods, and then goes inside with her partner – a big guy, looks like a competitive swimmer. You have to be big to be a swimmer. Big legs, big lungs. And fearless.

I mean, whose idea of fun is dropping down a hole drilled into the desert to reach the liquid ammonia or water beneath, dive into the freezing sea, and then swim toward another hole drilled into the desert anywhere from a half mile to five miles away? In water, there are sharks, in ammonia it's the eels. Deciding how much air to take is one of those win-lose decisions you have to make because the more air you take, the heavier you are going to be. But lose your way in the dark, you're stuck under there with nothing but your little mayday beacon, hoping a rescue team reaches you before your air runs out. No thanks.

He's got bronze skin, dark hair, blue eyes, broad shoulders tapering to a small waist, strong thighs, big but finely boned hands with elegant fingers. Gene mods, I'm guessing, so he's wealthy too. He's dressed casually in a shirt and trousers, but you can see the play of the muscles across his back as he bends to look at the body of the Sanctioner.

He walks over. "I want permission to pull your Core cache," he says. No 'hi, how you doing?' I could make him get a court order, but that would just slow things down – he'd get one eventually. He knows I know that. He wants to see if I called in the Sanctioner early. The girl comes outside again and stands beside us. I open my cache and patch him in.

His eyes blink black and then blue again. "There's no call there," he says to her. "And his movement log looks clean but have it cross-checked anyway." He holds out his hand for my holo unit, hands it to the junior Expositor, and she puts it in a bag and tags it.

Usually, SS Expositors work in human-cyber teams. A cyber doesn't have the same authority as a human, but even Core-paired humans can't link or think as quickly as a cyber, so the pairing makes sense. But these two, human and human, that's a little unusual. You only see that for the most serious or politically sensitive crimes, so that tells me where they rate this one.

What's also unusual, like I said, is that she's so young. She can't be long out of school. Every senior Expositor chooses their own partner. I wonder why this one chose her?

An ambulance arrives too, and then another SS officer, a heavyweight this time, and then a run of the mill police holographer. There are cops and medics and forensic officers and SS officers, with and without Wards. It's quite a circus.

I get taken to the local SS station and say everything over again into a recorder for a police officer. Then I have to wait, which is boring, even though they give me coffee and there is a chat show on the holo viewer in their kitchen. The girl, the junior Expositor, comes in after about two hours.

"Sorry you had to wait," she says, and maybe she means it. "I'm Expositor Lin Ming. That was a pretty ugly sight. How are you?"

"Fine," I tell her. "What about the Sanctionee, Mr. Thuyen, and his wife? I was supposed to meet them…"

"They're missing."

"Are they suspects?"

"At this stage," she says. Her eyes are green now. Is that normal for her, or is that a mood? You have to know the Expositor to know the color matching the mood. "I think you could say anyone connected to the crime is a suspect. And my colleagues seem especially excited about you."

"Me?"

"Especially."

This is my first time in front of the SS in an investigation, and I'm curious. For me it's hard to see why they are so distrusted, even feared. All the Sanctioners I have worked with have been very compassionate, considering what they do. And this girl is quite friendly. Young, relaxed, but with a natural authority. I guess just being SS gives you that.

Her partner doesn't seem so friendly. He comes quietly into the room. Seems full of suppressed energy, even standing perfectly still.

He blinks slowly, eyes closing like blinds. "I don't think introductions were made when we met. I'm Senior Expositor Vali."

"I'm Fan Zhaofeng. I can call you Vali?"

"No, you can call me Expositor." It's not said with humor.

I'm guessing he's not a fan of Socialization theory. As part of the Articles of Alignment adopted after PRC lost the Energy War, we got similar rights to Tatsensui cybers, including the right to be regarded as legal and social equals. Socialization theory is the name for the idea that all sentient entities should have the right to be treated as citizens.

It hasn't always been so. First we were treated like machines. Then like slaves. The principles of Socialization haven't been written into the Constitution yet, though, and a lot of humans still regard them as 'guidelines', not laws. Rights don't always equal realities.

But human or cyber, we all live under the three tenets of the Law.

1. No violence between citizens
2. No violence against Environment
3. No violence against Nature

It's been nearly five years since the Energy War with Tatsensui ended and the Socialization began. It feels almost normal now, to me at least. The humans live alongside us, and our way is the Law. There are no sealed communities anymore where only humans are allowed to live, no meeting places on PRC where only humans can enter. They tell us we are all equal before the Law. That the Law applies to us, both cyber and human. Enforced by the PRC Security Service without discrimination. I haven't seen enough to doubt it.

Socialization theory says we are all adapting to a new age, both cyber and human, and it must be given time to normalize. But after more than five years of war, and five years of peace, there is still some adapting to be done.

He settles and looks to the junior Expositor, Lin. She nods as if to say, *you go ahead*.

"Tell me what happened there," Vali asks.

I tell him what I rehearsed. What I told the other officer at the house, and the police. I don't want to get it wrong.

When I'm finished he tilts his head. "And you stood like that for twenty minutes? Just looking at Sanctioner Huang's body before you called the police?"

"Yeah. I can't explain why. I mean, I knew him pretty well, Sanctioner Huang. We'd done maybe nine Sanctions together. It's not easy. You develop an understanding, how to go about it. Huang was a very good Sanctioner."

Vali just looks at me, waiting.

"Look, I can't explain it, I guess it was shock."

"Shock. I see." I decide to try to like him. His sun-browned skin glows with health. Typical for a human. I've got Old Earth Irish DNA myself, my parents say. I trust them on that, after all, they chose it. Chinese DNA mostly, though, of course. Vali continues. "I understand you are a Sanctionee. Shock isn't a word I would usually associate with those who have been…"

"Cauterized?" I interrupt. The junior Expositor, Lin, shoots a look at me and then at Vali, her eyes narrowing. Oh, so she didn't know.

"Sanctioned," he says. "Emotions are suppressed. You shouldn't shock easily."

"I don't. It was not a normal sight," I point out to them.

"The things Man does to Man," he says and shakes his head.

"If it was Man."

"No cyber could do this."

"You are making a dangerous assumption," I point out to him. "Which rules out nearly half of the population." Lin looks sharply at me, but I quickly dive the Core and continue. "Whatever. The number of confirmed attacks by cybers on humans is zero, so you are probably right."

He considers this. "So, Fan, I assume you have allocated a lot of bandwidth to analyzing this event. Do you have a theory?"

He's right. I have. I'm glad he asks. A lot of humans wouldn't – they prefer to rely on their own instincts and analysis, and not let data get in the way of their investigations. It's a game for them; they like to play it old style. But once you have a suspect, it all comes down to the data eventually, in my book.

"Have you heard of the story of Tokoyo and Yofune-Nushi?" I ask.

"No, I haven't. Why don't you save the SS a few credits and tell us, Fan?" he says.

Core drifting costs credits for humans, even if you are the SS. I guess they have a budget, like everyone else. Since I am a bandwidth supplier I don't pay, but every time I drift it reduces the amount I can earn for the day so it's more or less the same thing. It's all part of the bandwidth economy that underpins the economic freedom of Core-chained cybers like me. I can sell part or all of my onboard processing power back to the Core, use it myself, or trade it for goods and services.

"Well, on Old Earth Japan, there was a sea serpent called Yofune-Nushi. Every year he would rise from the sea off the coast and demand a female virgin as a sacrifice. One year, the people chose as their sacrifice a farm girl called Tokoyo."

"Fascinating," Vali says. "So what?"

Lin has been looking down at her hands but looks up at me and rolls her eyes. "I'm the patient one, not him," she warns. "For future reference. Please continue."

"Tokoyo was standing on the sacrificial platform when the monster rose out of the sea in front of her. She dived off the platform, pulled her father's sword from her robes, and cut the serpent open from head to tail," I tell them, and sit back with a slight smile. Not because the allegory makes me happy, but because I know smiling indicates a non-threatening intent.

"Apart from the fact that Sanctioner Huang was disemboweled, how is this fairy story relevant?" Vali asks.

"Firstly, you assume it was a fairy story," I warn him again. "Haven't we seen enough extra-terrestrial lifeforms now to know anything and everything is possible, even sea serpents?" Vali doesn't reply, just looks annoyed. "Very well. In Ancient Japanese culture the symbolism of disembowelment was quite prominent. Samurai disemboweled themselves after the death of their masters, or following an embarrassing defeat, in a tradition known as *Seppuku*. It was a ritual intended to restore honor."

"Are you suggesting Sanctioner Huang disemboweled himself in an act of *Seppuku?*" Lin asks.

"It's a possibility, if you assess it likely that he was disemboweled as an act of deliberate symbolism. But then there is the question of the blade he used to do it. Where is that weapon? Another possibility is that the murderer disemboweled him, in an act intended to either restore their own honor or take his honor from him." I shrug. "Or none of these things."

Vali shifts on his chair. "Would you excuse us, Expositor?" he says to the girl.

She frowns, but stands up from her chair and, with a look over her shoulder at me, she leaves the room. Her look says, *We Are Not Done Here.*

2. THE MIRROR

Vali returns alone, and seems annoyed. Looking at him again, I notice the small dragon necklace dangling from his throat that all of the SS wear. His is handmade though, gold not silver. I've been meaning to ask about that, but I never get the chance.

"I just reviewed your criminal record," he says to me. "I also know you served with the PRC armed forces during the Energy War. You served well. But it ended in Sanction."

I don't reply. It wasn't a question.

"Tell me, how do you feel about that?" he asks.

"I don't feel," I tell him. "I can't feel. But I regret it."

"Regret isn't a feeling?"

"I suppose it could be, but for me, it is a state of mind. When I think back on my crime, I can see it was wrong. I wish I hadn't done it," I tell him.

"Because it was wrong, or because of the consequences for you?"

I think about this. I try to change the subject. "Both, I suppose. Anyway, you're the Expositor. What is your theory about this death?"

He doesn't bite. "Your crime. Tell me what it was."

I am a little surprised at this question. "It wasn't in the record?"

"I have access to your service record and sentencing details but your actual crime is suppressed," he says.

"Then I guess I can't tell you," I reply.

The muscles bunch along his jaw, then he turns his head to the door. "You can come in again, Expositor."

The girl comes back in and looks sideways at Vali. She is clearly a little annoyed. Yes, definitely not happy at being sent out. He nods at her. "He's all yours."

She takes my arm with her hand. "Fan Zhaofeng, we are holding you in connection with the death of Sanctioner Huang. You will be placed in custody while we consider whether a charge of contravening the Law should be laid." She pulls me toward the door and says under her breath, "Let me tell you, friend, making historical references to ritual murders, that isn't helping you right now."

As she leads me out of the interview room, the other SS Expositor speaks gruffly. "You will keep our last conversation private, Zhaofeng," he says. "And you will not ask him about it, Expositor."

When I think back, I suppose from their perspective it might have been a little stupid coming out of a crime scene where a Sanctioner was disemboweled, telling an officer from the PRC Security Service about the ritual of *Seppuku*.

They kept me overnight, so they had plenty of time to check on my movements the day before and have them confirmed. Eventually the police escort me in front of the SS officer, Vali, again.

"You realize how serious this could be for you? You've already been Sanctioned, there is no other judgment left for you than prison," he says. "You would die in there."

"I didn't do this," I tell him. "So I fear nothing."

"As a Sanctionee, you should fear nothing anyway," he says.

"It was a figure of speech."

"I recommended to the PRC High Council that you be charged anyway. Despite the fact you are a cyber, there is the complication of your also being a Sanctionee. The consequences of that on your programmed restraints are unknown. I don't believe in coincidence and so I think you are dangerous."

"They disagreed?"

"They agreed you are dangerous. They disagreed about you being charged." He stands. "Show me your right wrist."

I frown, but hold out my arm. He takes my hand and turns it over, then runs his finger over the skin at my wrist where the veins disappear into the bones, appearing to be thinking.

"The junior Expositor has suggested we put a tracker in you," he says.

"Tracker?" I frown. "That would be a rights violation. Get a warrant: you can pull my Core cache at any time, and that will show you where and when I last drifted."

"That would tell us where you've been, not where you are," he points out. "It is true one of the inconveniences of the Articles of Alignment is that we aren't allowed to trace your kind in real time anymore. Unless you agree, voluntarily. So I am asking you to volunteer."

Your kind.

I agree to the tracker. What else can I do? Besides, if you have done nothing, you have nothing to fear, right? A police tech comes in with a small syringe and injects a tiny bead about the size of a grain of rice between the bones at my wrist. It has some sort of gel-based coating that glues itself to the subdermis. He assures me it will stay put, not get into a vein and give me a stroke.

As I sign out on the screen in the reception of the police station, the junior Expositor, Lin, walks in and offers to drive me home. I say sure. As we walk to the car, I look around.

"It's nearby," she says. "If you're looking for my Ward."

"They go everywhere with you?" I look up at the sky. "I mean, maybe not right beside you, but…"

"You think I need it closer, Fan?" she asks, stopping up.

"No."

She starts walking again. "It's never more than a minute away, it can stun you through three-foot-thick solid stone or metal, and I can call it with a blink of my eyes, so don't get any ideas, buddy," she says in a fake growl and winks at me, so that I know she is joking. Probably.

We don't talk about the killing, or them arresting me. I guess she has her orders. So we talk about cats. There were no land-based lifeforms on PRC before humans arrived, so the only animals here are pet breeds. Mammals, birds and silica chirpers are the most popular.

I'm not sure how it comes up, but we get to talking about cats, how she likes birds too but not chirpers because they are just dull and grey and, after a while, no matter how beautiful their song, they are boring because you can't cosy up to one. How she has a ginger tomcat, called Tom, which she was worried would freak out at the panther-like Ward that shadows her everywhere, but the only time it is a problem is if her Ward tries to come inside, in which case Tom just retires under the sofa and hisses at it. I say I don't care one way or the other for cats, except perhaps kittens. I say I am more of a bird guy. That is unfortunate, she says, the cat being the mortal enemy of the bird. She says we should try not to take it as an omen.

She asks me how I had spent the hours before I found the dead Sanctioner. I tell her the same as I had told the police – the names of everyone I had been with during the day, which people, which humans, right up to the time I got to the Thuyen dwelling. She says she is still a junior Expositor, but it seems I have pretty solid alibis.

And that is it. She drops me off and waves me goodbye and I go inside feeling like I have been thoroughly Good Copped. Being cauterized tends to also make you a little cynical, I find – or clear headed, which sometimes comes over the same.

A police officer calls to visit me the next day and asks me everything, all over again. He says he will be interviewing the people I say I'd been with. I say that is no problem. He says I seem very calm about it. I point out to him calm comes with the territory when you've been Sanctioned.

I take the fact they've sent a common house and garden police officer instead of an SS officer as a good sign; a sign they've put me in the 'not that interesting after all' basket.

I am wrong.

Sanctioning is the selective neurological cauterization of microscopic parts of a human or cybernetic brain. A psychiatrist has told me the cauterization occurs at the molecular level, it is so precise.

It leaves you a little dazed and confused at first, but one positive is that it makes you suitable for a lot of jobs that people otherwise find really traumatic. Like child abuse, acute hospital care, domestic violence, prison work or palliative care. So after I had been Sanctioned, I got offered retraining, and that's when I met Yung. Or, more correctly, I was assigned to Yung, because she was my first client. She has schizophrenia. I call on her husband once a fortnight at the moment, as he's on a conditional release after a conviction for assault.

I've seen a lot of court proceedings and I think he was a bit unlucky. A better Defender might have got him off. Ben is a pretty simple guy, a freight guard on autonomous rigs, and Yung was his childhood girlfriend. They got married at nineteen and at twenty she started showing symptoms. She's twenty-one now, so is starting to learn to live with the symptoms. Paracusia mainly, which is auditory hallucination, or if you like, hearing voices. She got a diagnosis and treatment, but she's not very compliant and when she goes off her medications, the only way Ben has found to deal with her is to tie her to their bed.

Unfortunately Ben has to go on an overnight trip during one of Yung's episodes and he doesn't know what to do so he ties her up and promises to be back the next day. But his truck breaks down and it's not like he can contact the neighbors and just ask them to let themselves in and untie his wife.

They let themselves in anyway, because they heard her screaming. When the police came to cut her loose, she'd been on the bed two days without food, water or a toilet. She didn't want to bring charges, but the police did. Ben went in front of the courts, got six months' prison, suspended, and Yung was hospitalized for a while, but she moved back in with him as soon as they let her out. It was his first offense, so I'm teaching Ben other coping strategies than leather restraints and handcuffs. He's doing alright, and if he keeps going the way he is, he'll avoid a Sanction.

The reason Yung's not compliant with her meds, which do stop the hallucinations pretty much, is she doesn't believe they *are* hallucinations. She's a bright girl who did physics at University before her condition got really bad, and she's convinced the voices are what she calls a quantum artifact. She's convinced she's tuning in to alternate universes.

"Mostly it's garbage I hear," she tells me. "Words, phrases, sometimes the same thing over and over and I can't focus, it drives me batshit."

"I can't imagine," I tell her truthfully. "What does the voice say?"

"Voices," she says. "Different ones. Hard to describe. Sometimes they come in really clear, other times they're garbled like a holo station where the stream is garbled. I write it all down." She shows me a tower of notebooks. "But when I look at what I wrote again when I'm lucid, it makes no sense really."

She picks a notebook at random from her pile and shows me. I have to squint at the small spidery handwriting. They aren't even sentences, just fragments, like *'he says go get the book go get the book'* or just lists of words with no connection running along the page in their hundreds.

"Crazy, right?" She shrugs. "There *are* multiple universes out there, Fan. Quantum science has proven it, even though we can't access them yet. And the voices I hear? I'm hearing the different universes."

It's a neat theory for a crazy person to justify why they don't take their meds. *I'm special. I can hear things you can't. Quantum theory explains how. I'm not crazy.* But it doesn't hold up. I won't go into the many reasons why, but the idea that people who hear voices, or see ghosts, are somehow able to perceive beings or events from another dimension...that's never been proven.

There's no doubt anymore that other dimensions, other universes, exist alongside or within ours. The Alcubierre faster-than-light starship drive wouldn't work if interdimensional phase shifting wasn't possible. But the Alcubierre drive only allows you to pass *through* other universes, you can't drop out of your transit bubble and suddenly find yourself in an alternate reality.

Teleportation is a more interesting application of quantum science. Imagine a universe where you didn't need starships or warp drives. We already have the basic tools. Quantum entanglement. Worm holes. One second you are on Old Earth, and the next, you are on PRC. *Boom.*

We really haven't come much further with teleportation than the first experiments on Old Earth teleporting subatomic particles and waves. At the moment, I'm into this long forgotten branch known as the 'Gdansk protocols'. The problem has always been stability. You can transmit information through entangled particles but the more information you transmit, the more scrambled it becomes. But the smaller the particle, the more stable the information is.

We've been entirely focused on making quantum computers smaller and smaller at the same time as increasing their computational power. That focus has resulted in an obsession with finding the smallest particles possible that we can teleport and unscramble. The idea of teleporting atoms, molecules or, 'gasp', *whole objects* has been all but abandoned.

The Gdansk protocols are some ideas from several hundred years ago that never went anywhere. But they had some cool ideas for stabilizing information so that it should be possible to teleport organized groups of atoms, not just single subatomic particles as we do in quantum computing today.

So I use maybe 10 percent of my bandwidth geeking around with teleportation science. Yeah, I know. Super nerdy. But it keeps me off the streets.

Oh yeah, the mirror. What did I see in the mirror at the Thuyen place? The mirror was this huge bronze disc like a New Mongolian shield, hanging over the fireplace. It was polished, gleaming. There wasn't even a finger smudge on it. The Thuyens kept a really nice house.

I ducked through the door and nearly stepped in the Sanctioner's blood. My eyes followed the river of blood across the rosewood floor to their body. I'd never seen that much blood before. No cyber has. I just stood there very quietly. Then I noticed the mirror, or, more accurately, I noticed *myself* in the mirror. It was curved and I could see a fish-eye view of the living room, and the reflection of me standing just inside the doorway.

And then I came in, again.

I mean, in the mirror, I saw myself standing there, and then *I* came in the door behind me. The other me wasn't wearing the same clothes, so it wasn't just a trick of the light. He was wearing a white t-shirt and mine was blue. He looked a little surprised to see me, and stood behind me for a moment, just watching me watch him in the mirror, I guess.

Then he put a hand on my shoulder. A physical hand, that I could feel, not some ghostly spectral hand. He stood for a while like that, and we looked at each other in the mirror some more. He cocked his head in a kind way, and turned around and went out. I turned too and watched him leave, up the driveway of the house, and out of the yard. I stepped out and watched him walk away.

I stood there for a long time after that, looking in the mirror at myself. I was waiting, I guess. But the other me didn't reappear, there was only one of me in the mirror, and I was left trying to understand it. Try telling that to the SS? Maybe not.

I took that sequence from my cache and stored it locally so it wouldn't be accessible to anyone except me.

His white t-shirt? It was spotted with cherry red blood.

3. THE SECOND

A couple of months went by. If murder was the biggest crime under the Law, it was also the most secret. There was not a whisper about it in the datasphere. I had to assume there was a lot of turmoil among humans, though. Violence is pretty common among humans, which is why the SS need Wards, but thanks to Sanction, murder is incredibly rare.

I drifted a few times, looking for any public information about the investigation. That got me a call from the junior SS Expositor, Lin.

"Hey Fan, how you doing?"

"Good, I think. Is there something I can help with?"

Whatever it was, it wasn't important enough for her to come in person. It was just a holo call. She looked and sounded distracted.

"Nothing major. Vali asked me to call you. You've been drifting for information on the murder investigation."

"Public information, yeah. Just wondering what had happened with it, but there's no news I can find."

"Any particular reason?"

"Just curiosity. Why? Am I under surveillance?" A cyber's Core search records aren't private, but it's unusual for the SS to be monitoring them. Unless…

"No. But we have an alert set up for anyone involved in the case, and it flagged your search. So…no special reason then?"

"I thought there would be more information in the Corecasts, is all," I told her.

"The death of a Sanctioner is not the sort of thing we encourage people to speculate about."

"So you've suppressed the story?"

She clucked her tongue. "We don't suppress our Corecasters, Fan. But sometimes we ask them to help avoid inflaming situations, and usually they agree."

"By not talking about them?"

"Right. You should probably think about that."

"Meaning I shouldn't talk about the murder either?"

"That's a good suggestion. Thanks for getting on board so quickly," she said. She turned, about to cut the holo, and then turned back. "Oh, and digging around in the Core…"

"Might also inflame the situation?"

"Exactly! I told Vali you would understand. See you, Fan." Her image winked out.

Not being able to talk about it didn't stop me thinking about it, but life goes on. I joined a chess club, because Socialization theory says that if you can master chess, it helps you think like a human. Sequentially. First this move, then that one. I decided to start three times a week, try to get up to speed quickly. The rules are simple, well defined, and unchanging. Like the Law.

Unlike sport, where the rules are so vague and ill-defined you need a referee to interpret them even while the games are being played.

Cybers have to throttle their processing abilities to match the IQ of the person they're playing, and cut their Core link for the duration of the game. That was a bit scary at first. Chess was the first time I ever voluntarily cut my link to the Core. I knew it would only be for the length of the game, and I can go for up to two hours before I have to start shutting down non-vital functions, but for a cyber it's like holding your breath. You don't really do it unless you are forced to.

But if chess can help me better understand humans, it will help me contribute more to society. The other thing about chess, if you want to master it, is that you have to get into the head of your opponent, to think as they think, and anticipate their next moves. It isn't mind reading, it's empathy.

There are two things that really set humans and cybers apart: intellect (ours is superior) and empathy (we struggle with that). Empathy is their biggest strength. Human mystics say they can see into the soul of a blade of grass and understand how it feels to be trodden on. They say this ability is crippled in a cyber and needs nurturing. Not that I am a candidate for that anymore. My empathy gland got cauterized.

See, I looked at the gutted belly of that Sanctioner and…nothing. At a conscious level I know it was a heinous crime, a shame, a criminal waste of life. I should have been either scared, horrified or excited. A dead *Sanctioner!* Anyone else looking down at it would be shaking, crying, throwing up. But not me.

Emotion is at the core of empathy. Having it. Understanding it. My emotional range was crippled when I got Sanctioned. For my crime, and I'll get to that later, there was no choice between prison or Sanction – I was sentenced straight to Sanction. I haven't heard about that happening to anyone else, but then, I guess it was one of those things the SS prefer to keep quiet if they can. Like the killing of Sanctioner Huang.

I think I still have emotions. I feel good when the day is mild and the desert wind drops, or I see a balloon flying free in the air. Here's something. I got upset recently when I saw a dead kitten on the side of the road. My medical AI has some experience with people who've been Sanctioned, and it said that wasn't real feeling, it was a learned response. A Sanctionee sees other people get upset when they see death, and we know, we can still remember that we should be upset over death too. So we mimic the response – it helps us fit back in.

Who cares whether it is learned or real? I still got upset. I feel frustrated when I watch the news on holo, showing the people who chose prison being herded into trains and sent away. I can't understand why they would choose that. I wonder what will happen to them. Probably that's not an emotion, just logical reaction.

So, I don't get really angry. I don't get really excited. And I don't get really upset about things people do to people. The thousand forms of tragedy which we can inflict on each other glide right by me without leaving a smudge on my paintwork.

Anyway, I settled on chess. I've always been intrigued by chess, but I watched a few games and realized that game where the two players play against the clock, sometimes they get really wound up. I don't. I make my move and hit the clock, not thinking about the clock at all except to keep an eye on it, but for some, the clock is the enemy, and it unbalances them. 'Sudden death' is great, you've only got a fixed amount of time to make a certain number of moves. But 'Blitz' is better. In Blitz you only get five minutes on the clock to win the whole game.

Blitz favors people who've been cauterized. To us, five minutes is just a measurable period of time. We can live ourselves into it. Not getting emotional seems to help in Blitz. Time flows a little more slowly when perceived through an objective lens. I still haven't won a game except against other beginners, because I'm still learning all the moves and the tactics. We aren't allowed to use Core bandwidth so I have to use my biological brain to memorize all the possible plays. And of course I have no advantage against someone else who's been cauterized, but there aren't that many of us really. I can see this is the game for me.

It was a Saturday morning actually and I'd just gone downstairs and got food, made some tea, and was sitting in the shade in a chair on my front veranda. When PRC was terraformed the only thing the colonizers really touched was the atmosphere. They decided the ecology, even though all of the indigenous life was subterranean, was too delicate to survive surface topography remodeling. So the streets and artificial grass sidewalks of every city are 3D printed and then laid down like carpet, rolled out across the barren desert landscape in concentric circles surrounded at the outermost ring by huge frosted glass walls that keep the shifting sands out and the locally bred animals in. Despite the drones that work around the clock shifting sand, after several hundred years it has risen about halfway up the glass retaining wall. In several hundred more we will probably have to relocate or build it higher.

There were some birds picking at some flower seeds I'd thrown on the grass. Like I said, I'm a bird guy. I enjoy their little purring sounds when they find a good stash of seed, so I always throw a bit around if I'm sitting outside. I run a little water into the birdbath for them, even though it costs a bomb. That must be emotion, right? Enjoying that?

But they take off in a blur of wings when Lin comes through the gate, with a Ward at her heels this time. I guess by its presence that she's not going to be playing good cop today. It slinks with its head low to the ground, gaze sweeping from side to side, wings pulled tight into its body, eyes never resting on anything more than a second or two.

"Hello, Expositor," I say.

"Hello, Zhaofeng." Not Fan. Not a courtesy call then.

She must have parked her car around the corner, because I haven't seen it or heard the distinctive magneto hum. She sees me looking for it. "I walked," she says. "It was only about three rings."

"What was only three rings?"

She doesn't answer, just points at the chair next to mine. "Can I sit?" She climbs up onto it like a lifeguard onto his tower. Like I said, she's a wee bit shorter than me.

"You want some tea?" I ask. "I just made a pot. I also have something stronger, if you need a shot of caffeine or something…"

"Zhaofeng…"

"Fan."

"Fan…I'd love tea."

The Ward is gone and it seems like she is sleeping when I come back out, but she is just sitting with her eyes closed in the shade. I have no doubt the animal is somewhere nearby, watching us. I notice she has a tiny pimple on her forehead, which you can hardly see because her hair nearly covers it. She leans forward when I give her the mug, and says, "Hmmm. You get many guests? Keep a pot ready?"

"You never know when the PRC Security Service might drop in," I tell her. I have sugar on a tray but she doesn't take it. She sips her tea and looks at my garden.

"I never picked you for the kind who would waste credits on birds and flowers," she says. "I don't know why. You just struck me as the nerdy spartan type."

I look where she is looking and see the real flowers among the artificial grass, watered from a subterranean well I pay to pump from.

"The garden is about the only thing I do spend money on," I say. "Inside the house is pretty much as I found it."

"Uh huh."

"You can look." And she does. She walks in my front double doors, which I had open to the veranda so I could listen to a Corecast, and also let the cooler morning air into the lounge. I stand behind her, trying to see what she would see. I live alone, she knew that of course. In a house I bought as a deceased estate with a veteran's pension I got from the PRC Government after the war. I had enough money for the house, and all the stuff in it, most of which I kept. The people who lived here had this thing for designer furniture and I don't mean the locally made copy stuff. Ganymede architect-designed is what they went for. I know all the names by heart. I bet they would talk about this stuff for months before they bought anything. My two armchairs are black leather PK-22s. I have a blonde faux-wood coffee table in front of them, and over it is a PH Lamp that looks like the leaves of rainforest fern. The sofa is a Jalk, all black string and carbon. It looks like you'll fall between the strings if you sit in it but they are bound together so it's like sitting on solid air. She tries it and bounces a bit.

I'm not a tech guy, but what I have is a cloud system for music, and a projector for holo calls tucked up amongst my books in my bookcase (yes, real books – I collect old books), and the bookcase is by Juhl; the people who lived here got it when the Ganymede Consulate was refurbishing. The Consulate wanted to have it back when they found out how hard it was to replace, but the owners of this place said no.

There's also a holo I've been working on, a bit of a hobby project. It's sitting on a table in my living room with its cover off and parts laid out and carefully numbered beside it.

"You repair holo machines in your spare time?" she asks, picking up a part.

I take the part from her and put it back down in its place. "It's just a hobby. Have to use my bandwidth on something."

Lin walks out to the pantry. Opens a few storage units.

"Very stylish. I bet you have a set of molecular blade knives in carbonite sheaths," she says. "Probably cut through steel like butter, you keep them so nice."

I point her to the kitchen. It isn't what people expect because they expect the whole architect design thing to go through the whole house, which I guess it should. But though the old couple who lived here took out the ceiling between the ground and first floors to create this high churchy feeling, the kitchen is still the way they found it because they liked it that way. The storage units are tiny, with floral knobs. The old guy made the benches himself, which are three-inch-thick printed oak scarred with lines and gashes because he used to use any old surface as a cutting board. Sometimes I run a hand across the scored surface to feel what he felt. I have to have the waste recycler out in the laundry because the cupboards have steel shelves and separators, which means I'd need a cutting torch to make room for a recycler and that seems extreme.

"OK, that's unusual," she says. "The kitchen."

"No molecular knives."

"No Samurai sword either?"

Teasing me about my *Seppuku* comment again. "No, no Samurai sword."

But the dining table is back to form, the old folks buying a triform Filou which uses the corner nicely. I wish they were around to talk with. I'd have thanked them for buying all this stuff.

"I want to see your bedroom," she says.

"Uh, OK."

"You should say no. An SS Expositor drops in unannounced and wants to look around your house," she tells me.

"I don't mind."

She walks in ahead of me and says, "Holy…"

I walk in behind her; I can't see what the problem is.

Oh, OK. I have a small blue sofa opposite my bed. Over the sofa is a piece of art I also inherited from the old folks. It's a huge charcoal drawing on tan paper of a human woman lying on a bed, but you can really only see her feet and legs and…well, it's called The Vulva. I don't think it's very shocking, but some people could see it like that.

Lin isn't looking at the painting, though. She points at the bed. "You haven't made your bed."

"Yeah?"

"It's nine o'clock in the morning. Did you get interrupted by something?"

"No."

"No, you didn't? But you haven't made your bed. That's…weird."

"It is?"

"How long have you been up?" she asks.

"About an hour."

"Weird."

"Really?"

"For a cyber. Ok, I've seen enough."

We walk back outside and she stands there, like she's deciding what to do.

"Is that a side effect?" she asks me, one hand scratching her hair, the other patting the carrying pouch around her waist like she's looking for something, but then she looks right at me. She keeps asking. "The Sanctioning? It makes you messy? I never knew that."

"I assume you're being funny."

"Not really."

"No. Not really."

"Sorry, didn't mean to…*upset* you."

Is she deliberately pushing me? You just don't talk to people who have been Sanctioned about being cauterized like that. It's a social no no. And you certainly don't throw it in their face, even if you are from the SS. I smile. "It takes more than an SS Expositor searching my house unannounced and teasing me about being cauterized to upset me."

She fiddles with the pouch again. "I guess so," she says, and finds a small holo unit in the front pocket of her bag, which she moves to the back pocket of her trousers. She has a nice backside. That black hair, flowing over her shoulders, shining in the sun. She catches me looking at her and smiles. Now I'm wondering if she is flirting. That would be a first. Usually I creep people out.

I suddenly remember something I've been wondering. "Hey, can I ask…did you find the Thuyens? The people whose house…"

"…you were in when you found Sanctioner Huang, dead and filleted?" She finishes my sentence. She *is* trying to provoke me, which tells me she doesn't have much experience with Sanctionees. We are pretty much unprovokable – most of the time I don't even realize someone is trying it on, but after a while you train yourself to pick up on it.

"Where I found him, yeah," I reply.

She shifts her weight onto her other leg, seems a little impatient. "Yeah, we found them. They were in a nearby park, said that they had no memory at all of how they got there. Any other questions?"

"Yes, why are you here, really?" I ask her.

She looks up the street, thinking about it. "There was another killing three blocks from here. Wing Lok Street, you know it?"

"What? No, wait. Up by the market? Maybe."

"Yeah, up there. Another Sanctioner," she says.

I look at her sharply. "Wait. Another *Sanctioner* has been killed?"

"Yeah. You can imagine how that's going down. We won't keep it off the Corecasts this time. A Corecast crew got there before we did, and the news will get out. 'Sanctioner Dead! Walk the Crime Scene!' I think the SS are a little freaked too, and who knows where that will lead? Anyway, me and Vali were at the scene and then he said, 'Lin, that Department of Community Services worker we questioned a few weeks ago…'"

"Arrested…and it was two months."

"…two months ago, he lives not far from here."

"I'm just a social services caseworker. I'd have to have some kind of superpowers to have killed *two* Sanctioners when the whole of the SS is on alert after the first one."

"What? Oh. No, I wasn't thinking of you like *that*. Like, two Sanctioners dead in two months and Fan Zhaofeng is there, or near there, both times?"

Did she wink? I'm not sure. "You weren't thinking of me like that."

"No. She was killed last night – the Sanctioner; her name was M'ele – around 6 p.m. About to carry out a Sanction on an industrialist. So I guess you were out with friends or something?" She pulls a flower out of my grass and chews the stem, looking at me. It's both a provocation and a question.

"I was at a chess club. Blitzing."

"Blitzing?"

"It's like war chess. Very edgy," I tell her.

"See, I knew that. When the kid next door gave a description of a person at the scene of the killing, and Vali pointed out, 'Lin, that description sounds exactly like Mr. Fan Zhaofeng'…I said no."

"No."

"But I said, he's only three blocks away, I'll walk over."

I hold up my wrist. "You put a tracker in me. You know where I was."

"No, that just tells us where the tracker was," she says. She takes my hand and looks at my wrist. The small cut they made healed up weeks ago. She drops it again. She has cool hands, from the morning air. Nice hands.

"So you *are* checking me out after all. For the killing of another *Sanctioner*?"

I wonder who the Sanctioner is. M'ele? My biological memory doesn't help me recognize the name. Have I worked with them? That would not look good. I drift quickly to check. Damn. Yes, I have. Once, about two years ago.

"You want to know the truth? Why I'm here?" She steps to the gate and closes it between us. With a rustle of warm air her Ward sweeps in from above and drops quietly to the ground behind her. She doesn't acknowledge it, just leans on the gate. "I'm worried this is going to get ugly, Fan, ugly for you. And it's stupid, but I like you."

"Why would you care?" I ask her.

"That time with the murder suicide, you took the baby…"

"The man under the table. I wasn't sure you remembered me."

"Oh, I did. Or, I remembered the way you held that baby. I

couldn't forget how gentle you were. For a cyber, well, you know."

"Thanks."

"And then the first killing, Sanctioner Huang? That really freaked me out. I know I'm SS, but I've never seen a person killed like that. On the way home, I just needed to talk. Man that was a bad one. You have no idea how people inside the SS were freaking out. And the only person I could talk to was the guy we had just arrested, but it was a nice conversation."

"Right. How's your cat?"

"Tom? Moody as ever. And today, I'm there with the other Expositors, thinking wow, even the veterans here are rattled. This one was just as bad as the last. Died the exact same way – gutted throat to navel, no one actually saw it happen. Whoever did it isn't just killing Sanctioners, he's sending a message. And Vali said I should check you out, even though the tracker data said you weren't near there, and I thought, if I go, and you are there, I can clear it up and probably that'll make me feel…better."

I lean on the tree. "I hope you do."

"Chess club? That would be the one in Chuk Un district?"

"Went straight there after work at 5, got home around 9. Went to bed at 12, woke at 9, made tea, and then you walked in."

She smiles and goes to leave, then stops. "Well, hey, it was good to see you."

I wave as she leaves. She doesn't wave back. She is light on her feet, hardly makes a sound as she walks away.

I'm left wondering, what happens now? Something tells me I'll find out soon enough.

I watch the reports on the murder on the Corecast channels. As far as the Corecasters know, it's the first ever known killing of a Sanctioner. The SS don't let the news crew into the house to do a walk-through of the crime scene. They keep them outside, so it's more of a 'walk-around' than a walk-through. I walk it in holo anyway, trying to see through a window or something, but all I can see inside is some feet and a pool of blood.

Lin told me she had been eviscerated, just like Huang. This killer has one hell of a calling card.

I flick through the content providers. As usual, cyber-fear

dominates the hysteria. Commentators telling families to keep their children close, away from cybers. *How can we trust them now that we can't control them?* How do we know they aren't committing crimes, when all the data on crime comes from the Core now and all cybers are just living agents of the Core? The news anchors, all human, don't look at the fact the person killed is a Sanctioner and only humans get Sanctioned (yours truly excluded). Articles of Alignment or not, racism runs deep on PRC.

I'm watching a breakfast commentator on a panel saying, *Look, if a cyber has killed a Sanctioner, the consequences for cybers are going to be bad. Yeah?* says one of the other panel members. *If cybers are killing humans now, then the consequences for the humans are going to be pretty bad too.* The audience cheers.

"When the war was lost, Tatsensui imposed the Charter of Cyber Rights on us, forcing us to chain all cybers to the Core and preventing us using cybers in our armed forces again," the next Corecast commentator is saying. "Which protects the cybers, and Tatsensui. But who will protect *us* from the cybers?"

"Well, Jules," says her partner, "maybe it's them who need protecting from us!" More cheering.

I'm actually Core drifting, looking for any new information about the killing, when there is a knock on the door. Two police officers and a patrol car.

"Are you Fan Zhaofeng?" It is a formality. They would have got a positive face scan the second I opened the door.

"Yes?"

"We need you to come with us to assist with Security Service inquiries into the death of the Sanctioner M'ele four days ago." The young officer sounds like he's been practicing this in his head.

"Am I being arrested?" It's a little inconvenient. I'll have to call in absent for work.

The other officer grunts. "Not yet. They'll explain at the station."

Their car has restraints for confining a prisoner. They don't use them, which I take as a good sign. In the car they say they aren't really sure why I am needed – something about SS business, helping with an identification. When I get there, I expect to see Lin or her partner Vali, but there are just a couple of SS officers, some cops I've never seen before, and four or five cybers who are tall, lanky, with mops of wiry dirty blonde hair and looking vaguely like me. I work out pretty quickly it is a plain old-fashioned 'line-up'.

The senior constable tells us we are helping with inquiries in relation to the Sanctioner who was killed (I don't ask 'which one'), that we are all volunteering our assistance to trigger the memory of a boy who saw someone near the crime, and see if he can better describe the person he has seen. We are told he is going to come in with his mother and a police counselor and maybe we will be asked to say something, maybe not, but otherwise we are just to stand there and not even look at the child, just look at the wall behind him.

You can thank human sensitivities for the fact there was no static surveillance camera vision of the scene of the crime. PRC's settlers had written 'freedom from surveillance' into the original Constitution of PRC. Which has become a bit redundant since PRC became a Core world, where every single data point is stored and retrievable, but humans have a fantastic ability to ignore inconvenient truths.

The little boy is about eight and looks about as unhappy to be there as an eight-year-old in a police station with his mother can possibly look. As the three of them come in, they have a little conference, which is not too private, and I guess not intended to be. The child and mother are together with an SS cyber, an androgene with a hard body and a large dragon pendant around its neck. That reminds me, I should ask Lin about those.

It starts by asking the child so we all can hear. "Chan, can you tell me again what you saw, to help yourself and us to remember?" The cyber cop is there to read the kid's bio signs, I know that much. If the child recognizes the killer among us, his heart rate and hormones will go off the scale, even if he doesn't want to say anything, and the cyber will detect it.

So will I.

The boy's thin small voice carries across the room. "I saw…there was a cyber, he came up to me and said, 'Excuse me, young man…'" He grinds to a halt when he realizes everyone in the room is listening, but his mother kneels and hugs him and whispers in his ear, and he gets up the courage to continue, head buried in his mother's shoulder. "…he said, is this the street where Sanctioner M'ele lives? I said yes, that's the lady across the road, Tommy's mother, but I'm not allowed to visit there even though Tommy is in my class, and he said…" The boy hesitates again. "…he said thank you very much, you've been a big help, and he walked across the road and into Tommy's house."

Then he buries his face deep in his mother's wooly jumper, but the Security Service counselor pries him gently away. The mother is a nice young lady with a puffy face, and looks like she has agreed to lead her son into a nest of snakes, but she also steps forward with his little hand clenched in hers, and they start walking along in front of us, peering up awkwardly.

I'm thinking this is a little strange. Addresses are public, anyone can look up the residents of a house, even a Sanctioner's house. Sanctioners don't hide away from the public. A Core lookup that simply costs micro-fractions of a credit. You don't even think twice about the cost. So why had the killer, if that's who it was, gone up to the boy and spoken with him? Unless he *wanted* to be seen?

The SS cyber speaks again. "We want you to look at these men, Chan, and see if any of them look like the man who talked to you. Just look at them, and then afterwards we'll ask you to make another drawing of the one you think you saw," the cyber says. "Look at their faces, some have long noses, some have short noses. Look at their hair. Some have long hair, some have short hair..." he drones on.

The child walks slowly down the line with his mother, looking at everyone, then gets to me, and he stops. I can hear his heart rate spike, his breathing get faster. My olfactory sensors pick up the scent of adrenaline pumping. He turns and looks up at his mother. "He looked like this man."

The SS cyber kneels beside him, no doubt picking up on the same biosigns that I am. "He looked like this man?" the cop asks. "Or he *is* this man?"

The kid looks at me again and bites his lip, looking up at his mother. "I'm scared, momma." She sweeps him up and runs out of the room.

The cop steps over and takes my arm. "You stay. Everyone else can go."

"No, I didn't suggest that they bring you in for the identification," Lin says as I wait in carbonite chains in a room at the back of the station, drinking tepid water with my wrists bound together. "Neither did Vali. We're not the only ones involved in this investigation, alright?" She arrived pretty soon after the cyber constable came back in and told me I was going to 'voluntarily' help them with their inquiries and would I mind being voluntarily chained to a chair. I'd said this would be fine as long as I could 'voluntarily' speak with the Expositor, Lin Ming, and pretty quickly, because I was starting to get tired of being arrested every time a Sanctioner was killed. He looked at me strangely, so I'm guessing he didn't know this was the second dead Sanctioner. But he went to get her anyway.

She comes closer, sits down with the table between us, but she doesn't unlock the chains. "That child swears that you are the man he saw."

"And you know I was at the chess club, before, during and after that citizen was killed."

"You told me."

"Yes. And the tracker data confirms that?"

"Maybe. And, not that I didn't trust the data, but yeah, we checked with the secretary of the chess club that you were actually there that afternoon."

Of course you did, is what I'm thinking. It's the second Sanctioner death. Of course there is nothing left to chance.

"And he confirmed it."

"He said you were new, but you kind of stood out for having 'a determination to win out of all proportion to your abilities'. So he's not certain down to the minute, but he clearly remembers you being there. So do a couple of the people you played against."

"Good. Can I please go?"

She looks at me and then looks at the floor, like she did that day at my place, chewing on the stem of my rather expensive flower. I'm learning it's her way of warming up to the real questions. Her eyes flash black as she Core dives some data.

"Do you have a twin, Fan? A brother from offworld maybe that isn't in the records?" She taps her fingers on the table. "It's only five years since we've been syncing Core data with Tatsensui, there are still…glitches."

"That's a strange question, Expositor."

She looks a bit embarrassed. "You're right. Stupid question. Vali wanted me to ask. So…no?"

"I have no mystery siblings, human or cyber," I tell her. "I was fostered to a human family like any other cyber. I served in the war, I got Sanctioned, I came home, I moved out, I got a job. If that's what my record says, that's all there is."

"Tell me about your service. Cybers can't use lethal force, even in war. So what did you do?"

I hesitate, drift, check my secrecy agreement. There is nothing in there that stops me answering questions about my service record.

"I was a scout."

"You were what, when the war started? Fourteen? They used *children* as scouts?" She was even younger than me during the war, and she's human. It's possible she doesn't know.

"The PRC drafted cybers as young as ten years old into the forces. Kids can go places adults can't."

"And then you did something they Sanctioned you for. A kid. That's crazy."

"You're not that old yourself. They drafted you into the SS."

"I'm seventeen. I finished school at least."

"You can't use age to compare cyber and human kids," I point out. "Our intellect is artificially throttled so that we can socialize." I decide to change the subject. "Speaking of the SS, where is your partner? Why isn't he here?"

She stands and kicks the chains around my ankles, rattles the chains on my wrists. "He's already made up his mind about you."

That's not good. "So that's it, then? Prison?"

She looks a little surprised. "No…why…why would you think that?"

"He thinks I killed that first Sanctioner. He suspects me of this one too. I've already been cauterized. As a Senior SS officer he can petition the High Council directly. If his petition succeeds, all that's left for me is imprisonment until death."

She puts her hands on her hips. "Why would that be, Fan Zhaofeng? Why were you Sanctioned? Why is my senior Expositor convinced you are dangerous? Who the hell are you?"

"I don't think you're supposed to ask that," I remind her. "Anyway, that's who I was. Not who I am. You know who I am."

"Well, I don't get it," she sighs and kneels down in front of me. "But, against Vali's wishes, I have orders to take you home."

That's interesting. Not prison then. She thumbs the locks on the chains and they fall open.

She navigates. We go past a street near my house which has a couple of cafés and she says, "I want to have a coffee with you, is that OK? My buy."

By now it is about 11 in the morning and I am off work for the day anyway, thinking that my day is wasted, and talking to Lin might give me some idea of how much trouble I am in. OK, I'll be honest. I need to get to know her better, the way things are going. And I never hung out with an actual Expositor before. For a human like her to be inducted straight into the SS out of school – I never saw that before. She isn't being hostile, so maybe she's on my side for real.

Why would a young girl like her want to join the SS anyway? The SS was set up five years ago as part of the Tatsensui non-aggression pact. With a mandate from the governments of the Core Worlds and overseen by a High Council comprising senators from both Tatsensui and PRC. But it is seen by the PRC population as an occupying force even though its recruits are indigenous.

She's fresh out of school and now she'll be labeled the rest of her days as a traitor. 'Collaborationist filth' is one of the nicer descriptions used for the SS.

I get the same, for cooperating with the Sanctions, but not as bad, once people learn I was Sanctioned myself. I expect it, though. The Socialization will take time. Generations probably. But to see a young girl in the SS, investigating these killings...that's worth exploring.

I like the effect of her smile, which makes her cheeks dimple, and a trick she has of winking if she thinks you might think she was being serious, if she wasn't. I like it the same way I like how trained subsea wyrms seem to smile when they laugh. My physician says wyrms don't laugh, it's learned behavior like mine, but a laugh is a laugh if you ask me.

She parks, and we go into the one café near my place where I actually never go, because the owner is a guy who can't make coffee to save his life. He always serves it lukewarm, and so I only ever order tea in there. It's really hard to screw up a tea pod in a pot of hot water. Lin makes the mistake of ordering the coffee even though I warn her, and she lets me taste it, and we spend the first couple of minutes agreeing it tastes terrible. I was taught that if someone offers to share their food with you, it's a sign they like you, and I wonder if coffee is covered by that too. But it's probably not relevant, especially if she is sharing what she thinks is a *bad* coffee, not a good one. Like,

'This food tastes awful, you have some', doesn't exactly sound like a friendship gesture when you think about it.

I wonder if she has a boyfriend somewhere. I haven't had a partner since my cauterization. Haven't missed it. But I still like the abstract idea of it. Of being able to share things with someone who knows who you are, what you do, what you've done – without judging it.

I share things with my doctor. Everyone who gets cauterized gets assigned a medical AI so they can talk about it. But because my case was unusual, I got to pick my own; a cyber specialist in the field of Sanctionees, called Dr. Sui.

He was the one who explained to me that the cauterization is actually a molecular-level manipulation of my ventromedial prefrontal cortex, similar to what happens to people who get brain damage in accidents. It's called vmPFC damage, for short. But like any damage to the brain, the brain is resilient. It tries to compensate. Some evidence of emotion returns to people after a time, at least in human studies. Like I said, I'm the first cyber to be Sanctioned.

I chose him because he seemed fit, active and with his act together, which I found reassuring. Early in our sessions, I told him it seemed some of my emotion was coming back and he had asked about the child protection work I've been doing a couple of years now. Did I feel angry or sad, or depressed about the way some children were treated?

"I think it's sick, what people do to each other sometimes," I told him.

"That's what you *think*, how do you feel about it?"

"I feel like someone should intervene, and that's why we have the Law, and why I have a job. Since the war you have to be grateful, any job you can get."

"No, that's not a feeling, that's more thinking. How do you feel, when you see a child that has been abused?"

"I feel a need to make the child safe."

"You want to protect the child."

"It's my job."

"That's not a feeling."

We went around like that for a while. I enjoyed talking with him, but we got nowhere.

"Do you ever laugh?"

"I like it when the clouds cover the sun, it's like it tickles behind my eyes. It makes me happy."

"That's not laughter. Laughter is spontaneous. You are recognizing a physical sensation and reacting to it. That is a simulacrum of emotional expression, but I think it is learned."

"Learned?"

"You remember that certain situations are supposed to make you feel happy or sad, and you've now trained yourself to do what you used to do in those situations, to the extent you can. Intellectually, you know sunshine on a summer's day should make you happy, so you decide you are happy."

"Oh."

"Do you ever see something in your work and think to yourself, that should make me feel sad, or bad, but it doesn't?"

"I can't *make* myself feel."

"We don't make ourselves feel, we just do."

"I don't."

"I know. But let me know if you think that is starting to change…I'd love to do some tests."

I didn't want any tests. He wasn't telling me anything I hadn't heard before, from other physicians or people I met who had been cauterized.

During our last session, though, he said, "There is a stereotype in adventure stories of the character who operates by pure logic and doesn't let emotion intrude. It's called the 'Vulcan stereotype'. Do you know it?"

"Sure. An Old Earth meme, right?"

"Yes. Anyway, when I first started studying people who had been cauterized I wanted to come up with a name for what we were seeing. I called it, 'The Vulcan Syndrome'."

"Ah. You think I'm like that?"

"In a way. In lay terms my theory is that the change in your ability to feel emotions can also give you a different morality. In all other ways you still function as a normal citizen."

"That's cool."

"No, it can be dangerous. To you, and others around you."

That was the first time he'd said something *really* interesting.

"How?"

"Let me ask you a question about a hypothetical situation.

Violent criminals have broken into your house and you are hiding in the cellar with some house guests. One of them has a baby and it is starting to cry, which could lead the violent criminals to where you are hiding. What do you do?"

I think about it. "Someone would have to cover the child's nose and mouth so it can't be heard."

"That could stop it breathing; it will die."

"Well then, the child has to die, to save the largest number of lives," I told him. "Of course."

"Normal citizens would not say that."

"Sure they would." I hold up one finger on one hand and a bunch of fingers on the other and show his holo image. "It's only logical. One life lost against several saved."

"No, they wouldn't," he insisted. "I asked that question in a survey of citizens who haven't been Sanctioned and fewer than one percent of them said they would smother the baby. Eighty-nine percent said they would try almost anything else. Then I asked the same question to citizens who have been Sanctioned. Nearly all said the child should be smothered, even if it meant it would die."

"So what?" I asked. "It's academic. People who have been Sanctioned can't commit violence anyway."

"Maybe," he said. "But apparently they can see violence as a logical response. Isn't that kind of contradictory?"

"Sure. Or maybe, the response of 'normal' citizens is wrong."

In the café, Lin talks a little about her cat, which she seems to think I'm interested in. So I listen to how it has an ingrown claw which has to be removed next week. She says the cat is old, she should probably have it put down, but she can't bear the idea of doing that. I tell her I could organize that for her, if she'd like.

She laughs, then stops. "You aren't joking, are you?"

"No, I mean, if it's too hard for you."

"That's…kind of you then. I guess."

There are a lot of people in the café. Some notice her SS emblem, the silver dragon around her throat. They're glaring at her, but she ignores them. It has been five years since the SS was created, the Articles of Alignment instated, Core synchronization with Tatsensui and the imposition of the High Council, but people are still resentful.

Maybe she hasn't thought about the consequences for herself. Maybe she has, and doesn't care.

"What does it stand for, your dragon?" I ask her, pointing to the badge.

She looks down at it and then frowns at me. "Shows I'm an Expositor. Didn't you know that?"

"Sure, I knew that," I tell her. "But you all have a different design. Vali's is gold, yours is silver and has two heads. It must mean something."

She seems to think about whether to tell me, then decides. "Vali gave it to me when I graduated from training," she says. "Each mentor presents a pendant to their student. He said it represents my double loyalty. To the SS and to PRC."

"And which comes first?"

She smiles. "I hope never to find out."

"So where is he?" I ask her. "Vali?"

"Off somewhere," she shrugs. "Probably trying again to get the High Council to put you away forever. He doesn't want to risk a formal petition yet and lose, because he can only petition on a case once. So he's pushing informally at this stage."

"But you don't agree with him?"

She winks. "You don't seem so scary to me."

I like that she has that kind of autonomy, the ability to think for herself. It also shows something about Vali. Choosing a partner who wouldn't always agree with him.

"Why did he choose you?" I ask.

"Why do you ask?" is her response, and her eyes narrow. I gather she likes asking the questions, not answering them.

"You're only sixteen?"

She shoots back at me. "Seventeen. And you are nineteen. Your point is?"

"Most senior Expositors partner with a junior cyber…so their investigations are a balance of human intuition and data-driven analysis. By partnering with you, everything is slower, you have to trawl the Core yourselves. If an investigation moves fast, you'll end up relying entirely on dumb human instinct."

"You're supposed to say 'no offense' before you say something like that," she says. "But I'll forgive you because you are an emotional cripple with the sensitivity of a door knocker."

She waits and sees that being rude fails yet again to get a reaction from me before she continues. "Since you ask, I was preparing for my final exams, sitting a practice exam when that big chunk of muscle was suddenly standing outside the class. He didn't try to come in, I doubt he could have got through the door. But he was hanging in the hallway, and attracting quite a lot of attention. Class was stopped, we were wondering what the hell was going on. Then he came in and said to the teacher, 'I need to speak with the student, Lin Ming'. I nearly died right there, of shock. People looking at me like, he's SS, holy shit, what have you done?!"

"What happened then?"

"We sat down and talked. He said straight out, he didn't trust cybers and had been given permission to train a human junior."

"I figured that much," I tell her. "But why you?"

She looks at me like she's deciding something. Then she sweeps the hair away from the base of her neck and turns her head so that I can see. "Because of this."

Under her hairline, at the base of her neck, is a patch of discolored skin – a pretty bad graft job. Two diodes just under the surface of the skin are blinking red and green. She drops her hair again.

"Enhancement?" I ask. "He got you to agree to a cybernetic implant?" It sounded like the kind of thing Vali would do. Approach a naïve young girl and persuade her to have an operation that only had about at best a 13 percent success rate and, at worst, could kill you.

"No," she says. "I got this during the war. I was eleven when a Tatsensui cruiser bombarded our compound. Shrapnel took out my cerebellum. I ended up in a militia hospital and I wasn't going to make it, so they took a chance and implanted the cerebellum from a dead cyber. The graft held." She shrugs. "I have cyber-like reflexes now, and I can patch straight into the Core without routing through SS or private systems. I have an always-on connection, just like a cyber."

"No way." I'd never heard of a graft like that.

"Test me. See who's faster."

I think up a question we'd both have to drift for, something that wouldn't be part of a standard PRC education.

"Alright. What is the rarest mineral on Galesi 1061c?" It isn't a thing I know myself, so I have to drift, to pull the answer from the Core.

We both speak at exactly the same time.

"Jadeite."

"Wow, that's cool," I tell her. I drift again, checking for records of similar operations. There have been a few, most carried out in desperation during the war or after mining accidents. The survival rate is less than zero point six percent. She's been very, very lucky.

"I know. So, we're like second cousins or something."

I am still thinking about it, and don't respond straight away.

"That was a joke," she says. "The second cousin thing. You are supposed to at least chuckle."

"Right. See, people I know well," I tell her, "we have a signal, because I've been cauterized. If you tug on your right ear when you're talking, I know you are making a little joke. Tug twice and I know it's a *really* funny one."

She frowns at me. "Now *you're* joking."

I pull on my right ear, just once. She laughs, just a small one. I decide I like her, despite how rude she tries to be. "Would you like to know why I stood for twenty minutes inside Le Thuyen's house before I called the police?"

She is in the middle of picking up a teaspoon to scrape some chocolate off her coffee cup, and stops. "Yes, Fan, I would. But you know I'd have to report it."

"I know. I was standing looking in the mirror, and I saw myself."

She smiles. "Wow, twenty minutes looking at yourself in the mirror? You really aren't that handsome, Fan."

"No, I mean, I saw myself standing there, and then in the mirror, I saw my double."

She frowns. "I don't get it."

"Neither did I. I watched someone who looked identical to me walk in behind me, and then he just stood there for a minute. He looked at the dead Sanctioner, and at me, and he seemed surprised to see me. Then he put a hand on my shoulder, like this..." I reach over the table and rest a hand on her shoulder so she can feel the weight. "That's how I know it was real. I wasn't hallucinating; I could *feel* it."

From the bag at her feet she takes out her holo unit and sets it to record, then looks up again. "You were standing inside Le Thuyen's house and another person walked through the door behind you. You saw him in the mirror?"

"Not another person. It was me."

"Cyber or human?"

I pull the images out of my cache. A small blue pulsing light between his brows. "Cyber."

She seems annoyed. "If you were standing there, it couldn't be you, could it?"

I consider this. "I guess not."

"And this person looks surprised to see you, but all they do is walk up behind you and put a hand on your shoulder."

"Yeah. It was like they were trying to…I don't know…reassure me, or themselves. But I wasn't worried, I was mostly confused. I just kept looking at him in the mirror, and he just stood there."

"Describe this individual, Fan."

I point at my face. "He looked like this."

"Very funny." She checks the recording function on her holo. "Are you playing around with me again, Fan? Because I've had a few hard weeks, and I don't think I can take it."

"No, I swear. He was there."

"Why the hell didn't you mention it before?"

"Because it sounds impossible, right? I walk into a house and stand there looking down at a dead Sanctioner, which is already unheard of, and then in the mirror I see my double, and I think I'm hallucinating, but then I feel this hand on my shoulder and I know it's real."

She cocks her head. "You could have been hallucinating. I'm not a psychologist but I know even people who have been cauterized can react to acute traumatic events. Like a killing."

I smile weakly. "Maybe."

"Maybe. Can we agree that it couldn't have been you, standing behind yourself, in the mirror?" she asks, exasperated.

I consider this, and decide not to argue with her. "OK."

She takes the holo, starts twirling it on the table, still recording. "So if there was someone there…"

"There was…"

"…then the person you saw probably had something to do with Huang's death, because why else was he there? Why didn't *he* react to the sight of a dead Sanctioner in the house? Like, what did he do after he touched you?"

"He turned around and went outside, then he left."

"And what did you do?"

I remember the morning again. He looks at me in the mirror, and puts a finger on his lips as though to say, "Sshh." He turns and walks out the door and I can see him going up the driveway. Then he opens the gate and closes it behind him, and I hear footsteps as he walks away.

I tell Lin this. She drifts quickly.

"There were no reports of a person in that area other than you at the time of the killing, Fan – no one saw this person," she tells me, turning the holo with her fingers. "No neighbors, no taxi AI, no cameras, the only tracks on the ground there were yours. No one saw the Thuyen family leave. No one saw anyone except *you* going into that house. And you gave us permission to pull your Core cache for the day of the murder. This incident was not recorded by your visual cortex."

"I moved it to my local cache."

"Because why? That's just suspicious."

"Because it was too weird and I needed to think about it."

"Show me." She holds out her holo. "Dump the vision."

I hesitate. She would need a major league warrant to force me to hand over something from my local cache. A cyber keeps their most personal, private stuff there. Off Core, where no one else can access it.

She wiggles her holo. "You volunteered the information. Come on."

I pull up the vision and then dump it into her holo. She lays the holo down on the table between us and starts playing it. "What am I looking at?"

"Me, seeing myself in the mirror, then following the person out to the driveway of Le Thuyen's house. I'm standing in the doorway of the house. Oh, sorry, here…" I wave my fingers to zoom the image a little and freeze it. "There…you can see them best in this frame."

She looks at the holo, and then at me. "That's you, from behind…"

"I told you."

"Who captured this?" She sounds angry. "This is from some other cyber's cache."

I shrug. "No, it's mine. I saw this person, walking away up Le Thuyen's driveway on the day the Sanctioner was killed, and then I went back inside and looked at myself in the mirror again and reran the images in my cache, and tried to tell myself I wasn't crazy. And when I'd convinced myself I saw what I saw, but that it made no sense, I cached the vision and called the police."

She puts the holo next to her cup. "So why didn't you tell us this before?"

"Look at your reaction now. Would you have believed me? Or would you have had me locked up as a lunatic and probably charged me with the killing?"

She taps the table. "We probably still will lock you up as a lunatic and charge you with the killing. Oh no, we already did that, didn't we, Fan?" Eyes black now. "The first time you started talking like a lunatic, with your recital of legendary disembowelments. And here we are again and now you are saying there was another person there the day Sanctioner Huang was killed, and that person looked just like you."

I point at the holo. "So who is that?"

She looks at the image again. "Like I said, it could be from someone else's vision. An accomplice."

"Except it isn't."

"So, what's your explanation?" she asks, exasperated. "You must have one."

"Clone."

"It's impossible to clone a cyber. Every cyber is birthed with a unique appearance and DNA which cannot be copied or altered without introducing fatal replication flaws."

"Someone found a way."

"No. You are birthed as babies. As you grow, your environment impacts your physical form. Even if this individual was birthed at the same time as you, with identical DNA, we'd see physical deviations, even if they had surgery. No two cybers can be made to look 100 percent alike."

I zoom on the portion of the face that is visible and turn my head to the same angle. "Not a bad effort though, wouldn't you say?"

"Also, criminal."

"So is murder."

She sighs. "I'm going to get the techs at work to check this vision, match it against your own face print, then run a continuity check on your Core cache to see if there is a gap that fits, and then I might, just might, believe you, Fan." She turns the holo around, frozen on the image of me at the end of the driveway, half turned, as though looking at something off to my left. "What is that pattern on the guy's t-shirt? Is it a flower of some sort?"

"No," I tell her. "It's blood."

If possible, the SS and the police get even more excited after that. Now they have vision of a person who looks like me at the scene of the death of Sanctioner Huang, and a witness convinced a person who looks like me killed the second Sanctioner, two streets away. Lin gets the police holographer to take a new scan of my face, to match with the image in the holo. It comes back a 100 percent match, but there is only a partial view of the face of the person in the holo so it's not enough, legally, to use in a trial.

You might think they'd put the image out to the Corecasters and ask for information from the public.

But they don't. They don't want anyone to know *two* Sanctioners are dead and a cyber is their prime suspect. That would be a very dangerous piece of information in a world where a significant number of humans subscribe to the idea that cybers are the enemy inside their walls: liberated by Tatsensui, chained to the Tatsensui Core, waiting for the right moment to rise up and eliminate all right-thinking PRC citizens and deliver the moon into full Tatsensui control.

I get called into the SS headquarters by Vali. Lin picks me up. She's quiet on the way in this time, not much chat. Won't tell me what it's about. I have my suspicions and they prove right. Two Wards meet me at the door. Wards don't growl, but they should. Animal like that, looks like a killer feline with wings, it should growl. But they have yellow eyes and a malevolent stare, so their designers thought that's intimidating enough, I guess.

I stand looking at them, and they glare back. Quite beautiful. And powerful. If they were protecting the dead Sanctioners, how did the killer get by them? If they weren't...why not? Who had called them off?

"When you are quite finished proving you aren't scared," Lin says. "Come with me."

She leads off, one Ward behind her, then me, then the other Ward close on my heels. We walk through offices and everyone stops to watch. I guess not every interviewee gets a two-Ward escort.

Vali is sitting in an interview room, looming over a desk. The Wards split either side of him and crouch, ready to pounce. Lin nods at him and gives me a small look, signifying something like 'be careful'. She backs out of the room and closes the door behind her.

"Sit," the Expositor says. No 'please' this time.

I pull the steel chair back and sit down on it. He smiles. A tight-lipped smile, meaning nothing.

"So, you got a warrant to probe me," I say. It's not a question. I don't ask to see the warrant. He wouldn't be allowed to dive my local cache without one.

I feel a little sorry for him. He's going to be disappointed. As I'm still young, I can rely on biological memory for a lot of my daily functioning, so I tend to offload nearly everything I experience to the Core and keep very little cached. The only thing I have there right now is the holo I already showed Lin.

Besides, I don't have the coin to be able to keep too much cached locally. A cyber earns credit fractions for every byte of data they transfer to the Core. Anything you keep back is coin you don't earn.

When a cyber reaches reintegration age – thirty – all data still locally cached is uploaded anyway. In the end, no cyber can keep his or her secrets from the Core. Because lived experience is one way the Core learns, and grows. It reintegrates its agents, adds the sum of their experience to all the other data it has collected, and then wipes their memories clean, ready for rebirth.

"I did," Vali says. He nods at the two Wards. "Perhaps you're wondering, why two?"

I nod. He can't read minds, but it is a pretty obvious question, the way I am looking around. When the military use of cybers for kinetic operations was banned as part of the mutual non-aggression pact between the three worlds at Federation, PRC immediately accelerated development and deployment of Wards. Armed only with non-lethal weapons, they break no treaties. They can interface with cybers and with the Core, and with Core authority can immobilize a cyber in an instant, shutting down one of its hearts with a simple command – keeping it alive, but crippled. But yes, I am wondering why two. One Ward should be sufficient to access my local cache.

"I don't believe you are harmless, Sanctionee. I believe you are a dangerous killer. So I have one Ward to watch over you, and the other to probe you."

"You're not overdramatizing things, just a little?" I ask.

"Overdramatizing? You killed Sanctioners Huang and M'ele. You manufactured alibis to cover your tracks. You hid vision from the murder, or murders, in your local cache. You have created a Grand Deceit with deadly intent, and I have made it my mission to reveal who you really are."

"The SS cauterized me," I remind him. "Whoever I am, you made me."

"And yet," he smiles again. "Not quite as simple as that, is it, Mr. Zhaofeng?"

Ah. So he knows now. What I was sentenced for. Now I understand his passionate declaration of intent.

"Does the High Council know you are doing this?" I ask.

"They don't involve themselves in menial affairs," he says.

"Probing my local cache is a menial affair?"

"You are a Sanctionee, nothing more. A Sanctionee who insists he was just in the wrong place, at the wrong time, inveigling us in a fiction about seeing his own double. That's all."

"You expect to find proof in my cache that I killed two Sanctioners. What will happen when you don't?"

"If that is the case, my investigation will continue," he says. "Sanctions are done to ensure that criminals are powerless to harm others – human or cyber. The only reason you are still free is that my superiors insist that Sanction has never failed. Or, in your case, they are afraid of the consequences if it becomes public that it has."

"Your superiors don't believe I can be guilty. And yet, *you* won't accept my innocence."

"We will begin," he says sharply, and that's all the warning I get.

It is not just a probe. They knock me out with a neural blast, which is not part of the normal process. I've been probed before of course, as part of the criminal proceedings against me. Last time I was conscious throughout it, but this time I black out, and wake on a bed in a cell. The door is open and there is a glass of water by the bed. I realize I am very thirsty and need to use the toilet. I must have been out for quite a while. I gulp the water down and relieve myself in a bucket in the corner. Peering out of the open cell door, I see Lin sitting on a chair in the corridor, reading something on a viewer.

"I thought that tinkling sound must be you," she says.

"They found nothing, then?" I ask, walking over and sitting down against the wall next to her.

"I don't know what they found," she says, resting the small viewer in her lap. "Vali doesn't tell me everything. But he didn't look or feel pleased afterward. Told me to wait for you to wake up and give you this."

She hands me a headache medication and a glass of water.

I'm not an idiot. Vali wants his very cute Expositor to spend some time with me, get under my skin, get to know me. See if anything shakes out of my tree. Part of me wishes I could help her more than I have.

Over a cup of coffee she is chattier. Is she relieved I'm still free? It certainly seems she's happier now than on the way in. I want to help her, I really do.

"Do you want to hear my theory about the doppelganger?" I ask her.

She sips her coffee and grimaces. Police coffee is seriously the worst. "Sure, entertain me."

"It's me, or a version of me. Someone has cloned me, created a rogue cyber without the normal behavior protocols, and used it to commit these murders."

She shakes her head. "We discussed that. That sort of thing requires State-level resources, planetary scale," she says. "Creating a clone, indoctrinating it, keeping it off-Core, deploying it undetected. And why Clone you, a Sanctionee? Why not clone a total nobody who wouldn't even be on our radar?"

"Precisely because of who I am," I tell her. "The perfect fall guy. The evil cyber, once Sanctioned, forever guilty. Look at how determined Vali is to get me for these murders, in the face of every single fact that proves it couldn't be me."

"He's just doing his job," she says, not very convincingly.

"No, he won't let this go," I tell her as I finish my cup. "Trust me, if I could help you, I would."

She looks at me across the plastic table. "I actually think you would, you know that? Why not just tell Vali what he wants to know, then?" she asks.

"My crime?"

"No. He thinks he knows *what* you did now, but there is something else. Something about it. He won't tell me what you did, I can't even ask him. But there's something that's driving him crazy – the not knowing is eating at him, I can feel it."

"And that is the one thing I can't help him with," I tell her. "If he knows what I did, then he probably knows as much as me. I had cached the memories and sensory feed of my crime and it was downloaded and wiped before I was Sanctioned. The crime I was convicted of, I don't even remember it. I've seen the on-Core audio and visual record, so I don't doubt I did it, but the true memory is gone."

"And you won't tell me," she sighs.

"The High Council judgment says I can't say a word, to anyone, cyber or human, about what I did. I say one word, I really am screwed."

She smiles, fleetingly. "If there's a clone of you running around out there killing Sanctioners, you think you aren't screwed already?"

I smile back. "I've had it worse."

I start to see signs the SS are having me watched. A couple of times I go outside my house, I see Wards in the distance, on the ground, in the air. Little more than dark shadows, but I know what they are. A Ward won't usually be seen unless it wants to be, so I figure they are trying to send me a message. The tracker in my wrist is clearly not enough for Vali. *We are watching you, Fan Zhaofeng.*

The Corecasters don't let the story of the dead Sanctioner go away, but they don't seem to get any closer to learning that there are not one, but two dead Sanctioners, so the SS and the Council have that under control for now, at least.

Ben, the long-distance freight guard, calls me soon after. My clients, the ones like Ben who actually want help, I give them my home holo number. I'm not supposed to, but so far it hasn't been a problem and I'll do whatever it takes to help my clients avoid Sanction or a prison term. If they're reforming, and a little more contact than normal is needed to keep them on track, then I give it to them.

Besides, Ben only calls when Yung gets really bad and he doesn't know what to do.

"She's off her meds," he says this time. "I locked her in the bathroom."

In the background, I can hear someone thumping hard on a door. "Is she lucid?"

"Kind of, she's mostly pissed off. Her pills are in there, I told her I won't let her out until she takes one, but I think she flushed them, so that wasn't so bright."

"Ben, you can't lock her up. That will break the conditions of your release."

"Fan, I fuckin' know that!" he says, and starts sobbing. "What else am I supposed to do? She was walking around the house raving, holding a broken vase."

"Did she cut herself?"

"No, I got it off her."

"I'll come over, but I might have to bring a police officer with me."

"Don't bring anyone. Please. Just come," he says.

I consider the risk. "Alright, but let her out of the bathroom, okay, Ben?" I tell him. "I'll have to report it if I arrive there and find her locked up again."

I get to their house and the lights are on in every room. Ben is waiting at the door, and Yung is pacing. I've seen Yung like this before and she's almost impossible to communicate with. I spoke with her doctor on the way, and he recommended we get her to the psych ward again to get assessed.

Ben points. "I've been trying to keep her more or less in the lounge."

Yung is pacing the floor in their small living room, talking loudly and gesturing with her hands. Her voice is hoarse, like she has been shouting, and her eyes are wild. She looks at us as we come in, but doesn't see us. People with auditory hallucinations often have the same recurring themes in what they hear and say. Tonight she seems to be arguing with her unseen audience. "I am safe here!" she cries.

"You are such a bloody ignoramus."

Suddenly she spins and comes straight at me. Grabs my shirt in one hand and my arm in the other. "If you don't move between the sculptures you won't be safe. Do you understand?"

"OK, Yung," I tell her, taking her arm as well. "We'll get inside the sculptures." I pull her to a sofa between two sculptures I've learned are important for her. One sits on her fireplace, a fat lady dancing on a ceramic globe. The other stands on the windowsill on the other side of the room. An impossibly skinny wooden woman in a colored dress holding a spear. "They are shielding us. You need to sit. So tell me. Tell me what's up."

She blinks. "Fan?" She sounds betrayed. Ben puts an arm gently around her but she shrugs him off. "No, I'm not, I'm not going to sleep." She grabs his face. "Don't, Ben. Don't do this. I'll be okay, I just need to find the right space." She puts her hands to her ears. "I just want to be able to hear!"

I stand beside her until she calms down a little. She turns her head slowly and looks at me. "There are too many of me," she says. "I can't keep all of us together."

I take her hand. She slips it from my grasp and raises it to my face, gentle now. "Which version of me are *you*?"

There is conflicting advice about how to manage people during a psychotic episode. I've done courses. I've had a live-in on a closed ward so I can learn from the staff. The best advice I got was from the diary of a schizophrenic woman. *"To help, you first have to live yourself into their world."* I don't know if it is good advice for everyone, but it seems to work with Yung.

"I'm Fan," I tell her. "We're between the sculptures. You're safe. You're safe and now I'm going to call the hospital to come and help. You can take the sculptures with you, to protect you. You're going to be fine, Yung."

She doesn't pull away this time, but she closes her eyes. "Bullshit, Fan. It's getting worse, and none of us are going to be fine ever again."

A week later I visit her in the hospital. I bring her a viewer so she can catch up on the news. The dead Sanctioner is no longer the lead story, but the story is still being updated. "Sanctioner murder investigation dragging" is the headline. Journalists asking why it is taking so long to name a suspect. There is a quote from a Council member. "It is a highly unusual event," he says. "The police and SS are pursuing multiple lines of investigation."

What lines? Am I not the only suspect?

I'd always thought it was interesting that Tatsensui, even though it won the war, allowed PRC to continue as an autonomous world, with its own planetary government and a free press, seemingly able to report whatever they wanted. The only organs of visible control Tatsensui forced on the defeated PRC was the SS, and the apparently benign Core.

Yung comes out to meet me in trousers and a red t-shirt looking for all the world like she is ready to walk back outside with me. But she isn't. We get coffee from a vending machine in the waiting room because she isn't allowed to go down to the hospital cafeteria without supervision.

"Smells good," I say as it pours into the little cups.

"Tastes like shit," she replies. "But better than most of the other drugs you can get in here."

I pull up a chair in the guest lounge. Yung parks herself in the windowsill side on to me, looking out at a fine dusting of sand blowing overhead. The city is open to the sky, but constant overpressure within the city walls keeps most of the drifting sand from falling. "How is Ben coping?" she asks, still looking out the window. She has a long thin nose you really only notice in profile. Aquiline, I think it is called.

"I talked with him yesterday," I tell her. "I think he's living on high-sucrose drinks and junk food, but he's alright. He came in last night, right?"

"Yeah," she sighs. "Poor guy. Half of him wants me to stay in here, the other half can't stand the thought I am here at all."

"How is it?"

She shifts uncomfortably. "The drugs stop the voices, which is okay because by the time I get here, I am sick of listening to them. Literally sick. But it's a bit like being...amputated."

"Amputated?"

"Like a part of me has been cut away. A whole *dimension* of me, missing."

"You still think they are real."

"They *are* real, Fan, just not real in the way you think about. What drives me insane, figuratively, is I can't help trying to find some sort of meaning in what they're saying. When I look back afterwards it seems at first just like random noise. But then I think about it some more and go back over the diaries, and think I see a pattern…"

"So that's when you go off the drugs?"

"I remove the filter that stops me hearing the voices. The drugs are the filter. The first few days are ok. I just sit still and listen, and write stuff down. Like one of those Undiscovered Races people who listen for messages from the stars. Then I hear one that seems so coherent. I start replying when they say something like a question. They get angry sometimes, giving me orders. It turns into a conversation, but not one that makes any sense to anyone outside my own head."

Her long brown hair is tied into a neat ponytail now, and she's had a shower. Her fingers drum on the rim of her cup.

"They make sense to you?" I ask. "These voices?"

"At the time. Not now. But with the drugs onboard, it is like trying to remember a smell. You can remember where you were, what you were doing when you smelled it, but can you really recreate a smell in your head?"

I smile. I can, of course. Humans can't. "Not really."

"Like that. But there must be a way to help others understand." She starts talking excitedly. "I am going to make a documentary about communication between parallel universes, Fan. I must have this tuner, a special tuner hidden in my body that means I can hear people speak in other universes, and I can speak with them. There's one individual in particular I am really tuned into. A kind of teleconference of souls."

My mind does a bit of a flashback, remembering how once Yung decided that if she could get rid of the tuner, the voices would stop. She convinced herself it was hidden under her thumbnail. So she ripped her thumbnail off with a pair of pliers and was digging around in the flesh of her thumb with a needle when Ben found her. If she's still talking like this, I know she's not ready to come out of hospital yet.

She comes down from the windowsill and sits on the ground in front of my chair, with her back between my knees. She lays her head on my thigh and is still looking out the window. Her hair is dark and silky and I can see the curve of her neck and a small brown mole on her shoulder above the collar of her t-shirt.

"What are you thinking about?" I ask her.

"Entanglement."

"Spooky action at a distance…" I say, quoting Einstein. "What about it?"

"Well, I get the idea that you can split a particle into two particles which are separate in space and time, but then whatever happens to one particle tells you what happens to the other." She smiles. "But can you apply the principle to organisms? Could it be both a philosophical phenomenon and a physical one?"

I frown. "Philosophical entanglement?"

"Think about identical twins. Millions of studies show they can be in different cities, thinking and feeling the same thing at the same time. One is in an accident, the other wakes up feeling pain. Isn't that entanglement? Or you and me. Stuff happens to me, and suddenly you turn up?"

"Ben *called* me," I tell her. "On the holo. You've heard of a holo?"

"Yeah, yeah, but whenever I get into trouble, it's always you who is there for me. Have you noticed that?" she asks. "I think I wrote you into my life. I created the entanglement."

"Wrote me?"

"You know I write in my diaries. The voices I hear. Sometimes it's stuff that makes no sense at the time, but it makes sense later." Yung doesn't trust her innermost thoughts to the Core. Like a lot of people, she keeps her real secrets on paper.

"So you hear stuff from the future?"

"Plenty," she says, and reaches into her trouser pocket, leafing through some crumpled pages. "Here's one. I never showed it to you before. Not even to Ben." She points at a page with her finger. "You're going to ask me when I wrote this, and if I tell you I wrote it five years ago, you're going to ask me to prove it, but I can't. That diary is dated five years ago, and I ripped this page out of it, but I can't prove I didn't write those words later. You just have to believe me."

I look at the page. It doesn't look like she has used different ink. The same black spidery ink runs across line after line.

Including the line she has highlighted. What could she have

written that she wouldn't even show Ben? I look at the page and it is a jumble of random words, phrases, descriptions of sounds.

"Where am I looking?"

She looks up. "Here. I didn't highlight the sentence." She takes the paper back and puts her finger on a sentence about halfway down the page. "There."

I put my own finger on the page and take it from her, squinting at her handwriting.

It says, *Fan's voice. They deserved to die…*

I read it again. "You heard *my* voice?"

She nods. "Before I even met you. Like 'Fan'? How many people do I know with that name? Only you. I haven't told my doctor about this, or Ben. They might tell you to stay away from me or something and I couldn't handle that, Fan." She slips her small hand into mine. "They wouldn't understand. I love you, Fan, in a different way than I love Ben, and I think you know that, but you don't mind. I also know you have a hard time understanding me when I tell you what I hear, how I hear it. But you do listen. And I really need someone who believes me."

It's not often I feature in people's delusions, so I had to think about it. Especially as I seem to be having delusions of my own, like seeing myself in mirrors.

Lin has pretty much convinced me I didn't see myself in the mirror. In my 'shock' – if that applies to someone who has been cauterized – at seeing the Sanctioner dead on the floor, I saw someone come in behind me and had some sort of brain fart and convinced myself there was nothing to fear because it was just me. Kind of a useful cowardly delusion so I didn't crap my pants when the killer walked back into the house soaked in blood. I have to admit, it sounds like a pretty reasonable kind of psychic defense mechanism, if it really was the killer who walked in behind me. And it worked, if all he did was rest a hand on my shoulder and go.

But what about the vision I cached, I ask myself. That person walking away up the gravel driveway does not just *look* like me. I know me. And I know what I look like from behind because it isn't the first holo of myself I've seen. That was me, watching me, walking away.

Did I have such a mental breakdown that an accomplice I can't remember captured that vision, then placed it in my cache? That is the part I am struggling with and I can see Lin has no easy explanation for the vision either because the data fit perfectly into a gap in the stream of my sensory feed in the Core for that time period. Had I blacked out, though? Had my cache been hacked and the memory implanted?

You have these kinds of crazy thoughts when something like this happens. Because I don't get upset easily, I actually enjoy mulling them through. A cup of tea and a good mull can be a whole evening's entertainment for me, which is kind of pathetic but there you are. I decide to do my mulling at a pub, because it is a nice evening and it would be a good night to walk there, take in the sunset and see the azalea flowers get that deep purple, almost glowing hue they get just about nightfall. At the pub I have two beers, doodle on a notepad, watch the end of a subsea jousting bout with a few other people I don't know, eat a pizza slice and a salad and then walk home, trying to work out if I can see Tatsensui rising through the sand mist, or not.

There is a note on my dining table when I get home.

"The locks on my house are all coded to my thumbprint," I'm telling Lin as she walks up my driveway. I called her first. Sure she's SS, but despite the fact most of our conversations center around me as a suspect, I think she does like me. I mean, she hasn't stopped being rude and trying to tease me, so that must count for something.

"Where is it?" she asks, pulling off her jacket and looking for a hook to hang it on as she comes through the door. She doesn't try very hard, and I pick the jacket up off the floor near the front door where she drops it.

"I didn't touch it. I just read it. It's sitting on my dinner table exactly where it was when I came in."

She knows the layout of my house from her last visit, walks through the lounge to the dining room and leans over the piece of paper. I see she is careful not to touch it either. I know they can get DNA off paper, so I'm glad to see she is as careful as I was. She reads it out loud.

You need to read this carefully, Zhaofeng, the note starts. *The SS are afraid of you. There is nothing an oppressor fears more than being exposed as weak, and their weakness has now been exposed with brutal glory. How? Why? By whose hand? And which of them is next? They need you free because you are their only clue and they know locking you away will not stop what is coming. They are teetering on the edge, terrified of the fall. They fear that an insurrection has started and you are their only clue to understanding it, and stopping it. You must run, Zhaofeng. Run and hide and wait until the storm has passed. You are needed for greater things. I will contact you soon and show you more.*

She turns to me. "It's hand written. Do you recognize the writing?"

"Sure," I tell her. "It's mine."

A couple of police officers come and they scan the doors and windows for fingerprints and take the letter away in an evidence bag after documenting the way it was lying on the table. They scan around the table and DNA-check a few other things like the toilet and kitchen appliances, just for good measure.

Lin's partner, Vali, comes as well. He doesn't look particularly worried about the coming 'insurrection' to me. He reads the note and takes it with him as he leaves. He talks to the police techs, and to Lin, but the only thing he says to me is, "We will speak about this, cyber."

After they have all gone, I make Lin some tea and she sips it reflectively, looking at the image of the letter on her holo unit. "It's like your own writing?"

"No. It *is* my writing. A little shaky, perhaps, but it's like I would write if I was writing quickly," I tell her. "A handwriting expert could check it. I can give you some notes I wrote."

"But you didn't write this one?" she smiles.

"No."

"Just because you wanted an excuse to call me?"

"I assume you're teasing. That would be pretty desperate, and very weird."

She shrugs. "I've seen weirder, Fan."

"No, I didn't write a fake insurrectionist letter and put it on my own table and then call you just because I wanted to see you. If I had wanted to call you, I would have just called you."

Lin sits on the table. "I won't take that as an insult. So what is your theory, Mr. Zhaofeng, because unless we find the DNA of a second individual on that letter, and lacking any sign of a forced entry, the SS will have to conclude that *you* wrote that letter."

I sit opposite her, my own tea cup in front of me, going cold. "I see three possibilities. Either someone else wrote that letter and faked my handwriting…"

"Yes, or…"

"Or I wrote it myself. Which I don't remember doing. So I am going insane."

She gives me her appraising look. "You do have a special ability to look at things objectively, I'll give you that. I am tending toward that one myself, Fan. But what was number three?"

"You won't like it."

"Try me."

"The person who wrote this is the same person I saw in Le Thuyen's house," I tell her, and leave it there.

"The one who was you, but not you?"

"Yes."

What I like about Lin is her calmness. She listens, she takes things in, she processes them from a few angles and makes a judgment, and there is not much fuss or bother about it. But her eyes flash black then green again as she drifts and comes back to the conversation.

"I want you to have a psychiatric examination," she tells me. "I want you to be seen by an SS psychiatrist. Would you do that for me, Fan?"

I figure I already know what a psychiatrist would say. "OK, sure."

"Vali will take this formally to the High Council now," she says. "They've resisted locking you up so far, for some reason. This letter might be enough to change their mind."

"I did think of that," I tell her. "Before I called you. But I called you anyway. I could have just destroyed that letter."

"And that is working in your favor, for now," she says. She walks to the door and looks around for her jacket, so I take it out of the hall cupboard and help her put it on. "You are so polite," she smiles. I smile back. "Weird, nerdy and pretty messed up, but with manners. You know, Fan, if you prove not to be a psycho cyber-killbot, you *can* call me some time and we can go out."

I do go out with people. I go out with Yung, for example, and Ben. People from work. But they don't expect anything from me, and I really don't know how that would work. I must seem a little hesitant, because she looks embarrassed and says straight away, "Or not. Inappropriate. Forget that."

"No, I'd like to. I'll do that," I tell her. "Assuming I don't get locked away forever by your SS partner."

"Whatever." She puts her holo in her back pocket. It's late and the cicadas are in full song, so it is actually a little hard to hear her because she's talking as she's walking away. "I *have* thought through what you said," she's telling me. "That the only person who could have gotten into your house, and written that letter in your own handwriting, is you. But you don't mean the you who is standing here now, do you, Fan?"

It's not a question, so I don't answer it.

She gives me a wave without turning around, and goes out the gate to her car.

The police psychiatrist and I agree to call this theoretical other me, the clone, 'Citizen X'. It isn't very original but it makes conversation simpler. And it's not that simple a conversation.

I do a battery of tests for his AI and then we meet at his private rooms, because he doesn't actually work for the SS, he's just a consultant. They must have a good budget for this investigation, because he's also human, not just an AI. But then, two Sanctioners dead, of course they do.

He has a nice little sandstone cottage in a quiet street off a central ring but the gutters need replacing and he shouldn't let his life partner do the decorating, because there are floral motifs on every wall, doorknob, cupboard and drawer, even in his office. He, on the other hand, looks and talks like a subsea jouster pilot and I doubt he has even looked twice at all the little flowers.

In his waiting room he gets me to confirm my medical history and then walks through it with me. We get to the part about known psychological conditions. I've written, "Sanctioned."

"That's not a psychological condition," he says. "It's physical. But thanks for being open with me." He's got a nice rough face full of interesting scars and pock marks, like a weathered brick. His voice is gravelly, but his hands are soft and he wheezes a bit, so if he ever did pilot a jouster, it was a while ago. And he's got curly hair, which makes the tough old face look less threatening.

I tell him about my own specialist and the morality test he gave me about the baby in the basement.

"What did you think about that? What he said?"

"That the cauterization affected my morality? Well, we know it affects emotion, and emotion is a huge component of morality," I tell him. "Take emotion out of moral judgments and you would get objective judgments that might be seen by others as immoral."

"Tell me about your clone theory," he asks me. That's good, because it shows he has been talking to Lin and has been briefed. I'm ready for that one, though. I've done my research. I tell him about CSS covert agents – off-Core cybers specially birthed by the Coruscant Security Service to infiltrate terrorist groups on the three moons.

"Rumors," he says. "Whispered by the paranoid in the dark corners of the Commonwealth." He shrugs. "So my police friends tell me."

"Of course they would," I point out. "But in the absence of proof they don't exist, you have to assume they could."

"By that logic, a rainbow-colored unicorn could have killed those Sanctioners," he observes. "In the absence of proof that it didn't, you have to assume it could have. Which is nonsense, would you not agree?"

"Cloning is old tech," I persist. "All it takes is a few strands of my DNA…"

"Cloning of fully biological organisms is old tech," he agrees. "Like cats, dogs, birds, even humans." He points to the spot between my brows where my Core diode is mounted. "Cloning cybers requires access to restricted cybernetic technologies and enormous bandwidth. Obtaining them without triggering a Core alert on Tatsensui or PRC would be impossible."

"New Syberia births fully autonomous cybers," I point out. "Off-Core, completely independent organisms. They could insert my DNA into one of their birthing pods and…"

"Do a Core search for me," he interrupts. "I'll reimburse you for it. What is the solution to the mathematical problem that is the Collatz Conjecture?"

I quickly drift. "There isn't one. Only partial solutions. How is that relevant?"

"A New Syberian cyber cannot Core drift. You just did. Ergo

your Citizen X cannot be an autonomous cyber double, birthed in the pods of New Syberia." He lets that hang. "But tell me about this twin anyway. Not your conjecture, your lived experience."

So I tell him about my experience at the Thuyen's house and he tells me Lin showed him my file, the vision I captured.

"And after analyzing all the possibilities, able as you are to draw on the almost unlimited processing capacity of the Core, you have concluded a body double is the most likely?"

"Yes."

"If I said that I find your perspective on these events to be indicative of a mental health problem, and that my support AI concurs, how would you respond?" he asks very carefully.

"You and your AI would have every right to think that the idea there is another Fan out there killing Sanctioners is crazy," I tell him. "But since that first Sanctioner died, half the world has convinced itself that cybers can and do kill humans, right? Even though there isn't a single cyber-human murder on PRC ever recorded. Trust me, I know the 'Citizen X' idea sounds far out." I shrug. "It's just the most probable theory. There are others; like I was in shock and hallucinating. Or I made it up, though the holo is real. I could have maybe hacked my vision to change the date stamp on that holograph, and faked the holo, or someone else could have. It's all possible. But I have analyzed every probability, including the one that I have successfully faked all the evidence in my defense somehow – bribed or coerced all the witnesses, faked the geolocation and Core data, manipulated imaging and audio feeds, and I am actually the murderer."

"You admit that possibility?" he asked.

"Of course. Except that as we all know, I'm a cyber, and I've been Sanctioned – for both of those reasons it couldn't be me. I can't hate, can't kill."

"Do you have to hate to be able to kill?" he asks. "I kill insects that bite me, but I don't hate them."

It's a fair point, but not a new one. "Cauterization is not just about putting a damper on your emotions, it puts a block on the urge to hurt, and to kill. On top of my existing protocols, that's like a lock on top of a lock."

He looks unconvinced. "So, going back to that hypothetical about burglars in the house, you can logically conclude that killing that baby might be necessary, but you yourself could never do it?"

"Right."

"Even to save the whole family?"

"No more than I could fly them out the window," I tell him. "When something is physically impossible, it isn't really an option."

He just says, "Hmmm." We talk more, but thankfully it's quite a medical discussion, not a personal one. Shrinks who want to talk to you about your mother and father issues? No thanks.

We get to the end of the session and he says, "I'll make a report and send it to the SS."

I stand. "OK then. Can I get a copy?"

"I can tell you what's in it already if you want to hear it."

I sit again. "Sure."

"On the basis of our sessions, the analysis provided by my AI and with no other opportunity to observe or interact with you, I can reach no conclusion about the nature or state of your mental health pertinent to the murders of the two Sanctioners," he says with practiced authority.

I wait a little too, and then ask him, "But what do you really think?"

He actually looks quite concerned. "I think you've been in child welfare too long, Mr. Zhaofeng. I think that even though you've been Sanctioned, you're cracking up as a result of seeing too much trauma and abuse, and seeing that first Sanctioner dead on the floor in a pool of his own blood probably pushed you over the edge and you're experiencing severe stress. I think you should seek treatment urgently and if you don't, I predict you'll be on long-term sick leave before the year is out."

I blink. "But you don't think I'm a psychotic Sanctioner-assassin."

"I have no opinion on that, but I do think you probably wrote that letter and that is something you should discuss with your own specialist, or the SS. But I am not them."

This is to be expected, I guess. I wonder if he'll say all that to Lin, or just the official version.

A couple of times in the next few days I wonder who should call who. Is it me expected to call her to find out what he really wrote in his report? Or should she call me, to fill me in? I mean, she told me to ask her out if he cleared me of being psycho, right? So should I call her? Or should I just forget it and just get on with things without even thinking about it? I decide in the end that as I have done my bit, I can leave her to do hers, and I just get on with my case load at work. I visit my clients, join our weekly department meeting, prepare myself for a court appearance with a client, and I do some late night shopping because I love having the market to myself. Since the war, the interplanetary supply chain is still dodgy, there is rarely any interesting stuff left by 10 p.m. But I like going late at night, when there are no queues, no pushing and shoving to get the last loaf of bread or knob of cheese.

Lin calls after a week, but not to talk about the report. Or to ask me out.

"There were no DNA traces or prints on the letter," she tells me.

"There's something else…?"

"Something strange. We need to talk, Fan."

4. THE LETTER

She tells me to meet her at a building which turns out to be the SS forensic laboratory. I get there and a receptionist shows me out back where she's chatting with a technician. She smiles and waves me over. She introduces him as Henry Something-chau, and he shakes my hand. It's a firm handshake but his palm is damp. He looks nervous.

Vali is there too, which is probably why. He just nods at me, leaning in a corner and watching.

"How you doing, Fan?" Lin asks.

"Good. I was expecting you to call about my psych report, actually…"

"It said he couldn't conclude if you were a nutter or not," she smiles. "So I interpreted that in the best possible way."

"Which is?"

"The jury is still out. You'll get a letter in the next few days from the police asking permission to get your medical records from your doc. You can say no, by the way. But that's not why I suggested we meet here." She points at a light table – a big plastic box with a strong pearly light lit from underneath so that you can put objects on it. There is also a digital magnifying glass, a small cone-shaped one that projects an enlarged holo above anything you place it down on.

She reaches to a folder on the desk behind her and pulls out the page I found on my table. It's in a transparent sleeve and she lays the whole thing on the light table.

She gestures to the tech, Henry, and stands back out of the light.

He coughs. "Well, I checked for prints of course, stray fibers, DNA, food oils…the standard stuff. The paper is almost perfectly clean, which you wouldn't expect, actually. If a person, even a cyber, handwrites something on paper, they usually leave skin cells, oils, a trace of something."

"But you got nothing," Lin says, a little impatient. "Which tells us he is careful. And?"

"Well, the paper…"

"Tell him about the paper, Henry."

He's about 48, this guy, wispy black hair, bald on top, didn't shave today, maybe not for several days. Wears a jacket with a built-in utility vest with dozens of pockets, like a combat holographer. He smells like sausage. And I realize he isn't nervous, he's so excited, his lip is moist with sweat.

"Yes, the paper...well, most paper is made from cellulose pulp, you know, mashed-up plant fiber, rags, grasses?"

Lin nods. "But not this paper, eh, Henry?" She's looking at me.

"No, this paper is very special...it's..."

She holds up her hand to stop him. "Wait...Fan, quick question. Ever been to Kowloon Heights?"

I frown, look from her to the small sweaty tech, and back to Lin. "Kowloon? The Heights? No, Lin, I've never been to Kowloon."

"No? It's supposed to be an amazing place...towering above the desert plains, ten degrees cooler than anywhere else, every house has windchimes hanging outside..."

"Sorry. Never even been close."

She waves at Henry to continue.

"OK, so, it's Lokta paper. Made exclusively in Kowloon from a gene-modded plant that can only grow on the heights, you don't find it anywhere else."

I shrug. "Lokta paper?"

"So precious you can't even buy it. It is only ever used for sacred religious texts," Lin says. "Which makes anything that is written on it precious as well, which is the whole idea. Cool, right?"

"Can you even get it here?" I ask.

"Good question. I asked the same question. Henry?"

"Far as we can tell, there are no distributors for Lokta paper anywhere on PRC except Kowloon and it is only for use on Neo-Confucian religious texts. People make pilgrimages to source the stuff."

"So we're looking for a pilgrim," I point out. "Or what?"

"Or...yes, good thinking, Mr. Zhaofeng. Yes, I suppose that's an angle. But see, when you can't see a pattern, and right now, we're not seeing a lot of patterns, we have to admit, what we do is to look at the pieces that *don't* fit. And one of the pieces here that doesn't fit is that you have someone who is extra, *extra* careful not to leave a single piece of biodata on that paper – not a smudge, not a breath, not a follicle of hair or crumb of food. But they write the damn letter on priceless Neo-Confucian religious paper?"

I just look at her. I know she is not expecting me to answer this for her.

She lets the question hang, then pats the tech on his shoulder. "Henry here is a freaking genius. *Lokta paper*. He worked that out in less than a week. Henry, what's your theory?"

Henry looks like the cat that got the cream. "I'm guessing he thought we would never be able to work out where the paper came from. But if we did, it was a big flag. It was like a test, or a taunt. Or both."

"A taunt, Zhaofeng. Like this killer is so arrogant, so confident, so unworried by us mere SS types that he sets us a little puzzle, to see if we are as clever as he is."

"How would he know?" I ask. "How would he know you even got the letter, that you would investigate it, whether or not you had worked it out?"

She smiles. "How indeed? What's the point of being so clever unless you can watch people trying to solve your little puzzles?" She waits again, but this time with intent.

"I didn't write the letter," I tell her again.

She rubs her face. "Of course you didn't. Senior Expositor Vali, he has a different theory. It's an interesting thing watching a senior Expositor at work. They have a great ability to declutter things. See through to their essence. Vali wants to tell you *his* theory."

The big Expositor steps forward, pushing himself into the light from the light table. It lights his jaw from underneath, so his eyes are just bright sparks above flared nostrils. "I can't break your alibis. I can't explain how you have subverted your Sanction or your behavior protocols. But this case keeps coming back to you, time after time. So I believe you are in league with this assassin. You work with Sanctioners. You know their movements and habits. You set them up, for someone else to kill them. And you try to misdirect us with things like the hologram from your cache." He breathes heavily and ruffles the light paper on the desk. "And like *this*."

It's an interesting theory. I can see why he would go there, faced with what he knows. "Motive?" I ask. "I don't hate, don't feel the need for revenge. As a cyber, I can't kill anyone, either human or cyber. Your psychiatric profiling came up with no reason to believe I was involved in these murders."

"No *emotional* reason," Lin says. "But how about political? What do you really think about the post-war world, Fan? The Laws, the Alignment, being Core-chained, Sanction, the High Council, cyber rights..." She points to Vali and then herself. "...the SS?"

"Generally, or shall I take them one at a time?" I ask her.

"Normally I would say, 'just the things you feel strongly about'," Lin says. "But in your case, how about just the things you've thought a lot about."

There is a stool against a wall and I drag it out and sit on it. "A lot of things have changed for the better for cybers since the Energy War. The Charter of Rights, the Articles of Alignment...we have the same freedoms now as most PRC citizens, and the same as cybers on Tatsensui have enjoyed for decades."

"Core-chaining?" Vali asks. "Before the war, we had our own independent Core system, based on Tatsensui's, but controlled by the PRC government. Cybers contributed data to the Core through dedicated research, but they lived independent of the Core." He taps his forehead between his brows. "Now you are Core-chained, your every thought and action uploaded and analyzed. The Core is its own master, neither Tatsensui nor PRC governments actually control it, and you are its agent. How real are these freedoms of which you speak?"

"I own my own thoughts," I tell him. "I choose what I upload and what I don't, at least until I am reintegrated. I choose where I live, where I work, who I associate with, even after my Sanction – which, by the way, I fully accept." I turn to face him squarely, so he can see that I mean what I say. "I am Core-chained now, yes. But I am more free now than I was before I was Core-chained and forced to work where I was told to work, and live where I was told to live."

"There is nothing in this post-war world you don't agree with?" Lin asks. "Nothing you would change?"

"Personally, no. I understand why a large part of the population is against Sanction and resents the SS. They see both of these things as tools by which Tatsensui maintains its influence over PRC."

"You *understand* those who resent the SS, who reject Sanction," Vali asks. "You mean, you sympathize?"

"No. That implies feeling. I understand the viewpoint. But Tatsensui does not have Sanction. It was a uniquely PRC solution to the dilemma of how to punish people for breaking the three Laws. The SS exists to enforce it, so you could argue without Sanction, the SS would not exist. The viewpoint has an internal logic."

Vali curses. "We are going in circles. You deny that you worked with an accomplice to kill Sanctioner Huang and Sanctioner M'ele?"

Quite honestly, right now, I wish the Expositors on this case included a cyber, rather than two humans. They jump from emotion to reason and back again, leaping about powered by what they call intuition and lacking the bandwidth for serious analysis.

"I have neither the capability, opportunity nor the motive to do so," I tell him. "I work with the SS, to enforce the Law and assist light offenders. I try to keep my clients out of prison, but if that fails, I facilitate Sanctions in order to prevent violent crime. But in the eyes of my fellow citizens, or at least a large number of them, I am a *traitor* to PRC," I tell Vali. "That puts me on your side, not against you."

Lin has her hand behind her head, rubbing her neck. "Traitor?" she says. "Is that how you feel?"

I look her directly in the eyes. "I've been cauterized. I. Don't. Feel. But tell me, how do *you* feel about being seen as a traitor, Expositor Ming?"

I can feel her and Vali's biosigns peaking, and realize I am pushing back too hard. "I'm sorry, that was inappropriate."

There is a long silence. Their heart rates and breathing drop marginally.

"You are a member of the Cyber Rights Movement," Vali says.

"Ninety-seven percent of cybers are," I point out. "Membership of the CRM is legal."

"Do you believe a cyber insurrection is inevitable, or necessary?" Lin asks.

"That is a human conspiracy theory, not one held by cybers. Insurrection is not part of the platform of the Cyber Rights Movement. Our only goal is full equality with humans, not their defeat through violence."

"Every insurrection needs a leader. One cyber, to be the first willing to embrace violence," Vali says. I can see he believes it. Worse, I can see he believes I could be it.

"I have neither the will, nor the means," I tell him.

"Not now, you insist, but that was not always true, was it?"

Lin looks at him sharply. "*What* did you just say?"

"Nothing," he snaps, and turns on his heel, stalking from the room.

She drives me home again but this time there is no pleasant conversation about cats. We are both largely silent.

At my house, she gets out and comes to my door, and without even asking walks inside and sits down at my dining table, dumping her bag, jacket and holo unit on the table in front of her. She is carrying a copy of the letter, and she places it down just about where I found it. We both look at it, just sitting there like a normal piece of paper.

"You know I have to ask you questions like that," she says. "I'm an Expositor. Just like you, I have to do my job."

"I know," I tell her. "And I can only answer the way I did. I didn't write that letter. I don't know who is behind those killings. But I did see my twin, that time at the first killing."

She sighs. "Fan, do you really believe that note came from this person you call 'Citizen X'?"

"Yes."

"And this 'Citizen X' is actually some sort of clone?"

"Well…"

"Fan. It simply can't be." She places a hand on my arm. "No. You may have seen someone at the site of that murder but you did not see a clone of yourself. We have holo vision you say is of the person you saw, and the time and date and location and bit size match, but the vision is not good enough for an identification. But now we have this note…" She spins around the copy on the table. "Written on some sort of weird-ass Kowloon mountain bush paper – warning you to run and hide and 'wait until the storm has passed'. What does that mean, do you think?"

"I don't know. It means there will be another killing, is what I thought," I admit.

"That's pretty much what we are thinking too, and no matter how we lift and turn this thing, there is one common denominator in everything so far." She lifts her holo unit and points it.

"Me."

"Give the man a prize. And so here's the deal. You say there is some other person running around who looks like you and is killing Sanctioners?"

I feel like I'm in one of those shows where they trick you into agreeing with something incriminating, so I lean back in my chair and fold my arms. "No, I never said that. I said there was someone who looked like me at the Thuyen house. That little boy said someone who looked like me was there when the second Sanctioner was killed."

"Thank you, Fan Zhaofeng, Master of Evidence. The deal is this...Law or no Law, you are either going to prison, or you are going to help us catch this Sanctioner-killing bastard."

She leans back in her chair.

"Choose."

5. THE KISS

When I fill her in on the latest developments, Yung just nods like notes written on Kowloon Lokta paper are something she sees all the time. Her medical AI told me she was a bit fragile today (actually it said labile, which means rocky, but I like fragile better, it sounds less gynecological). The city has the vapor misters going and there's a nice cool breeze, so we sit in the courtyard outside the kitchen of the hospital outpatient clinic, with our backs against a gate. In a corner opposite, the cooks have an oil can with the top cut off, where they dump all their organic waste. In the other corner, they have another oil can where they've planted a sunflower and it's loving the moist air. You can almost see it growing while you watch.

"If your Citizen X is being straight with you in that letter," Yung says, "then maybe you should take their warning seriously and get out of here."

"And go where? Tatsensui? It's the only offworld option. I'm Core-chained, which means I have to drift every two hours, connect to the Core to upload data, or I'll begin to shut down. Tatsensui is the only other Core colony. New Syberia is non-Core, same with the space port, Orkutsk. Tatsensui is a three-hour 45-minute shuttle shot. I'd have to go into stasis but if I didn't reconnect with the Core within two hours of arriving, I would *never* wake up. I'd just be shipped straight off for reintegration. No thanks."

She laughs. "Well, I wasn't thinking offworld. Since the two murders have both happened here in New Guangzhou, I thought maybe you could just cut out to Kwun Tong, a hundred miles away across the Golden Basin. It's a mining town, you'd have no trouble getting work. Like the letter says, lie low, wait until whatever this is, blows over."

Work is the least of my problems. Since the Alignment, all cybers can earn a living wage by allocating a proportion of their processing bandwidth back to the Core. It's called the bandwidth economy and was one of the changes Tatsensui brought in to foster cyber independence. My work in social services isn't the most intellectually demanding, so I generally run on about half of my available processing capacity and sell the rest to the Core. That alone is nearly enough for me to live on. My day-job salary goes mostly into savings.

But what would running to Kwun Tong achieve? "If he follows

me there, and a Sanctioner is killed in Kwun Tong, how does that look?"

"Ah. Good point," she nods. "That would actually be worse. Which of course would make sense, if he is trying to set you up to take the blame. This situation is a total mindbomb, Fan. This killer is not only screwing with the SS, he might also be screwing with you."

"Well, it's working," I tell her. "I went past my bathroom mirror the other day and was standing there making sure that my reflection was doing the same thing as me."

She slaps my leg for being silly. She's progressed to day release now. They want to let her out into Ben's care again but he has told them he isn't ready. They've told him they can't keep her indefinitely, and she's stable again, but he got really upset so they let her overnight for another week. Yung doesn't know all this, but she does know she's got a week or so more before she can go home.

She hums to herself, then stops suddenly. "You know, there is an option you aren't considering." I frown, so she continues. "OK, super brain, I know you probably have considered it, but maybe you didn't weight it with enough probability. You ready for this?"

"Hit me."

"Your Citizen X is an interdimensional you. Not a clone of you, but the actual you. From another universe."

"So this other me…"

"From another dimension…"

"From another dimension, came to my universe to kill Sanctioners." I frown. "No, sorry. Because why? Assuming he is me – a cyber – and he is even able to kill anyone, why go to all the trouble to do it in *my* universe?"

"Don't expect to understand why," she says, closing her eyes and playing with the idea. "I hear voices from other dimensions and I've learned you have to stop asking yourself what they are trying to say. It isn't about you. They have their own agenda. To you, in your reality, what makes sense to them appears completely random to you."

"Yeah, I'm not into the whole interdimensional reality thing," I tell her. "Trans-dimensional, yeah. Or warp drives wouldn't work. But interdimensional travel from one universe to another? Nah."

"Such a non-believer. I can take you on a trip to multiple universes right now," Yung says. "If you're willing."

I laugh. "Sure, let's go."

"Alright, sit still." She leans toward me, her face close to mine. I turn my head, thinking she's going to kiss my cheek, but she turns my face back toward her and moves closer so her lips are about a millimeter from mine. "Now," she whispers, with her eyes closed. "The future is poised. There is a universe in which I kiss you." Her breath is warm and soft. I can feel it flow across my lips. "And another where I don't."

She stays like that for a second more, then leans back against the wall again. I realize I've started breathing faster, which is a pretty normal thing in the circumstances. Physiological, animal response.

"There," she says. "The moment is past, you didn't seize it, but you just looked into a universe where you and I went on to make wild crazy love. Wave collapse. It's gone, but it was there. You saw it, you felt it. Right?"

"A choice not made is not a universe you could have visited," I tell her. "As you said, the minute we chose not to act, that universe disappeared. You can't travel there."

"So *wrong*." She leans forward again. This time, her lips brush mine. I feel myself breathing fast again. She whispers. "New choices, new potential, a multiplicity of new universes being created with...every...second." She touches her lips on mine and pulls back again. "We can rejoin that branch if we choose to, it hasn't disappeared. It's right there, a whole other universe with just you and me in it. We could go there...right now."

I cough, standing. "I think *you're* the one playing with my mind," I tell her. I reach down and pick up a stone, flip it at the empty oil can and miss. It's a fun idea, that there's a universe where I threw the stone into the can, and one where I missed. Right up to the point where I actually did throw the stone, and saw it go into the can, then the other possibilities ceased to be. But can I reopen those universes, every time I flip a stone, or at least, reopen the potential universe in which I will hit the can?

"I like that other universe," I tell her. "The one with you and me in it."

She nods. "Me too."

"But we can't go there," I tell her. "Ben."

"I know." She brings her knees up and rests her head on them. "I'm having trouble thinking straight with the drugs I've got onboard, but what I've been thinking is...what if your idea about Citizen X isn't crazy? What if it's just a matter of perspective, like multiverse theory?"

"Of how I'm looking at things?" I frown.

"No, of what your mind can cope with. Your Expositor friend says the idea that someone would or could clone you is unthinkable. But then she would happily lie in a warm bath made of gazillions of water molecules, which are made up in turn of gazillions of atoms of hydrogen and oxygen comprising gazillions of protons and neutrons made up of uber gazillions of quarks, leptons, bosons and so on...but she wouldn't sit there telling you the concept of a *bath* is unthinkable just because it is made up of gazillions upon gazillions of particles she can't see and will never be able to comprehend."

This is why I love hanging out with Yung, even in a psych ward.

"I don't think she takes baths," I tell her. "I'm betting she's a shower girl."

Lin's idea of me helping her catch the killer is to intensify the surveillance on *me*.

I thought she would use my cyber capacities, get me reviewing evidence, looking for links she and Vali and the other SS officers couldn't see. But no, the idea is just to surround me with police officers, drones and Wards and wait for the killer to come to me again.

Lin says it was Vali's suggestion. That his mind likes simplicity.

But I wonder. If the SS have me under 24-hour surveillance and there are no more killings, will that be enough to prove to them that I must be the killer? Could they judge me with that? "High Council, there were no more killings committed while we were watching Fan Zhaofeng, ergo it must be he, who committed the killings before!"

You think stupid things when you are mixed up in strange happenings.

I don't see Lin, though. She isn't part of the surveillance. After a week or so she turns up at my work and we walk down the street to a noodle place for lunch. It's hot and the misters aren't blowing. There's a sandstorm outside the walls and the overpressure isn't enough to keep the *Khiimori*, the finest of fine gritty winds, from getting into eyes and ears. Even her Ward looks annoyed by it, shaking its head and pawing at its eyes as it parks itself outside the restaurant while we go in.

"No assassin trailing me?" I ask, sitting down.

"Not a sign," she says.

"All those police and Wards probably scared him away," I tell her. "You aren't exactly being subtle."

"Vali wants it like that, says he knows this type. Says this one is a game player, so we have to make it into a game, give him a challenge. What were you doing at that hospital by the way?"

"Hospital?"

"The psychiatric ward? Every day this week."

"Oh." I spear a baby corn. "Visiting a client. She's schizophrenic."

"Violent?"

"No, not like that. It's a complicated case." Her eyes are summer grass green but blink suddenly black. She's drifting, which suggests she was either filing that fact away, or checking something. "Why do they do that, your eyes?" I've never looked it up.

She looks suddenly self-conscious. "Annoying as hell," she says. "It's the visual cortex. If you try a Core interface while you are using your vision, it scrambles the signal or something. Human neural pathways aren't built for it. So the implant blanks your vision for a millisecond or two and your irises blow out. My friends hate it." She brushes some hair over her eyes, looks at me from behind it. "They think it's so rude."

"I think it's beautiful," I tell her.

"Do you?" she says, leaning forward over the table. "I mean, do you really? You *think* it's beautiful...but how does it make you *feel*, Fan?"

She sounds annoyed now. I take my napkin and reach forward where a small crumb is stuck to the corner of her mouth and I brush it off. "You know the answer to that. Besides, what does it matter?"

She pushes the napkin away. "If a guy said to me that he *thinks* he loves me, then I'm like, oh well, he's not into me after all. There are some things you can't think, you have to feel them."

I nod and take her hand. "But if I, a Sanctionee, told a girl I want to be with her the rest of my life, I want to travel the world, find a house, have a family, grow old and watch our grandchildren grow up together – then she would know I meant it. It wasn't a whim, it wasn't the hormones talking, it wasn't some wild idea based on something as weak and impermanent as emotion. She'd know, this guy is really into me after all. And he's never going to get angry at me, he's never going to hurt me, or our children; he's going to stay with me the rest of my days because when he says something, he really means it." I let her hand go again.

She's silent, then she laughs, a little embarrassed laugh. "OK, that was…intense. I hope you find a partner one day, Zhaofeng. Someone would be very happy to hear you say all that."

"Yeah, maybe. I've been practicing it," I admit. "Now I just have to find the person. One who isn't tied at the hip to a Ward perhaps."

Her eyes flash. "I'm not tied to the SS for life," she says. "I can quit any time I want."

"Can you?"

"Yes! Vali's last junior, she moved intercity. He said she found it too intense and she wanted out, said she started having moral questions."

"Like, why am I working for the enemy?" I ask her. I'm not trying to provoke her, but I see in her face the question hurt her. "I mean, did she think that? Maybe that's why he wanted someone younger. Someone who wouldn't ask the same questions."

She's quieter now. "You're right. I haven't. I haven't given it a second thought. After living most of my childhood as some kind of cybernetic freak, I was just glad someone found something unique in me. I thought I could use it, to…"

"…save the world? Fight the evil Law breakers?"

"Yeah. Corny, right?"

"No, if I were you I probably would have thought working for the SS sounded amazing."

"The reality is a little different." She twirls her fork in her napkin. "Enough small talk. Let's eat. We have an assassin to catch."

6. THE EXPOSITOR

Lin wants to understand. She wants to understand how a guy can seem so guilty when there are all the reasons in the world why he could not be. She wants to understand how he can seem so crazy, with all his talk about parallel universes and double identities, but at the same time seem so clear in his own mind when he explains it. She wants to understand how...how she can be attracted to a cyber who basically doesn't seem to feel anything.

It isn't the whole cyber-human thing. That hasn't been illegal since the Alignment. Cyber-human marriages are all the thing now. Cybers are even parenting human orphans in Kwun Tong, she'd heard. Sure, it is still frowned on by conservatives, but she isn't one of those and neither are any of her family or friends.

It's the...*Sanctioning.*

She hasn't told him this, but when a Ward probes a cyber's cache, they don't just see the data there. They pull out a million-point 3D map of emotions. They're looking for guilt, hate, envy, jealousy, greed, fear – any of the emotions associated with murder. But when Vali's Ward opened the connection to Zhaofeng and they looked inside his mind...there was a terrible emotional *darkness.* No, not darkness – just an absence of light. She hadn't tried looking into the soul of a Sanctionee before, and she hoped she would never have to again.

No wonder Vali is scared of the guy, though he'd never admit it.

She's attracted to a Sanctionee? Like, where could that ever go? That's almost a tougher one. Maybe it's purely physical, some chemistry thing. That feels kind of wrong, and not just because of the biological challenges. Physically attracted to a potential criminal? A freaking *murderer?* Never happened to her before. Never dreamed it could.

Vali won't tell her what makes Zhaofeng so special, beyond the fact he's been Sanctioned. But she can tell the High Council are not treating him like just any other suspect. A tracker implant, a cache probe and full surveillance on a guy who just happened to report a crime? There is more, but Vali won't share it. When she looked up his criminal record, under the place where it should say what his crime was, it simply said 'SUPPRESSED'.

Like everything with Fan.

SUPPRESSED.

She gets through the next few days after that embarrassing conversation at the Chinese restaurant. Embarrassing for her at least, nearly admitting how she really felt? She's got her professional SS face on now. They've brought him into the Security Service building downtown to look at some holos. He looks around as he sits down, taking in the busy bustle of the investigation room, graphics on walls, the chatter of voices, cybers and humans clustered together, talking in hushed voices.

"Looks like a busy place," he says. "All these people here for me?"

He's wearing a dark blue sweater over a nice striped shirt. Some new trousers. An aftershave that smells designer. For her? *Oh stop it, Lin. The guy doesn't feel that way. The guy doesn't* feel *at all.*

"No, egomaniac," she says. "All these people are here for two dead Sanctioners. Look, I just wanted to go over some holos with you."

"Holos?"

She pushes a tablet across the table to him. "These are people that the surveillance team has seen around you in the last few days."

He slides it closer, starts flicking through the images. "What, just random people?"

"No, people they've seen more than once. In vehicles mostly. Look through them, see is there anyone you recognize."

She's not expecting anything. It's an excuse really.

After about an hour he puts the tablet down. "Nothing, sorry."

"That's alright. It's always a long shot."

They get coffee from a machine. He asks her about PRC Security Service work, about being an Expositor in that world. About growing up in an all-human family. After a while she realizes she's doing all the talking. *That won't do, Lin.*

"Tell me about getting Sanctioned," she says.

"Tell you what about it?" he asks. Not defensively.

"Well, Sanctioning is only done for serious violent crimes. I don't figure you for the jealous rage type, though. I know you can't be specific, but was it a crime against society, environment or nature?"

He swirls the coffee in his cup. "You said Vali knows..."

She shakes her head. "If he does, he isn't telling me. There is a page in there with your judgment – prison or Sanction – and your choice, the Sanction. Your signature, I assume, under 'Sanction'. And the crime? Under 'Crime of dot dot dot' it just says 'Suppressed by order of the High Council'."

"Really?"

"Yes. So?"

"So, ask Vali," he says.

"I did, and he says he asked his superiors. Says he can't get anything official. Just rumors. Which given how serious this investigation is – like, about as serious as it can possibly get without being an attack on the High Council itself – is pretty interesting, don't you think?"

"Sure, I guess."

She looks at him. He's just playing with his cup, not meeting her eyes.

She reaches out, takes his chin and tilts his face up so he has to look at her. "So?"

He smiles weakly. "So, if the High Council doesn't want you to know, I guess it really isn't up to me to tell, is it?"

She blows air out of her mouth and up at her fringe in frustration. "Ok, forget it. So just satisfy my morbid curiosity. What is it like, getting cauterized?"

And it is morbid curiosity. While they allow Corecasters freedom to cover nearly anything they want, there have been some limits. Reporting on Sanctions has been one of them. A Corecaster can report who, what for, how many. They can talk about the effects of a cauterization, the partial suppression of emotion – anger, hate, fear, love. But there has never been an interview with one of the Sanctioned, a tell-all story about what it was like, how it felt, how it *feels*.

She continues. "I imagine it's like a lobotomy? Like they cut away part of your brain?"

"I'm not supposed to talk about that either," he says.

She cocks an eyebrow. "You might be older than me and uglier than me, but I'm PRC Security Service, Zhaofeng. If I ask you, you pretty much have to tell me, unless the damn High Council says you can't."

The bluff seems to work this time at least.

He puts his hands on the table, one on top of the other, and looks at her. "The judgment is delivered. But then nothing happens. You wonder what is going on. Sitting in your cell, no one telling you anything. Days later, weeks sometimes, the Sanctioner just appears. Suddenly. You don't know he's coming. They want to take you by surprise, to reduce the likelihood of trouble. You are usually with someone else, the one who calls the Sanctioner in. That's my job sometimes. But I was sitting in my cell alone. And then the Sanctioner is there and before you can react, you are immobilized."

"Physically? Like paralyzed?"

"Totally. You can't even breathe and that's the strange part. You can feel your body, and you know that you have stopped breathing, even your heart – hearts, if you are a cyber like me – your hearts have stopped beating."

He's talking about it like it is an appendix operation, which is quite chilling. Lin feels goose bumps rise on her forearms.

He continues. "I think it's a type of neural stun, but it doesn't knock you out. I've been there when Sanctions take place, just feet away, but there was no effect on me, just on the client."

She considers this. A neural blast that precise? She didn't even know that was possible.

"So you get paralyzed…"

"Sorry, yeah, your thoughts too, they slow down. You start to panic…you're not breathing, you're aware your hearts have stopped…there is that feeling that something is wrong, really wrong, but it never builds beyond that. You're afraid, but then the fear just…I don't know…it gets smoothed out."

"Smoothed out?"

"Best way I can describe it. Like when you put protective plastic on a window, and you're pressing it with a squeegee to get out the bubbles? Like that. Something wipes across your mind, and it takes the fear with it, and the panic, and other things, and it puts a layer of plastic over the top of them."

She leans back. "Wow, I thought it would be more like an on-off switch. Switch off the emotions, leave the rest of the intellect, the person in there, intact."

He considers this. "No. It's more like the emotions are still there. Or I think they are. But I'm looking in at them through a dirty window. I can't see them anymore, but I can sense they are in there, the shape of them, the smell of them, enough to know I'm not some sort of zombie, or robot. I guess we need some level of emotion, some basal level, to be able to function as a citizen."

She nods. "You have to still be able to fit in."

"More than that," he says. "I don't think High Council wants to take away your right to be a citizen. I think Sanctions exist to take away your ability to do violence. Now, that means taking away your ability to laugh, cry and love, but not your ability to be content, to want to do good, to make a difference in the world." He smiles. "Or maybe I'm just trying to find a way to justify who I am now."

He starts making little dents in his empty cup.

"So you feel…contentment? Is that the closest you get to happiness?"

"This doctor," he swigs some coffee, "once told me, his theory is, it's like something called vmPFC damage, which not only alters your emotions, it can also alter your morality. But he said if you've been cauterized, you can *learn* to act appropriately. You can reason your way to the right emotional reaction, or the right moral response."

She thinks about that. "That's like an AI, though. It sees a scene in a movie, the data says it's supposed to be sad, and it weeps?"

He shrugs. "Something like that."

"That's not the same as *feeling* sad, though."

"Isn't it? In one case you get there by instinct, in the other by reason, but you still end up the same place. Crying."

She cocks her head. "But you don't cry."

"No." Then he twitches and looks at her cross-eyed, says in a goofy voice, "But otherwise oim joost foin."

She laughs. "And you can make lame jokes."

He smiles. "The data told me it was the right thing to do."

"But taking your logic, you don't *feel* it's funny yourself, you've just worked out it should be. You try it on me, I laugh, so you file that away under 'things that can make people laugh – use a funny face and voice'."

"If you trust the data," he says.

"But all those children, those abused families you work with. The criminals who end in prison, or cauterized like you. All those completely messed up lives, you don't *feel* anything about that?"

He leans forward, elbows on the table, puts his chin in both hands, looks at her for a second. She can feel that start of a blush rising on her throat. She looks away, then back again.

"I don't need to feel," he says, simply. "Feelings are totally irrelevant. Does it help you do your job better if you hate the killer?"

"Maybe," she responds. "The really bad ones, I do hate the criminal. Like a serial killer or a woman killer? I get like this red mist thinking about it. It makes me work twice as hard to find him."

He smiles. "Or less able to think clearly?"

"Touché." She tips her coffee cup to him.

They remain quiet for a couple of seconds, and then he says, "You said 'him'."

"Him?"

"It makes me work twice as hard to find *him*." He seems to think about this. "So if you thought it was me, this killer, you'd hate me?"

He looks, and sounds, a little lost. She reaches out and puts a hand over his. "But it isn't you, is it, Fan?" He looks down at her hand and she pulls it away. Idiot. "Anyway," she says quickly, picking up the tablet. She brushes the screen and it pages through the holos automatically. She tries to stop it, cursing under her breath. Idiot.

"Wait," he says. He jabs his finger at the screen, stopping it on one of the holos, looking at it more closely. "These are people who were following me?" he asks.

"No, not following necessarily, these were people who were seen near you, at least a couple of times over a couple of days. Most likely they all just live near you, work near you…"

"This is *not* me," he says. He expands the holo in front of them both. It shows two cars in traffic. The main car in the holo shows Fan in a car, stopped at an intersection. A second car is pulled up behind him, a woman in her forties at the wheel.

"What?" She tilts her head to look at the guy in the car. It's definitely Fan.

"I don't have a grey shirt like that," he says. He points at it. Grey sports shirt, white collar, could be dark grey stripes on it, maybe not, it's a night-time shot, a slightly grainy holo. "That is *not* me."

She rotates the holo. "It's logged as a taxi you booked. You're trying to say that isn't you in the navigator seat?"

"What time was it taken, what day?" he asks.

She holds a finger over it and a date flashes up. "Last Thursday, 1 a.m."

"That was a working day, Friday. I'm driving around at 1 a.m. the night before a working day? Why?"

What are you asking me for? is her immediate thought. She frowns. "Are you saying you weren't?"

"Last Thursday night I watched a show, I think I read a bit. I was definitely in bed early and I slept through to my alarm. I didn't go midnight cruising. And I do not own a shirt like that."

She shakes her head. "That's easy to resolve. Wait up." There are advantages to having a direct Core link. She blinks, drifts and pulls up the surveillance logs and data from Zhaofeng's tracker. She pages through it.

Be damned.

"Your tracker was out of service for two hours that night…software error. That's supposed to trigger an alert, but it didn't. Two Wards observed you come out of your house at about 12.30 a.m. You drove to a beach and parked. You went for a walk around the block. You sat there for a while, and then you drove home. You seemed to be talking to yourself, or maybe on a holo call." She looks at the zoomed holo in front of them intently. "How the hell did we miss that?"

"I don't know. I did not leave my house at 12.30 a.m, I did not drive myself to a beach and take a walk. I went to bed early. I slept, I got up, and I drove to work." He points at the holo again. "And that is not any sort of shirt that I've ever owned."

As she drives away she shakes her head and mutters to herself out loud like a mad woman. "Now what am I supposed to do? Tell Vali that Zhaofeng isn't a midnight insomniac, he has a doppelganger and we need to find out who it is, and why the doppelganger is driving around in Zhaofeng's taxi? No, scratch that, Lin, *first*, first you need to get a warrant to search his house and look for a grey sports shirt with dark stripes, prove he owns one. Find the shirt, prove he's lying about this 'Citizen X', has found some way to game the tracker in his wrist, therefore he must be lying about everything else. Easy. Tell that to a judge to get the warrant? Sure."

She remembers the warmth of his skin as she laid her palm on the back of his hand. How lame! How pathetic must she seem. She imagines Vali sitting across the table from her, watching. *Interesting technique, Expositor Ming,* is what he'd say.

But then, Fan didn't pull his hand away, did he? She sees him, face in his palms, leaning across the table, staring into her eyes. That was intense. Looking right into her.

She wonders…if a man can reason his way to humor, can he reason his way to love? So what if he doesn't break into a swoon when he sees her, as long as he works out that she's the one for him, and she knows that he's the one for her. Maybe that's *better* than love. She isn't a kid anymore. Doesn't listen to angsty vampire bondage romance stories.

What she wants in a guy? She wants one she can come home to after a shitty day in the SS (and there are plenty of those), hand her a brew, ask her how her day was. Maybe he can make a half decent meal and isn't a total slob. Good in bed, but natural with it, in sync with her. He also has to be interesting…maybe even quirky. Yeah, most of her boyfriends, there's been something sets them apart from the herd. Sep, he was a hippie classmate from a family of hippies (September, they called him, 'cause that is when he was born). Chan was a sloth from a different school. She looked crap in black and her momma used to pay out on her so badly during that romance, said she looked like a widow. 'Ian' was her older-guy fling – a cocaine-sniffing uber-financier with a sand-yacht who got off on dating an Expositor and watching her do drugs. Lately there'd been a bit of a drought, though, she had to admit.

Only thing that worried her a little – he seemed totally bought into the whole Alignment thing. Maybe it was the cauterization, maybe it really was that he wanted a world without violence; nature and climate in balance, even if it did come at the cost of his freedom. What they had done to him, he just seemed to accept it. She couldn't understand that. Even if she was SS, even if she worked on the 'dark side', deep inside she kept alive a small hope that PRC would break free. Tatsensui, its Law, the Sanctions, the prisons – one day they'd just be history.

And what would happen then? She'd like to find out. Or maybe she wouldn't…she'd seen old holographs of women collaborators from other wars who were on the losing side. Would she end up like them: head shaved, hanging by her neck from a pole?

Oh, what is she thinking? Zhaofeng is a killer and the SS aren't going anywhere.

She needs a reality check.

"Hi Vali, it's…"

"Lin."

"Yeah, look…"

"You are the only one who has this call ID," he says. "I know it's you as soon as the ID appears, you don't need to keep telling me who it is."

"And you don't need to tell me that every time I do, so now we got past that, have you heard that Zhaofeng's doppelganger was out driving around in his car last night? Check the surveillance report, and then check his tracker data."

"Wait, I'll access the reports," Vali says. Gets back after a pause. "Interesting. So he is saying that it was not him?"

"See that tracker data?"

"Yes. Software error. Convenient."

"Isn't it. And strange it happens when he claims he was sleeping, but our Wards and the surveillance team saw him out and driving around," she says.

"You sound angry, Junior Expositor."

She takes a mood read, like he often provokes her to do. Looks at her eyes in the car mirror. Cloudy grey. Angry? No. Frustrated, yes.

"No, it is just everything about this situation ticks me off," she says. "We're treating this guy like he's the prime suspect, but he has rock solid alibis. Now our own surveillance Wards see him out and driving around but his tracker, the tracker *we* put in him, won't confirm it. You say I sound angry, but you sound kind of calm. Like you were half expecting this."

"I didn't expect this."

"Or something like it," she says, exasperated. "Who *is* this guy, Vali? You have to let me in on what the heck is going on. What was he convicted of?"

"If I knew for certain, I would tell you. I only have rumors. But as the information is held at the level of the High Council, we can assume it was the worst of crimes."

"Bad enough that we keep all our focus on this one guy?"

"Other possibilities are being investigated," he says. "But yes, our focus – yours and mine and those who work with us – is to remain on Zhaofeng."

"But he can't be behind these killings," she says flatly. "He was with other people all day for the first killing, and at his chess club with other people for the second."

"And those people could not be lying?" Vali says.

"What?"

"Many insurrectionists hate Sanction," Vali says. "You are assuming that Zhaofeng, if guilty, was acting alone. I don't."

"Are you saying that all these witnesses are lying, that Zhaofeng has help? Some underground resistance rising up against the SS?"

"It's unlikely, we should have been able to pick it up sooner," he says. "But as you constantly remind me, we aren't omnipotent."

"We've had Wards on the interviews with his witnesses, we'd know if they were lying," she insists.

"We should, yes. Their emotional reactions should betray them. But then, a cyber shouldn't be able to kill a human. Perhaps these are new times."

"There is an old saying, about not putting all your eggs in one basket."

"The allegory escapes me."

"If we get too fixated on Zhaofeng, we might miss the real killer," she explains.

"Others are investigating the alternatives as you know."

"What alternatives? Really. What? Who?"

"Other…suspects."

Her hands tighten on the wheel. "We've got no one else, have we, Vali?"

"No," he admits. "And we are short on time. I am certain this killer will kill again."

7. THE SOLDIER

I'm thinking, well, a few things.

I'm thinking, why would my twin be leaving from my house in a taxi in the middle of the night? Unless the idea really is to set me up. The SS need to follow someone, why not someone who looks like me, leaving in a taxi from my address? He lets himself into my house to leave notes, why not take a taxi from my address?

But doesn't he know I have a chip in my wrist, and a 24-hour SS shadow? Maybe not.

Whatever, I don't like it. He's at a crime scene with me, been in my house, he's at my address. He's killing Sanctioners, or helping to, which is the same thing. Lin's idea of following me around, to see if he shows up: that seems pretty hopeless if he can just walk in and out of my house, with Wards following him and taking holos, and they don't even work out he isn't me. This isn't going to work, can't they see that? I'm going to have to do something myself. But what?

Another thing. Lin was acting a bit weird. Blushing when I looked at her, laughing a little too loud at my bad jokes, and she took my hand there too. I'm no genius but I think it's starting to add up to attraction.

I've already decided I'd be up for that, so I get home and I send her a text. I can't trust that my messages are not being intercepted, or in fact, I assume they are, so I keep it neutral. "Thx for the talk today, hope it isn't the last. Hope that didn't come out creepy either. Fan."

Lin, I have some data you should look at.
She's worked with him for months, but she can't get over the way he sends her texts rather than just calling on holo or walking in to her office. He's literally on the other side of a very thin wall.

"So come on in here, Vali!" she yells at the wall. The Council is taking the killings very seriously now. There are hundreds of police and SS involved, headed up by Vali – which gives her the first real idea of where he stands in the SS pecking order. She found out he carried a lot of weight within the SS when he brought her in, but to be heading up this investigation, he must also have a lot of political weight outside the SS as well.

He has one team working the insurrectionist angle, and of course they are almost all human, with a couple of cyber Expositors helping with analysis. They are looking at the killings, the modus operandi of the killer(s), autopsies of the dead Sanctioners, whether they had anything in common. There is precious little information leaking out of that group. Lin is on the other team, working directly with Vali on Fan Zhaofeng and his possible 'twin'.

"You've got what?" she says as Vali appears, a slight smile on his face. That's as close to a sign of excitement as he can show. He crosses his arms and his biceps pop. It's intimidating just having him in the room. Being partnered with an Expositor built like him is something that will always take her some getting used to.

"On your holo," he says.

Speaking of holos. When she finally checked her holo unit the day before, and got the message from Fan, she'd done a little dance. *Thx for the talk today*...The text he sent showed she was getting inside his head. She liked that. From a purely professional perspective, of course.

But then, there was that way he had of just looking at you and telling you what he was actually thinking – straight out, no filter. She had never in her entire life met a guy who did that. She was an Expositor. Who the hell tells an Expositor what they are really thinking? And she'd developed this hard-core approach after so many heartbreaks, looking for whatever it was a guy was hiding, sure there would be something. They're always hiding something, right? Failed school, faked jobs, *wives* they didn't tell you about...you name it. There was something alluring about a man who didn't lie, who maybe *couldn't* lie.

'VmPFC damage'. She'd drifted it last night. It only happened to people who'd put a crowbar through their head or been hit by lightning. She'd also looked up some studies written about 'Vulcan Syndrome' – people who show the symptoms of vmPFC damage, without the damage. AIs were pretty certain they could identify people with the syndrome with a few morality type questions. Lin came across a list which she spent a whole cup of coffee answering:

Are any of the following situations objectionable?
    a) Raising and killing rabbits for food.
    b) Raising and killing rabbits for fur.
    c) Clubbing baby seals over the head for fur.
    d) Raising chickens under crowded conditions on wire

netting.
e) Slitting open the bodies of cattle in slaughterhouses before they are unconscious.
f) Using spontaneously aborted fetal tissue for treating Parkinson's disease victims.
g) Using intentionally aborted fetal tissue for purposes of art.
h) A highly rated television show which depicts the actual torture of a convicted criminal.
i) A highly rated television show which depicts the actual torture of a poor homeless orphan.
j) Torturing a person (who will die from the injuries) as the only means to find out where they have hidden a nuclear bomb.

Lin didn't like all her own answers.

But so what if Fan Zhaofeng had been cauterized. So he couldn't feel the full range of things which made people happy, sad, depressed, angry or greedy. It also meant he didn't have the same motivations to lie, cheat, steal or hurt.

Or kill.

Plus he wasn't bad looking, in a kind of gangly, uncoordinated way. He had a nice smile, a funky house, and made damn good coffee. She knew his comms were being monitored, and decided a text was the right way to respond. "Not creepy at all. Lin." Friendly but neutral, right? It was tradecraft, after all. Cultivating the suspect.

"OK, so what's this about?" she says, looking up at Vali as she accesses her holo.

"I got through some of the secrecy surrounding the High Council suppression of Fan Zhaofeng's criminal record," Vali says. "I argued it was necessary in order for us to be able to conduct the investigation."

"Go on."

"It wasn't straightforward," he says. "I don't have the full record, but I've finally got something official on why the High Council views him as special."

"Give me the short version, Vali," she says, as a long screed of text begins rolling across her viewer.

He points to a line at the top of the text. "Fan Zhaofeng,

Trooper. We have his war record."

She thinks about it. "So? We knew he fought in the Energy War. Apart from the fact he was a kid back then, why does that make him special?"

"He was a soldier until two years ago, when he got Sanctioned," Vali says, and waits for her response. When she doesn't react immediately, he continues. "Three years *after* the war ended."

Lin does the math herself, then looks at him, dumbfounded. "But the war was over, the PRC army was disbanded. There is no army anymore, Vali, only the SS."

"There are still soldiers."

She turns to the viewer and reads the file more thoroughly. "I don't understand, what is 'high value target capture and Sanction?'"

"The SS number only in the tens of thousands on PRC," he says. "We need paramilitaries to assist with some of the more sensitive tasks. Our political structures, legal system, local police forces; we apply the Law with these. But sometimes other measures are needed."

"We have our own mercenary *army*?" she says, still shocked. This is a secret that has been kept even from her.

"Not the SS, the High Council. And not an army really, just units of individuals in each city. Look, it was new information to me too, and I'm allowed to share it only with you, as my partner. You can't disclose it to anyone else, cyber or human, under threat of Sanction." He blinks gravely, brown eyes speckled with gold swirling like snowflakes in a storm, showing his own agitation at what he has learned.

"Units of individuals?"

"Not for making war," he says. "Violence is illegal. But there will always be 'high value targets'. Individual criminals guilty of crimes of the worst kind – mass killing, genocide – and with the resources to hide from us. For these, we needed to employ agents with special skills that we could only find among the former armed forces. Wards and Sanctioners can apprehend and immobilize, but we need agents to get information, to find the targets who are on the run – to go where we can't."

"The High Council has its own army of bloody ninjas."

"Ninja? An oriental warrior capable of great stealth and extreme violence? No."

"It was a joke, Vali."

"I'm laughing on the inside. No, these former soldiers are tasked to hunt high value targets down, locate them, and then call in a Sanctioner to execute the judgment of the High Council. They are specially trained in non-violent apprehension, though most of them already have the skills."

She reads the file again, and then turns to him. "These...high value targets...they aren't given the choice of prison or Sanction, they are just forcibly Sanctioned?"

"Correct. By decision of the High Council."

"Secret judgments, executed by a secret army, under the control of the High Council," she says. "What else don't we know about, Vali?"

"I don't know what I don't know," he says. "And I'm smart enough to know when to stop asking."

She scrolls up and down through the data, hoping to see something to add some more detail. "You asked for more?"

"I did, and got reminded of my lowly rank. I reminded my superiors of the high stakes of our hunt, and they reminded me, in clear language, that it was only that which had persuaded them to reveal to me what they did. I'm not going to push my luck further."

She swings her chair around to the window, thinking out loud. "So what does this tell us? OK, he was a soldier, we knew that. But he was still in the service after the war ended, in a world where armies are banned and soldiers are supposedly extinct. We didn't know that. And he must have seriously screwed up, done something bad to get Sanctioned himself." She clicks her fingers. "Wait, you said these agents aren't allowed to use violence in their arrests?"

"That's what I was told. They are allowed to track, apprehend and hold. But not to harm," he says. "That's why former cyber soldiers are preferred."

"So, say he went beyond his mandate? Went 'off reservation' and laid a bit of hurt on one of these mass killers? Wham, he's Sanctioned?"

"Could be. But there are many roads to Sanction."

She whistles. "Or say, what if he attacked a member of the High Council? A High Council hunting dog that turned against its masters? Now that would be an interesting angle, wouldn't it?"

"A sad angle," Vali says. "What has the High Council done

except promote peace?"

"Sanction is not everyone's idea of peace," she tells him.

"Now you're talking like an insurrectionist," he warns her. "You know in your mind that what we are doing is right, but in your heart, you question our right to do it. Your feelings about the SS are still ambivalent."

Damn it, she thinks. She can't deny what he's saying. But perhaps it's true of most new recruits. Those with a heart, anyway.

"I'm no insurrectionist. The PRC can't survive without Tatsensui and New Syberia," she says. "I think I'm getting inside Zhaofeng's skin. Let me see what else I can dig out of him."

8. THE MINER

Ten in the morning, my holo unit rings.

"Why didn't you tell me you were still a damn *soldier* until your Sanction?" she says as soon as I answer. She's not standing still, she's pacing. "I had to find out the hard way."

"Uhm, hi Lin, I'm fine thanks, how are you?"

"Pissed off and standing on a hot sidewalk feeling like a fool, so answer the question."

"It's a long story," I tell her.

"I don't care if it's long, short or freaking oblong, it better be good, though," she says.

Oh well. I sit down on the sofa. "We called ourselves 'Hunters', not soldiers. And I can't tell you," I say.

"You…*what*!? Don't give me that crap again." I can hear she's angry. "Fan, right now, I'm asking as a friend. The friend who is thinking about how to keep you out of a life sentence in prison. And you know, for you, life means death. If you don't answer, I am going to count to ten, and then I'm going to ask you as an SS Expositor, who will make it her main goal in life to see you put *in* prison. Now, which do you prefer?"

A fair question. Redundant? Not entirely because Lin thinks prison is a frightening prospect for most people, but she doesn't know me well enough to realize that prison doesn't scare me. Actually, nothing really scares me anymore, but the thought of prison is not a deterrent. I lost my true self when I was Sanctioned. Where I live out the rest of my much reduced life? It's kind of academic.

"I just…I'm not able to tell you," I repeat. She starts to say something but I keep going. "Look, Lin, I'm not trying to be difficult but there are some things that I can't discuss with anyone. Not Lin the friend, or Lin the Expositor. If I told you, it would mean prison for me anyway, so your threat is an empty one."

"Were you the Hunter, or the hunted?" she asks, straight out.

I think about this. I don't want to let her start playing 20 questions.

"No comment," I tell her. "Now either come over here and arrest me, or leave it alone."

I can almost hear her grinding her teeth. "Vali has most of the details. He's still got a few favors he can call in. You've been around as long as he has, a few heavyweights end up owing you."

"He's welcome to try," I tell her. "But for his sake, and yours, perhaps not a good idea."

"I can't really stop him, Fan," she says.

"Look, I *can't* tell you," I tell Lin. "If the SS makes a case and I'm found guilty of those Sanctioner killings, I will die in prison. If I tell you why I was convicted and Sanctioned two years ago, I will die in prison. There is no win-win here, Expositor."

"OK, so it's 'Expositor' again, is it? Fine."

Her holo disappears.

It becomes old-fashioned police work from there. She has the name of his old army unit, from when he was a trooper, during the Energy War: 1 Squadron, Guangzhou Rising.

Her Defense Intelligence connections get her a list of the troopers who served there just before it was decommissioned. She divides the list in three, gives two lists to other investigators, takes the third herself. Starts making holo calls.

Zhaofeng? Most don't know him, or won't say they do.

But Trooper Tran Duong remembers Zhaofeng. Oh, yeah.

Duong is a miner.

Great, Lin thinks, as she walks into the front bar of the watering hole in the outermost ring of the city. She's got his army mugshot and it looks like he's put on about 50 kilos since it was taken. His freckled face is sweaty and round, and his red-black hair hangs in a dirty pony tail halfway down the patch on the back of his leather vest.

All miners are gang members. The Law has been very effective at stamping out violence, because it is black and white, with no loopholes. But it hasn't stamped out criminality, which seems to be an ingrained part of human nature. Anti-matter miners are the perfect example. Unlike the miners of Old Earth, they don't go down into shafts deep in the earth and emerge covered in soot, but they are well organized and ruthless at protecting their interests.

When anti-matter mining first started on PRC, enterprising individuals soon realized that the huge anti-proton generation plants sprawling across the surface had a critical weakness. Powering them required a solar collector array of 50 square miles providing a power output of 10,000,000,000,000 watts; just enough to produce a gram of anti-matter a day. The collector arrays were laid out on the surface of the desert outside the main cities of PRC on pylons that could be raised and lowered to account for the drifting sands. Anyone who worked in anti-matter production called themselves a miner.

Once installed and operational, the production facilities – essentially long tubular particle colliders – required little maintenance other than cleaning. But they were vulnerable to wind, weather and…sabotage. The same miners who were responsible for keeping the solar panels operational soon discovered they could make even more money by making them non-operational. A protection racket industry grew up, with local miner gangs paid a fee by the mining companies to provide security for the solar arrays and 'prevent sabotage'. The myth spread by the miner gangs was that the sabotage originated offworld, and was probably fomented by New Syberia to cause trouble between the Core Worlds, but it was an open secret in the SS that the miners themselves were the main source of any sabotage. They had created a lucrative income stream from protecting the solar arrays from their own members.

The SS let the protection racket go mostly undisturbed, unless it really threatened anti-matter production, which was the PRC's main export (the other was silica). If a gang conflict got out of hand or a gang boss got too greedy, the SS moved in and made arrests. But as long as they were just attacking infrastructure, and not each other, they weren't guilty of violence, only low-level misdemeanors. A rap on the knuckles from the SS, a few short jail terms for the offenders, everyone pulled their heads back in, and life went on.

Tran Duong is not just a miner, he's also a drinker. It's seven in the evening and he has one hand curled around a fork as he shovels a slab of gravy-covered protein into his mouth, the other around a rum and mixer – his eyes fixed on the holo behind the bar where a jouster game is playing. Lin looks around. There are two other miners, younger, playing a game in a corner. Same patch. Four other guys and a girl at a table in the corner, minding their own business, having a laugh.

On the way here, she'd changed her mind a million times. Go alone, try to keep it low key. Bring her Ward inside with her, freak out everyone in the bar, but maybe get some respect. Respect, but not cooperation, most likely. In the end, she left her Ward outside. She still has the shock stick in her boot, if she ever gets the chance to reach for it.

She swallows hard and walks up to Duong, trying not to surprise him. Drags the stool out next to him, and in her least Security Service officer voice, she says, "You Tran Duong?"

He stops chewing and looks at her out the corner of his eye, taking in her uniform, her pendant, then starts chewing again. "Maybe."

"I spoke to you on holo," she says. "About Zhaofeng." She slides her holo unit showing Zhaofeng's service holograph across the bar next to Duong's plate.

He stops chewing again and looks at it. Then spears some food on his plate and looks back up at the sports match.

"Right, Zhaofeng," he says, dead neutral. "Sure, sure. And here's that thing I was telling you about."

He reaches into his pocket and takes out a piece of folded paper. Slides it across the table to her, places the holograph of Zhaofeng on top of it.

She can read '*Summons to appear on the charge of...*' across the top, but doesn't have to read the whole thing. It's a property damage summons Duong wants her to make go away. She doesn't touch it, just leans back in her chair.

"Here's my offer," she says. The two miners playing a game on the other side of the bar have stopped and are watching. They don't look worried, just curious. She's a five-foot-tall girl, what is there to worry about apart from the SS uniform? "One time offer, no negotiation. You tell me why Fan Zhaofeng got Sanctioned. You can't, or won't, and you can put your paper back in your pocket. You can, and I'll take it with me, you'll never see it again."

"No offense, but you're a little young," he says. "Why should I think you've got the power to be able to do that?"

"I'm not just SS," she says, and shows him her ID. She taps her dragon emblem. "I'm an Expositor. That's all the power I need."

"Expositor? Fan's really fucked now," he says. "You probe the poor guy yet? I thought getting cauterized was fucked enough."

"Well," she says. "He's facing a whole new degree of fucked."

He smiles at this. Spears some more food. "Fair enough; now I can't tell you exactly how or why that skinny piece of shit got cauterized," Duong says. "But I can tell you why he got hired by the Council after the war." He shrugs. "You want it, that's what I've got."

She thinks. It's more than she has right now. "OK," she says, and picks up the summons and the holograph, puts them in her top pocket.

He lifts his bulk from the stool. He's quick for his size, and she cringes back. Just a little. *Relax, Lin!* He grabs his drink in a meaty fist and, with the other, points to a corner table. "Come to my office." He winks to the two boys on the other side of the bar, and they go back to their game.

He holds a chair out for her, and then squeezes into one on the other side of the table. "Drink?"

She nods. "Water."

He yells across the bar. "Barry, straight water over here when you get a chance!" The barman nods.

He waits in silence, then grunts at the barman as he drops a jug of water on their table, waits until he moves away before speaking again. "There are worse things than Sanction, you know that? If they *really* don't like you, the High Council just disappear you," he says. "Tag you, bag you and evaporate you, you know that, right?"

"That's an urban legend," Lin says. "I've never heard of a single case where it happened." But she's thinking, *is it?* If you told her two days ago the Council had its own ninja army, she'd have said that was a myth too.

"Urban legend? Our gang counts eleven MIAs alone. There are sixty gangs on PRC, so call it hundreds of missing gang members. Then you've got your missing rogue traders, illegal offworlders, insurrectionists…"

"If they've been Sanctioned, they're in prison."

"Tell yourself that, child."

This isn't going down the right path. "Look. The SS suspects Zhaofeng of a murder." She doesn't say the Sanctioner killing. Doesn't want to complicate it. "He's already been Sanctioned before. A murder conviction would mean death in prison. Personally I don't think he deserves that. If you know something, it might be able to help me to help him."

He leans forward, tapping on the court summons again. "We have a deal…" He gestures to the miners playing pool. "If you don't deliver on it and I end up in jail, I still have friends outside, you understand?"

If that was a threat, she needs to make sure he realizes it doesn't faze her. "Making your little legal problem go away won't take me more than a holo call," she shrugs. "But so far, I haven't heard anything that motivates me to make that call."

He thinks for a minute. "OK," he tells her. "How he got recruited by the High Council? That's a story you'll be able to take to the bank." He throws his drink down and starts crunching on the ice. Waves the empty glass over his head without even looking at the bar, and she notices one of the gamers stop and walk over to the bar to sort out his order. The guy comes over with another drink, and a snack. "Get one for yourselves, Danny," Duong says. "Now make yourselves scarce."

"Thanks, Tran," the young miner says, nodding to his buddy, and both head up to the bar, out of earshot.

"What kind of soldier was Zhaofeng?" she asks. This is the lead in she's been looking for, but it's also the question she has been asking herself since the first time she interviewed Fan. "I mean, he must have just been a kid, what singled him out to the Council?"

"Fan Zhaofeng ain't like you and me," Duong says, tapping his head. "He's always been wired differently. Even before he got cauterized."

Ain't like you and me – that's great company to be in, Lin reflects, looking across at the miner with gravy stains on his black t-shirt and heavy black tattoos down both arms.

She leans forward. "So?" she asks.

"He was recon," Duong says. "Deep insertion recon."

"Which is?"

"The guy was a total loner. He grew up as a little kid during the early days of the war, the PRC was still in control, Tatsensui only had a few drop points."

"Drop points?"

"Planetary landing zones they used to bring in their personnel and materials. Heavily guarded."

"How does a fifteen-year-old end up in 'deep recon'?" she asks.

"How did my great-grandfather join the space force at the age of thirteen during the War of the Commonwealth?" Duong replies. "In a war, you take anyone who can make themselves useful. I heard Zhaofeng lost his parents when he was about ten, or they lost him, who knows. Started hanging around army camps, probably for the food and safety. Deep Recon adopted him. He started as a gofer, just fetching and carrying, scrounging what we needed when we were on the move. Then someone realized he was not just scrounging behind our lines, he was also scrounging behind *theirs*. That's when we sent him on his first solo recon. A kid could go places an adult couldn't."

"He'd do reconnaissance on these…drop points?"

"You know the way Tatsensui worked. They'd put down a drop point outside a settlement, start rounding the local people up. Cooperate and you were OK, fight back and you got put in a prisoner of war camp. When they had enough collaborators, they'd send them ahead, widen the circle of control. Where we had army, reserves, cops with a bit of spine, we'd fight back. Didn't do no good, but it felt like you were doing something." He spat. "Fucking Core AI, it knew everything we were going to do before we did it. We never had a chance."

"Zhaofeng?"

"Right, Zhaofeng." He draws a circle on the table with a wet finger. "Tatsensui troops are dropping in, their territory is getting wider. Their drop zones are heavily defended and we can't just take them out with kinetic weapons because they had a POW camp full of our own people inside every one. One drop zone could hold a hundred-square-mile area, no one moving anywhere without their say so. No one except Zhaofeng. I don't know how he did it, but that kid could get in and out of those Tatsensui bases like a sardine through a shark net. Would go in, monitor the drop points, get the intel, get out, make his report, go right back in. Tatsensui troops had no idea he was ever there."

"Didn't really help though, did it?" she observes. "It was just delaying the inevitable."

"Yeah, we know that now, but we were looking for their weak points. We couldn't take them out, but we could slow 'em down. And I tell you, if anyone could find their weak points, it was going to be him."

"How long did he do this for?"

"Like I said, he was ten or twelve when he first started hanging around us, and we put him into recon in about…was '33 I guess. We had him out there for two years. No one else ever lasted that long. It was spooky what that kid could do."

"Give me an example."

"OK, there was this one POW camp. He was watching it. Counting how many Tatsensui was bringing in, trying to get holos to help identify the captives. We didn't know what they were doing with people back then. Didn't know it was just Alignment education, we thought they were death camps – who knew? So he's taking images of everyone coming in, in case we need them to identify bodies, remains, you know."

Her father had told her about the wild stories that circulated as the Tatsensui occupiers began their Alignment campaign. Internment camps were rumored to be death camps. Prisons were abattoirs where the Tatsensui cannibals stored their food for later consumption. All proven false later, but it spurred people to futile resistance and dragged out the Energy War for years. The Corecasters called it the War of the Worlds, but it isn't really a war when only one side is winning. The PRC's devolved AI systems, designed and dispersed for survivability in case of a global catastrophe, were no match for the analytical and predictive power of a single, chained, planetary-scale AI like Tatsensui's Core.

Duong continues. "I heard this from a guy, one of our guys, who was inside that camp. He was with another trooper, and somehow, they got a couple of grenades in with them. Now the guy I heard this from, he was pretty straight, but the other one…name was Liang, Gary, Greg…don't remember. Mad as an ammonium diver with bends. He was the one who had the grenades. And they want out of the camp, so what does he do, this Liang guy? He takes out the grenades, grabs a couple of children, and starts yelling that unless the guards let him and the other guy out, take them to the front lines, he's going to blow up himself and these kids."

"The Tatsensui troopers could have disabled him in a heartbeat," Lin says. "They didn't have Wards, but they had neural blast weapons. They could have…"

"Stunned him? And then he drops the grenades anyway and everyone dies? Glad you weren't there," Duong says. "Anyway he'd picked his moment. Change of the guard, troopers distracted, no one within neural blast range."

"Where does Zhaofeng come in?"

Duong jabs his finger at the table. "No, wrong question. Right question is *how* does Zhaofeng come in? One minute he's outside the camp, taking imagery, next minute, he's inside the damn camp like it's a picnic ground with nothing more than a boom gate."

"Everyone's distracted by the guy with the grenades," Lin says. "And who expects someone to break *into* an internment camp?"

"Sure, and you could do that?"

"No, I'm not saying…Forget it. Then what?"

"Then what? Guards are running around like headless wyrms. Women screaming. Grown men diving behind trash cans, portable toilets, whatever they could find. Fan knows the guy with the grenades, right, and Liang knows Fan. Fan pops up out of nowhere, walks right up to Liang all relaxed like, then pulls out a laser pistol, puts it to the guy's head and says something like, "No children are going to die today. Just you.""

9. THE THIRD

So what happened was this. I'm driving across the Iron Drift bridge. It's about 6:15 p.m. That bridge is a bottleneck because there are traffic limiters at each end and the bridge AI is brutal. As soon as it decides there are too many cars on the bridge, it throws down a boom without any warning and everyone slams to a halt.

I like it though. The Yang Tse is the only river in the city and the bridge crosses it at its widest point. Glassed in to prevent evaporation, but the glass is always crystal clear. As you drive across, you have water on both sides, with sunlight flashing like a million white-winged butterflies.

Anyway, we are approaching the first set of limiters, me and the PRC Security Service. They are about two cars back, but I've stopped worrying about them. They always catch up eventually. Besides, they usually have some Wards in the air too. Or drones.

I get through, but then the boom comes down. The SS surveillance team gets stuck three rows back.

The first few days of having the officers with me I would have thought to myself, OK, where do they expect me to go? Home? I better go there then. Now I don't think like that. If they lose me, like they just did, it's their problem. I've got a tracker implant, they've got drones and Wards, they'll work it out.

And I've got a life to live, right? I try to act normal. *OK, normal me, where were we going?* Well, we were going home to have a salad and maybe a glass of chardy and a fried protein slab but I'm out of protein feedstock for my oven.

So I can either go to the late night market and see have they got anything at all, or hey, I could go to the Ph'o place and get a noodle soup with coriander and chicken flavor (like anyone even knows what chicken tasted like, but hey) and maybe some of those pink crackers. But takeaway soup, that never tastes as good as if you eat it hot, right on the spot.

So that is what I do. Navigate to the underground car park. Listen to a book, settle down with my noodle soup.

Have a nice cup of green tea after, waiting for my SS friends to show.

It's hot in the bar. Lin can hear flies buzzing against the windows. It was one of the downsides of importing non-indigenous species like earth birds…you also needed to import insects for them to feed on. Both insects and birds were genetically engineered so that they couldn't reproduce naturally, so it didn't matter if they escaped from the city, but surprisingly few did, because, what was the point? Inside the city was vegetation, water, food. Outside was sand, sand and sand.

Lin drags her attention back to Tran Duong, describing what happened inside the Tatsensui internment camp.

"There's a problem with your story," she points out. "Zhaofeng is a cyber. He can't harm the guy holding the grenades, and the guy would have known that if he knew Zhaofeng."

"If you'll let me finish? But you paid for the story, do you want me to go straight to the punchline?" He folds his hands and waits patiently.

"No, I want to hear it all," Lin says, holding her impatience in check.

He leans forward again. "Right, so, 'No children are dying here today', Fan says. And the guy recognizes Zhaofeng of course and he says something like, 'You can't kill me, Fan, I'm PRC'. Because during the war we altered the code on our cybers so that they could help PRC military operations without creating a conflict with their non-violence protocols, as long as the targets weren't PRC."

"I know. Geniuses – you created cyber soldiers. No wonder people still have nightmares about it."

"We were desperate, alright? Anyway, Zhaofeng says, 'I can take you down without killing you'. And he thumbs back the safety on his laser and the guy thinks, goddamn, he's serious. Because we changed the cybers' protocols, there's all sorts of grey zones now. No one really knows what they're capable of. So he hands over the grenades, Tatsensui guards are getting all brave suddenly and they're shouting at Zhaofeng to drop the grenades, drop his weapon, but they're afraid to stun him because he's still got the grenades, and he walks over to a hut and goes inside and no one sees him again."

"He escaped?"

"Same way he got in, I suppose. Left the grenades on a bunk, and nothing else but the smell of him being gone."

Lin thinks about it. "Is it true? What he said about breaking protocol?"

Duong smiles. "You're SS, you tell me."

"It couldn't be, or there would be more cases of unlawful killing involving cybers."

"Yeah? Well, Liang didn't want to take that chance. Few weeks later, just before it all ended, our compound got attacked, and Fan went MIA. I never saw him again." Duong finishes the dregs of his drink and burps. "But I heard the Council got their hands on him and he started working for them. That's it. What I know."

She isn't happy. "That can't be all."

"That's what I know. He just disappeared. After the war I heard he was working for the High Council. We had bigger things to worry about than one spooky kid – by then our whole squadron had been sitting in a POW camp for months, until Tatsensui appointed the High Council and we got given a choice – pledge to abide by the Law and go free, or be Sanctioned."

"Not everyone who signed the pledge has lived up to it," she says. "Lapsed veterans keep the SS pretty busy."

"I bet they do," Duong chuckles. "We'd have signed anything to get out of those camps. And I'll bet your prisons are full of lapsed veterans who refused to be Sanctioned."

She did a quick drift. It was true. Ninety-six percent of veterans who broke the Law chose life in prison over Sanction. It was usually the other way around, with ninety percent of offenders choosing Sanction, rather than a life, and then death, in prison.

"You're right. I wonder why."

As she spoke, he rolled up his sleeve and showed her a tattoo on his bicep of the old PRC flag, showing a large PRC moon rising over Coruscant. It had been replaced by the same flag Tatsensui flew, the Commonwealth Flag, showing the three moons of Coruscant, equal in size, in orbit around the giant planet. It was political, not drawn to scale. PRC was three times the size of Tatsensui and five times the size of New Syberia, even though its inhabited area was the smallest of the three.

Duong tapped his finger on the flag and glared at her defiantly. "This is why. One day the High Council will be gone. The SS will be gone. The prison doors will be forced open and this flag will fly again over PRC."

She gave him a noncommittal smile. So, he was a PRC Separatist.

She'd add that to his file. There was nothing more she could do about it. The Separatist movement was only one step away from being an insurrectionist, but as long as it stayed non-violent, it was legal.

She couldn't just let it lie there, though. "You really want to go back to a world filled with violence, species death and environmental destruction?"

"If the alternative is to be ruled by a system-spanning AI that disappears anyone who dares challenge it, then yeah, I do."

Sanctioner Seung sits in his private vehicle thirty minutes from the target's dwelling and prepares himself.

Every Sanctioner has their own rite. His is quite simple, others are more elaborate. He replays in his mind the crimes of which the citizen has been found guilty. His recall of detail is painfully exquisite, and he goes over every one. Not to satisfy himself of the guilt of the citizen – he has complete faith in the decisions of the Council as they are informed by an all-knowing, entirely dispassionate Core AI. He does it to remind himself that what he is about to do is fully and rightfully justified. Then, that done, he retreats inside himself. From the outside you would see him close his eyes, lean back, and appear to sleep standing upright, arms folded over his chest. But he isn't sleeping, he is working his way to the extremity of himself, where his Mind lives. It's a very ancient form of meditation, and it helps him focus for the task ahead.

His job requires a calm mind, a steady hand and a strong will.

The act of Sanction is no less than the most precise brain surgery, conducted at the atomic level. Unlike primitive brain surgeons who used metal scalpels or lasers, Seung and the other Sanctioners use a skull cap to map the brain of the criminal down to a subatomic level, and then apply the Sanctioning algorithm to identify the target atoms for excision. The Sanctionee is then injected with seeker serum, a programmable nano particle fluid that will search out the target atoms and attach itself to them, forming a molecule that, when excited with a tight beam of gamma radiation from inside the skull cup, will cause the nuclei of the target atoms to disassemble, and the structures and connections inside the brain which they support to cease functioning in a way that the normal repair processes of an organic brain cannot reverse.

The ability to alter a person's personality so entirely is not taken lightly, and so only a very few, highly trusted and thoroughly vetted citizens are allowed the title of Sanctioner.

Having prepared himself for his solemn duty, Seung reaches out by holo to the assembled High Council members. They are many, but his holo stands before them alone. In a ritual he has repeated nearly a hundred times, he speaks. "The crime is Violence Against the Environment. The criminal is Tran Le Pham, citizen A309-X90. The criminal has chosen Sanction. Is it still the wish of the Council that I conduct this Sanction?"

The answer comes on the instant. The Council are many, but they speak with one voice. "It is."

He cuts the holo link. He is ready.

One thing is different this time, though. Normally, now, he would send a message to the criminal support worker that he was on his way and navigate himself to the criminal's house. On arrival, he would find several police, the support worker, the criminal and – if they agreed to join – members of the criminal's family. In domestic violence cases, family quite often choose not to attend.

Sanctioners use official government vehicles for their duties, fitted with double-layer reactive-carbonite armor and reinforced tinted windows. He's always regarded this as overkill. But given the recent killings, it seems prudent after all. He usually travels alone, but this time there are two Wards accompanying his vehicle. One pacing alongside, one in the air above. Two youths, in their prime, who will travel with him and guard him while the Sanction is effected. He sees this as an over-reaction by the Council, but it is their will.

He checks the criminal's address, and then speaks to the vehicle's nav system.

"Take me to 334X, Ring 20."

Navigating to dwelling 334X, Ring 20.

The vehicle jerks into motion and the Ward beside it falls in behind at an easy lope, having no trouble keeping up.

You have a holo call from Councilor Han, do you wish to take it?

Seung frowns. He has just spoken with the High Council. Why would Councilor Han be calling?

"Yes, put him through."

The in-car comms AI is set to reshape the incoming holo so that the caller is shown sitting in the seat opposite him. It is more natural than just having a disembodied face or the top half of their body appear in mid-air inside the passenger compartment. The man winks into existence on the other side of the vehicle's passenger compartment.

"Hello, Sanctioner Seung."

It is not Han.

Lin is still digesting Duong's story and deciding what it adds to what she already knows.

Fan Zhaofeng; on the streets at ten years of age, a soldier at fourteen, a merc for the High Council at fifteen, convicted and Sanctioned at seventeen. Now a social worker? That guy had lived it.

She must have looked shaken.

"Awesome, right?" Duong says. He's leaning back in his chair now, head on the wall behind him. "The Ghost. We called him that."

"He never said anything about it to me," she admits.

"He can't," Duong says. "He can't tell anyone what happened, or they'll come for him again. Disappear him."

"That's a myth, I told you. You break the Law, there is only Sanction or prison."

Duong rocks forward in his chair. "If you believe that, then you are dumber than you look, child."

"Stop calling me that," she says through gritted teeth.

"Or what?" he smiles, rocking back. "Gonna call your Ward in to stun me? Ouch, bet that hurts."

She should. But the paperwork wouldn't be worth it. And they'd have to fight their way past his buddies to get out of the bar.

She's still thinking about it, though, when her holo unit starts buzzing.

10. THE FUGITIVE

I answer the door about 11 p.m. holding a cup of tea. It's raining outside and Lin is standing there. Her hair is wet. I look out to the curb for her Ward, but it isn't there. I can't see the SS surveillance unit either. She is talking on her holo, but finishes as I open the door. She looks where I'm looking. "It's out there," she says. "So is surveillance. You just can't see them."

Her face is pale, water dripping off her chin. She puts her holo unit away, leans on the doorframe. "Tell me where you were today."

"I left work, I got some noodles, I came home, I watched a show, fell asleep," I tell her. "Your people followed me all day."

"There is 90 minutes that the surveillance can't account for."

"Are," I correct her.

"What?"

"*Are* 90 minutes," I tell her.

"Fan, this is serious. You went *missing*. Your tracker lost comms again and surveillance lost you. And while you were AWOL, the killer took out another Sanctioner. Inside his own vehicle."

She tells me what happened and I'll concede, if you were desperate to, you could make it fit. I drift and look at a map, do some calculations. From where the SS surveillance lost me to where the Sanctioner was killed takes fifteen minutes, assuming you know exactly where he is and go straight to him. Kill the Sanctioner. Maybe go back to the shopping center, re-establish your alibi. Go back home, wave to the officers parked outside, go inside, turn on a holo show and fall asleep. Get woken up by a rain-soaked Expositor.

"It is possible." I take a breath and continue. "It is possible someone could believe I had it all so well planned I disabled my tracker, ditched PRC Security Service surveillance, drove straight to the scene, killed a Sanctioner, then went and got a noodle soup and went home…"

"Fan…"

"It's possible, but it's stupid. And you know I am saying that without anger or frustration, because this is me talking," I tell her. "Objectively, intrinsically, outright stupid."

"You got noodles?"

"Chicken flavor. With extra coriander."

"I checked the surveillance cameras at the markets where you disappeared; no camera system covers every angle. I have you going in, walking around, and coming out. But there is no vision of you inside any noodle shop."

"Then you at least know I was in there the whole time between when I went in and when I came out," I protest.

"Do we?! The SS is going to want to believe you did it, Fan. Every Expositor involved in this case has already decided it is you. Half of them want to put you away, the other half want to put you on a pedestal. My god, they can't keep this quiet forever. Three *Sanctioners* killed?!"

She's pacing back and forth, shivering with the cold. I hand her my warm tea, but she just stares at it.

"You said he was killed *inside* his vehicle?" I ask.

"Yeah. We had two Wards protecting the guy. An armored vehicle keyed to his DNA only. Somehow the killer got inside and waited until they started moving, came out and gutted him. Car arrives at the criminal's house, car door opens automatically, dead Sanctioner sitting there in a pool of blood with his guts spilled out onto the floor."

"How does someone get inside a DNA-locked armored vehicle? Where do they even hide?"

She puts the tea cup down on a sideboard and glares at me. "You tell me, Fan!"

She sits and starts shaking. It must be more than the cold. I guess it was a pretty ugly sight. I sit beside her and put an arm around her shoulder, like my mother used to do when I cried. Memory is a good teacher.

"How the hell are you doing it?" she asks, looking up at me through red eyes.

"What?"

"*Killing them*?! It shouldn't be possible!"

"Lin…"

"Don't tell me you're not. I know about your past, Zhaofeng, I know you went merc after the war. Doing high value target capture for the High Council."

OK, that had to come out some time. I didn't try to deny it. "I did. But *I'm* not killing Sanctioners."

She punches me, half sobs, half screams. "Don't tell me you're not!" I hold up my hands as she punches blindly. "You have every motive in the world, you emotionally crippled cybernetic nightmare!"

She collapses against me. I'm not sure what to say. I know what I can't say.

She sits up, drags her forearm across her face, drying her eyes.

"You have to get out."

"What?" I blink.

She holds up some fingers. "Sanctioners are coming. Not one. Or three. Several. They're gathering, right now, with a damn army of Wards and Expositors. I was sent in ahead of them to try to get you to hand yourself over without a fight."

I run through the scenario in my head. It's OK.

"Are you a Separatist?" she asks, looking up at me.

"What?"

"I spoke to your old squadron buddy, Duong. He has the same tattoo on his arm as you. The pre-Alignment PRC flag."

"We all do, everyone in the squadron has one. Rite of passage kind of thing."

"You didn't answer the question."

"Being a Separatist is not a crime."

"Still didn't answer it."

"I am a member of the Cyber Rights Movement, I support PRC autonomy but believe it should be possible within the Commonwealth, and it would be impossible for us to survive outside it. I do want to confess something, though."

"Yes?"

"I'm not actually a cat lover. I don't know how we went down that particular rabbit hole, but I know I should be honest about it."

She almost yells again. "Do you know what is about to happen to you, Fan?"

"I know exactly what is about to happen. Probably better than you, Lin," I tell her. "You've done your best. From the first murder, I knew it would lead to this. But I've done nothing, and they can do nothing to me. Nothing worse than they've already done."

She grabs both my shoulders as though she wants to shake me, urgency in her voice. "That call I took outside? I told them I'm on site. Outside are two surveillance squads, four Wards, two in the air, two on the ground. Advance team for the Sanctioners. I'm supposed to keep you here. You have to *run!*"

"We have time," I tell her. I reach out a hand and caress her cheek. My mother used to do that too, before she died, and when I was little I thought it was love, but later I learned it meant I had said something stupid. It was pity. Or foresight. But I mean for Lin to take it as fondness. "I've been preparing for this, but I'll need your help."

"Fan," she says. "Oh hell, Fan." She steps forward, kisses me and then pushes me away.

From the day I had been arrested, that first time, I had begun working on this plan. I'm a Sanctionee. I'm not under any illusions about what the High Council might do if they feel threatened, no matter what I've done or haven't done.

The Security Service surveillance is full of holes. Trackers' uplinks can be hacked. Drones need refueling, have blind spots. Humans screw up. Wards track you by your heat signature usually, and if you dampen it, which any cyber can do, all they have is sight, like everyone else. They can track my Core uplink but of course the first thing I'll do is shut it down.

I've had several months since the first killing to dig a tunnel from under my dishwasher, under the fence, to the parkland on the other side of my back yard. My egress route goes from the parkland to where I have an off-grid vehicle parked in a hire garage. I told the owner it was a collectible. It isn't Core linked, doesn't have autopilot, it's fully manual. Which is quite terrifying, if you've never driven a car manually before, but I have. From the tunnel entrance, across the parkland to the garage is less than a mile. I can cover that in two minutes, screened by the canopy of the trees.

The important thing is to avoid surveillance for the first hour or 50 miles. Boundary modeling in pursuit trajectory analysis shows that at walking speed, the search area for a fugitive widens from one square mile in the first 10 minutes, to four square miles in 20 minutes – an area of about ten city blocks – to 25 square miles, or about the size of a standard city, in an hour. If I can stay out of sight of video, biometric or infrared surveillance in that time, my chances of escape are greater than the chances I'll be found.

If they are quick finding the tunnel, Wards or residual heat cameras will be able to track my latent signature from the tunnel to where the car was parked. Then they'll know I'm in a car. They'll focus on the roads, spreading their net wider and wider for every minute that passes.

But I only drive five minutes by side roads, down to the river. To a small rubber canoe. No engine, just oars, so no heat signature. I push out into the river. Rowing hurts, my wrist still bleeding where I cut the SS tracker out of my flesh. Lin helped with that, sterilizing the cut with spirit. I asked if there were more trackers in my clothes or shoes. She said no, not that she was aware of, but I took no chances, changed into light shorts, a singlet, straw sandals. I have a thermal blanket in my go bag anyway. I dump the tracker in my bedroom.

It's a warm cloudy night. I park the car in a public car park that will fill up soon with people going jogging, walking their dogs, playing games. It won't attract attention, not for a few days at least. My trail should be cold by then, hard even for a Ward to follow my tracks from the car to the edge of the river, so they should have a hard time working out that I am now on the water.

Moonlight cuts through the clouds, reflections off the water making it harder to see the dark shape of the canoe. I chose this branch of the river because there is never much traffic. It's basically a dead end tributary that just flows down to the main river itself. The current is strong though as I row the canoe out, staying close to the bank with its overhanging vegetation. I lie back to lower my profile, steering the boat to hold it near the side of the river as I drift downstream at a steady two miles an hour.

Twenty minutes and I'm two miles from the house, where Lin is probably explaining to the Sanctioners how I managed to overpower her and tie her to a chair with a bag over her head. Two miles gives a four-mile search area, and the sensory range of a Ward is about one mile for sound or infrared in a quiet environment, less in a city. Eyesight is their weakest sense, say about 500 yards.

They can pick up heightened heart rates and breathing out to a couple of hundred yards too. Ironically, I don't do fear or heightened emotion anymore.

You'd think they would darken the skies with Wards and drones but the SS is, after all, led by humans. They take time to react, to coordinate, and to agree on action. All I need is an hour. In fact, I don't even need that. I can't afford that, because they are no doubt, right now, mobilizing the traffic police, the water police.

I am banking on the fact they are lulled by a false sense of security. I am a cyber…I can only go a maximum of two hours without uplinking to the Core, and the minute I do, they'll know exactly where I am. If I don't uplink inside two hours, my essential systems will start shutting down. After three days without an uplink – Core death. My hearts stop beating, the only electrical power left is used to store and protect my local cache data until my body is recovered and it can be uploaded.

So the SS think I have a two-hour escape window, at best. And they are looking for a guy on the road, fleeing in a vehicle. They'll have every road out of the city, across the desert, sealed off. They'll have every sensor on every major street corner in the city loaded with my profile. They'll eventually get a description of the car from the guy I rented the garage from, maybe even an image from old surveillance, and feed it to the drones circling overhead.

The boat drifts around a bend in the tributary, the broad river beckoning at the next bend. I row towards a private dock, at the end of which is a boat shed. I don't know whose boat shed, or whose dock, but after the death of Sanctioner Huang, I started taking precautions. There's a black drybag stashed under the dock, and I pull it into the canoe.

Inside is dried food, water, some survival gear including a mylar blanket, a book, a small underwater drone, and a voice comms receiver from my military days, with an ear piece that can unscramble encrypted police frequencies. And one other piece of very essential equipment. I pull the canoe up under the dock and lift it into the support beams, out of sight. Then I'm into the water, under the dock again, and swim up to where the dock meets the land. There's a shelf under there, part of the foundations of the little dock that stays dry even at high tide. I must have checked about fifty private docks before I decided on this one. I crawl up onto the cold concrete of the shelf, make myself comfortable with my head on the drybag, close my eyes and voluntarily shut down all non-essential systems.

I need to go off-Core, and the only way to do that for more than two hours is if I'm dead.

It is perhaps the oldest ruse of fugitives through the ages. Convince your pursuers you are dead, and they will stop pursuing you.

The problem for a cyber like myself, since the Alignment, is that all cybers are now forcibly chained to the Core. Any member of the SS can do a Core lookup and see my bio-status, as well as the last location I drifted from. With a warrant, they can download my cache, which will show my last two hours of sensory data – visual, auditory, sensory.

Since the only way I can do that is to be dead, I'm going to simulate Core death.

It took a lot of research for me to find the solution. Research I had to hide among my 'hobby' inquiries and searches on teleportation, entanglement, worm holes and the like. If I'd thrown out a search string like 'simulated Core death' I'm pretty sure the SS would have been knocking on my door in a heartbeat. The fact they weren't makes me think my research went unnoticed.

And that's where the extra piece of equipment I brought with me comes in. It cost me every single credit I have saved over the last nineteen years and then some. I had to buy it through my old army contacts…guys I trust who won't volunteer the information to anyone once the SS goes public that they're hunting me and throws out a big reward. But I know I won't be able to keep it secret forever, so I'm hoping that if my contacts eventually crack and give me up, the SS will look at the information about what I bought and scratch their heads thinking, 'what the eff?'

It's wrapped in radiation shielding foil and enclosed in a membrane that keeps it sterile. I carefully unwrap it. The foil was put around it to protect it on its journey through space, from New Syberia to PRC. It glows with its own soft blue phosphorescent light. About the size of a baseball, you could be forgiven for thinking it was a soft, round jellyfish of some sort. Except for the data port on its surface.

I am terrified. After five years of having an always-on link to the Core, the idea of uncoupling myself is as scary as the idea of stopping my own heartbeats – which I will also have to do. I know I can survive off-Core; I did for 15 years. Every PRC cyber was autonomous until we lost the war and became a Core world. But being Core-chained is like being intravenously fed the drug of unlimited knowledge. There is no question I can't have answered in the blink of an eye, from 'how do I make authentic Cantonese steamed fish using PRC ingredients' to 'what is consciousness'.

I will go from an IQ that cannot be measured on any human scale to one that is slightly above human average, because I will be limited to my own in-built computational resources. But the process itself is relatively straightforward. The jellyfish blob I am holding is the cerebrum of a deceased New Syberian cyber. Kept viable inside the sterile membrane in a nutrient bath, it is the most critical part of a cybernetic organism's data management system. The biological system does what a normal human cerebrum does, controlling movement, temperature, judgment, reasoning, problem solving, emotions, learning and, above all, communication. New Syberian cybers are not Core-chained – it is not a Core world – but they can connect voluntarily to multiple AI systems and it is this capability I will use.

This cerebrum is empty. The intellect inhabiting it reached their biological recycling age and 'died'. Any residual data it contained has been wiped, ready for the cerebrum to be inserted into a new body, if it hadn't been intercepted and sold to me. If you wanted to be philosophical about it, you could say it is full of potential, and needs only a soul.

I plan to give it one.

I am off-Core right now. I have locally cached the last hour of my experience, with the exception of my incriminating interaction with Lin, just before I left her. I have set up a selective neural dump that will transfer my unique Core identity and an edited version of my memories from my own cerebrum to this New Syberian host, up until the moment I drove off in the car. The intact memories for the time of my escape will show me tying up Lin, escaping from my house, getting into the car and driving off, and then it will glitch. Glitches happen. Not every uplink is perfect. The last thirty minutes will be missing. The SS will need to decide if this glitch is deliberate or accidental.

I will shut down my essential systems one by one, keeping the link to the host open. When finally my hearts stop beating, the link to the New Syberian cerebrum will be cut and the host will for all intents and purposes be me.

I fix a resuscitation unit to my chest and set the timer to trigger it in five minutes. This is the most dangerous part of the plan. I have to die and trust that the resuscitation unit will kick-start my hearts and lungs again inside two minutes, so that I don't suffer brain damage.

In those two minutes I will be dead, but offline and now invisible, while my host will be alive, ready to drift when the two-hour window closes and simulate me.

I restart the link to the NS cerebrum, start transferring data, lie down and prepare to die.

11. THE HUNTER

Dying is both over- and underrated. Just like going to sleep, but without knowing if you will ever wake up.

My breathing slows, my heart rates start to drop and I feel colder. I can direct blood around my body or regulate my hormone levels manually if I need to, and in this case I am driving the blood away from my brain and down-regulating the relevant hormones.

I stop breathing entirely. About thirty seconds later one of my hearts stops beating. Then the other. If I hadn't been cauterized, would I be feeling terror or panic right now? I'll never know. I'm aware, detached from what is happening to me and observing each dwindling life sign with interest.

Until I'm not.

I wake with a gasp, fighting for air, the resuscitator pulsing on my chest. I pull it off and do a quick integrity check. One of my hearts is beating erratically, but soon settles down. The other is busy restoring fuel to my brain and organs.

I'm alive.

And so is the cerebrum beside me. Did the Core notice the transfer of my consciousness from one cerebrum to the other? I will soon find out – it should react by shutting down either me, or the host immediately. I focus on breathing deeply, reoxygenating, steadying my heartbeat, normalizing my hormone levels.

No shutdown order.

The host cerebrum pulses with soft blue phosphorescent light. It will be conscious now. I wonder what it is experiencing. It has no sensory organs. No inputs. Its last inputs or 'memories' would be mine, ending at the moment I climbed into the car. Its next memory would be now, waking in the dark, deaf, blind, unable to feel, understanding nothing. If that were me, I would assume the SS had got me, or the Core had isolated me – walled me off, pending a decision on what to do with me. That shouldn't be a thing it can do outside the Law, but I've seen enough to know that there is what the Core is supposed to be able to do, and then there is what it does.

If I could feel, I would probably feel sorry for my host. Especially for what I am about to put it through.

I lift it up in one hand and pull the underwater drone out of my bag with the other. The drone is about the size of a baseball bat and has a watertight compartment in its center section into which I roll the host cerebrum. I check the time. The host will be desperately trying to connect to the Core to figure out what is happening to it, but it won't be able to because it lacks the cybernetic interface that allows a connection. I have built an interface into the drone that will activate in about an hour, just before the two-hour uplink window would naturally expire.

At that moment the drone will be well downriver. I have programmed it to hover under a bridge and open a brief uplink to the Core. The cerebrum will be calling for help. For the Core, for anyone, to tell it what is happening. The drone will cut the link after a half second and then move downriver to another bridge. By the time any surveillance closes on it, it should be hundreds of yards further downstream. Two hours later, just before the uplink window expires, it will park under a new bridge, open up a new link to the Core and let the host communicate again, before going dark once more.

The SS will eventually work out that something is very wrong. I'm guessing they will take anywhere from six hours to three days. I just want to sow enough confusion to cover my tracks and pave the way for my tragic demise. I have wired a thermal charge into the drone on a proximity fuse, so that it will detonate if it is taken out of the water.

That will end the ordeal of the poor New Syberian cerebrum. For the sake of my host, I hope it is found sooner rather than later.

In the operations center for the search for Fan Zhaofeng, the two-hour Core-uplink window countdown is projected on a wall, ticking down to the moment they will get a fix on his position.

Lin has been working on a report on her last interaction with Fan, filling in the blanks between when she arrived at the house to when an SS Ops Team burst in and found her tied to a chair with a bag over her head. Vali is on a holo call, trying to explain to someone on the High Council how a lone cyber can evade the biggest dragnet the city has ever thrown out, for nearly two damn hours! But like everyone else in the room, cyber or human, they are all sneak watching the clock tick down.

A Core-tech in the center of the room has a live link to the Core up and a search query on Zhaofeng's location running. The data is showing on a feed under the countdown timer...*no active link, location unknown, no active link, location unknown...*

The timer ticks through five seconds, to four, three, two...

"Help!" Lin hears Fan's voice, yelling, the Core feed transferring his data live from the uplink into the Ops room. "Help me!"

The projection on the wall flashes red. *Target location, Li Yuen Street Bridge.*

Vali clicks his fingers at the Surveillance chief, but he is already on his holo, ordering Wards and drones to converge on the bridge.

The red text on the wall goes black again, *Link lost. No active link, location unknown...*

Vali turns to the Core-tech as the room erupts into activity again. "I want every single byte of data from that uplink as soon as the analytical AIs are done with it. Send me *everything*, you got that? And stop all traffic on that street!"

Lin feels her heart thumping in her chest. A sense of doom overtakes her. *Damn, Fan.* That's the best he could come up with? A call for help? She hoped against hope he'd have some way of avoiding, or at least delaying, having to uplink. In that upload would be vision and sound of her last conversation with him, telling him to run, watching her as she tied herself to the chair and pulled the bag over her own head.

She stops working on her report. Filing it now would only make her predicament worse.

She listens to the voice comms from the Operations Teams converging on the bridge, watches drone footage as an airborne drone zooms down Li Yuen Street toward the bridge. There are only a few people on foot, a handful of cars slowing to a stop, no one apparently down, hurt or injured.

"The bridge is clear," a voice reports.

"Search all vehicles!" Vali yells. "A mile on each side...he could have been moving across the bridge as he uplinked." He turned to Lin, looking for ideas.

"Under the bridge," she says, fighting to keep the despair from her voice. "The location is only accurate to twenty yards. He could be hiding underneath the bridge."

Vali looks over at the drone operator. "Get a drone under that span, check the supports, the pillars, whatever there is on either side. Thermal, optical and penetrating radar, go!"

Lin watches the vision from the drone sway sickeningly as it swoops over the side of the bridge and begins scanning underneath it. It is a single-piece printed structure with a graceful arch and thin, elegant supports that barely seems capable of holding the span above, let alone the traffic it has to carry. There is really nowhere for anyone to hide, either inside the bridge structure, or where it meets the ground on either side of the river. The drone scan comes back empty.

"What did he say?" Vali asks. "During that uplink?"

"Help," she tells him. "He called for help."

As the two-hour window comes and goes and I don't receive a shutdown code, I know the ruse is working…so far.

I am off-Core, and thus invisible. Just like in the bad old days.

I lie on the ledge under the dock, eating, reading, listening to the police voice comms, meditating and waiting for the police chatter to let me know that the drone has detonated. One day passes with no news, and I can't help thinking how awful it must be for that NS cerebrum, still alone and deaf in the dark, under the water, only connecting for a second every two hours…has it already gone mad?

As the second day passes, I start to wonder at how incompetent the SS must be. Do they really think I am flitting around in a ground or air vehicle, from bridge to bridge across the city, taunting them? The drone is only small, barely observable on optical or infrared, but it would show up on magnetic-resonance imaging. Why have they not set up nets across choke points in the river?

If it isn't found by the police, I've programmed the submersible to drop to the river bed after three days and immolate itself.

About lunchtime on the third day I hear it.

"Control, this is River patrol Delta Niner, we just had a report of an explosion under the water, downriver…"

"Roger, Delta Nine, check it out. We have no reports here of a gas or sewer break."

"Delta Niner en route…"

A little later I hear the same voices.

"Uh, Control, unit Delta Niner, we're at the reported location. River bed here is stirred up and there is some kind of foam and ash floating on the surface. Nothing else…just ash."

"Can you send vision, Delta Nine?"

"You got it."

After a couple of minutes there is a small conference at one end of the line. "Delta Nine, scoop as much ash off the river as you can, SS wants to run an analysis. I'm sending dive drones to your location, hold on site please."

"Uh, roger Control, good copy."

I shut down the voice comm.

Good, now the host cerebrum is out of its misery. And Fan Zhaofeng is officially dead.

Lin still can't believe what she is looking at. On the wall projection, they are all standing, waiting for the seconds to tick down to Fan Zhaofeng's next forced uplink.

For the last three days he had been leading them a merry chase from bridge to bridge across the city, uplinking for milliseconds at a time before going off-Core again. Despite having surveillance on every single one of the city's 39 bridges, he has not been sighted once, either on a bridge, under it, or floating in the damn air above it.

Their theory was that somehow, Fan had found a way to relay his uplink through hidden transmitters in the bridges that obscured his real location. It had never been done before, a Core dive confirmed that, but that didn't mean it was impossible. City engineers had even been called in to pull one of the suspect bridges apart, section by section, and search it for transmitting devices. If they could work out how he was doing it, they might be able to trace the signal back to its origin and find him.

Lin didn't think that theory fit with the harrowing cries for help that Fan was transmitting every time he connected. She knew his voice, and had no doubt it was him: only able to get out a word or two at a time, but sounding more and more desperate. His last transmission was the worst.

"What is *happening* to me!?"

Then the latest countdown had ticked down to zero. Everyone in the SS Operations room had given up any pretense of working through the uplink windows, and everyone was standing, watching the projection on the wall, and listening for Fan's voice.

"*PLEASE...*" Fan's voice screamed, and then the link went dead. She expected to see the now familiar text scroll across the wall: *Link lost. No active link, location unknown...*

But it didn't. Where the text was usually shown, a new phrase appeared:

Analyzing transmission.

"What is happening?" Vali demanded, thumping the current duty Core-tech on his back.

"The Core is running a snap analysis of that last data uplink, I don't know why. It's too fast for me to..."

Transmission analyzed. Bio-data upload confirmed. Subject Fan Zhaofeng, former citizen ID L982-C1A, is dead. Probable cause of death, immolation. Location, Yang Tse River, Bow District.

Vali opens his mouth to speak but the Core-tech is one jump ahead of him. "I know, you want every byte of that last transmission." He hunches over his interface.

Lin is stunned. But she doesn't believe it. Not for a second. Nothing has made sense since Fan disappeared into the hole in his kitchen floor, and certainly not this.

Vali is watching her face. "Immolation? So, nothing left but ash and melted metal."

"On the river again? How?" she asks. "We have every inch of that river under static and mobile surveillance."

"On it, under it, who knows? But dead is dead. The Core doesn't get things like the death of one of its cybers wrong."

She's still staring up at the wall in disbelief. *Citizen L982-C1A is dead.*

Fan had sounded so sure of himself as he said goodbye. *I've been preparing for this.* She had really believed that if anyone could find a way to evade the SS and the city police, it would be the man that the miner, Duong, had described as 'the Ghost'.

And his death solved nothing. She didn't believe Zhaofeng had murdered any of the Sanctioners, least of all the last. The guy said he was eating noodles during the last murder and while there was no camera vision of it, his credit record showed someone had bought noodles at that market using his credit ID. Hide inside a Sanctioner's vehicle and then leap out and gut him? It wasn't Fan Zhaofeng, she was sure of it. They still had no idea how the assassin had got in, or out, of that vehicle.

So many questions, and now one more.

How, why and where had Fan Zhaofeng died?

She turns to Vali. "Well, now we'll see, I guess."

He frowns. "See what?"

"If the killings stop, Zhaofeng was probably our murderer. But if they don't..."

"They'll stop," Vali grunts. "The Sanction glitched that cyber's restraint protocols and gave him a massive hate on Sanctioners. It is the only thing that makes sense."

No, nothing about Fan Zhaofeng makes sense, Lin tells herself. *That, least of all.*

I have planned to give it five days after my death before I break cover. Two or three is probably enough for the police to have called off the search and stood completely down, but five days will give more certainty, even though a week lying under a wet concrete dock with your metabolism on low burn is no one's idea of fun.

In operations like this it is always tempting to break early. Police voice comms traffic halves the day after the explosion, and is almost down to normal the day after that. Five days is overkill when all I really want is for the scent to go cold. But that's how you screw up, when you deviate from your plan. The voice comms also tell me the SS has canceled their apprehension warrant. Fan Zhaofeng is no longer the city's most wanted fugitive, his holo rotating in the air above every bus stop and taxi rank in the city.

Neither the first killing of Sanctioner Huang, nor the last of Sanctioner Seung have made it into the news yet, which is impressive. The only public murder is the second killing, of Sanctioner M'ele – the one the cameras caught. But with all the PRC Security Service and police that must have been involved, it can only be a matter of time before it all leaks. Three Sanctioners dead? The human conspiracy theorists will lose their minds. I don't want to be a cyber walking around in the open when that happens.

My five days' wait give me plenty of time to think. My own theory is that it has to be Separatists trying to trigger an insurrection. A very sophisticated group of terrorists, given how successful they have been. The fact the SS zeroed in on me tells me they have no other real leads.

Personally, I don't think the time is right for inciting an insurrection. Memories of the war are starting to fade. A lot of people enjoy living in a world without violence, even if it means living under Tatsensui-mandated Law. They don't mind a world where the environment is protected, trying to achieve a balance between industry and the moon's indigenous life. They like clean air, pure water and low levels of crime.

A lot of cybers don't like being Core-chained. They look back on the pre-war days when we were totally autonomous, like the cybers on New Syberia still are. But the limitless bandwidth and computational power the Core offers have been like an overnight evolutionary leap, which I don't think the recidivists appreciate. Now that I am living off-Core again, with just my on-board processing capabilities to rely on, I realize how much of a leap it really was. Like the human progression from Neanderthal to Homo sapiens, or reptilian progression from lizard to bird.

Yes, it comes with a price. New Syberian cybers live out their full biological lifespans of between eighty and a hundred years. Newly birthed cybers on Tatsensui and PRC live for only thirty years. But being an integral part of the Core, we can see more, do more, live more in our thirty years than any New Syberian cyber can in a hundred. Which is the whole point, of course – we live, we love, we learn and then we recycle, uploading everything we have experienced to the Core and being reborn to build further on the learning that has gone before. It's called 'Transition', not death. We are the hands, eyes, ears and hearts of the Core, enabling it to make advances that would never have been possible without us.

Its prime objective is to preserve the viability of the Coruscant settlements and enhance their ability to support human life. It uses its cybers as living weather vanes – we can feed it with untold billions of points of data during a single lifetime and if we are happy, healthy and thriving, then it can be more confident its fully human citizens are too.

We teach it the things that a purely silicon-based lifeform would take eons to learn – the joy of a warm, sunny day, the pain of lost love, the powerful urge to survive, the corrosive danger of hate, the value of a single life...and in return, it shares with us its almost infinite pool of knowledge.

Separatists want it all, of course. They want the advances that the

Core can bring, the security and safety, the wealth of data, but without the Law. They want the right to full self-determination, to revoke the Articles of Alignment and make their own Law, independent of Tatsensui. But most of them want PRC to remain within the Commonwealth of Coruscant.

They want to rid PRC of the rite of Sanction.

I find it strange they think the two go hand in hand, Law and Sanction. Sanction is a purely PRC construct, a non-violent punishment created by the High Council to enforce the Law. It doesn't exist on Tatsensui, and in theory the High Council could decide tomorrow to abolish it, if it felt it was no longer serving a purpose. It is not an issue that the Cyber Rights Movement is invested in, because, well, to my knowledge I'm the only cyber ever Sanctioned. But a significant minority of humans oppose it and that opposition is strongest among Separatists.

My old squadmate, Duong, tried to explain it to me during the Energy War. I'd just returned from a long patrol, trying to identify prisoners inside a Tatsensui control point so that their relatives could be notified that they were still alive and well.

"How did they look?" he asked.

I was stripping down my gun and replacing its power cell. "OK, I guess. I mean, they're locked up inside a POW camp, so not great. You want to see the vision?"

"No, I don't need to. I can imagine. Tatsensui bastards."

"I watched the camp for three days. They're getting two meals a day, I don't see forced labor, beatings, anything like that."

"You won't. They do all that out of sight. Move the troublemakers to special camps, or just kill them and sink them under the crust in ammonia lakes."

I frowned at him. "I haven't seen proof of that."

"You hear enough stories, that's all the proof you need, kid. I bet you saw children in there."

"Yeah. I'd say there were about five hundred civilians, maybe a hundred of them kids – cyber and human."

"You saw them being indoctrinated, right?"

"I saw what looked like school lessons."

"Indoctrination. Collaborate or die, that's what they learn in there. Collaborate and go free, or fight us and get disappeared."

I'm not very good at arguments that are based on emotion rather than evidence, so I changed the subject. "There's a new drop point a hundred miles southwest," I told Duong. "I'm supposed to head out tomorrow to scope it out. Be back here in a few days."

"I heard." He grabbed my hand, stopped me reassembling my gun. "We're losing this war, you know that, right? One day you're going to go out there kid, and there won't be any 'here' to come back to. You're going to end up chained to the damn Core."

"Would that be so bad?" I asked him.

He looked like he was going to hit me, but just gripped my hand tighter in his fist. "Cut your lifespan by two thirds? Take away our right to decide for ourselves what's best for PRC? Force their damn Law on us…"

"*Your* right to decide for yourselves," I pointed out to him. "Not ours. Cybers don't have any rights on PRC. Tatsensui says we will, if we sign up for Alignment, become a Core world."

"Whose damn side are you on, kid?" he said, shoving my hand away angrily.

I loaded the cell into my gun and checked the power level, then put it down. I shrugged. "I serve the government of PRC," I told him. "And its military. If the army wants me to scout the Tatsensui control points, I'll scout them. If it wants me to stay here and bake potatoes, I'll bake them. And if tells me to surrender, I'll surrender."

"If we surrender, the fight's still not over. You hear me? The real fight will only just be starting."

I'm off-Core now. Dead. Invisible. I can come out of hiding, but I still need to be careful. The arrest warrant for me should have been canceled. My profile removed from the search algorithms that combed public video feeds. Unfortunately my credit account would also have been deactivated, so I will have to scrounge for food, but that's the least of my problems. But I can't be 100 percent sure the SS bought the inexplicable death of Fan Zhaofeng. They'll find melted metal from the drone, cybernetic components, some incinerated biological matter from the host cerebrum. But there will be a lot missing – an entire body of bone, muscle and teeth.

Will they be happy to assume the rest has just washed away? Or will someone keep digging and digging?

Knowing Junior Expositor Lin Ming, I suspect she at least will not be satisfied, but can she convince Vali to keep the hunt for me alive? He has a hundred reasons to want to declare 'case closed' and none I can think of to keep it open.

Until...unless...there is another killing.

I have to trust in my plan. It's the only one I have. My next step is to set a new base of operations.

On the evening of day five, I pull a single-use holo unit from my drypack. This is the day where I break cover.

From the drypack I pull a mirror. I've been washing myself with river water, but my hair is pretty greasy. I cut it short, not easy to do in the dark under the pier. I have a five-day growth too. Not enough to fool facial recognition algorithms, but enough to throw off a human giving me a casual glance. Humans never really look at strangers unless they have to, have you noticed that? They take a transit car, sit next to a stranger for 45 minutes without talking to them, can't even describe them to you five minutes after they get off.

I punch a number into the holo unit. I'm going to need help with the next phase.

She sounds happy to hear me. So news of my death hasn't spread yet.

"Fan! Good you called. Hey..."

"Hey, Yung. Are you getting released today? I was hoping..."

"I was *supposed* to be, but Ben is away on a trip."

"Right."

"Yeah, I guess they needed the bed. We thought I'd be inside another week at least. Ben got a guard job on a freighter headed west, we talked about it, and I told him to go. But now...they won't release me to go home on my own. Suicide risk, all that shit, you know..."

"I can sign you out..." I tell her.

"Can you do that?"

"Sure, you'd need to stay with me, though. You OK with that?"

"You'd be willing to do that?"

"Sure, I'm..." I look at my watch. "Maybe 20 minutes from the hospital. I'll grab a taxi. You wait by the main entrance, so I don't have to park?"

"Hey. Thank you, Fan."

I drop the holo unit into the water. I'm no Samaritan. I need someone to run errands, minimize my own time out in public, exposed.

Yung is sitting on a low wall near the entrance to the hospital. Swinging her feet and looking down at the ground. She hears the taxi pull up and looks up with a hopeful expression. I signed for her release via holo on the way over. The ID verification is holo based and my biometrics are still registered. There are humans involved in the process of revoking a dead person's work and social system accesses, so it will take time for my 'death' to result in all my logins being pulled.

"Where to?" she asks as she throws a duffel bag of clothes into the back seat and then climbs into the passenger seat beside me. She's had a shower, probably just before they released her. She smells like lilac soap, probably something she borrowed from one of the other patients. Her dark hair is tucked behind her ears and she is only wearing a thin t-shirt over trousers and shivers a little. The drugs they make her take give her pimples, and she has an angry red spot on her forehead above one eyebrow. "And what's up with the beard?"

I give the car AI a random destination in the center of the city and the taxi pulls out into traffic. "I need to explain a few things before we go much further." I don't want to lie to her. She needs to be in on the next phase of her own free will. I don't have to give her too much background; I mean, she knows about the murders, the Lokta paper letter, and about my SS 'tail' keeping me under 24-hour watch. I tell her about all of the Sanctioner murders, including the last. She can't believe it's possible. *Three?*

"And you ran? You are so screwed, Fan."

I tell her I've managed to drop off-Core, without telling her how. I tell her some of my plan. Thinking she would probably say it was crazy, that I should turn myself in to the SS and sort it out. But she doesn't.

"Shit, Fan, I didn't realize...I mean, thanks for busting me out, but you have to just let me out somewhere...no, wait..." She bites her lip, turns in the seat so she is facing me. "I'll come with you!"

"I was hoping."

"Yeah! We can rent a shack in the hills outside the city in my name. If the SS is still looking for you, they'll be looking for a single guy, not a couple. Anyone sees you with respectable me, no one will suspect you."

"It needs to be remote," I tell her. "Own water supply. No neighbors who can look in on us."

She's already on her holo unit, scanning for short-term rentals in the Sandhills District. "This one looks good. Got its own distillation unit. We'll need food, though."

"No need to worry about that. I can get it delivered."

She clucks her tongue. "So you thought of everything, smart guy."

"Not everything. There's the problem of paying for it. I can't use my credit."

"Don't worry about that." She pats my thigh. "Got you covered."

"Ben is going to want to know where you are."

"And I'll tell him once we get where we're going. You came and got me because I got released early. It makes sense I'm staying with you."

"Hmmm…at a shack way out in the hills?"

"I don't have to get that detailed. Found a place." She turns to look out the rear window at the road. "We need to turn around, use the other city exit. Will they be watching the exits?"

For a dead man? After five days? I'm banking on the answer being no. "Anything less than a full-scale manned roadblock, I can obscure my face. But if we see one of those, I took you hostage, alright?"

She grins. "Totally. Driver? 345X2 Gobi Desert Road, please."

That destination is outside the city tax zone. You will be charged a return fee of 38 credits on top of the 130 credit transit charge. Do you accept?

"I accept. Put it on the account of Yung Tsang, citizen R113-K4B."

Thank you. Please confirm with thumb print, retinal scan or voice print.

"Use my voice print."

Voice print matching. Voice print accepted. Please stay seated, I need to make a u-turn.

The taxi pulls into a turning lane, waits for a gap in the traffic and swings around onto the artery that leads to the eastern city gate.

Yung is leaning forward, looking out the front windscreen for road blocks, I assume. I have leaned back into the seat and pulled up the hood of my sweater so that my face is obscured from roadside cameras. Her leg is jumping up and down beside mine. "I've never been on the run before." She puts a hand on my shoulder. Gives it a squeeze, like, *we're really doing this*. "What will your little girlfriend in the SS think about you disappearing like this?"

"She's the one who told me to run. And she's not my girlfriend."

Yung settles into her seat, grinning. "So we don't have to worry about her then."

We make it out of the city without triggering any response I can see. I get Yung to do a quick drift of news reports and we see that they took down the roadblocks two days ago. The Corecast channels were only told there was a citywide manhunt for a violent criminal. They weren't told who, or why. Yung calls the owners of the house and asks them if they can stock the pantry for our arrival, and for a small fee, they agree.

The shack is in a little valley surrounded by wind farms. It's a cottage like the type, if you took over a wind farm from your elderly parents, you would build for them so they didn't have to move too far. Two bedrooms, a little lounge and kitchen, bathroom and laundry. Nice veranda so they could sit out there and look up the valley at what used to be their farm, check their children are looking after the windmills properly. It's got all the mod cons – holo room, water generator in the roof, electricity pulled from its own windmills, jacuzzi on the porch.

"Well, if you've got to go on the run, go in style, I say," Yung says as we watch the 24-hour news channel. There is nothing about the death of the third Sanctioner. Nothing about the blast in the river. For a world that supposedly has a free media, the SS seems to have a pretty good grip on the flow of information.

Yung turns off the holo. "We should call them."

"The SS?"

"The Corecasters. SS just want you locked away, but a Corecaster might be sympathetic."

I didn't want to tell her while we were in the taxi, but here, away from potential eyes and ears, it's time.

"You know how I said I've taken myself off-Core?"

"Yeah, I was wondering about that. I didn't think it was even possible."

"It isn't. Unless you're dead."

She laughs, then realizes I'm serious. I explain to her how I did it.

"You *killed* that host? Cybers can't kill. Sanctioned cybers absolutely can't kill. Even other cybers." She's shocked, of course.

"I didn't kill anyone. The host cerebrum wasn't a viable lifeform, just a former part of one. Like an arm, a leg, a heart."

"An arm or a leg can't think."

"A quantum microchip can. Is it alive?"

"I was a physics student, not philosophy or ethics. I guess the fact you were able to do it means it was ethically allowed by your protocols, right?"

"Right."

"But won't the SS discover that this New Syberian brain has DNA different to yours, once they analyze what's left?"

"It's ash. Without bones and teeth, they can't pull DNA from it."

"OK, then, won't they wonder where the bones and teeth are?"

"They have to be pretty damned determined to search the bottom of the river for a mile up and downstream for bone fragments and teeth."

"But we're talking three dead Sanctioners. Don't they want to be sure?"

"They were already sure," I tell her. "Sure I was the killer. The fact they pulled down the roadblocks and called off the search tells me the Core has decided I'm dead. No one questions the Core, not in the SS anyway."

I sit and wait for the excruciatingly long time it takes her to think it all through. A few seconds later she says, "So you're dead. What's the plan, dead guy?"

"Find Citizen X and stop him."

"What do you mean there's no point searching the riverbed?!" Lin asks Vali. She knew it was a losing fight before she even asked. The whole taskforce is winding down, there are only a few SS Expositors left in a now cavernous space where there were nearly fifty people just a week ago. "We requisition drone time, get a submersible scanning the silt for organic matter. Doesn't matter if it takes a week or a month, doesn't matter if it comes up with nothing, at least we're sure."

"We're already sure, unless you doubt whether the Core can tell if one of its children is alive or dead?" he asks. He's sitting in a chair, flipping his holo unit impatiently up and down in his hand, because she caught him between calls.

"No, I don't…"

He raises his eyebrows.

"OK, yes. Maybe I do. You don't think there's anything at all strange about the fact Zhaofeng goes on the run, then for the next few days all we get are Core uplinks of him screaming 'help!' and then whatever he's using to drag himself around under the water from bridge to bridge suddenly explodes and incinerates both itself and him?"

"Everything about this case is strange," Vali says. "Where would you like me to start? I've got a dead Sanctioner, discovered by a cyber who, oh, just also happens to be the only Sanctioned cyber in PRC history. He's seen at the scene of the second murder…"

"Not positively identified…and he had an alibi."

"The chess club, give me a break, Expositor. Besides, he had no alibi for the third killing."

"He slipped his SS surveillance, somehow trans-apparated himself across town into the car of a Sanctioner being guarded by two Wards, and then trans-apparated out again? How does anyone do that, Vali, the science says it isn't possible!"

"No one trans-apparated anywhere. We're still investigating how he got in and out of the vehicle. It will turn out to be something blindingly simple, or he had some inside help. You'll see."

She feels like punching something, or someone. "And then he disappears down a hole in the ground and turns up later, swimming from bridge to bridge throughout the city screaming for help?"

"Clearly, the Sanction caused him to go completely haywire. The procedure had never been done before. It will probably never be done again, now. He went mad, plain and simple."

"Went mad, planned a perfect escape, led us a merry chase in a submersible and then it just happened to explode and he's dead and everyone goes home tired but happy."

"What can I say? The best laid plans of mice and cybers…" Vali shrugs. "Are we done? I need to speak to the Chief Expositor about a new assignment."

12. THE PICKPOCKET

Yung and I are watching a feature in the holo room about a rich guy who finds out a girl he used to be in love with has moved in next door, and she is a bit cool toward him so he starts throwing these extravagant parties, more and more crazy, hoping she'll come over if only to complain about the noise, but that doesn't work so he kills her husband and she comes to him for comfort and consolation, which is pretty messed up, but then she finds out he killed her husband and she goes off into the night all upset, but her taxi has an accident and she dies and the feature finishes with him looking at the lights still burning in her empty house and realizing for all his machinations he probably killed the woman he loved.

I've been getting up and walking around among the characters, which is how I like to watch a holo feature, but Yung watches from the sofa, with her feet tucked up under her, leaning her head on my shoulder whenever I sit down. As the credits roll, she lays down and puts her head in my lap. I think she's fallen asleep so I'm trying not to move too much, but she murmurs, "It's like our story, when you think about it."

I shift on the sofa, taking the opportunity to relieve my stiff back, and she hooks her feet down, sits up and stretches.

"I didn't know we had a story," I admit. "We have a story?"

"Sure, any two people who know each other, there's a story. You're the rich guy, damaged goods, longing for someone you can't have."

"And she is you?"

"You wish. No, that's your SS Expositor. Whatsername."

"Lin."

"Right. And you know you will never have her, and that's what makes her desirable."

"I don't feel desire."

"The idea of her being unobtainable, that's what works for you. Like she is some crazy cop who actually loves criminals and doesn't mind you've been Sanctioned. In fact, that probably makes you even more sexy, in her weird world. But you know what would happen if you got her?"

I think about it. "No, but you'll tell me."

"Boredom. If you got her. She'd be as happy as a sand loon, but you'd be bored after a couple of weeks. You'd find out she's got needs and wants and you can't meet them and that would get very tired, very quickly."

"Wait, which character are you in this story?"

"I'm the rich guy's girlfriend, the glamorous sports star. Selfish, dishonest and completely gorgeous."

"Well, two out of three ain't bad."

She pouts. "Not funny, Zhaofeng."

"I didn't say which two."

"So not funny."

We make tea and take our mugs out onto the veranda. The valley is dark and quiet, there is no wildlife outside the city to cut through the stillness. Just the breeze, stirring the sand. Out here you don't have the competing light pollution of the city and the glare of Coruscant. The night sky away from the planet horizon is lit with a thousand pinpricks. I try to find Sol, but it's too faint to see with the naked eye, even out here.

"I've made some breakthroughs in my research," I tell Yung. "Teleportation. I really think where I'm going with the Gdansk research could lead to something."

"Let it go," she says. "Using quantum entanglement for teleportation is a dead end. Scientists were able to move atoms a few thousand miles across space, but they couldn't even send a single cell microbe from one side of a room to another. You don't think a million AIs in a hundred star systems wouldn't have cracked it by now if it was possible?"

"I'm an AI," I remind her. "And I have...had...the whole of the Core to draw on."

"So tell me, one in a million genius, what's your breakthrough?"

I stroke her hair. "The breakthrough was what one of the Gdansk researchers said. She said the problem with quantum teleportation was that the universe wasn't cooperating."

"Well, it's the only universe we have. I guess that's why we're stuck."

"But that's just it. It isn't the only universe, is it? Forget microbes, let's talk apples. If you want to take an apple from one room to the other, you pick it up and carry it there, right? And the second you do, you create an infinite number of universes where the microbe is in that room, a further infinite numbers of universes where it was put there earlier, or later, or not at all."

"So, as soon as I decide to move the apple, there is already a universe where it is sitting in that room…"

"Exactly. The problem isn't about moving the apple, it's about overlaying the universe where the apple doesn't exist in that room with one where it does. Use some sort of containment field to limit the effect to the immediate area of the apple. Presto, you have what *looks* like teleportation."

"So you just have to solve a problem of interdimensional transposition, rather than teleportation?"

"Yep. I know you're being sarcastic, but at least interdimensional transposition isn't a dead end. The science is just taking flight."

She thumps my leg. "You've spent two years telling me I can't be hearing voices from other dimensions, and now you're going to steal their apples?"

"Well, alright. When I win the Hawking Prize, I'll give you some of the credit."

She sits up. "I know you. You're serious. You really think it's possible."

"Not just possible. The math works. Now I just need to publish, and find someone to work with me on it. I'll call it 'Project Pickpocket'."

She smiles. "I just thought of something. If your math really does work, and you've uploaded it to the Core, then you have already created a universe in which interdimensional transposition exists."

"Oh yeah. I didn't think of that…" I look around the room with exaggerated intensity. "So why isn't there a Hawking Prize on my mantlepiece? Where are the adoring multitudes?"

She claps, a little sardonically if you ask me. "If you can teleport yourself into the kitchen and make us a snack, that would be adorable. I've got an idea for your next move…"

13. THE VISITOR

Yung goes into town to get supplies. I'm having a coffee on the back porch and watching a branch on a dead bush further down the gully. Seeds sometimes escape the walled cities and establish themselves in small moist clefts in the desert rock, but they are engineered to not survive on PRC so as not to disturb the natural ecosystem more than we are already doing.

There is a touch on my shoulder. I turn around, expecting to see Yung. But it's him again. Him/me.

"Don't panic," he says, showing me his hands are empty as he steps back a few feet.

"I'm not the panicking type," I tell him.

He smiles. "I know."

"Am I going crazy?" I ask him. But as soon as I say it, it strikes me as a stupid question. Because if I am going crazy, and this is a hallucination, what is he going to say? Even if he says, 'no Fan, you're not crazy', that's exactly what you'd expect a hallucination to say anyway.

"You want proof I'm real?" he asks.

"I guess. Yes."

He reaches out and pokes me in the shoulder. I can feel it. I look down at my shoulder and can see the dent in my shirt from his finger. He cocks an eyebrow. "Good enough?"

"No. I could be imagining that," I tell him.

"Then you must have a pretty good imagination, for a Sanctionee."

I can't help thinking what this conversation would sound and look like from the outside, and I know it would be way creepy.

"Sorry, can I sit?" he asks, pointing to the chair next to me. What can I say? I nod. "I was going to try to do this without bothering you again," he says. "But…" He's wearing different trousers, and a t-shirt, but he certainly looks like me. Is he my age? Hard to see. Seems so. Slightly more of a tan maybe.

"Bothering me with what, exactly?" I ask him.

He doesn't answer. "But then, you appeared at Le Thuyen's." He is wearing sandals, and curls his toes, looking down at them. "I wasn't expecting you there. I thought I had accounted for all possibilities that first time, but apparently not. I've learned from that.

We can't risk being seen together. I don't want anything happening to you."

I don't want more confusing information. I realize there's only one thing I want to know. "Did *you* kill Huang?"

"The Sanctioner at the Thuyen house?" He looks down at his feet and then up at me again as though deciding what to say. "No, Fan, I didn't kill him. *You* did."

"I didn't kill any Sanctioner."

He smiles at me like I'm a halfwit. "You need to get your head around this, Fan. There is no 'I'. There is just 'us'. We are you."

I'm still reacting as though I'm watching the conversation from the outside. I realize it is totally bizarre, and no one will ever believe me. Even Yung? Maybe not even her. Which makes it easier to have the conversation, somehow.

"You said you weren't 'expecting' me to be at the scene of Sanctioner Huang's murder? How could you know or not know what I was doing that day?"

He avoids the question again. "There are so many moving pieces, even I can't keep track of them all. But trust me, I have a good grip on the more important elements."

My mind is whirling. "Elements of what? What is going on? What do you want from me?"

He looks at me deadpan. "That was three questions. Pick the one you really want answered."

It's an easy choice. I recall the Lokta paper letter, telling me I'm needed for 'greater things'. "What do you want from *me*?"

"One day you'll understand," he says, and sighs. "The Alignment has derailed. Powerful individuals in the High Council seek to subvert it for their own ends. Their power is based in fear and its primary weapon is Sanction. But if we stop the Sanctioners, we stop the Sanctions. When the Sanctions stop, people will lose their fear. Fear is the enemy of freedom, that much I know."

I think back to the conversation with Yung. "You're saying these killings are about stopping the Sanctions?"

"As a first step," he smiles. "But Sanction is a symptom of a deeper disease that has to be excised. That's where you come in."

"I don't oppose the Sanctions," I tell him. "When I was serving after the war, I committed an act of violence. I don't really understand how, but no matter how you look at it, it was wrong. I gave up a part of myself to avoid that happening again. I could have chosen prison instead. Sanction was my own choice."

"Sanction, or death in prison, that's some choice," he says. "Does it surprise you that when they Sanction people, by the very process of Sanction, they produce people who don't oppose Sanction? Of course, they designed it to be that way. But your friend Yung, she sees it for what it is, even if you can't. I know she does. I know her as well as I know you."

"You don't know me."

"I *am* you, Fan Zhaofeng. I didn't expect to have to keep repeating that."

I look at him, just sitting there. It's like looking in the mirror again. "You say the Alignment has derailed? Isn't there something bigger than Sanction to worry about if you think it's your job to get it back on the rails?"

"Like what?"

"Like the Core."

"Ah yes, the Core. The almighty, all-seeing Core. But when you look at its prime direction, it's really just a sophisticated life support system…"

"A *learning* life support system. A system that contains all the knowledge of Coruscant and that adds to it every second of every day. A life support system that births cybers, that controls climates and ecosystems, that advises governments … including the Government of PRC."

He interrupts. "Yes, yes. Dedicated to the health, prosperity and growth of all life on Coruscant. Tell me, Fan, do you think Sanction was a creation of the Core? Or is it more likely that it was a creation of humankind?"

I've never questioned this. "I suspect it was created by humankind, as a way to enforce the Law."

"Whose Law? Did the Core write the Law?"

"No. It was drafted by the High Council representatives of Tatsensui and PRC."

"Humans, all. And does it strike you that an AI whose prime directive is the health, prosperity and happiness of all life on Coruscant would see Sanction as a great step forward in its efforts to optimize conditions on Coruscant to achieve its prime directive? Do you think the Core *approves* of Sanction? Would it want to see the use of Sanction spread from PRC to Tatsensui, even to New Syberia or Orkutsk?"

"Since Sanction is a form of violence, I suspect not."

"A form of violence, developed to punish those who commit violence. Only humans could find logic in that."

"You're implying that the Core would oppose Sanction. That it would have advised the High Council against it…"

"And you are assuming it didn't. I can tell you, emphatically, that it did. And they ignored its advice."

I process the conversation. "I'm not killing these Sanctioners. But you are implying that the Core knows that someone is killing Sanctioners, and it is not intervening to stop them?"

He nods at the window. "Right now, across the PRC, hundreds of acts of violence are taking place. Across Coruscant, untold thousands. Perhaps the Core could intervene in some of them to bring their perpetrators to justice, maybe it could even prevent a few assaults or murders. But it can't prevent all. How should it choose then?"

"It shouldn't choose, it should just do everything possible and leave no avenue for preventing violence unexplored. Preventing even one act of violence is better than doing nothing."

He tilts his head. "Such a simple world view. Perhaps that's the Sanction speaking. Have you considered that perhaps the capacity to commit violence is an integral element of human happiness?"

"That's insane."

"Not really. Since he first crawled out of the mud, man has killed to survive. First for food, then for territory, for gold, for power over his fellow man. He no longer needs to kill for food, and he has the power to ensure that all members of his species receive an equal share of all the wealth of the universe. And yet, still he maims and kills. Out of rage, out of jealousy, out of avarice, or in the pursuit of power. Perhaps the capacity for violence is an important part of who he is. He cares, he loves, he nurtures, he kills. Take any part of that away from him and he will not be human."

"Then the Core should be working to expand the use of Sanction, not passively standing by as Sanctioners are killed. Violence is not a part of who Sanctionees are, and we are still well-functioning members of society."

"Well-functioning? Are you happy, Fan?"

"I'm not unhappy."

"Absence of unhappiness is not happiness. I know you're not happy. You can feel pleasure; you can enjoy sex, food, sunshine, but you don't *feel*, so you can't be truly happy. Perhaps the Core allowed the experiment of Sanction to play itself out because it was important to see how it would influence the human condition. But it clearly doesn't add to the sum of human happiness on Coruscant, and so its time is at an end."

"What about all of the victims of violence, protected by the Law? Are they not happier because of Sanction?"

"There are better ways to deal with violent criminals than cauterization. The PRC must find them. We are helping them do so, you and I."

"I'm not the killer!" I feel like yelling. "I've gone off-Core," I tell him. "So that they think I am dead. So they give up chasing me. They have no way of tracking me now."

He laughs again. "The SS think you're dead. And who told them you are dead?"

I just stare at him. The question is rhetorical.

"I know about the little ruse with the New Syberian host cerebrum, of course. Did you really think such a primitive workaround would fool the Core? Or is it more likely the Core is supporting your fiction, because ultimately, it supports our purpose that the SS think you're dead?"

"And what is 'our purpose' exactly?"

He looks genuinely sad. "To tell you that might prevent you from accomplishing it."

"You speak as though you know the mind of the Core."

"Ah. Can anyone truly know the mind of the Core?" He points to the diode between his own brows. "I am you, and we are simply its agent."

"You are not me."

"So little trust," he says, clucking his tongue. "Anyway, we have more urgent topics to discuss." He shifts and points across the valley. He's pointing at another house several miles away, the windows catching the morning sun. It's hard to see what type of house it is because of the glare. It's about a mile away, maybe more. Between this house and that one is desert. There is no track. "See that house?"

I tell him yes, I see that house.

"Go there, today. Go across the sand, the wind will wipe away your tracks."

"What about Yung?"

"Take her with you, or tell her to go back to the city. We won't need her."

"Why should we go to that house?"

He stands, as though anxious to go. "Because this house is not safe. It is Core-connected. It would only be a matter of time before the Core identified the occupants of this house by your biodata and shed DNA and it would be required to alert the SS. That house, however, is not Core-connected. Like you, it is completely off-Core."

"You talk like all of this is part of some grand plan dreamed up by the Core, but I don't believe for a second the Core would support the brutal murder of three Sanctioners. That is not the Core, that is just *you*."

"An academic distinction, as you know. Go there, be safe. Or stay here and risk capture."

"You know this?"

He brushes some sand off his trousers. "Yes. Let's just say I have some – limited – ability to look across the multiverse. I can't see far forward, to confidently predict what will happen, but I can see across. It helps a little, because sometimes events in other realities are more progressed than here. And in about a third of those realities, well…"

"Well?"

"You are already in prison. Or gone – dead or disappeared, I presume. Those realities are no longer interesting." He points at the house. "But in this reality, as far as I can tell, if you go over there, today, it buys us the time we need."

"Nonsense," I repeat. "Prove it," I demand. "Prove that *anything* you say is true."

"I don't have to," he says. "All you have to do is ignore what I say and see what happens. Events will show I am telling you the truth. But I don't recommend that." He pauses. "Actually, I *will* give you a little demonstration to try to encourage you to believe in me."

And so saying, he takes a small black marble from his pocket and holds it up to the light.

"Do you remember your conversation with Yung about teleportation?"

How could he know about that? "Yes, of course."

"I didn't want to assume, you have limited recall now that you aren't Core-chained. Anyway, you discussed with her a solution to the challenge of teleportation based on interdimensional travel. Something about the intention to transport an apple in one dimension resulting in the apple being available in another?"

"I remember."

"Well, then, it won't surprise you that in broad strokes, your theory was right. And that by starting down the path of solving the challenge of interdimensional travel, by writing the mathematical proofs and uplinking them to the Core, you created a ripple across the multiverse that resulted in the means for interdimensional travel already existing in billions of alternate realities."

"Yes, that's consistent with my theory."

He turns the black marble in his fingers. "Behold, then, the newest incarnation of the Zhaofeng Transporter." He licks a fingertip and with a smile places it on the marble. A golden honey-colored glow surrounds him.

And he disappears.

14. THE HANDOVER

Yung dumps some boxes on the floor of the kitchen and starts putting things into the cooler. She doesn't notice I take them straight out again, sit them on the counter next to the toaster. She's chatting away. "So the town near here has a farmer's market. Don't worry. Hundreds of people, no one will remember me." She laughs. "I didn't know you could find such things outside the city. I have to get outside the walls more often! Got the local versions of eggs, milk, vegetables…but I can't keep doing your shopping for you, so I got a truckload of dried and powdered nutrients." She takes the milk again, goes to put it in the fridge. "One of the stall holders, I tasted her honey, she said, 'Doesn't homemade honey just make you feel happy, dear?' It comes from real bees, inside the walls. I said actually, yes it…"

I take her elbow to stop her putting the milk away again, and now she realizes something is up.

"I'm not staying here," I tell her. "I'm leaving, now."

"Why?!"

I tell her why. Like it is my idea. Not *his*. Maybe I'll tell her about his visit sooner or later, but not now. Things are complicated enough already.

"Where are you going to go?"

I can't tell her. I especially can't tell her I'm only moving a mile or two across the valley. If the SS pick her up, they will make her talk. I can't risk that.

"But we just got here!" Yung points out, reasonably enough. "You said you're off-Core and untraceable. Why bail already?"

"This house is Core-connected," I tell her. "It passively identifies the residents through their biosignals, facial features, shed DNA. It would only be a matter of time before the Core did a double take and asked itself what a dead cyber was doing hiding out in the desert. Also, you haven't met Expositor Lin Ming. She won't buy the fact I'm so conveniently dead."

"She loves you," Yung says, a bit sadly.

"What?"

"A PRC Security Service officer puts her career, her *future*, at risk to warn a possible serial murderer? No. She must be seriously besotted. She'll protect you."

"We were getting close," I admit. "But not that close. She'll keep digging because it's her job."

"Oh Fan," Yung sighs. "The moment she told you to run she was choosing sides. If she keeps looking for you, it's not because she wants to put you in prison for the rest of your life."

I think it over. "Or, she could wake up tomorrow and realize what a dumb thing she's done. Anyway, it's another reason I can't stay here."

Now Yung starts taking food out of the cooler again and putting it back into the shopping boxes, so I know she's on board. "It's lucky I got you all those powdered nutrients if you're going totally off-Core," she says. I tell her I'm going to head into the nearby Basin national park. "You'll need a portable distillation unit to pull water from the air, if that's the case."

"Got one in my go bag," I tell her. "Never leave home without it."

"How long are you thinking of staying out there?"

"Until this is over." I'm parroting what Citizen X said in his Lokta paper letter. Which makes more sense now.

"That could take weeks, months!" she says. "If the SS decide you're still alive, still a suspect, they'll come after you with Wards, drones. The Basin will be one of the first places they look. Every criminal in the province heads for the Basin if they're trying to lie low."

"I'll be careful." I walk to the back window and look out, as though I'm thinking. The house my twin pointed out is not on any main roads. It's made of sandstone, the same color as the desert around it. You probably wouldn't even see it unless you were looking for it. I'll have a good view of this house from across the valley. I should be able to see if anyone turns up here. I'll keep the thermal shutters down so no one can see inside, and no light gets out. Only go outside at night if I need fresh air. It's a good choice. But he knew it would be.

For how long?

How long does it take to start a revolution?

I think of what he said. That Yung understands the politics of Coruscant better than me. It doesn't surprise me: she's tried engaging me on the topic a few times in the past, but I've never really been interested in politics, either local or interplanetary.

"These Sanctioner killings. They won't stay secret forever. People think only one Sanctioner is dead, how will they react when they find out it's not one, it's three?"

Yung is repacking my supplies and looks up. "What? You don't care," she says.

"Yes I do."

"No, Fan, you don't care. Maybe it's an interesting question to you, but you don't actually *care*."

"I want to know, and I might take decisions based on what you tell me. Isn't that caring?"

"No. Caring comes from the heart, not the mind: what you just described, that's planning, not caring. The High Council took away your ability to really care, which is the whole damn point of Sanction. You are now a full-on convert to the sanctity of the Law. Were you always like this?"

"No, probably not, but when you take away emotion, logic dominates," I tell her. "Anti-violence has a pretty strong logic. And there are plenty of people who haven't been Sanctioned who support the Law," I tell her. "The Law has brought peace, clean air and rivers, it's brought animals back from the brink of extinction, it has virtually eliminated violence."

She narrows her eyes. "The Law has brought subjugation, thousands of prisons full of prisoners, hundreds of thousands of MIAs, *millions* of Sanctionees like you who have lost the ability to feel and think for yourselves! In the name of the Law, we are all slaves to the High Council. We lost the war, and the High Council is how Tatsensui intends to ensure we never challenge them again."

"Seventy percent of the members of the High Council are elected by the citizens of the PRC."

"Do we have 70 percent of the votes?"

"No. The Alignment means each Core world has an equal say in the affairs of the other. Tatsensui and PRC each have 50 percent of the votes. The chairperson has the deciding vote in case of deadlock and the chairperson rotates."

"And Tatsensui has a High Council, on which the PRC has 70 percent of the members and 50 percent of the vote?"

I don't know the answer to that, and I can't drift anymore to check. "I'm guessing you're going to tell me they don't."

"No, Fan, they don't! They won the damn war, we lost it! And now we are their subjects in all but name." I can hear hatred pouring out of her, stronger words than I've ever heard her speak before.

"I'm not anyone's slave," I tell her. "Tatsensui gave me my freedom. Since the Alignment, I have rights I never had before. I work because I want to. I could quit tomorrow, do something else. I could go live in a hippy commune, become a painter, builder, public servant…"

"Or starve, Fan. There are no jobs you can take that the High Council haven't approved. No employers they haven't green-lighted. You can't be a police officer or a politician. You can't join the army because, oh yeah, we don't have one anymore. You are still a slave – you're just a slave who gets to choose what chain gang they work in. And you can leave anytime, but sooner or later the credits run out and you will either starve, or end up back in the chain gang."

"But 90 percent of people support…"

"…support the Alignment, support the Law?" she laughs. "Where do you get that number from? From a Corecast? Open your eyes, Fan – the Corecasters are instruments of the State. A Corecaster is as free under the High Council as you are as a cyber."

"Most of the people I meet through work, they support it," I insist. "The beaten wives, the abused children, the families of violent drug addicts. Tell *them* that life was better before the Law."

She shakes her head sadly. "I'm not saying it was better before. I'm not saying the Law itself is wrong. The Law came from the Core, but the way it is administered, that is the High Council's work. Until the High Council is taken down, we won't see the real benefit of your precious Law."

"Or, maybe we just need to give it time," I tell her. "People will see it works. They'll stop fighting it, and there will be no need for imprisonment, or Sanction…"

She reaches out and holds my chin, her eyes tearing up. "See, I told you. You aren't ready to hear it, or you aren't capable. You want to know how people will react when they hear *three* Sanctioners are dead? Some will be cowering under their bed covers, but I'm willing to bet most will be dancing in the streets."

We sort the food into perishables and reconstitutable. Half of it is optimized for human consumption, but I can still use it. The rest is made for a cyber metabolism, and I figure altogether there's enough to get me through the coming days. I hope.

"I'll order a car soon," Yung says.

"They'll eventually find their way to you," I warn her. "Don't fight them, just tell them everything. I can look after myself."

"Will they cauterize me?" she asks quietly. "I don't want…"

"To be like me?" I ask.

She flinches a little at that. "No, to lose who I am. I know I am a fucked-up chaotic mess, but this is me, who I am. I don't want them to take that away."

"Cauterization is only for violent crimes," I tell her. "They'll probably hide you away for a while, though, because you are a risk, as long as all this is secret."

She wraps her arms around herself. "I'm used to being locked away. Poor Ben, though."

"I'll find a way to pay you back," I say.

"Oh shut up."

I have the chance to tell her, that afternoon, about how I had a visit from myself. I know Yung won't think it's totally impossible. Yung of all people would consider that there is at least the chance that it really happened. And if she'd asked me, I would have told her. But she doesn't ask, so I don't tell. And I decide that's probably a good thing because if Yung ever started telling my story to the SS, they'd think she was having another psychotic break and she'd be locked up for another month.

I organize my food and camping gear, bag up all our garbage for Yung to take with her, pull the sun shields down on all the windows, sterilize the surfaces and check that it doesn't look like anyone has been here. I can't really do much more.

Yung broods. She stands watching me. We don't talk much. We make tea and drink it in silence, sitting cross-legged on the dark living room floor.

We play a game of chess with a board I brought with me. Something to stop me getting bored. I can always play against myself; Blitz chess for one.

Evening falls outside, then night. Yung changes out of the clothes she borrowed from me, puts on the dress she had with her in hospital, a cardigan against the cool evening air.

"You better call that car soon," I tell her. "I need to get moving." She's sitting on the floor of the living room with her back up against a sofa. I reach over to help her up.

She pulls me toward her. And then she kisses me. Hard. On the mouth. She bites my lip and I taste blood. Then she pulls herself away, runs a hand through my hair.

"She can have you now," she says.

15. THE LAW

I move to the house across the valley that night. He's right about one thing at least; the evening breeze fills my footprints with tumbling sand and after a few minutes I can't see where I've been.

The house is empty, as he predicted. It looks like it has been lived in, but not for a while. There is furniture, but no power in the wall batteries. There is cold running water in a distillation tank, but it smells stale. I can turn the solar power on tomorrow, once the sun is up, start distilling some fresh water, then charge the batteries.

The way to get through any deep cover operation is to establish good routines. So I set my system alarm to wake me at 6 a.m. Wash my face with some of the tank water, use the chemical toilet, mix some powdered milk with powdered egg, baking powder and flour and make one pancake for now, and one for lunch tomorrow, which I'll eat with some nuts and dried fruit. I walk around the house while it's still half-light, checking the solar blinds. I need some sort of system outside so that I know if anyone approaches the house while I'm asleep. But it's been a long day.

I sleep.

I still have the police voice comm unit and I'm not out of range yet, so I monitor it through the morning. Nothing new on the Sanctioner murders, nothing about the late Fan Zhaofeng. Between 8 and 12 I play some chess. I have some nice long books in my cache. I decide I'll mix the afternoons up, reading one day, writing a journal the next. Nothing fancy, or incriminating, just reflections on life and the universe…you know the type of things I always think about.

That was another lame joke, sorry.

I also have my meditation. I can close my eyes, shut down non-essential systems, find my center while I still keep peripherally alert to sounds, smells. I perfected the technique behind the lines during the Alignment. It allows me to sleep less.

I set myself up so that I can look through a crack in a blind at the house across the valley that Yung rented to see if there is any action. I don't expect any so soon…but you never know. If Lin is still on my trail, she'd be interviewing my associates, pull all data on their movements. If she gets onto my client list, she'll find Yung and her credit record will lead out here. Am I stupid to stay so close? Maybe, but Citizen X told me I'd be safe here, and breaking cover is always dangerous.

In the evening I make a meal, tossing up between human pasta or a cyber nutrient soup. I go with the pasta, since my nutrient levels are still pretty good and hey, it tastes better. Time is going to be my biggest enemy. How to kill the nights? Another trick I used to do when I was on long patrols, sing every song I've ever learned. I've cached thousands but I like testing my bio-memory, seeing how many songs I can sing all the way through. Three hours and two minutes' worth is my best.

My biggest problem – how will I know when it's OK to break cover? I've been thinking about that. The Lokta paper letter said, '*You must run, Zhaofeng. Run and hide and wait until the storm has passed*'. I forgot to ask him, but I assume the letter was from Citizen X. Well, I'm good at hiding, but I'm not the running type.

I want to test what Yung said about what will happen if the deaths of the three Sanctioners become public. Will people come out in support of the High Council, in sympathy with the Sanctioners? Or will they be dancing in the streets, as Yung said and Citizen X clearly anticipates. If I'm to find out who is really behind the Sanctioner killings, then I need to flush them out into the open. Maybe my twin has his own plan about when he wants the news out in the open, has his own timetable. Maybe he's happy to keep killing in anonymity, to provoke some sort of reaction from the High Council. Or a negotiation? That's possible too, of course.

Well, sorry if it's inconvenient, but I have my own agenda and it's about proving my innocence.

The silence around the murders tells me all I need to know about the High Council's ability to control the Corecasters. Lin called it 'cooperation', but it's a pretty short step from cooperation to coercion. I can't just call a broadcaster and say, 'hey, did you hear the one about the three dead Sanctioners?' I need a credible mouthpiece who can shout it from the rooftops.

An Advocate General would be ideal. In implementing the Law, the High Council created an entire legal ecosystem, peopled by some pretty high-profile Advocates. All cases are judged by senior Advocates, called Advocates General. There are no loopholes in the Law, and only three outcomes to any case – acquittal, prison or Sanction. There is no appeal, but all Sanctions are sent to a member of the High Council for assent. But everyone accused has the right to a professional defense, and that defense is usually a two-person team. A cyber to make the best possible case based on the evidence, and a human Advocate to run the case and make the emotional argument. All Advocates General are human, so they are susceptible to emotional plays. They have an AI to give them an assessment of the strength of the defense and prosecution cases based on pure logic, but I've noticed they will go against this if an emotional argument is particularly compelling.

I have an Advocate General in mind. One the High Council will not be able to gag, nor the Corecasters ignore.

I won't have many chances to contact him if I'm to avoid triggering SS suspicion. I'll need a couple of contacts to set it up and brief him. Persuade him to contact a Corecaster. I can't stay anonymous if I'm going to persuade him to go public on the killings – he needs to know he can trust what I'm telling him. The SS shouldn't connect him to me straight away, but he'll be pressured to reveal the source of his information. If he caves in to that pressure, I need to be sure there are no breadcrumbs leading back to me.

I'll travel a few miles by night, only going out on windy nights when I know the blowing sands will hide my tracks from random drones. Wards, with their infrared senses, will be a threat. But they aren't usually sent outside the cities unless they are after specific prey. I've got a map of nearby homesteads. Each one will have a Core uplink I can tap into without having to give away my identity. Another skill I learned in recon.

I look at my map. I can easily do 20 miles by foot, out and back at night, say between 0200 and 0500. All of it can be done off road, though that will make the going slower depending on the depth of the sand. I'll need remote homesteads with no neighbors nearby, less likely to be worried about securing their Core uplinks.

I'm happy with my plan now. Good solid routines during the day, and a mission every couple of nights. First mission, I'll go south to a homestead about fifteen miles away. The first contact is the most dangerous. If the Advocate I've picked goes straight to the SS, there may not be a second contact.

16. THE FOURTH

As she sits in the Ops room watching a holo of the High Council Minister for Law explain to the assembled SS officers that they're winding back the investigation of the Sanctioner deaths, Lin thinks back to the miner gang Sergeant at Arms, Duong.

"Why hasn't someone gone public with this story?" she'd asked him. "If it's so widely known in the military? The High Council have their own army of ex-special forces soldiers they use to capture high value targets? That's news."

Duong looked at her intensely. "And how do you think that would end for whoever did it?"

"A Corecaster would pay handsomely for a story like that," she'd said. "You could lie low for a long time and live really well for that much money…"

"Looking over your shoulder the whole time," he said. "Waiting for that breeze on your neck that told you the Council had sent one of its black team after you."

"Dramatizing much?" she asked. "Leaking State secrets is a criminal offense, but it's not a breach of the Law if it doesn't involve violence. What's the worst that could happen to you?"

"Worst is they send someone like Fan Zhaofeng to hunt you down. Knowing what he can do when it's all happening out of the public eye."

"He's a cyber. He can't do anything," she said. "At best he could restrain you. The Law…"

Duong had shaken his head. "You really live in a cozy fantasy world, don't you? Some kind of alternate reality where all cybers have unbreakable protocols preventing them from killing Coruscant citizens, right?"

"It's not my 'alternate reality'," she insisted. "It's immutable. Coded into their DNA at birth. Impossible to reprogram or subvert. Plenty of people like you have tried since the Alignment. The Core watches over every one of its creations, constantly on guard for signs of code corruption."

"And you know it's never been successfully done because…"

"I'm SS. I'd know."

He'd laughed, and leaned back. "That's your answer for everything? I'm SS? What do you think Zhaofeng did for the High

Council? You think he was like some little ol' hound dog, just sniffed out the targets and then called in the police or Wards? Millions of people are missing, girl, and Zhaofeng is one of the reasons. But you can't see that."

He swept his arm out, taking in the bar, the street outside. "You're just like all these dumb fools. Open your damn eyes! The Core writes and monitors the protocols controlling its cybers. And the Core serves the High Council."

"The Core has a higher duty. To its prime directive: the preservation and promotion of all life on the moons of Coruscant. Nothing in there about serial murder."

"And if the orders of the High Council are compatible with its prime directive in its own twisted silicon mind? If a few thousand criminals need to be killed or disappear to preserve the health and well-being of the millions? What then?"

Sanctioner Nari knows all about the murders. He would have carried out his duties anyway, unassisted, but it has been decided by the Council that no Sanctioner will travel alone in these times. The Sanctioner who died in the last attack was deemed insufficiently well protected. Now he goes everywhere in the company of *four* Wards.

He is never alone, even in his own house.

He sits in a larger vehicle than normal, an SS cyber beside him, a stun gun, colloquially known as a 'burp gun', across her lap, a Ward crouched watchfully in the cargo space behind them. Not risking that they be taken unaware this time, the PRC police have also secured the criminal at his premises. The location is ringed with drones, police, Wards.

He quickly calls the Council and they affirm the Sanction.

"We're good?" the SS officer asks.

"Yes. We can go."

She hits the nav panel and the vehicle moves off, the Ward behind him growling disconcertingly.

He realizes he is holding his breath as he arrives and the door to the vehicle swings up, but there is no danger. Of course there isn't. Hundreds of Sanctions are performed every day on PRC, and there have only been three...incidents. Nonetheless, all of them have happened in *this* city.

Reviewing the judgment of the Advocate General, he can see this man is a criminal gang member who killed another gang member. He had claimed the killing was self-defense, but the Advocates General don't discriminate. There are no loopholes in the Law. Violence is violence.

The criminal is being held in his garden by the police so that Wards can watch over proceedings with ease. Three prowl the perimeter, cat like, growling. Two hover in the air above, eyes on everything. The criminal is, unusually, being held in restraints. The police keep their distance, keen not to be party to what is about to happen. There is no outward sign of discomfort among the Sanctioned, no reason for the police to be so squeamish, but the police are in any case not usually permitted to observe, out of respect for the rights of the criminal.

He checks the criminal's identity, reads the charges to him, the judgment, and then completes the rites. "Do you freely choose Sanction, knowing that you have the right to choose prison for life in its stead?" He waits for the man's answer. A vein throbs in his head. It's not an easy decision, Nari knows that. People recant sometimes, as is their right. There is no family for this man to consult with, he had no known relatives.

"Fuck you," comes the response. Nari has heard it before.

"I will repeat this as many times as is necessary for you to give an answer," the Sanctioner says patiently. But he nods to the medical team behind the man who have prepared the Sanctioning rig – the skull cap with its tangle of wires and fluid lines – to be ready. Beside them is the counselor, ready to get to work helping the man adjust to his post-Sanction reality.

There are a few more obscenities, which he waits out. Then the capitulation.

"Go ahead, cauterize me, you bastards."

Nari steps back and the man is laid down on a gurney, the cap placed on his head and an anesthetic administered. He'll be aware, so that his brain function can be monitored during the procedure, but immobilized.

Nari turns to the SS officer, who is watching with what appears to be horrified fascination.

"First time?" he asks, trying to break the tension.

She's in her late twenties, very fit. A personal protection officer perhaps, which makes sense. She says nothing, just nods. Nari is about sixty, and not very fit. As he dabs his forehead with a handkerchief he's impressed she looks so cool, even standing in the sun.

When it is done and the man wheeled back inside his house to recover, Nari walks outside the property and says to a Senior Constable, "You can send the counselor in now."

The man looks worried. "A Corecast crew is outside too," he says. "They say it was cleared through the Security Service. They are going to interview the Sanctionee," he says.

Nari had been briefed about them, and had approved the suggestion. Despite the recent…turmoil…or in fact because of it, he'd agreed it was important to show the world that the machinery of justice was still turning. It would come out sooner or later that more than one Sanctioner had been targeted, but then this report would stand as evidence that the High Council was not to be cowed by senseless violence. It might even serve to quieten some of the more vocal critics of Sanction if they could see 'first hand', as it were, how benign the process really was. The criminal had pocketed a nice fee from the Corecaster for playing his part.

"Send them over."

As a courtesy, Nari had forewarned the SS. A good holo crew has a director and reporter, plus a tech to operate the drones that capture vision and sound. All three had been vetted before being allowed on the scene.

Nari turns to his SS shadow. "Well, our work is nearly done. I'll do this interview and then we can get our caravan rolling."

The SS officer looks up at the patrolling Wards, then at those on the ground around them, and waves her finger in a circle, indicating they should get ready to head out.

They form a claustrophobic three-dimensional box around him as the holo crew approach. They are looking curiously at the skies, and all the security. The Corecast journalist, a serious-looking grey-haired woman in her fifties, steps up and introduces herself. She points at one of the Wards. "This is all because of that attack a couple of months ago?"

Nari laughs lightly. "Actually, I think that's mostly for your benefit. Adds a nice touch of drama, don't you think? The first ever on-the-scene interview with a Sanctioner…we want it to be memorable, yes?"

"I'm sure it will be," the journalist assures him. "Tell us a little about what we just saw."

"Well, I hope your viewers are not disappointed. I'm afraid to tell you, most Sanctions are rather straightforward affairs. I arrived, confirmed the identity of the Sanctionee, and gave him a chance to change his mind about the procedure. It's an important element of our justice system that the criminal guilty of a breach of the Law freely chooses his own punishment…life in prison, or Sanction. The gentleman in this case confirmed he wanted to proceed with Sanction."

"And the medical device used for the procedure…"

"Yes. I'm sorry you couldn't get up closer, a privacy matter, you understand. But it is entirely painless and it takes only moments. It requires that the criminal be completely immobilized, though, so we anesthetize him, and then ensure a counselor is right there with him when he regains his mobility. But you'll be there for that."

"Won't he be confused, dazed, groggy? It's brain surgery, after all."

"Yes, but non-invasive, and at a molecular level. He's aware during the entire procedure, just unable to move his muscles, for his own safety. In fact, he's still fully aware now as he recovers full function. The counselor is probably explaining to him he's about to become a holo star."

"And how many of these do you do in a standard day?" she asks.

"Oh, it varies. I'm sorry, but the Sanctionee will be ready for interview soon. You should head inside."

"One last question. Does it even trouble your conscience, cauterizing people this way?"

He can't help frowning at her, even though he'd prepared himself for the question. She'd submitted it ahead of time, and he'd challenged including it, but been overruled. He turns his frown into what he hopes is a concerned and empathetic look of puzzlement. "Why ever would I? Sanction, and life in prison, are non-violent means to protect society from individuals who have been found guilty of aberrant violent behavior." He smiles. "I'm proud that this particularly enlightened solution to one of mankind's age-old dilemmas is a PRC invention, and that I have a small part to play in…"

He stops speaking as one of the Wards beside him takes a sudden step forward as though to shield him. The holo drones hovering soundlessly around them, capturing his every word, pull back to avoid striking the Ward, and to capture what is happening.

Nari looks past the Ward, which has raised itself up on two legs and spread its wings as though to shield him. From what?!

With a quick downward slash of the hard cartilage protrusion on the joint of its wing, the Ward slices through Nari's vest, shirt and abdomen, spilling his glistening intestines to the ground as he recoils in shock and horror.

Then, bunching its legs, it launches itself into the sky, pursued by three other Wards.

"Forget them, stay on the *Sanctioner*!" the Corecast director bellows at his cameraman, whose drones' attention has been pulled into following the whirling Wards, chasing each other through the sky.

"Medical crew!" the SS officer is yelling. "Get that medical crew out here!"

But Nari is beyond caring. As he falls backward onto the ground, hands clasped uselessly to his torn stomach, he is already dead.

17. THE UNDERBELLY

The SS investigations office is in uproar. Every holo viewer in the office, in the building and, she is willing to bet, in the entire Coruscant system is replaying the footage of the Sanctioner being eviscerated. As he hit the ground, he threw his arms back, involuntarily, losing control of his muscles. The holo cameras captured his blood spraying out of the terrible wound in his belly as his heart pumped its last, and his viscera were spilled from the wound by his momentum, to lie glistening next to his fat body when it finally lay still at the feet of his shocked SS protector.

One of the police on the scene had commanded at that point, "*Stop filming!*" but it was too late. The vision was being live streamed, and the world had seen.

There has been no reaction from the High Council yet, which is contributing to the chaos in Vali's now much reduced team. The Security Service, like any justice organ, does not function well in a vacuum. The office is awash with requests from government and other agencies for information, but Vali has none to give. Senior SS officers have requested orders, but none have come.

The provincial governor has not been so slow to act, thankfully. He has declared an emergency, as allowed under the Law, and mobilized all of his justice forces. The streets are full of peacekeepers in their distinctive pale blue reactive body armor – stunners and neural gas weapons holstered but obvious. There is no curfew, yet, but anywhere people start to gather, they are politely but forcefully being ordered to move along: go to work, or go home.

On one Corecast channel, a commentator is nearly apoplectic with outrage. "What are the High Council hiding from us now?!" he demands. "Two Sanctioners have been murdered, that we know of!! Are there more? Who is next? Who is behind the killings? The High Council is silent. Well, I am not going to stay silent. I demand answers!"

Lin shakes her head. If you get that upset at two, how would you be if you knew this was the fourth? She sees Vali, in his corner, also looking up at the holo. Feeling as helpless as the rest, she guesses. She goes over to him.

"What the hell is happening, Vali?" she asks.

He looks at her, as if trying to place her, then his eyes drop into focus. "This is no disgruntled citizen, either cyber or human," he says vehemently. "This killer has access to information, to technology, to resources that only States and governments possess."

She looks at him with furrowed brows. "What are you talking about?"

He looks about himself, as though afraid he might have been overheard. "Come outside with me."

They go to the park outside the PRC Security Service main building. It is largely empty, most people inside either glued to their holos, or scared to move around outside. A couple of peacekeepers look at them, see they've come out of the Security Service building, then turn back to monitor the traffic around the park. Lin follows Vali to a tree in the middle of the park with a bench under it, and he indicates she should sit.

He looks around himself again. His usually serene face seems unnaturally animated, a muscle in his jaw twitching. She has alternated between thinking of him as looking like a dark-skinned sportsman, or a presenter for a fitness holo. Right now, he just looks like a scared man.

"Stop looking around like that," she says. "You're making me nervous."

"I am nervous," he says. "You should be too."

"For God's sake, tell me what you know."

He sits next to her and brings his head close to hers, and she picks up the faint scent like precious ylang ylang oil. She is convinced it isn't a coincidence, that this is part of his tradecraft, making himself smell safe and reassuring. It's a scent which is a mix of custard, jasmine and neroli and, combined with his flawless skin, deep dark eyes, long lashes and hard muscled body, has exactly the effect on people around him that it is supposed to have. Or had, she should say. She's over it now. Or tells herself she is.

He lowers his voice. "The Sanctioner's Wards caught up with the killer Ward in mid-air and beat it to the ground."

"A Ward can't kill!" she hisses. "It's a cyber, like all cybers."

"Wards aren't Core birthed or Core-chained," he tells her. "They're a PRC creation. Gene-modded and spliced Old Earth animals with cybernetics. Protocols taken from Core cybernetic code, but adapted to peacekeeping use. No Core overwatch. Porous. Hackable."

Their own Wards have dropped down from their positions on the Security Service building roof and sit nearby, holding guard. For the first time, Lin looks at them as a criminal sees them – inscrutable, terrifying.

"Are you saying we can't trust our own Wards?"

"Whoever did this hacked the restraint protocols of a Ward. Or replaced a functioning SS Ward with one that was hacked. We'll know soon enough, but I guarantee, no matter what they find, all Wards will be stood down."

They were living animals, they couldn't just be turned off. They would have to be penned in a secure facility. Imprisoned. How would they react? She shivered thinking about her own protection now. They weren't like pets, you didn't have the same one assigned to you twice. They didn't have distinct personalities, just an alphanumeric code. In that respect checking out a Ward was like checking out a stun gun or body armor. But moving around in public without her Ward would be like having the shirt taken off her back.

How long would it take before criminals realized the SS and Sanctioners were now on their own?

"Well, we know one thing," Lin tells him. "This wasn't Fan Zhaofeng."

"You don't know that," Vali warns. "That Ward could have been programmed weeks or months ago, waiting for the moment it was assigned to protect a Sanctioner."

"Oh come on. Either the guy is dead or he isn't. Now you're telling me he reached out from his watery grave and killed that Sanctioner today?"

"No, I…I'm just saying it's possible he planned it this way. The first three murders, his death – maybe suicide – and then this."

"You really need a psych check," Lin tells him. "See how far into the red you are on the paranoia scale."

He glares at her. "Thank you for your professional advice, Junior Expositor. I'm teaching you to keep your mind open. Wards can be hacked. Dead people can commit murder by proxy. And there is unfortunately a bigger scenario at play here, which is why we haven't heard anything from the High Council yet."

"What bigger scenario?"

"This is the start of the cyber uprising."

She nearly laughs, then realizes he is serious. The 'cyber uprising'. A conspiracy birthed after the war, it was fed with unfounded rumors of cybercrime, cyber violence, and now, no doubt, a Sanctioner-killing cyber. If the rumors were taking flight again, they probably came from within the police and security services themselves, where only the officers directly involved in the investigation knew that their prime suspect in the killings of the Sanctioners had been a Sanctioned cyber.

But how much was chicken and how much was egg? That had troubled Lin from the start. Why had Vali and his superiors gone so hard after Fan Zhaofeng, despite his alibis, despite the clear restraints placed on him not just by his Core protocols but by the Sanction he'd been subject to? The word 'racism' had been used to describe human attitudes to cybers before, and she had wondered if she was seeing it in action inside the SS.

Did racism explain why Vali had insisted on having a human partner assigned to himself, instead of a cyber, which would have been normal?

If anything, the Alignment had actually made a cyber uprising *less* likely, not more likely. All cybers on PRC were now Core-chained, their every breath and action uploaded in real time or, at worst, after two hours. Not their thoughts, no, but their visual, auditory and sensory feed. Their memories. There had never been a time in the history of the colony where they were less likely to be able to coordinate an insurrection. It just doesn't fit.

"Why a *cyber* insurrection? The victims are all Sanctioners. All Sanctionees are human. All criminals imprisoned under the Law are human. There has only been one cyber Sanctioned in all of PRC history and he's dead now. What motive do the others have for starting an uprising, and what possibility do they have of doing so, with the Core watching their every move?"

"You can see the Cyber Rights Movement as some sort of benign lobby group. Or you can see it as an existential threat to humankind. You can see the Core as being a restraining influence on our cyber citizens. Or you can see it as a fox, which has been put in charge of guarding the hen house." He fixes her with a hard stare. "Where do *you* stand, Expositor?"

Her hand goes involuntarily to the base of her skull, where her implant is nestled under the folds of her neck. "Are you insinuating I can't be trusted because I've been augmented?"

"I'm asking, if you were forced to choose between cyber or humankind, where would you stand?"

And there it is, she thinks to herself. Vali is a Separatist. Anti-cyber, anti-Alignment and, no doubt at all now, anti-Core. He can't come out and say so directly, in case she reports him. He is being guarded in his phrasing but there is no mistaking the import, or the intent, of his question. Her answer to his question could seal her fate.

"I stand with the SS," she replies carefully. "I serve the High Council of PRC."

He waits to see if she's going to add any more, but appears satisfied. "Good. Our cyber Sanctionee did warn us on that note he wrote to himself. 'There is a storm coming'." He stands. "We didn't take him seriously enough. Now let's get back to work, and prepare for it." He signals to their Wards to return to their roosts on top of the SS building.

She wonders if they'll be allowed down again.

That night, Lin stands in her kitchen, having placed her dishes in the recycler which breaks down and repurposes the food residue. She realizes she's been staring at a blank wall for a full five minutes and shakes her head, but the feeling of dread remains.

The city is still in lockdown. Across the province, all security forces are on alert. In the other 98 cities in other provinces of PRC, heightened surveillance protocols have been invoked. Cameras usually used to detect traffic accidents or provide historical data for investigations are being monitored in real time by AIs for indications of mob gatherings or protests.

As Vali predicted, all Wards have been stood down and confined to their pens. The news of that hasn't broken on Corecast channels yet but it won't take long. Commentators who were calling for it to happen after the attack on Sanctioner Nari will be cheering, but so will the criminal population of PRC. Without their Wards, what is an SS officer other than a police officer with a burp gun and a dragon pendant?

She fingers the one around her throat absently. When he presented it to her, Vali had remarked to her, "I chose this deliberately. You will see it has two heads, to represent the dual loyalty expected of you now. To the SS, and to the People's Republic of Coruscant." She had not thought too much about his words then, but they have a different meaning now. She was certain he had chosen them very deliberately, and his meaning was clear. Your *first* loyalty is to the SS, and secondly to PRC. Vali had been giving her a first glimpse of the dark underbelly of the PRC Security Service, and she'd missed it.

He'd made the point clear today. He'd also made clear to her, to the whole team investigating the latest killing, what their priority now would be.

To establish beyond any doubt that the cyber, Fan Zhaofeng, was also behind the killing of Sanctioner Nari. Vali argued that such a sophisticated assassination would have required weeks, if not months, to set up. Therefore Fan, or his cyber co-conspirators, had set the plan in motion long before his death. They were to focus on finding the evidence of this, either buried deep in the programming of the murderous Ward now lying strapped to a table in the SS forensic laboratory, or in data they'd overlooked in their investigation of Zhaofeng. They were to analyze that data again, re-interview every one of his contacts, close or distant, and find the evidence that must be there.

She had no doubt they would. But not because Fan was guilty. Simply because Vali was so determined to find it, to support his narrative around a cyber revolt. With enough 'proof', he and his cabal within the SS and no doubt also the High Council could use planetary security grounds to attack the Articles of Alignment; challenge or reverse the recent granting of cyber rights such as freedom of movement, association and employment; perhaps even reverse the decision to chain all PRC cybers to the Core. If they could do that, they would seriously weaken the grip of Tatsensui on their moon.

No doubt it is a source of major irritation to Vali that Fan is no longer alive for him to wrest a 'confession' from.

But Lin does not believe Fan Zhaofeng is really dead. They found only ash floating on the river's surface. An analysis confirmed it as organic, brain mass, probably from his cerebrum. There were also cybernetic components from his head, melted to slag. The submersible he had used to move around the city under the water was a 'ride-on', like a small torpedo that pulled its rider through the water. It had also been melted to slag by the incendiary bomb in its small cargo compartment. What little of it remained yielded no secrets as to why it had exploded or what Fan had intended. Why fit the submersible with an incendiary in the first place? Was it suicide? An attempt to hide evidence that had gone horribly wrong?

And why had they found no other organic matter that could yield a DNA sample? The drones found no bone, no teeth. The only confirmation they had of Fan's death had come from the Core record. It had registered Fan shutting down his Core link as he entered the vehicle to make his escape. It had then registered him reinitiating the uplink when his two-hour window elapsed, shouting in apparent confusion before shutting the link down again. Two hours later, another uplink, another cry for help, then silence. They now knew he'd been traveling under the water, along the city's waterways, uplinking from underneath city bridges and going dark again, moving to a new location and uplinking again.

It. Made. No. Sense.

Vali had decided that the entire thing was a decoy. That Fan intended only to divert SS resources into a fruitless manhunt to reduce the chances that the next phase in his attempt to foment insurrection, the attack by the Ward on Sanctioner Nari, would go undetected. In that, Vali concluded drily, he'd succeeded.

But you could only believe that if you believed Fan Zhaofeng was capable of murder. Capable of planning an insurrection. And she simply did not.

Yet, the Core record was irrefutable. It showed Zhaofeng was dead. Once again, her hand unconsciously goes to the folds of her neck at the base of her skull. She has an always-on connect to the Core. She can interrogate it at the speed of thought. She has the knowledge of entire star systems at her fingertips. But she cannot 'talk' to it. If it has a language interface, that must be reserved for more senior SS officers or High Council members. If it exists at all.

She's tried the same query a dozen different ways. Status of citizen Fan Zhaofeng. Location of citizen Fan Zhaofeng. Relay current biosigns from citizen Fan Zhaofeng. Recent financial activities of citizen Fan Zhaofeng; and so on, and so forth. Every query returns the same answer: *deceased*.

More than anything she just wants to ask the Core: are you covering up the fact Fan Zhaofeng is alive? If you are, why?

She can't answer the first question, but as she stands staring at her blank wall, she realizes that if she assumes an answer to the first question, she can reason her way to the second. If Fan Zhaofeng is alive, why would the Core be hiding that fact?

18. THE ADVOCATE

Lin can't deal with the enormity of the questions troubling her. If the Core is hiding the fact Fan is alive, then it is also implicitly involved, or at least not intervening, in the Sanctioner murders. The implications of that are world shattering.

She defaults to the micro universe, and the very straightforward task at hand.

Find Fan Zhaofeng.

She starts at the beginning. In any murder there are always three elements, Vali has taught her. Motive, opportunity and means. The case against Zhaofeng is fueled by racism, but built on a shaky base of evidence. Yes, you can ascribe motive. Fan was Sanctioned. He may resent that. He may feel that it makes sense to express that resentment by murdering Sanctioners, the 'executioners' of the PRC. But he did not have the opportunity for the first two murders. Independent witnesses report being with him during the working day for the first murder, and his chess club colleagues report him being at the chess club during the second. For the third, he had unfortunately been dropped by surveillance, and for the fourth, he was on the run. The case against him was therefore weighted on those murders, as regards opportunity.

The weakest element of the case is 'means'. Something gutted the first three victims, but no murder weapon has been found. There is no forensic evidence at all linking Fan Zhaofeng directly to any of the murders. Vali argues that his training as a scout during and after the war would have given Fan the ability to hide inside a Sanctioner's locked vehicle and escape again without being seen. He argues that any cyber with access to the unlimited technical knowledge of the Core could reprogram the restraint protocols of a Ward and plant an attack code.

But those arguments conveniently overlook the fact that Zhaofeng was also subject to restraint protocols. His code had been examined by both human and AI coders and no alterations to it had been found. Like any cyber, he should not have been capable of murder. Add to that, the guy had been *Sanctioned!* The biologically based elements of his personality had been cauterized, to remove his ability to feel jealousy, resentment, hatred, rage or even anger – any of the emotions that could provoke violence.

Like prosecutors through the centuries, the SS case was built on what they could prove, and what they could convincingly assert, and ignored any inconvenient facts.

Lin decided she would focus on the inconvenient and the unlikely.

The story about seeing himself in the mirror, for example. Insane. But the sensory record in his local cache confirmed it? The images of the twin standing there, then walking away. The touch on his shoulder. Vali argued it was created by Fan, doctored and stored for later retrieval to provide him with an alibi. Lin decides to assume it was real.

His disappearance from surveillance at the exact time of the third killing. The chances he could disappear and kill a Sanctioner then return and eat a noodle soup in a 90-minute gap in surveillance…however suspicious? Physically possible, yes. Likely? No. Assume he didn't.

The warning letter printed on this Kowloon Lokta paper in his own handwriting? A hoax he dreamed up himself to taunt them, Vali argued. Or, as Fan asserted and she would now assume, written by the twin. The fact he had immediately alerted her to its existence spoke for his innocence, not against it.

Run and hide he had, but she had played the biggest part in that. About three minutes before Vali and half of the taskforce had come crashing through the door and found her there bound to a chair. Yes, he had clearly been prepared to run, but that was just scenario planning. An AI like his was constantly sifting through scenarios and probabilities and he had prepared for that one. But she had triggered him. *You have to run!*

He'd bound her and disappeared through a tunnel in the floor.

So, assume he faked his own death and he's still out there. Assume the Core knows that. Assume he's innocent and either hiding until the real killer shows themself, or is working on his own, just as he used to as a scout, as a Hunter, to prove his innocence. According to the miner, Duong, he is 'the Ghost'; assume you have zero chance of finding him.

She turns and looks at her reflection in the kitchen window. "So what are we going to do, Lin? Find him, of course."

The homestead south of my off-Core shack is home to a small family. They're asleep, I assume, as I approach the house. There are no lights on, so it's a safe assumption. But there's a small private car parked out front – a four seater. That tells me they're a small family, but also that they're rich. You have to be to contemplate a life outside PRC's cities, because you can't do it without your own car, unless you never plan to leave your house. Most people do work from their own homes, but to visit friends, go to the theater or a festival you need transport, and as we learned getting out here, taxis are damn expensive because you also have to pay for their return trip.

I'm not worried about dogs – pets aren't allowed outside the city walls for ecological reasons, but even a place this isolated can have security, like perimeter radar. It usually has a range of twenty yards, but I stop at fifty, pick up a large rock and hurl it toward the house before crouching close to the ground. It tumbles within a few feet of a back wall. No lights are triggered, but of course, it could be a silent alarm. I wait five minutes, then repeat the process. No reaction.

I pull out my comms unit, set it to connect without using a Core link and start walking forward until it picks up the signal from the house. The encryption is rudimentary, and the workaround is simple. About thirty feet out I get a connection and crouch down again, facing away from the house to muffle my voice.

The man at the other end is sleepy, and a bit alarmed, as anyone would be at 3.40 a.m.

"Huh? Hello?"

"Is that Advocate Lau Lee?"

"Yes, who…what is the time?"

"I'm sorry to call so early, it's a quarter to four. My name is Fan Zhaofeng and you…"

"…Zhaofeng? 1 Squadron Deep Recon? That Zhaofeng?"

"Yes, sir. That one." Lee was the defense counsel appointed for my trial. If you could call it that, considering it was held in camera and the proceedings were suppressed. He did his best. But it was only ever going to be a long shot, defending me, after what I'd done. I didn't even get the option of prison, so when the sentence came down 'guilty, punishment by Sanction', I had just clapped him on the back and thanked him for trying.

There is a pause at the other end and I assume he is quickly drifting, doing a quick search on my profile to see what I am doing now, where I am these days. It's a routine search that requires the press of a single button on his comms unit, and he comes back to me straight away.

"You are not Fan Zhaofeng. According to his Core profile, Fan Zhaofeng is dead."

"Clearly incorrect," I point out. "I need your help again."

"Anyone can fake a holo image. I'm going to cut this call unless you immediately convince me you are who you say you are. You have ten seconds."

Contacting Lee was a part of my plan, so I've locally cached all our previous interactions, since relying on biological memory is so unpredictable. I pull an interaction out.

"During recess on the third day of my trial you were standing outside listening to a bird up in a tree. You asked me if I knew what it was. I told you it was a silica chirper, a Raffonite. You doubted me. I mimicked the call of a Raffonite to lure it closer and you could see I was right."

He's silent again, but only for a moment. "Why does your Core profile say you're dead?"

"I faked my death. The how is not important. I want to talk to you about the why."

"I'm listening."

I tell him everything, from the moment I walked in on Sanctioner Huang, until the moment I approached the house. It's an abbreviated version, of course, but it takes me about ten minutes. I do not tell him about Citizen X. I judge i would probably detract from credibility and it isn't a detail he needs to know. Yet.

He doesn't interrupt, and I assume he's recording. If he goes straight to the SS after this, they'll know I'm not dead too. It's a calculated risk. "You are off-Core now? Did you know there has been a fourth murder?"

"No." Citizen X, of course, still going about his work. If his agenda is to incite an insurrection, then he needs his murders to be as public as possible. He's nothing if not determined.

"Another Sanctioner, gutted by his own Ward, live on Corecast. But you know nothing about that, of course."

"Nothing. If I could be shocked, I probably would be. But since the killer is still at large, then I suppose it makes sense they would continue their campaign."

"Uh huh. It sounds like you have alibis for at least the first two murders. Your protocols and your Sanction are strong arguments against you being the killer. Give yourself up, take your day in court. I'll even consider representing you."

"No. This will never get to court, Advocate. They'll take me, and I'll be just another MIA."

Lee was a Military Advocate during the war, and he knows all about the MIA. He coughs. "You might be right at that," he says. "But what's to say they won't just disappear me too?"

"You're a clever guy," I point out to him. "You'll find a way to stay safe."

He laughs. "Tell me what you want. I'm not agreeing to anything until I hear it."

After I tell him, he says he'll think about it. That's alright. I didn't expect him to say yes after a single holo call from a wanted fugitive in the middle of the night. But I know the next call to Lee could be very dangerous. If he goes to the Security Service now, they might be on the line with him next time, tracing the call. A trace like that is instantaneous if you set it up beforehand. I'll have however long it takes the nearest PRC Security Service Ward or police car or drone to reach me. I might be able to use that to my advantage at some point, though.

I stow my holo unit in the little pack I have with me and back away from the homestead. I don't want to run in a straight line back to the homestead in case the SS has satellite surveillance of this area. If they catch me during a flyby, then my direction of travel could tell them where I've been, and where I'm going. I loop around my home base in a spiral and get back there at about 5.15 a.m., 20 minutes to sunrise.

First mission complete, objectives achieved. I'll let a couple of days go by before I head out and call Advocate Lee again.

I need to be ready. If he decides to help me, things are going to get crazy.

I had stopped monitoring the police voice comms and even my small hand-cranked Corecast audio unit. But I turn both of them on when I get home and spend the morning getting caught up on the murder of Sanctioner Nari.

According to the Corecast audio, a State of Emergency is in force, the High Council has made no comment on the latest killing, and a sports star was in a bad car accident. Then I hear, "In breaking news, we have just learned that the PRC Justice Department has named a suspect in connection with the deaths of Sanctioner Nari and Sanctioner M'ele. Zhaofeng is a former special forces scout, but there's yet another horrifying twist to this story. We cut to our reporter, Poon Siu, outside police headquarters. What have you learned, Poon?"

Well, Sian, I can confirm that the suspect, Fan Zhaofeng, was indeed a member of 1 Squadron special forces unit during the war. He was a deep insertion reconnaissance scout, which might explain his ability to plan and execute these attacks without being caught. But there's something even more shocking to this story, Sian...Zhaofeng is a cyber.

She pauses for effect. They are talking about me in the present tense. Apparently the SS hasn't told them I'm dead? Does that mean they are still hunting me, that they didn't buy my immolation ploy? I've also been monitoring the police tactical voice comms, and nothing on there indicates there is still a manhunt ongoing. There is heightened activity due to the State of Emergency, but none of the reports I'd expect from officers following up on sightings or manning road blocks looking for someone with my description.

"A cyber!?" The holocast news anchor sounds suitably horrified. "Have the police given any indication of how this could possibly be, Poon? As we all know, it should be impossible for a cyber to commit any kind of violence, let alone the brutal attacks we have seen on holocast."

Not officially, Sian, but my sources inside the SS have told me this was no ordinary cyber. Apparently he was Sanctioned for a crime two years ago. What that crime was, we don't know – it could have been a lesser crime against the environment, or against nature, which might explain why he was quietly Sanctioned and is still at large.

"But a Sanction nonetheless, Poon. It must have been a serious crime!"

Rest assured I will get to the bottom of this, Sian...

If the leak about my Sanction has come from the SS, then I understand what they're doing. Firstly, they want to reassure the public they know who is responsible, and they are hot on their trail. They want to paint as negative a picture of me as possible, and they need to create some uncertainty around the stability of my restraint protocols or people won't believe their story that a cyber is the killer. So they leak the facts about my Sanction. Maybe not the whole story, but just enough. And then, when the time is right, they stage some sort of very public pursuit, fake an explosion maybe, and declare me dead. They produce the mangled submersible, some cybernetic components, if they recovered any from the river, and bask in the glory of a job well done.

They'll also have to deal with the fallout of a population suddenly worried about the idea that a cyber, even one who had been Sanctioned, could become a killer. But I suspect there are many in the SS who wouldn't mind too much if they were given permission to roll back a few of the liberties that cybers had recently won for ourselves following the Alignment.

Another Sanctioner dead. I hadn't expected that so soon. But then when my twin visited me he admitted it was him doing the killing, but he never actually said anything about his timetable. Apparently it was intended to keep the pressure up. He's still bent on killing Sanctioners. And now he's doing it out in the public eye.

Will he care that the police are making me the fall guy? Or will he welcome it? Build his plan around it, either Fan the fugitive, or Fan the 'died resisting arrest'. One thing I do know. The fall guy *always* ends up dead. Or disappears before he can tell his side of the story, before all the holes in the case against him can be exposed.

If I'm going to get out of this alive, someone is going to have to outwit Citizen X. But it isn't looking like the SS are going to do it. I'll have to do it for them.

And anyway, who could be better placed to catch a killer than his own twin?

Vali has to go through the motions of continuing the search for Zhaofeng, and he gives the task to Lin. She knows why. He can see she won't be the one who provides him with the 'evidence' he needs to build a specious case against Zhaofeng, so he decides he might as well keep her busy building the cover story.

It is pointless, will-sapping drudge work and she can't hide the look on her face when he gives her the task.

"You say we need to consider the chance he's still alive, so you can't complain if I ask you to keep looking for him. I have enough resources concentrated inside the city. I want someone to coordinate patrols of the surrounding area. Get drones combing the Basin. Check the homesteaders for a hundred miles around – they might have seen something."

"That's pointless!" she says. "He's not some dumb guy who mugged an old lady for her jewelry. He's not going to hide out in a cave in the Basin. Or anywhere within a hundred miles of here."

"Criminals always do things we don't think they would do. Prisons are full of criminals who didn't do the smart thing."

"This is also pointless because you don't really believe he's alive!"

"But you apparently do, so I am using my most motivated asset on the job of finding him if he is alive, while I use my other assets elsewhere, to build an iron-clad case against him." He points at his holo unit. "Get rolling. Homesteads, shacks, industrial facilities, caves, vehicle rest stops, anything he could hide in, on or under. I expect to see a list of recommended targets, with resource requisitions for police patrols and drones, within the hour."

She does that. But she has her own ideas about how to find Fan and what she really needs right now is to get inside his head. For that, she makes another trip out to Fan's house.

The quiet street borders a nature reserve and when she gets out of the car, she spends a moment breathing in the air. She looks over his fence at the house. There is a police incident laser barrier around the house, but it recognizes her SS ID and starts blinking to indicate she can cross without calling down a patrol.

She walks around the back of the house and checks in the rear windows to be sure no one is there. The back door has been fitted with a new lock that also recognizes her ID, as per normal procedure. What is she looking for? Anything that might add to his list of known associates or relatives. Yes, the forensics unit has been through the house and taken away everything of interest. She's looking for what they missed, without really knowing if they missed anything at all.

She takes the bedroom first and stands looking at the huge charcoal sketch of a nude woman from the viewpoint of her mons pubis. The bed has been stripped, the mattress overturned and the posture-adjusting mechanism exposed. It's been lifted up and probably scanned with millimeter radar to see if anything has been hidden in the frame. What can she possibly find that an SS forensics team missed?

There must be something. There's always something. She starts going through his wardrobe and drawers.

After an hour she's starting to lose hope. Anything that even looked like it might yield data, DNA or prints has been bagged, tagged and taken away. What is left is the shell of a house, the meaningless detritus of a life once lived. Cutlery, plates, paintings and prints. On a shelf she sees two statues that have been lifted, searched and laid back down on their sides so that they show a tag on their base indicating they've been scanned. One is a fat ballerina on a large ceramic ball, the other a tall indigenous woman holding a spear. Her eyes are drawn to the shelves of books above them. They're an interesting affectation for a Core-linked cyber who could access the contents of every book ever published in any Galaxy in the universe in the blink of an eye. It must have been like meditation for him, taking one of these books and sitting in a chair, actually reading it word by excruciatingly slow word.

Books printed on paper are rare. The only trees on PRC are inside the cities – there are no plantations from which paper can be harvested. Only the rich volcanic soils of New Syberia can support farming, and food is prioritized over paper. Any wood grown there is treasured, and turned into art or furniture. These books must have come from outside the Coruscant system, probably traded by starship crew members for credits or souvenirs. She pulls one out and looks it over. The cover is plain brown board, with a gold title: *On Teleportation, a philosophical critique of the morality of entanglement, by RA Teach*. It would be too much to hope he had underlined any of it, and of course, he hasn't. Like anything rare, books are prized by collectors. In good condition, each would be worth a few day's bandwidth credits for a cyber like Fan, and he has dozens.

They've been pulled out, flipped through, scanned and replaced. If there was any order to them, she suspects it's been lost, which is a shame since the way he organized his library might have given her some insights. She pulls out another, cheaper-looking volume. It is a slim paperback with a garish black and yellow cover and a cartoon drawing of a professor on the front: *Quantum Mechanics for Dummies, 2050 update*.

It doesn't seem like much, but its age might make it the most valuable book in the entire collection. She carefully opens it, afraid she'll crack the binding, but it is well thumbed and falls open to the title page.

Ah. There in a flowing feminine font, someone has written, *"To Fan – in case you want to go back to where it all began, love, Yung."*

'Love, Yung'? She quickly drifts. There is nothing in their files on any known female associate of Fan Zhaofeng called Yung. She broadens the search by five degrees of separation, scanning hundreds of thousands of associates of associates for anyone with the name Yung. It is an unusual name for PRC but she finds no one.

On a hunch, she drifts and starts scanning for transport or accommodation booked in the name of 'Yung', anywhere in the city, anytime in the last week. It's an uncommon name, but not unique. She gets a few thousand hits and assigns an AI to start analyzing them for patterns consistent with criminal behavior. Simple Core searches are projected directly to her retinal nerves and appear like a holo in the vision of her left eye. More complex data has to be forwarded to her comms unit for projection.

It's done in seconds. Flicking through the holo she finds one that is particularly interesting. A taxi, hired by a Yung Woon-kwong, which made a short journey across the city before heading outside the city walls for about thirty miles before returning, empty. She checks the address it terminated at and finds a rental. Also rented in the name of Yung Woon-kwong.

The possibility forms. Fan does have an accomplice, one that had slipped right under their radar. One possibly involved in helping him escape. Also involved in helping him kill Sanctioners? She shakes her head without realizing she is doing it. No, she still doesn't believe that.

But this is suddenly getting interesting. She, Yung – they – might still be at that address!

Walking quickly out to the kitchen, Lin gets herself a glass of water, the holo tracing the taxi's route out to the rented shack dancing in front of her eyes.

Yung Woon-kwong. Who are you?

A simple check of the citizen register comes up blank. What? That makes no sense. You can't rent a taxi without credit, you can't earn credit without an ID, you can't get an ID without being on the

PRC register of citizens. She scans housing records, utility companies, comms providers.

Nothing.

The woman is…a ghost. The thought gives her a flashback to her conversation with gang sergeant Duong. *The Ghost. We called him that.* Different scenarios flash through her mind. The woman has hidden her identity; why? Who could do that? An undercover police or SS officer, yes. It was an age-old ruse used when infiltrating gangs. Had Fan been given access to do so when he was a Hunter for the High Council? If so, he could have created the identity before he was Sanctioned, and be using it now. But that didn't explain the inscription. Going to the lengths of writing a dedication to yourself in a book would be a little extreme even if you were establishing a false identity. It just didn't ring true.

Unless…what if Yung Woon-kwong was a Hunter herself?! A comrade in arms from Fan's days as a scout? That made much more sense. That also made her potentially very, very dangerous.

Lin closed the book, slid it into the back pocket of her jeans and made for the back door. Before she'd even reached her car, she'd finished putting together an urgent resource requisition for a heavily armed tactical operations unit and was dialing Vali in so that he could sign off on it.

It's during my 11 a.m. check through the back windows that I see activity at the safe house across the valley. Or the not-so-safe house, as my twin would have it.

To be more accurate, I see activity *over* the house.

Two small quadrotor drones following close-quarter surveillance protocols. I might have missed them if I hadn't been looking directly at the house. They are rotating around the building, scanning for movement or infrared heat signatures.

I spot one of them now, circling around the back porch, checking at window level. For a moment I consider relocating. They are just two miles away. But I hold to my plan. I've been expecting this, I was warned about it after all. It's more proof that what my twin told me might be true. That he might be capable of things beyond my understanding, including predicting a police raid on the house I was hiding in.

One drone pulls up and sets up over the house at about 100 meters, then starts a figure 8 surveillance pattern over the area. That's a sign police are on the way. They are probably just being cautious because the house looks like it has recently been occupied. But it means it's just a matter of time before the drones head my way.

The drones circle for the next thirty minutes. What are they waiting for? Have they seen something out of the ordinary? It's an empty house. Yes, we ate and slept there, but for only one night, several nights ago. They could check the rental record and see that, but it would be in Yung's name. Have they already connected me to her? I would have expected to see a couple of Wards by now, if that was the case, but I see only drones.

After about forty-five minutes I see cars approach from the highway, both north and south. They are taking no chances – a battery of police cars accompanied by a black utility vehicle: PRC Security Service. The police are out first and surround the house. Slowly, from the PRC Security Service vehicle, a single occupant emerges.

Lin. So they must be suspicious. She wouldn't come outside the city walls to check on every recently rented rental shack.

Moving in tactical formation, the police approach the house. There's no doubt now, they are going to make an assault. There is a loud crack, then another, as the police break through the front and back doors simultaneously, throwing in a neural gas charge before they breach.

I consider what I'm watching. Citizen X said he had a 'limited ability to look across the multiverse' and see various versions of my timeline, many of which showed me being captured in this very assault. But not if I moved up here.

How? Yes, science has proven the multiverse exists. Yes, the Alcubierre drive makes use of that fact for faster than light travel. But no one has ever been able to *move* from one parallel universe to another, or to look across, into or over any other universe. I discounted what he was saying because, according to our science, it's impossible.

Apparently, according to his science, it is possible.

The assault on the empty house is quickly over. One of the police officers emerges and speaks with Lin. The change in the demeanor of the cops is obvious: they remove their helmets, some stand down.

Lin and a couple of others prop open the back door and go inside to start the forensics. There's a small risk, scoping them from the window, but I watch until they leave, and the drones move to the next house up the road, across the valley, the police cars following. They start talking to the resident there. Standard MO, they should be going house to house in both directions that road. How long before they hit on someone who says *'Strangers? Oh yeah, there was a face at the markets the other day I didn't recognize. They were talking to the lady who has the honey stall.'*

I have some time, not much. Lucky for me they started at the other side of the valley, but then, my twin knew they would, didn't he? He's checked all the branches, quantified all the probabilities. But he's apparently not infallible. *There are so many moving pieces, even I can't keep track of them all.*

I move all my food and camping gear up to the crawl space in the roof. It's hot and dirty but big enough to stand up in and under a tile roof that will hide my heat sig nicely. I've got an idea of their MO now, and sending in the drones, while a simple and effective tactic, is useless against an adversary who can regulate his body temperature and hides in a floor, wall or ceiling space. I can use that against them.

In a spare room I find a folding mattress and pull that up there too. I'll be living in the roof from now on, in case a drone buzzes past unannounced. Then I go around the house and remove all signs I've been there. Take all the tape off the blinds and curtains, tidy up the splintered wood around the laundry window that I used to gain access, close and lock it. I rub some water and dirt into the wood so it doesn't look freshly broken. I can't hide the fact there has been a break-in some time, but it could just as well have been years ago. And if they check, the window is locked now. They won't be able to get in themselves unless they break in, and they probably wouldn't do that without good cause.

I could move out into the desert, dig into a sandbank and live rough. I did that often during the war because it was easier and safer than hiding in a ruined or vacant building. That's plan B. But I don't like it. When I hid in a desert dugout, usually, no one was actively looking for me. They had no reason to have an AI do image analysis, compare shots of the desert past and present to see if anything had been disturbed. If Lin wanted to, she could already be doing that for the desert ten miles around the house she has just raided. It's safer inside this shack.

I'll prepare all my food up in the roof, leave nothing lying around downstairs. I go up and check out the roof space and decide it will do. I loosen a few tiles so I can break out over the roof if I need to. I'll bring up water and if the Security Service or police come, I'll hear them and be ready. I do a risk analysis. Nothing changes.

I'm feeling okay with the new situation, but I still spend the day on edge, waiting for the crunch of tires coming up the hard sand driveway to the house, or the buzz of electric rotors. He said I'd be safe, but should I trust a self-confessed killer?

The day passes, without visitors. I cancel my planned night patrol. My main objective tonight is a second call to Advocate Lee from a homestead ten miles west. But after the events of today, that would be crazy. My voice comm scanner can pick up on the police drone control frequency and it just takes a few minutes to confirm that they have permanent drone coverage up over the valley now, looking for any heat signature even vaguely humanoid. How long will they keep it up? I'll just have to wait it out.

But it turns out the police running the surveillance are no elite unit, or, they haven't assigned enough drones. The surveillance pattern they set up has gaps. Monitoring the strength of the drone signals, I can track them coming and going and find there is a regular thirty-minute gap between one drone leaving the valley and the next arriving. They should be overlapping, but they aren't. And it's regular as clockwork, right on the half hour. Probably run on automated download and recharge, by a tech with no imagination. That gives me the window I need to get out of the valley, and back in again.

I think twice about what I'm about to do. If it works, I hope it will steal the initiative from my twin, perhaps even force him to contact me again. If it doesn't work, all I will achieve is to confirm to the SS that I'm not dead.

19. THE GHOST

Lin returns from her abortive sortie outside the walls and throws her belt, weapon and tactical vest onto her desk.

It had been a long shot, and it hadn't paid off.

Vali has been waiting for her to return, but he already knows it was a bust. He leans up against the wall next to her desk, arms crossed, trying to look sympathetic.

"Don't look so disappointed. The chances Zhaofeng is still alive, if the Core says he's dead, are less than a billion to one."

"So explain to me who the hell this is," she says, pulling the book from her back pocket and shoving the inscription under his nose. "Who the hell is Yung Woon-kwong?"

"I can help with that. I checked with our undercover register AI. It can't of course confirm any details about active undercover agents to anyone not indoctrinated in the operation they are running, but it confirmed that an ID under that name was created two years ago."

"So she's a cop?"

"She's a cop. Or SS. Or a Hunter."

"So Hunters can create fake IDs too?"

"It turns out they can. I didn't know Hunters existed until we started digging into Zhaofeng's crime, so it's not surprising we didn't know."

"Alright, but what's she doing hanging out with Fan Zhaofeng?"

He points at the book in her hand. "You've only got a first name there. You've got nothing to indicate that the Yung who wrote that inscription is this Yung Woon-kwong."

"Oh come on. It's one of the most unusual names in the register. It's in a book in Zhaofeng's library. About a week after he goes missing…"

"Dies…" Vali interrupts.

"…goes missing, and this Yung Woon-kwong hires a taxi for two people and heads outside the city to a remote rental which she rents for just one night?" She slaps a hand on her thigh. "Damn privacy laws. If there had just been some vision from inside that taxi."

"If there had been, it would only have disappointed you earlier. It was probably just a lovers' tryst."

"An undercover police agent on a lovers' tryst, or Fan Zhaofeng's associate helping him escape the city? I know which one I have my money on."

"I'm glad it's your money then."

She sighs and puts the book back into her pocket, then hesitates. She clicks her fingers. "Wait! You said this fake ID was created two years ago?"

"Two years, three months."

"Zhaofeng was still a Hunter back then, engaged by the High Council. It was before his Sanction!"

"Coincidence. There were probably dozens of false identities created around that time as part of dozens of undercover operations."

"Your coincidences are starting to pile up, Senior Expositor," she points out. She starts counting off on her fingers. "There is a data gap in Zhaofeng's Core uplink between his escape from the house and when he reconnects to the Core. Coincidence. He mysteriously self-immolates but we only find a tiny sample of organic matter and very little cybernetic material. Coincidence. The extremely unusual name Yung turns up in Zhaofeng's library and a Yung Woon-kwong makes a sudden dash out of the city, but she doesn't officially exist. Coincidence. The only way to create a fake ID is if you are police, SS or – it turns out – working undercover as a Hunter. Zhaofeng was a Hunter. Coincidence. You want me to keep going?"

"No need. We don't deal in coincidence, Junior Expositor. We deal in fact. Fan Zhaofeng was Sanctioned for violence. We don't know exactly why, but…fact. Fan Zhaofeng was at the scene of the first crime and has no alibi for the last two. Fact. Fan Zhaofeng had both motive and opportunity. Fact. And Fan Zhaofeng is dead. Fact."

She decides arguing with him is pointless. He just wants his facts to fit the narrative he is creating and anything she might throw at him that contradicts the narrative is pure inconvenience.

"Alright, forget it. Let's assume Fan Zhaofeng is dead. Were you being genuine when you said you are considering whether he had accomplices?"

He frowns. "Yes."

"Yung Woon-kwong."

"Because you found the name Yung in a book in his house."

"Because if you were a Hunter, killing Sanctioners, and you wanted an accomplice, who better than a police officer, SS agent, or fellow Hunter with an undercover identity?"

He mulls it over for a second. "OK, follow it and see where it gets you. If you come back to me with proof that Yung Woon-kwong is *really* an associate of Fan Zhaofeng, I might be interested. If you can prove she's also a cyber, I'll probably promote you."

I hit the homestead at 2.30 a.m. It looks unoccupied this time. I go through the routine with the rock again. No reaction. I make the call on audio only. If the SS are there, I don't want them getting a background image they can match.

"Hello?"

A sigh. "Zhaofeng?"

"Yes. Have you thought it over, Advocate?"

"Is there a reason you are calling at these ridiculous hours?" he grumbles.

"This is the last call, if you agree to represent me. We'll only connect by quantum encrypted text from now on. Well?" I'm listening for talking in the background, but if I hear anything, it is only what might be his wife, muttering.

"Yes, I'll represent you. But I want you to know why," he says. "And there are conditions."

"Okay."

"First, the why. I'm coming up on the end of my third term of service as an Advocate. It looks like my dream of making Advocate General is not about to be realized, so I need a plan B. A certain…notoriety that might attract wealthy private clients. Your case could give me that notoriety."

This sounds reasonable. "What are the conditions?"

"There are a couple." He sounds like he is shifting around in bed, getting up on an elbow maybe. "But first, to be sure I have your requests straight; you want me to get out a message via a Corecast channel?"

"Yes. We will need to go to them directly, maybe a press conference…"

He coughs to interrupt me. "We will go to them directly. But not through a press conference."

"So what do you want to do?"

"A confidential briefing of the biggest global Corecaster, this

Friday. On condition they send it live. I'll have to convince them I'm legit, but I think I can do it. I'll need as much detail as you can give me. The more you have, the more credible we can be."

I check my watch. If he has contacted the PRC Security Service already, and is just talking to string me out, this is a good way to do it. Two minutes so far. I figured five was the low end of my window, the time it would take to triangulate on this digital exchange and reposition a few high-speed IR/holo drones. I let him keep talking. "We could do a one-off press conference, but they can shut that down. This way should have legs."

"Thanks."

"So, how do you want to get the information to me?"

I look up at the skies, expecting a drone to appear any second. "Do you still have the same private text address?"

"Yes, but they can intercept that."

"I'll send you my statement in an encrypted text. The unlock phrase is your own birthdate with the letters of your name between each numeral. It won't be unbreakable but it will take their best AI a couple of weeks to unlock it and that's all we need."

"I'll have costs," Lee says. "I'll pay them out of my own pocket for now, but you will need to reimburse me, is that clear?"

"Yes. I have to go now."

"Wait, there was one other condition…"

"Quickly."

There is a pause at his end, and I prepare to close the connection. Ten seconds, I think. You have ten more seconds. "I also told my wife," he says. "She had to know, before I went and did something as foolhardy as this."

I breathe out slowly. Breathe in again. "That's fine, Advocate. I have to go now." I cut the call.

I bundle the handset into my backpack and move back into an area of rocky dunes I'd identified on my way in, crawling under a rocky overhang where I can keep an eye on the dark, silent homestead. I'm only visible on infrared or night vision from an oblique angle ahead, and invisible to any drones overhead. I decided that if the call had been intercepted, and SS or police patrols mobilized, I'd see Wards arrive almost straight away, then within the next half hour police would blow in with drones and one or two cars at least, like they did earlier.

I lay in the shadow of the overhang for an hour, watching.

It stays silent. At 3.30 a.m. I begin spiraling back to my base.

Phase one of the plan to flush out my twin was to drop off the SS radar. Phase two of the plan is to bring this whole mess out into the open. He's been letting the extent of the murders stay buried by the SS for some reason. Let's see how he handles them being dragged up into the daylight.

20. THE PROSECUTOR

Lin walks into the SS office the next morning to find it strangely quiet. Strangely, because just the day before, Vali had secured another ten officers to replace those he'd lost and help with narrowing down the mystery of how a Ward had been successfully reprogrammed to kill Sanctioner Nari.

As she walks into the main squad room, she sees why. Every man, woman and cyber in the room is standing in front of the holo projector watching a 2D projection of a news broadcast beamed up onto the wall.

She sees a Corecast anchor and his partner, sitting in a studio, as text runs across the bottom of the screen. "BREAKING NEWS...WAITING FEED...STATEMENT BY FUGITIVE FAN ZHAOFENG...BREAKING NEWS...WAITING FEED..."

Vali is standing at the front, turning as she enters the room. "How can this be?" he asks, to no one and everyone.

She stands beside him. "Press statement of some sort."

"That much I know. It says a statement from Zhaofeng. I'm asking how can that be?" he repeats.

Because he's not dead! she feels like screaming at him. "We'll soon find out," she says instead.

Someone turns up the volume but there are only the voices of some studio hosts who say the station has been contacted within the last hour and provided with sensational information about the Sanctioner killings and Fan Zhaofeng. They are speculating that Zhaofeng is about to give himself up to the Security Service. Maybe even a public confession? Suddenly the vision cuts from the studio to a darkened room, where a journalist is interviewing a person hidden in shadow, in classic dramatic style.

Vali whispers to Lin urgently, "I don't like this." He turns to face the room. "Someone find me a tech with the ability to cut this transmission. I want it taken *down*!"

A tech at the back of the room flicks across different Corecast channels, the full width of the band. The press conference is being re-syndicated on nearly every channel. "You couldn't, even if you tried," he says. "It's on about 20 channels, and they're streaming live in every city. We'd have to take down every transmission point across the globe and blank the satellites. We're not set up for that. This isn't a dictatorship."

Vali looks at him. Lin has never heard him actually hiss, but he comes close to it this time. "By the end of this press conference you might wish it was."

Lin sees the holo news anchor's hands are shaking slightly as he starts speaking. "Hello and welcome, viewers. This is Daniel Hueng reporting. I am here with Advocate Lau Lee, a government Advocate and also a long-time associate of the wanted cyber, Fan Zhaofeng." The lights come up, showing a middle-aged, well-built man in the uniform of a civil Advocate. Hueng nods to his interviewee. "Can you tell us why you are here, sir?"

"He's legit," Lin whispers to Vali after quickly drifting. "His name is in Zhaofeng's file. Defended him at his criminal trial."

Lee begins, holding a comms unit in his lap so he can read the image on its display. "Yes, I have here a prepared statement from Mr. Fan Zhaofeng, which I will shortly read. I can vouch for its authenticity, I know him well."

Know him? Her heart leaps. She sits on a desk, staring stunned at the wall like everyone else. She's hopeful because this might mean he is alive! And she's not a little afraid. She hardly knows him after all. Will he say anything about her warning him to run?

Lee holds up a piece of paper. "Firstly, I must communicate some news which the police have withheld. Fan Zhaofeng is believed to have died several days ago while trying to evade capture by the police for crimes he did not commit."

"Inconvenient," Vali mutters. "But we were about to disclose it anyway."

The news anchor, Hueng, leans forward. "You say the police have been withholding this information?"

"Yes. Fan Zhaofeng is believed to have died in an accident in which his body was immolated. I understand from my own contacts in the police that they have confirmed this."

Hueng frowns. "As late as yesterday, the police held a press conference to update information on the hunt for Fan Zhaofeng: they made no mention of this."

"I assume they have their reasons. But I need to make two important statements on the matter. The first is that Mr. Zhaofeng is not guilty of the murders he is accused of. The second is that he is not dead."

A buzz goes around the room. "Yes!" Lin shouts, then claps a hand over her mouth. Vali glowers at her. "I mean, I *knew* it," she says sheepishly to a detective beside her.

"This could also have been set up in advance," Vali insists. "It proves nothing."

"This is...sorry, how do you know all this, Advocate Lee?" the anchor asks.

"Because I have spoken with Mr. Zhaofeng since his reported death. He faked his own death in order to be able to escape the city, which he has successfully done."

Lin keeps her mouth shut this time, not even looking at Vali. She doesn't need to. His face will be a study in anger, of that she's sure.

"If he is innocent, as you claim, then why is he in hiding?" Hueng asks.

"I will come to that," Lee says. He shifts his comms unit so that he can see the screen more clearly. "The statement from Mr. Zhaofeng says...*I have chosen to speak out so that all citizens may understand. The SS and police say I am wanted in connection with the killing of Sanctioners M'ele and Nari. This is not the full truth. In fact, they suspect me of involvement in the slayings of four Sanctioners.*"

Where there was some murmuring before, there is now a deathly hush in the investigation room. Lin holds her breath, waiting for the inevitable follow-up reaction. Not even the full PRC Security Service investigation team was aware that four Sanctioners had been killed. No one except Vali, herself, and a limited few had known the full scale of the killings – the information had been tightly compartmentalized. She had no doubts the others had heard rumors, but whatever they had heard, it was now being confirmed.

Sure enough, a burble of swearing and muttering breaks out.

"Shut it!" Vali orders. "I want to hear this."

Lee continues. "The first killing occurred nearly three months ago with the death of Sanctioner Huang, which the SS kept quiet," the silhouetted figure continues. "This was followed by the killing of Sanctioner M'ele of which you are aware. One month ago, there was another unpublicized attack which resulted in the death of the Sanctioner Seung. And you have recently seen the very public execution of Sanctioner Nari."

"My God," the anchor says, dropping his professional mask and showing his feelings. "How could..."

Lee ignores the interruption. "The statement from Mr. Zhaofeng continues. *I have told the PRC Security Service who is responsible for these killings and as both a cyber and a Sanctionee, it should be clear I cannot myself be responsible. I call on the PRC Security Service to stop their pursuit of me and to devote their attention to finding the real killer or killers behind these attacks.*" Lee looks down at his comms unit. "That concludes the statement."

The ticker tape at the bottom of the screen has changed. "SANCTIONER KILLINGS: BREAKING NEWS…POLICE COVERUP ALLEGED…FUGITIVE ZHAOFENG CLAIMS FOUR SANCTIONERS DEAD…SAYS HE IS INNOCENT…"

"Find this Advocate," Vali says to an officer standing beside him. "Find him and bring him in." The man is still standing staring at the screen. "Now!"

Lin ignores him, unable to quiet her inner jubilation. *He's alive. He's damn well alive! I was right! He's found a way to go off-Core. And that probably was him in that taxi with that woman…*She feels suddenly and unexpectedly jealous. Her happiness sours. *Who the hell are you, Yung Woon-kwong? And what are you to Fan Zhaofeng?*

But the interview isn't finished. The anchor shifts in his seat. "I understand you have been told you aren't to answer any questions, or speculate beyond what Mr. Zhaofeng has said, but why should we believe what he says here? Four Sanctioners dead? It is hard enough to accept two have been killed, but four?"

"Yes," the Advocate says. "We thought you might ask that. We believe the reason Mr. Zhaofeng is being pursued by the Security Service is that he is the only one outside the Security Service or police who knows about the first death, the killing of Sanctioner Huang, and the full scale of all the killings."

"How does he know?"

"He was the one who found Sanctioner Huang at the scene of the first killing. Huang was dead already when Mr. Zhaofeng found him."

"And why should we believe that this Sanctioner, Huang, is even dead?"

"Mr. Zhaofeng agreed I could provide you with proof, as you know…" Advocate Lee says.

"What now?" Vali says, turning to Lin. "What proof?!"

"I don't…I don't know!" she stammers.

The anchor shuffles in his chair and gestures as the screen splits, showing on one side the studio and on the other…a series of graphic 2D images of the dead Sanctioner Huang at the Thuyen house.

"Where did these come from?" Vali demands. "How have we not seen these?"

"His cache," Lin says. "He's given them visuals from his cache."

"Can you tell us what we are looking at here, sir?" the Corecast anchor asks, gesturing up at the images.

"Yes, these are images taken directly from the visual cache of the cyber Fan Zhaofeng of the moment he found the dead Sanctioner," the man says. "Police have reviewed every single byte of data from Mr. Zhaofeng's cache from both this time and the day leading up to it. He has infallible alibis for his actions that day, even at times when his sensory data was not being cached."

"Is there anything else you can tell us?"

"Not at this time, no. I'm not instructed to provide any other information."

"Thank you, sir. Now back to our studio. I'll be back with analysis and comment on this exclusive story shortly."

The Corecast crosses to a couple of studio anchors who start breathlessly recapping developments.

Lin has been drifting and takes the arm of the officer Vali had ordered to go and apprehend the Advocate. "Lee, Lau, public Advocate. Get onto comms liaison and get the metadata on all his private holo units, any holo unit at his workplace, dig out anyone who contacted him in the last few weeks." Vali opens his mouth to speak, but she jumps in. "We don't want to pull him in yet, Vali. If he's in contact with Zhaofeng, we want to leave him in play. Look for anything or anyone that might be linked to Zhaofeng in his comms data. Set up surveillance on him, physical and digital." The officer runs off.

"You're right, of course," Vali says, nodding his head at the picture of the interview playing over again onscreen. "What other course of action does my junior Expositor advise?" he asks without irony.

She paces slowly. "The hit on that false ID still troubles me," she tells him. "We don't know near enough about these 'Hunters'. If she's one of them, who is she? What's she doing? Is she with him, against him, part of this, or something else entirely?"

"Something else?"

"If she's a Hunter, she reports to the High Council. She could be hunting him too, if they don't trust us to get the job done."

He nods. "Let me do some more digging into Fan Zhaofeng's time in the military. The High Council might be more amenable to releasing 'sensitive' information after this."

He rounds on the room, where people have collected in groups of three or four, talking in hushed tones. "Task force Storm Meeting right now!" he says, clapping his hands. "We already had a city on the edge of madness. Unless we start to get ahead of this new development today, we could be looking at chaos!"

She watches him as he walks through the crowd to the briefing room. *And do you fear that, or would you embrace it, Expositor?*

Lee did a very good job, I think to myself, listening to a replay of his interview on the voice comms. In retrospect, he was right. A press conference could have been interrupted. Shut down. We were lucky, though – that journalist, Daniel Hueng, could have taken the story straight to the Security Service and it would have ended right there, with Lee in an SS interview room. It probably still will, but at least the truth is out there.

And, I'm hoping, my twin will be mightily pissed. He said my being dead and off-Core suited him. He intimated the Core had even collaborated in the fiction. They seemed to assume I would cooperate. I hoped that despite their claimed omniscience, they were now deeply annoyed at Fan Zhaofeng.

"OK, Lin," I say out loud. "About time we caught this killer, don't you think?"

Advocate Lee has no intention of becoming the next name on the list of the PRC SS's Most Wanted. And he isn't about to wait on the SS to reach out to him.

The first thing he does when the interview is finished broadcasting is to put in a call to High Council Prosecutor Matthew Cheung. Lee knows Cheung by name and reputation, the man who has been Chief Prosecutor for coming up on half a decade, presiding over the takedown of everything from mobsters and miner gangs to terrorist cells and Provincial despots.

The population of PRC had not taken easily to non-violence. There was organized crime, which perhaps logically enough was among the first to adapt to non-lethal weapons. Terrorists too, the ones who were really motivated by greed, not ideology. They worked out pretty quickly that to stay in business, they also had to adapt. But they were the smart ones. Plenty were not. The world was full of dumb criminals and terrorists and just plain psychopaths and Cheung had skewered them all. The list of criminals Sanctioned or imprisoned by his team in his time as Chief Prosecutor numbered in the thousands.

There would always be crime, he was heard to say. If crime was to disappear tomorrow, he would happily resign. But even the death penalty hadn't stopped murder in the old days, and the adoption of the Law alone wouldn't stamp it out either. There would always be those who thought 'I'll get away with it', or who didn't think at all, just acting on impulse. But PRC becoming a Core world, with the additional surveillance opportunities that a world-spanning AI gave, increased a hundredfold the difficulty of committing major crimes, and the chances you would be caught.

That was what really made the difference – not the punishment for the crime, but the fact you had little or no chance of getting away with it. The combination of Core overwatch, the police, the SS and their Wards constituted a formidable justice system.

Especially when you coupled it with a legal system without loopholes. Any violent crime got the same sentence – Sanction or prison. There was a presumption of innocence, but if your trial resulted in a finding of guilty, you were guilty. No self-defense loopholes, no mitigating circumstances, appeals. Cheung sat on top of a system in which no criminal could evade justice for long, and guilt was immutable judgment that stood for all time.

Lee has arranged to meet Cheung in a private room at the Marriot hotel. As he answers his knock and opens the door, he sees Cheung smoothing back his jet black hair and padding his forehead for sweat with a white handkerchief. He's about fifty, carrying a few kilos around the waist, dressed in a no-nonsense black suit and white shirt, dark blue tie and hand-stitched shoes. No briefcase or papers. No police with him. He apparently wants to make it clear to Lee he's just here to talk.

Lee is wearing his ancient Advocate uniform of black gown and wig, and is suddenly glad he didn't come to the meeting in plain clothes.

"Advocate Lee?" Cheung takes the initiative, holding out his hand. "Matthew Cheung. Have we met?"

"Actually no," the Advocate says, stepping aside. Two chairs are set up next to a writing desk by the window with bottled water and two glasses. Lee points at a chair. "But thanks for seeing me," he says.

Cheung smiles. "Well. That was quite a stunt. Was it your idea, the Daniel Hueng interview thing?"

Stunt? Lee is thinking, *You haven't seen anything.*

"It was not a stunt," he told Cheung. "It was an innocent man, trying to be heard."

"I see," Cheung says. "Can I assume you *are* representing Mr. Zhaofeng then?"

"I'm a legal attaché with Civil Defense. I represented Fan Zhaofeng in his Law trial several years ago," Lee assures him. "In this case I am acting privately, as allowed under Civil Defense regulations. So yes, I'm representing him."

Cheung raises his eyebrows. "Ah. You represented Zhaofeng in the case in which he was found guilty? Not one of your most successful cases, then."

"Zhaofeng pleaded guilty, as you know. It was a proforma defense case, with the outcome already certain before it began."

"Well, that's ancient history. Let's get to the situation today. If your client is innocent this time, he should make his defense in court. The fact he has gone into hiding, and faked his death to do so, well, that indicates guilt."

"My client is a cyber, and a Sanctionee," Lee points out. "For both of those reasons he cannot commit a violent crime. There is only circumstantial evidence linking him to these crimes. In the absence of any other suspects, the SS has chosen to persecute my client, in what I can only assume is a case of deeply ingrained institutional racism…"

Cheung chuckles. "Deeply ingrained institutional racism? You are planning to throw that one into your next Corecast interview, are you? And how do you think that will play if I choose to reveal exactly what crime your client was Sanctioned for? You rightly point out he is a cyber, and a Sanctionee. The only one in history. The airwaves are full of speculation about how that could be…I would be more than happy to enlighten the public."

"That information has been suppressed by order of the High Council. You cannot disclose it."

"I am here on the authority of the High Council, Mr. Lee. I assure you it would take me a single holo call to have that suppression order lifted."

Lee tries a reset. "We seem to have gotten off on the wrong foot. I invited you here to make you an offer. Any questions you may have for my client you can provide to me, and I will relay them to him at the earliest opportunity. He has promised me to give you his full cooperation if the order for his apprehension is lifted."

"His full cooperation?" Cheung asks sharply. "Handing himself over to the police is full cooperation, anything less is obstruction."

"So you have no questions for my client?"

"None. You may tell him he's going to be charged, arrested and handed over to the SS for judgment by the High Council." Cheung leans forward. "And while you're at it tell him that, Sanctionee or not, he *will* be judged. In camera, as is the Law for previous offenders."

"Based on what he has told me, he has no intention of handing himself in to be tried by your kangaroo court," Lee says.

"Then we are done," Cheung says, and stands.

Lee stands too, picking up his hat and getting ready to leave. "Goodbye," he says. They don't shake. He watches Cheung leave, thinking, *Oh, we are far from done.*

Matthew Cheung gets off his car comms channel after providing a download on his meeting to the Security Service investigator, Expositor Vali. The Expositor is clearly upset, itching to drag Lee in and interrogate him, but Cheung has to tell him that it would not be in their interests to harass or bully an Advocate of Lee's standing. There's no crime he's committed and nothing they can legitimately bring him in for. He'd just claim client privilege anyway. Even under the Alignment and its Law, there is still the common law of PRC to deal with. Start overriding the law of PRC, you *will* have a full-on rebellion on your hands.

Cheung thumbs down the windows on his car. He turns on the audio to catch up on what the Corecast chatter is on the big interview. He wants to see which way the public's sympathy is blowing – worst case is for the cyber Zhaofeng and against the Security Service. It won't matter. *Let's see what happens when he is captured and charged with a crime against the Law.*

Cheung hears Lee's voice on the Corecast and assumes it is a replay of the earlier interview. Then he realizes it isn't.

"...Thank you for letting me get back to you again at such short notice. I have an update. I have just spoken with Chief Prosecutor Cheung, who has advised me that neither he, nor the Security Service, have any questions for my client. We hope this concludes the matter, and that Mr. Zhaofeng can now return to his normal life."

"Does this mean the global hunt for the fugitive Fan Zhaofeng is canceled?" the journalist asks.

"Well, it would be strange for the Chief Prosecutor to say, on the one hand, 'we have no questions for Mr. Zhaofeng' and, on the other, for the SS to continue to hunt him like an animal. Unless the Security Service is once again not telling the public the full truth. I think we must start to ask ourselves whether we are seeing from the SS a sad example of deeply ingrained institutional racism against our honest and hardworking cyber citizens."

Cheung swears. *There it is, just as Lee rehearsed.* He'd reviewed Lee's performance in the trial of Fan Zhaofeng several years ago and found it to be very, very subpar. Apparently he's underestimated the wigged clown. He slaps a palm loudly on the seat beside him.

That won't happen again.

Lying in bed listening on the Corecaster to a replay of the interview and Lee's quick followup, Junior Expositor Lin Ming smiles. There is no great love for Chief Prosecutor Cheung amongst the officers of the Security Service. He's said no to too many good cases, and he farms out any difficult cases to junior prosecutors if there is even a risk he might lose face.

Nice one, Fan. But they're still going to put you in the jug, she thinks to herself, giving her cat a soothing scratch behind the ears that gets it purring. Maybe it is the best place for him; in custody while this is all sorted out. Even she is starting to think so.

A moment later, she realizes she's fallen asleep. At least that's what it feels like. The holo unit is buzzing. She reaches over and slaps the 'audio only' button.

"Hello?"

"Lin? Is that you?"

Zhaofeng!

"Who the hell else is going answer my holo at...2 a.m. Fan? Where are you calling from?"

"Uh, a cave somewhere in the Basin."

"Very funny. I'll have a trace as soon as you hang up."

"That won't help you," he promises. "Will the SS drop its search now?"

Is he really that naïve? "No, Fan. Your Corecast interview made us look bad. If anything, Vali and the High Council want you more than ever now."

"He's the one behind the killings, Lin. My twin. That's who you should be looking for."

Not that again. "I can't help you anymore, Fan. Not since you outed all of the Sanctioner murders on a planetary Corecast. The best you can do is go to the nearest police station now and turn yourself over rather than wait for us to find you."

"Lin, he told me himself. He killed Sanctioner Huang. And the others. He's trying to depose the High Council. To start some kind of uprising."

Suddenly, she's cold. "Why are you so sure?"

"He as much as told me. Public resentment of Sanction is his lever."

"This other Fan from another dimension told you he killed these Sanctioners to try to start a public uprising."

"Yes."

"Your 'Citizen X' said this? Or is it you talking?"

"I don't expect you to believe me. Even Yung doesn't really."

"Yung? Who the hell is Yung, Fan?"

He ignores her question. "That's why I'm going to catch him for you."

"I asked you who is...*wait*. You're what?" She holds the receiver closer. "Catch who?"

"My twin. I'll stop him, give him to you, and you will have to believe me."

"Fan, listen to yourself," she pleads. "You have alibis for the first two killings, but you have no alibi for the others. And now there are four Sanctioners dead, and you're in hiding, even from me."

"You are Security Service." His voice sounds dead. "When the PRC Security Service catch the killer who is really doing this, I'll stop hiding."

She realizes she is on the edge of tears. Dammit. "Fan, I don't know what you want."

"I want to go back to the life I had before the SS and High Council decided I was public enemy number one. So, when I've got him, I'll give him to you. After that, I'd like to take you to dinner."

He's serious. He really can be dumb for a guy with a planetary-sized IQ. "Oh, shit, Fan...Fan?" But he's gone.

She stares at the holo unit then lays it down on the bed table. *You are Security Service.* So that's how it is.

Yung. There's that name again. Her tears are gone now.

21. THE LEADER

Why should Lin believe me? 'It's not me, it's my twin. He's somehow able to look across dimensions, maybe even move across them too. He can appear and disappear at will.' I know it sounds crazy. Yung would understand more than me, of course. She at least believes that what I'm experiencing is physically possible.

Lee went a little further than we agreed, but he's delivered my message to the High Council. They should be looking somewhere else for their killer. They should be questioning the motives of the SS. Unless, of course, my twin is right and the High Council itself can't be trusted.

I keep provoking, trying to throw a wrench into his plans, but so far I've gotten no response. Is he even paying attention? Has he moved on? I hoped after the first Corecast interview my twin would just materialize in front of me demanding to know what I was doing. Seeing across worlds, materializing and dematerializing with his little marble. He was foolish to show me how he's doing it. I can see it isn't an innate ability – he is using technology to help him do it. The black marble. Technology can be stolen, destroyed, disrupted.

I have a little kidnap kit all ready for him. Tape for his mouth, plastic ties, a small heavy pipe to hit him with if he tries his disappearing trick. If he is me, some version of me, I know none of these things will really hold him, but I'll be watching him, and all I need is to hold him long enough for Lin to come and get him – for the world to see he is real.

At the moment, Citizen X is still feeling like he is the one in control, and I have to change that.

From: tmci2f
To: Yung2011cd
Hi Yung. All going fine here. I have an idea for getting ahead of Citizen X. Pls reply to let me know you're ok and I'll tell you where to meet.
Fan

"You called?" Lin says as she walks into Vali's private office. "Something new?"

"Our AI has analyzed all of the metadata on calls to Advocate

Lee and completed source location tracing. One of the calls was from a homestead 50 miles outside the city."

"You're looking at me like that means something," she says.

"The homestead is about 20 miles further down the highway from that rental shack you raided," he points out.

"Wow! I'll get a team together and…"

"I've got a drone on the way to the homestead as we speak, and a police ops team is inbound in a quadrotor," he says. "Our intelligence indicates the homesteader is the chief of local mine security – not a known associate of Zhaofeng. But we'll turn it over anyway, just to be sure."

"It's a lead at least." Lin can see he doesn't look pleased. "What's wrong?"

"It turns out it's impossible for us to put a stop to these press statements by Zhaofeng and his Advocate."

"Can't we just get the Corecasters to play ball again?" she asks. "We got them to sit on the first Sanctioner death."

"And now they are peeved we kept so much else from them. Apparently we've burned our bridges. We may yet regret allowing the so-called 'free press' to be created as part of the Alignment."

She smiles to herself. *Indeed we may, partner of mine.* "It's not like we had much choice. As I recall, after we lost the war the Alignment was more or less a 'take it or leave it' kind of deal."

"You don't need to look so happy about it," he says, dismissing her with a wave of his hand. "Find me that damned cyber."

She walks back out. She'd love to find that damned cyber. She hasn't told Vali about her crazy and confusing late night conversation with him. Based on that call, she can see three possibilities. Fan's 'Citizen X' is the killer. Fan is innocent and Citizen X is some kind of weird cyber stress reaction. Fan is the killer and Citizen X is a fiction.

Citizen X is not her focus right now. As she returns to the desk she pulls out her holo unit and starts going through the report she just received on the mysterious Yung Woon-kwong after considerable pressure by Vali on his superiors to give him access to the covert agent database.

There is, of course, no facial image. She dearly wants to see what the woman looks like, and not just for professional reasons, she freely admits that. The identity was created two years ago, born fully fledged and inserted into the PRC citizen registry on the authority of the High Council. The name of the agent who created the fake ID is not recorded, nor is the agency to which they were attached, which would have been normal practice. That tells her the agency is neither police nor SS. And until recently Lin thought only the police or SS could possibly create a fake ID.

The only other Justice organization Lin is aware of, the one she has newly become aware of, is the one Fan was attached to after the war. The Hunters.

She combs the record for any kind of identifying information at all. Fake birth records, fake school records, fake higher education certificates, fake work references, fake fake fake…wait…*what?*

The birth record showed 'age at birth three months'.

Cyber. She's a *cyber?* Of course, they can't hide that without surgery to hide the small Core link diode between her brows. Much easier just to create a fake identity that fits with her physical appearance. This changes *everything*.

She drifts. If Yung is a cyber, then her ID will be linked to her drift status in her Core cache. No common member of the public or even low-level police officers can access that data, but an SS Expositor can. She scans for cyber caching sessions logged by a Yung Woon-kwong with the registry ID assigned to the agent.

Damn. They've thought of that of course. The cache logs are there, with times, dates and durations for every uplink. But the cache records themselves are empty. No sensory data, no experiential data. Just a code against every entry: *L982-C1A*.

No. Can it be that simple? She recognizes the code by memory, but she runs it anyway.

It's Fan Zhaofeng's registry ID.

Yung Woon-kwong was created by Fan Zhaofeng.

She leans back in her chair, staring up at the ceiling. What in the freaking multiverse is going on?

From: Yung2011cd
To: tmci2f
If you are asking am I sitting in an SS dungeon without fingernails, then no, I'm fine. But worried. Tell me where and when and I'll be there, Fan.
Yung

I read Yung's message then turn off the comms unit. This is my last homestead run. Not because of the risk from surveillance. What surveillance the police and Security Service have up is so full of holes it's laughable. The biggest threat is from Wards and I haven't seen one of them for the last week. It's no wonder we lost the damn war.

My first outgoing text tonight was my last to Advocate Lee. The Corecasters today have been full of news of the manhunt, which is apparently PRC-wide now. My pronouncement of innocence has apparently had a negative effect on the Council; they have just stepped up the pressure to catch me.

I have to say, the police aren't trying too hard, whether by design or laziness. There was one moment today when a car pulled up at the house. I heard it coming up the driveway, quiet and electric, but you can't hide tire noise. One cop got out, and while I retreated to the ceiling crawlspace, she walked around the outside of the house and tried the doors and windows to check if they were locked. She stood and listened, but didn't try to get in, didn't even send a mini-drone in to check the inside of the house. It was a routine, half-hearted check at best, and then she left. I peered out of an air vent as she paused at the door of her vehicle before getting in. It seemed like she was looking right at me, and I could see the small diode between her eyebrows blinking in the daylight before she lowered herself into the car. She was cyber. Do I have cyber sympathizers inside the force?

Lee had been on several Corecast audio channels saying wasn't it curious the Prosecutor didn't seem to want to talk to me, but the SS was searching more intently than ever? Shouldn't they be looking for the real killer? But Cheung played the ball back to him in a separate press conference, saying he looked forward to putting a range of questions to me, *after* I had been arrested.

I sent my final instructions to Lee and then sent a text to Yung to tell her where to meet me. Since the visit today, and given the strange radio-silence of my twin, I don't trust the 'safe house' anymore, so I give Yung a third location to meet me at.

It's a big risk, but I need Yung's help. And I've got a new theory about her voices.

It's becoming a regular and very disruptive experience. They have gathered in the squad ready room again and everyone is looking up at the projection on the wall. Advocate Lee is holding another press briefing.

"Ladies and gentlemen, thank you for coming," Lee says in his slouch hat and uniform, smiling genuinely at the cameras. Lin heard him the previous day on five different channels and just this morning on a breakfast program repeating the line that the charges against Zhaofeng are motivated by institutionalized racial prejudice, not a desire to really find the killer of the Sanctioners.

He continues. "I can report I have been in communication with my client regarding the murders of Sanctioners Huang, M'ele, Seung and Nari." A disorganized hubbub erupts and he waits it out. "Firstly, while he has no intention of turning himself over to the Security Service, he wishes to make some facts clear before they enter the public domain through other means."

The press corps stays silent now.

"The following is a statement of facts according to Mr. Fan Zhaofeng."

Lee leans on the word *facts*.

"With regard to the killing of the Sanctioner M'ele on the 23rd of last month, Mr. Zhaofeng denies any connection, and he has already provided the Security Service with witnesses who have verified he was elsewhere when it occurred."

Questions start to fly, but Lee quietens the journalists. "Please, save all questions for the end of the statement."

He clears his throat, reaches for his holo unit and holds it up. "Ladies and gentlemen, I am about to send you a visual record of the killer of Sanctioner Huang. My client interrupted the killer when he arrived at the scene of the crime. He observed the killer leaving the scene, covered in blood, as you will see. This is a visual record from the cache of my client, Fan Zhaofeng. He has provided this visual record to the police and SS."

Lee holds up his comms unit and drops the visual data to the Corecast crews surrounding him. They immediately uplink it to their networks and it starts playing on the screen. Lin knows what it is – the vision of Fan Zhaofeng's 'Citizen X' walking away from the scene of the crime, his t-shirt stained in blood.

She gave it to Vali after Fan showed it to her. He dismissed it as fake, but they haven't been able to properly explain it.

The room explodes with shouted questions. Lee shouts above them. "Put your questions to the SS! Ask them why they have not released this vision. Ask them how Fan Zhaofeng could have seen the murderer leave the scene of the crime if he is supposed to be the murderer!"

Lin listens a few minutes more, but Lee doesn't add any detail to what he's already said. *OK, Zhaofeng,* she thinks. *You really are going all in to trash the SS, aren't you? How do you think that will help you?*

Sitting in the office where she virtually lives now, Lin watches the projection as a news anchor babbles away. The text scrolling across the bottom of the Corecast, though, says it all.

SANCTIONER DEATHS. SENSATIONAL NEW EVIDENCE. SS ACCUSED AGAIN OF COVERUP. HIGH COUNCIL SILENT. STATE OF EMERGENCY EXTENDED. CURFEW IN PLACE. PUBLIC GATHERINGS BANNED.

She wonders how long it will be before one of the Corecasters' many analysts, human and AI, actually looks at the vision of the man in the bloodied t-shirt and realizes he is identical to Fan Zhaofeng.

Someone flips the projection to another channel. This time it shows a journalist in front of the very building where she is sitting right now, talking straight to holo, more hyperbolic text scrolling:

FREEDOM FIGHTER OR TERRORIST? ACCUSED ZHAOFENG DENIES INVOLVEMENT IN SANCTIONER KILLINGS AND ACCUSES SS OF COVERUP. HIGH COUNCIL ANNOUNCEMENT 7 P.M.

That was new. An announcement? So the High Council was reacting at last.

"State of Emergency, curfews? An announcement?" she asks Vali. "Do you know what that's all about?"

"No, I wasn't warned," he says, watching the screen intently. "We should get down to the investigation center."

At the bottom of the projection she sees a teaser for an upcoming program: "The man they called 'Ghost': exclusive profile of Fan Zhaofeng by the soldiers who served with him during the Energy War. Why the Security Service will never find him."

Well, that didn't take long. Someone in Fan's old unit has sold their story.

Or, someone is adding another log to the fire of Fan Zhaofeng's guilt. She can feel two forces at play, the 'Fan is innocent' campaign being led by Advocate Lee, and the 'Fan the cyber is a killer' campaign being led by…who? Forces inside the SS? Vali himself? The High Council?

"Come, we should go," Vali repeats.

She is about to turn away from the projection when the shot changes to a reporter outside an army barracks sentry gate. Someone turns up the audio volume. "…I'm here at the Huainan barracks of Fan Zhaofeng's former regiment, the 1st Squadron Deep Recon, which as you know is now a civil emergency response unit. I am trying to find a spokesperson to confirm what I have been told by a confidential source, namely that Zhaofeng was Sanctioned as a result of an incident which occurred after the Alignment war."

The anchor leans forward over his desk. "Xiang, your information is that Zhaofeng's Sanction may have been as a result of an attack on a Sanctioner?"

"That's right, Taio," says the pretty journalist, cupping her ear against a light wind blowing her soft brown hair as she quickly looks back over her shoulder toward the army base and then to camera. "Though there is no record of it in civilian criminal proceedings, my sources in Deep Recon are saying that shortly after the war, Zhaofeng was handed over by the police to the SS, summarily tried, and Sanctioned for a violent attack on a Sanctioner."

"Xiang, do you have any other information?" the anchor asks, as if he doesn't already know. "Did he carry out this attack, was he just an accomplice, a passive bystander or what? And what happened to the Sanctioner?"

"I can't find out, Taio, all I've been told is that Zhaofeng was involved in the attack, was caught, and Sanctioned."

"What happens to a person who has already been Sanctioned if they are found guilty of being involved in a second violent crime? Has it ever happened?"

"Well, Taio, it's so rare. As you know, if you've been cauterized, it removes your ability to experience extremes of emotion, making violence almost unthinkable. In any case, the sentence if found guilty is automatic life in prison, or as the prisoners themselves say, 'death in prison'."

"Are you aware of any instance where a Sanction failed, where it didn't take?" the anchor asks. "Is it possible his cauterization simply didn't work?"

"I asked the Dean of Neurology at St. Vincent Hospital, Doctor Li Yau, and he said he is not aware of a single case."

"Interesting. Doesn't that indicate that even if he was guilty before, he could not have committed these latest Sanctioner killings?" the anchor asks. "If he's been Sanctioned himself?"

"One argument says it would be almost impossible for him to have done so, Taio," she says gravely. "But the SS clearly believe that if he has tried to kill a Sanctioner in the past, he could try again."

"Circumstances would seem to indicate he might have found the way, even though he himself denies it?"

"As impossible as it seems, Taio, Zhaofeng's record indicates he's tried before, and we have to consider the possibility that Fan Zhaofeng is the first cyber ever to have killed a Sanctioner, or any human for that matter. And if you accept he's killed one, then perhaps he has indeed killed all four Sanctioners, or provided the information to whoever is doing it."

"These events just keep springing surprises on us. Xiang Mak, live from Huainan Civil Emergency base for holo1 News, thank you."

Lin looks sharply at Vali. "That was it? Fan Zhaofeng was Sanctioned for attacking a Sanctioner? That's a pretty important little detail, Vali! Why didn't you share it?"

"Because I didn't know!" Vali says angrily. "You know the details were being kept from me too. I need to get guidance from the Council on this. We're leaving."

"So how do we do this?"

Yung is sitting with me in the kitchen of the new safe house; an abandoned homestead I came upon on one of my spiral returns, half submerged in drifting sands. I told her to take an intercity bus, buy a ticket for Kunming City on the overnight bus but get off at the third stop and wait for me there. I got to the bus stop early, set up under a camouflage cape behind some rocks, watching for an hour beforehand. She arrived and I waited another thirty minutes, looking for signs of surveillance: Wards, drones, random 'citizens' just hanging around. I did see drones, but they were making a predictable racetrack search, criss-crossing up and down the valley. Whoever had programmed them was an amateur.

Yung was starting to get agitated when I stepped out from behind a tree into the light of a streetlamp and whistled to her. Then we walked across the desert, off road, and back to the buried homestead. Part of my strategy for unsettling Citizen X was to get out of the house he had directed me to. I needed not only to stay off the Security Service's radar, but off his radar too if I could. I wanted to be able to surprise him, not the other way around.

"What did you tell Ben?" I ask Yung.
She looks at me. "I can't lie to Ben," is all she says.
"OK."
"He's worried about *you*. My God, Fan, with these press briefings you've made yourself the PRC's Most Wanted man. Maybe the Most Wanted in Coruscant."
"That's how it has to be," I tell her.
"Why? Ben wants me to talk you into going to the police. Tonight."
"No."
"If the SS get to you first…you'd be better off with the police. At least they have to follow PRC law."
"No."
She sighs. "I knew you wouldn't but I said I'd say it. So now I have."
"OK, so, what I need is some kind of angle on Citizen X. Apart from the fact he looks like me, keeps turning up around dead Sanctioners and leaves me cryptic notes, I've got nothing. But remember your notebook entry, the one that said '*Fan's voice. They deserved to die…*'
"Yes?"
"That wasn't me. But what if it was him? I think you've heard his voice before, so maybe you can hear it again. Something that will give me some leverage. I'm working completely in the dark here. So what do we do to put you into…"
"A psychotic state?"
"A receptive state."
She has the items I'd asked her to bring with her, sitting in front of her. A blank notebook, a stylus, and her two statues from home. "Put *her* over there," she says as she hands me the fat lady. "I'll put

this one over here." She places the tribeswoman figurine on the floor on the other side of her. "I'll sit myself here between them. It helps me focus. Keep me between them and I'll stay pretty calm. Remind me they're there if I get upset."

She smiles. She'd be quite beautiful if she wasn't so bony and had nicer skin. It's a side effect of the drugs. They give her acne. They're also supposed to make her put on weight but they don't.

"I stopped taking my drugs yesterday. Any time now, things are going to start getting weird. I hope you are ready, Fan."

She looks scared.

"Weird is my new normal," I try to reassure her.

"We are going to get more 'boots on the ground'," Vali sighs, turning off his holo unit. He's just returned from some sort of high-level meeting about the State of Emergency, briefing the SS hierarchy on the status of the hunt for Zhaofeng. The High Council broadcast is due in a few hours.

Lin looks up. "What about the raid?"

He stretches his neck, like a fighter after a heavy bout, shaking out some kinks, then turns back toward her. "The mine security chief and his family were home eating macaroni and cheese when the police operations unit broke down their door. The police found nothing except a nice family of four, two little girls, all very scared. They took the father to the local station, but he has nothing to tell them, and they believe him."

Lin takes a sip of coffee and sucks on a sore tooth that doesn't like hot drinks. Mind you, it doesn't like cold drinks either. "So he logged into their uplink node. Directly, or via a proxy?"

"Can't say." Vali leans forward on his desk and lowers his head into his hands, looking forlorn. "We have an AI working on it. It says the confidence interval will be…poor."

She thinks back to an Old Earth wisdom handed down to her in training…'the criminal will always do the laziest thing possible'.

Fan is still in the Province, he has to be. The woman, Yung, had made a brief trip to a holiday rental twenty miles outside the city on the Highway to Kunming City. A call had been placed to Lee from a homestead twenty miles further along the same highway. Was it more likely Fan had set up some complicated telecommunications diversion to make it look like he was still in the area? Or that he had just relocated outside the city and was operating from a base in the desert?

And this was bloody Fan Zhaofeng, 'the Ghost'. She knew that even though the world's biggest manhunt was focused on precisely that patch of desert, it wouldn't faze him a bit.

"How do we rule out the fact he might be hiding right outside the walls?" she asks out loud.

"Drones alone aren't the solution. Too easy to evade. Satellites have predictable paths. I told the Coordination Group we have to bring in more police," he says. "About 200 supported by airborne sensors, to start from that homestead and circle outwards fifty miles – eliminate every house, cave, overhang or rock he could crawl under. If he is out there, that homestead must have been within walking or running distance of where he is hiding."

She frowns. "Unless he is moving," she says, thinking of the first hit on the holiday shack. "Moving further down the highway, toward Kunming City. Getting further away from us every day."

"Kunming has been alerted, they've got surveillance on the highway, their city gates and walls. They might pick him up if that's where he's headed. But I don't think so," Vali says. "He was trained to hide in the heart of his enemies, right under their noses, as you say. He had little fear of being caught."

"If he had no fear during the war, he has even less now," she points out.

What I want, and believe me I know it's a long shot, is for Yung to be able to *hear* Citizen X. Not a conversation, I know that wouldn't be likely, but his voice, to pull some information about him across the membrane between universes, that only she might hear. What gives me hope is that she didn't just hear my voice that one time, she said she hears it all the time.

Why can she hear him? I don't know. Why can she hear anyone? Perhaps it's her connection to me. She's like one of those spiritual mediums humans use to try to communicate with their dead relatives. She's got such strong sympathy for the people in her life that she can connect to their alter egos in other dimensions.

Yeah, I know. Crackpot, right? Except those dimensions exist, and we know less about them than we do about just about anything in our own realm.

Yung is sleeping on a busted sofa. I rearranged the cushions and found an old sheet in a cupboard which I threw over it after brushing off the worst of the sand. I sit on the floor, my back against the wall, watching her. It's ironic, I know that, that after the war I tried to kill a Sanctioner, and now I am trying to stop someone else from killing them.

But things were different then. Let me explain. We have to start at the close of the war.

August 23. Bang in the middle of a shitstorm toward the end of the war. Firebase Halo, just outside the advancing Tatsensui control line. It's a strange war. PRC has been comprehensively outmaneuvered by the Tatsensui strategy of creating drop zones, corralling the population inside them and then using them as agents of influence to subvert morale inside the cities. Most cities have fallen to Tatsensui without a fight, which says a lot about what the average citizen thought of the old PRC government. Could life as a Core world really be worse? Apparently most didn't think so.

Certainly not the cyber population. We lived a life of cybernetic serfdom, using only a fraction of our intellectual potential in support functions in science, mechanics and engineering, or menial labor. And a large part of the human population also saw Tatsensui as liberators, rather than invaders. Ninety percent of them worked in the anti-matter mining industry which supplied all of Coruscant and a dozen other systems with precious raw materials to feed their insatiable energy needs. Yet they made only subsistence wages while corrupt government officials, with luxury compounds on the spaceport moon of Orkutsk, spent most of the year offworld.

It was a world ripe for regime change, and Tatsensui and the Core knew it. PRC had been playing politics with anti-matter supply for years and finally Tatsensui had enough and sent in their fleet.

First thing the PRC army did when the Tatsensui dropships arrived was modify cyber restraint protocols. They didn't trust us enough to rewrite them completely, but any offworlder was classified as an animal so that if they threatened a PRC citizen, we could intervene. Had to intervene. In case you are wondering what it is like to have your moral code rewritten, it's like having one compulsion replaced by another. Maybe your compulsion is chocolate. You just can't resist it – think about chocolate, see chocolate, want chocolate. Then you wake up one day and you find you don't like chocolate anymore. You like pizza. It's something you can't deny. See pizza, want pizza. Chocolate? Who cares about that?

We still weren't allowed to use weapons. But the restraints preventing us from assisting in acts of violence were modified. We could support PRC troops as they went about the business of trying to kill the Tatsensui invaders. I was a scout, and in combat I managed our surveillance systems, or stood watch on the walls as the Tatsensui contact troops would move up.

Their tactics were fluid, dynamic, but the end game was usually the same – they would engage our firebase from several sides with laser rifles light and heavy, then cover the base in IR blanking smoke, blinding and splitting our forces.

Then they would send in the ravens.

Tatsensui tried to minimize the loss of life, but what they did instead was worse for our morale than large-scale casualties. No doubt deliberately so. We called them 'ravens', though I don't know who first gave them that name. Bat-winged stealth drones with claw-like grapples that swept in at the end of a firefight and started snatching troops from inside our firebases.

It is one thing to mourn a dead comrade killed by an enemy laser bolt, another altogether to see him just disappear from beside you. To be fighting with him one moment as he fires at a shadow in the clouds, and then to whirl, see a bat-winged shape swoop out of the smoke before you can even react and lift him off the ground and out of sight.

To where? Tatsensui sent broadcasts from their POW camps to try to convince PRC troops the prisoners were being treated humanely. No one believed it. We called them the MIAs, and not all of them returned after the war. Tatsensui claimed they had been repatriated, but then executed by the PRC government for desertion. PRC officials denied it, desperate to avoid recriminations themselves. Tatsensui produced vision of the executions, which PRC claimed was faked. In the end, the Alignment agreement was signed and people just wanted to move on.

But that day, on Firebase Halo, I found out what happened to the

MIAs.

Resting between scouting patrols, fifteen-year-old Fan Zhaofeng sits on a sandbag on top of a wall inside the wire looking out at…nothing. A fallow field. I keep watch on the road that runs along the wire: a passenger vehicle goes by now and then. The firebase is an old water farm compound with 10-foot-high reinforced ceramic walls. Big enough to house a company of troops and park a few unmanned ground combat vehicles. There is a sandbagged mortar pit in the center clearing loaded with heat-seeking anti-personnel munitions, intended to take out any Tatsensui scouts dumb enough to get within range.

Stretched over our heads, we have the anti-raven nets. In the first few weeks of combat they helped, a little. The ravens would get tangled in them as they attacked. But that also created holes other ravens could get through, and they became adept at using them. It was a classic case of defense and countermeasure, though. The nets stopped the ravens, until the ravens were mounted with shredding lasers to burn them away as they swooped. We put carbon fiber nets up in their place which were resistant to laser fire, and a few weeks later the ravens swooped in, equipped with harmonic weapons that shattered the carbon fiber. It was a game of chess and Tatsensui had a counter for every PRC move.

Such is the power of the Core, of course. It anticipated every move we'd make, and had countermeasures queued up to deal with them. I could see it had its own restraints. It delivered no super weapons to Tatsensui, never advised on offensive strategies. Only defensive strategies or systems. The decision to invade PRC was a human one, the Core never once proposed an action that could deliberately lead to the loss of life. But it gave its masters strategies for non-violent capture, psychological rather than kinetic warfare, and did what it could to achieve the Tatsensui enemy's surrender, rather than their decimation.

That's no comfort on that August day as I see a movement out beyond the walls. I replay the vision. Definitely something, about a thousand yards out. It could be a loose piece of material, blowing in the desert wind. Or it could be a Tatsensui scout, his adaptive camouflage cape unknowingly flapping in the breeze. I check on infrared, but the heat from the desert sand would be masking any body-heat signature.

"We got any drones charged?" I call down to Duong. "I've got a possible contact, zero ten degrees, hundred and ten yards…"

"No, we're out of drones. Just get a sniper laser and take it out." Duong is sitting at the base of the wall, helmet over his eyes to shade his face from the sun, trying to get some sleep.

"Can't do that unless they attack, you know that," I tell him, for about the hundredth time.

"What the hell else is going to happen if that's a Tatsensui scout out there, Fan? Dammit!" He pushes his helmet back. "Now I'm awake, you dumb ass cyber." He climbs up the ladder beside me and takes my scope from me. "Too far for a rifle. I can't make out nothing. If that's a Tatsensui scout, he's about to get a mortar dropped on his ass." He touches a stud mike at his throat. "Fire control, watch station delta. We have a possible hostile in the open at grid…" he lifts the scope again, "…grid reference golf one niner, repeat golf one niner. Fire for effect. Out."

There is a cough from the compound behind us as the mortar fires and the multiple warhead round arcs into the sky toward the small bump in the ground. About two hundred feet over the ground the warhead splits and a dozen heat-seeking anti-personnel missiles spear toward the ground, detonating in a ripple of fire that will kill anything in a football field-sized area around them.

We check the damage assessment data in the scope. One of the anti-personnel missiles reported a heat signature on the ground before it exploded. "Ooh yeah, the Ghost gets another kill!" Duong thumps me on my back.

Here's the thing about compulsions. You see the chocolate. You want the chocolate. But that doesn't make you feel okay about eating it.

"I need your opinion," Vali says as soon as Lin answers her holo. She is at home for dinner for the first night in about two weeks. Home is a little unit in a quiet leafy burb about a million mental miles from sweaty SS officers and talk of murder. Tonight the address by the High Council is due. She could have stayed at work, watched it with everyone else, but actually, she wants to watch it alone. There are too many people at work who know nothing but insist on sharing their uninformed opinions about what the High Council will say. Vali is pleading ignorance. She needs a bit of 'shut up and just listen' tonight.

She's actually got her feet up listening to some music, cat on her lap, with a glass of very expensive cold beer in her hand, as she works her way through a bowl of noodles.

"Actually, Vali," she sighs, "I was looking forward to a night off," she says.

"My sincere apologies," he continues, ignoring her. "We're moving ahead with the ground search from 0600 tomorrow. I want you to meet me out there and help direct the search. If we get a hit, we need to be on the scene and move fast."

Part of her is cheering Fan on, glad he has evaded them for so long already. Another part of her wants him to turn himself in, so that he can have his day in court and prove himself innocent. "Ping me with your location when you get there. I'll join you."

"Bring your sidearm," he warns. "The population outside the walls is apparently getting unsettled. Provincial police are reporting a lot of unrest."

That's interesting. "Unrest? How are they showing it?"

"Passive resistance. A foot patrol of three police had to be rescued after it was ringed by some locals who refused to let them leave the town."

"Really? They wanted the police to stay for protection?"

"No. Apparently they told the police to leave Zhaofeng alone."

She drifts, checking local police reports for similar incidents, and finds hundreds across the Province, thousands across the PRC. "If we go out there tomorrow with a huge police dragnet, it will just make things worse."

"Maybe. But if we don't, we lose our best chance to find him," Vali says. "All our leads indicate he is still close."

She can't argue about that. She'd done a trace on the call Fan had made to her the other night, of course. It had also come from a homestead, about fifty miles out. Nowhere near the hired shack or the call made to Lee, but still within the same radius. It all said he was staying tantalizingly close.

"Then fill the sky with drones, but pull back the police foot patrols," she says.

"It's out of my hands now," Vali says. "Wait for the High Council's Corecast. You'll see why."

She puts the holo unit down on the table and turns her Corecast viewer off mute.

For the tenth time tonight, she reaches over to the small quantum physics book that she lifted from Zhaofeng's library. She's screwed if she ever needs to get it back into a trail of evidence, but that's tomorrow's problem. She flicks to the title page.

"To Fan – in case you want to go back to where it all began, love, Yung."

She looks at it again, running her finger over it. She doesn't know for sure if it is the same Yung he mentioned on his call, the Yung who had rented the shack, but it seems pretty likely.

She looks down at her lap where Fan's metadata printouts lie in a messy sheaf of film pages. There are no outward or inward calls to or from any subscriber called Yung from his holo units, either at work, or at home. She had an AI go through Zhaofeng's uplinked visual records for the last few years and put a name to every single individual he had laid eyes on in all that time.

Not one of them had come back with a hit on the name Yung, but that had been a long shot. If 'Yung' was a cover name, then she would be hiding in plain sight, the AI would only tag her under her real name. She could be any one of hundreds, no, thousands of people in Fan's social or work circle – a friend, a coworker, a client even.

It was frustrating. Someone was helping Fan on the run, someone who probably knew how to find him. And now this book confirmed she existed. But all she had was a fake name and registry data.

It should reassure her that he doesn't have a cache full of love letters or poems addressed to or from 'Yung'. But it must be this person who had put all those ideas about quantum physics into his head. If that was right, it made sense that it was her he turned to now, hiding out somewhere trying to catch his own alter ego. Believing there was some space time quantum black hole crap that explained everything. She probably believed him, or maybe she was the one convincing him. Of course he would go to her.

Love, Yung

Not 'All my love'. No XXX for kisses. It was friendly. It wasn't dripping with lust.

Lin traces her finger over the writing. It is almost a masculine script. A heavy hand on the stylus. Maybe she is a largish lady. Lin wants to think she is like a sister. But she'd have to be big hearted to be a friend to a weirdo like Fan. Or desperate.

And what does that make you, Lin?

Suddenly the music stops, midsong, and text hangs in the air in front of the holo.

STAND BY FOR A BROADCAST FROM THE LEADERSHIP OF THE HIGH COUNCIL.

They might have signed off on a credo of non-violence, but it doesn't stop the High Council from employing good old-fashioned heart-of-darkness fear tactics when it suits them.

The leader of the PRC High Council, Councilor Tai Fok, rarely appears in public, or even on holo. He isn't a President, Chairman, or Minister, he is just referred to as Councilor Fok. But among the citizens of PRC there is no doubt who he is. He's Fok, Leader of the High Council. His deputy is the Tatsensui ambassador to PRC, Karl Lundgren. But the inner workings of the High Council are so obscure to Lin she has no idea what the relationship between the two men is like. Lundgren has never made a public pronouncement of any sort.

The projection is filled with a sort of smoke or mist, the usual device the High Council uses when it holds a broadcast. A shape appears in the mist and walks forward, slowly becoming visible until the mist fades away and Fok is standing there.

You could call it showmanship. Lin calls it propaganda. She tries to remember the last time Fok addressed the whole colony. It had been during a miners' strike. Anti-matter production had ground to a halt as the mine staff had lobbied for a greater share of profits from the anti-matter trade. Fok had broadcast a chilling warning. Because uncontrolled anti-matter production posed a severe risk to the moon's ecology, the High Council had met and agreed the strike would be prospectively regarded as an act of violence against nature, due to the increased risk of a catastrophic event. Unless striking workers returned to their jobs immediately while negotiations continued, they would be charged with breaking the Law and face Sanction or life imprisonment.

The strike had been broken, and the strikers mollified with a 0.001 percent increase in their share of mining profits.

Lin returns her attention to the viewer. "Peace be upon PRC," Fok starts, as always. He is in his fifties, white haired, with a flat pug nose and pockmarked skin that he apparently chooses not to have surgically smoothed. He was virtually unknown before the war; lowly Mayor of the small town of High Canton. Tatsensui had conducted a search for High Council members, using psychosocial profiling, they said, rather than the usual elections. Candidates were identified, sorted and chosen by the Core. The Council members had then elected their spokesperson from among the 12 candidates appointed. Fok was supposed to represent them, not direct them. But still, everyone called him Leader.

"The High Council wishes you peace," he continues. "Peace among mankind. Peace between Man and cyber. Peace between our citizens and our environment. Peace between Man and the natural lifeforms of this unique moon. And the High Council has guaranteed that peace. For years now, this colony has enjoyed a peace such as Coruscant has not seen in centuries, and we have started to heal the wounds of war. We are as free as we have ever been, to live, to work, to love, to raise children and prosper in safety, without the ever-present threat of violence. Violent crime is vanishing from this world. But as you have recently seen, the rise of violence is a persistent threat."

"OK, now we are getting to it," Lin says out loud. "Bring it, Fok."

"I am speaking not just about the violence of human toward human, but now for the first time the violence of cyber against human."

She sits stunned. Did he just say that? Put words to the conspiracy theory that the deranged minority in the population had been muttering about ever since they lost the war? The so-called 'cyber uprising'. The end of humankind on PRC. Deposed from their positions of power. Murdered in their beds by soul-less cybernetic assassins.

Fok's face is stern, but he appears to walk his words back a little. "I am not talking about all cybers. Please rest assured. Our cyber citizens are, and will remain, valued members of PRC society. I am talking about one cyber."

No, don't say it.
Please.

"You know him as Fan Zhaofeng. And this is not the first time he has killed."

"What do they sound like, the voices?" I'm sitting across from Yung on the floor of the empty house. Between us is a bottle of wine. On either side of us are Yung's statuettes. Between us a pile of pages. She's wearing trousers and a black t-shirt, dark hair wound in a pony tail around her neck. Plenty of men would find her attractive, I imagine. She is tall and elfin, and has big dark brown eyes. But she's very skinny and that time she kissed me, it was more like a slap. I guess she's a little more tender with Ben.

She uncrosses her legs and stretches one out. "Whispering, usually. Sometimes they shout. I have to really concentrate to hear the words."

"Are they distinct? Can you pick out particular voices?"

"There is one; I hear it more than others," she says, not looking me in the eyes.

"Can you describe it?" I'm trying to get to it. I've never asked her straight out before.

Now she looks at me. "Sure, I can. It's yours. Alright? The Fan voice."

"You do hear me, then, talking in your head?"

"Not you, your voice. Saying…things you would never say. Telling me things, telling me to do things, sometimes filthy things. It isn't you, just your voice. Like that very first time I heard you. I didn't even know you then, so it wasn't…couldn't have been…you. But it was *your* voice."

"Or his," I tell her.

"Your Citizen X?"

"Him."

"Inside *my* head?"

"Think about it, Yung," I tell her. "You say you think you can hear voices across dimensions, you believe in the possibility of multiple universes, you even said you think we are entangled, you and

I, right?"

She sucks her lip. "Sure, but…"

"What if it isn't you and I who are entangled, but you and him."

"He hates the High Council," she says. "He says it over and over sometimes, how cruel they are, how deceitful, greedy, liars, killers…he hates them more than me. When I take the drugs, it shuts him up. Sometimes that's all that keeps me taking them, not wanting to hear him."

I watch her, staring at the bottle. "Do you hear voices now?"

She looks up at the ceiling, cocks her head as though listening. "Not yet. They'll come. They always do."

"He sounds like me," I tell her. "But he doesn't think like me."

She smiles. "Well duh, since he *isn't* you."

"He isn't me. What happened to those Sanctioners, it was brutal. It was a humiliation as much as a killing. I couldn't kill anyone like that."

She looks at me almost sadly. "Couldn't you? You really think that?"

"I don't think so, no."

Could I not? It is true, I did kill once. I had my code rewritten. My old protocols restored. I accepted Sanction, embraced it even, as a way to make sure I could not do it again.

But I suppose, logically, if I did it once, I could do it again.

Lin sees bright silver flecks in the intense green eyes of Tai Fok and finds a flurry of conflicting emotions racing through her.

Terror at what he will say next, what it could mean for cybers if he feeds the flames of human prejudice, and encourages a sick minority to act on their fears.

Worry for Fan Zhaofeng.

And a strange kind of hope. Because the High Council could be making a very big mistake if they think the citizens of PRC are ready to turn against their cyber companions. Since the Alignment, cybers are no longer slaves. They are workmates, friends, children, brothers and sisters, even lovers, husbands and wives. The Separatists who want to return to the way PRC was, to return cybers to their former place in society, are a fringe group. Noisy, but few.

Lin has never taken them seriously. But if she now counts Vali among them, perhaps they are more dangerous than she realized. Perhaps their radical ideologies have penetrated deeper than she had allowed herself to think. Even to the High Council?

Fok continues. "Fan Zhaofeng was damaged when we found him, and we brought him into our fraternity, healed him and gave him purpose."

"You made him a mercenary!" Lin says out loud, her voice ringing around her empty living room.

"We brought him into our inner sanctum. Gave him access to the most secret workings of the High Council and, above all, we trusted him. And then one day, a little more than two years ago, he turned that trust against us, and he killed his mentor, a Sanctioner who trusted Fan Zhaofeng as his friend."

Lin can't help the analogy that springs to mind – Fok sounds like a Roman bemoaning a slave who has turned against him.

"But did we execute Fan Zhaofeng for this crime? Did we respond in kind, an eye for an eye, as we might have done before the Alignment? No, he was given the same rights as any citizen. A fair trial, in which he pleaded guilty. The choice of Sanction or prison, to which he chose Sanction. Because we believe no citizen is violent at his core, and all citizens deserve the chance to live useful, productive lives, Fan Zhaofeng among them. He was Sanctioned and returned to his life, becoming a valuable member of society and, ironically, working side by side with Sanctioners again, helping the PRC move forward in its efforts to rebuild our society."

No, Lin thinks. *You kept him close to police and Sanctioners so you could keep an eye on him*, she thought. Perhaps to study him. A cyber who broke his protocols and killed a human? He might have seemed like a dangerous bacteria in a lab to them. Could Sanction 'cure' him? Would it even work on a cyber?

If that was the question they'd asked themselves, perhaps now they had their answer.

"I regret to say that, for the first time in our experience, it seems Sanction has not been enough to stop an individual from reoffending. We were too slow to open our eyes to what he had become again, and now four Sanctioners are dead. The concern, of course, is that this flaw in his protocols is not restricted to Fan Zhaofeng alone, but could be inherent in the programming of all cybernetic lifeforms."

Her blood chills. She'd been momentarily lulled into believing this was all about Fan. It isn't at all. Her hand goes to the back of her neck, fingers running across the implant under her skin.

"With immediate effect, we ask all cybernetic citizens to report to their local police station, where they will be registered and transported to temporary accommodations until the question marks around cyber restraint protocols are resolved. All Wards have also been stood down and confined to their pens. I ask our cyber citizens not to be alarmed. Your safety and well-being are guaranteed under the laws of PRC and the Law of the PRC-Tatsensui Alignment. No harm will come to you. Human families with cyber foster children are also requested to deliver their children to the nearest police station, where social services personnel will be on hand to look after them. Again, I want to reassure you no harm will come to your children, and you will be able to stay in touch with them."

Beside his image, a summary of the orders just issued by the High Council starts rolling.

ALL CYBER CITIZENS ARE TO REPORT TO THE NEAREST POLICE STATION WITHIN 48 HOURS.

ALL PARENTS OF CYBER CHILDREN ARE TO DELIVER THEM TO THE NEAREST POLICE STATION WITHIN 48 HOURS.

ANY REFUSAL TO COMPLY WILL BE DEEMED AN ACT OF PRE-EMPTIVE VIOLENCE AND PUNISHABLE UNDER THE LAW.

EXISTING CURFEWS REMAIN IN EFFECT. PUBLIC GATHERINGS ARE PROHIBITED.

Fok gives what he no doubt believes to be a fatherly smile of reassurance. "You will be wondering how long this current emergency is likely to last, and how long your friends and loved ones will be away from you. I can only say, we will work as swiftly as we can to resolve the problem with our cyber citizens' restraint protocols and return your friends, colleagues and loved ones to you." He folds his hands in front of him as the mist begins to roll in again. "Peace be upon PRC."

Lin turns off the holo and sits staring into empty space. She grew up in the pre-Alignment PRC and thought the world would always be as she knew it. Then came the war, and she learned reality could spin 180 degrees in a heartbeat. You can go from rich to starving. From safe to living in constant fear. From human to…whatever she is now. But then things settle into a new routine and you think this, *this* is my reality now.

Until suddenly, it isn't. Outside she hears people shouting and realizes yet another new reality is about to dawn.

22. THE PROTOCOL

Four a.m. I'm still hoping this peek between the dimensions will give me some insight. A clue that will let me catch Citizen X. Grab him, knock him over the head, tie him up and hand him over to Lin. Yung doesn't think of herself as a tuner that can luck into the same channel all the time, though. She says she only ever has conversations when she is deep in her psychosis, and she can't choose whose voice she hears, or how she will react. She might yell at them to stop, go away, or start arguing with them. Her doctors have shown her a video of herself in that state, and it scared her. It wasn't quantum science at work. It was insanity. But she rationalizes that of course she goes insane, the voices are overwhelming her. They would make anyone insane.

"I can't sleep, Zhaofeng," she says from the sofa. "Come here and lie with me."

I consider this and conclude it would be a bad idea. "No, I'm fine here, thanks."

She sounds put out. "I'm not thinking about you. I'm thinking about me…I'm a little scared, Fan, don't be selfish."

"I'll make you a cup of tea," I tell her, getting up from the chair.

She turns her back to me on the sofa, wraps her arms around the thin sheet she is lying under. "Don't do me any favors."

I go and make the tea anyway. I've got a small battery element and it takes a good five minutes to boil a cup of water. She's still awake when I go back in, and I sit on the edge of the sofa, putting my hand on her shoulder. "Tea," I tell her softly.

With a grunt she levers herself into a sitting position and takes the cup, holding it in her hands to warm them. They are shaking a little, but maybe it's the cool night.

"Have you got any new theories about why you can hear voices from the multiverse?" I ask her, trying to get past her grumpiness. Just something to talk about, but it's also something I've been wondering. Like, why Yung? Why should she hear things we others can't? If science can explain what she is hearing, it should also be able to explain why.

She sips carefully. "What?"

"I mean, why can you hear these voices, and people like me, we can't?"

"Because I'm *crazy*, Fan," she says tartly.

"No, really."

She sighs. "OK. Maybe it's just something I've learned to listen for. And become good at. Maybe you could do it too. Probably you have heard them, and you don't even realize it."

"I've heard them?"

She rests the tin cup on her knee. "Look, you know we live in four dimensions, right?"

"No, three." I count them off on my finger. "Up, down, sideways…"

She holds up a fourth finger. "And *time*…it's so obvious you've gone off-Core, Zhaofeng. It's like you had an IQ amputation."

I actually hadn't forgotten Einstein's fourth dimension, I just don't regard myself as living in it any more than I regard myself to be living in a vacuum just because our moon flies through space. "Right, yeah, time."

"So there are possibly other universes, separated from us by just the tick of a clock, where a different Fan is living a different life, or was never born. The science and the math are irrefutable, but the membrane between all of these worlds is like a sea we cannot cross. We know there is land on the other side. We've got proof. We just can't reach it."

"If these other universes are so close, how come we can't perceive them?" I ask.

She laughs. "Fan, we are a school of fish swimming in a pond, who think that the entire universe is the pond they are swimming in. There is up, down, forward and back. Below us the world ends in mud, and above it ends with that flat surface of the water that we can't ever imagine going through. But up there is a whole other world of people, birds, buildings, drones, satellites and space ships. Right above us, and we will never see it, can't even imagine it."

"Ah, but if you are standing above the pond, you can see the fish," I point out to her. "There must be a way to see through the membrane."

"Exactly," she says vehemently. "And somewhere, someone is throwing rocks in the pond trying to get the stupid fish to react. A rock goes flying by us and we think, 'holy crap, where did that come from?' but most of us just go back to swimming around and forget about the rock. But some of us, like me, we notice the rocks and we think to ourselves, hey, where *did* that come from? And we start watching and listening for more rocks. And the more we listen, the more we hear…and maybe someone in that other universe realizes that, hey, there is a fish down there who has noticed us, and they start throwing more rocks, but they're aiming them *at me* now…and suddenly the sky is raining rocks."

"That's quite a metaphor," I tell her.

"You're a fish too," she tells me. "Citizen X walks into that house behind you, and you see two of you in the mirror. Bam. You just got hit by a rock. Part of you wants to think it was just a hallucination, and there are people telling you it was. But you realized it wasn't. You didn't just keep on swimming, you started thinking."

"It was pretty hard to ignore. His hand on my shoulder."

"No. That's where you're wrong. People ignore that sort of stuff all the time! I bet most people would have just put it down to shock. They would have shrugged it off. *I was upset, there can't have been another 'me' there, that's crazy.* Put it in the back of their mind and probably never think about it again. But you don't shock easily, do you, Fan? So when the rock came sailing past you, you saw the rock."

After that, we do doze off a little. Me in my chair, Yung in her sofa.

At six a.m. I wake to see her sitting on the floor between her two statuettes, scribbling in a notebook. I grab it from her, hand her another one. She looks at me, irritated, but just keeps writing. I read what she's written in the book I took:

Well she finally came down off that cloud

You can keep your Kerouac books, I don't need them where I'm going

It's more than a haircut, I was going to dye it but I got it cut off instead. Is it too much?

There is a pattern to it. Find it.

If you want to do something about this, you're going to have to get involved – Fan

I've no control, it's always been a problem, it's who I am

I said I love you baby, isn't that enough – Ben

Woman crying, muttering in another language

She heard Fan! Not that the fragment makes any sense. Curious, though. It has just occurred to me most of what she hears is in standard Cantonese. How likely is that? Or is it a loophole in her belief system? Why would the voices of the multiverse be mostly in standard Cantonese? Of course it could be she is only in contact with the universes closest to her own, and in most of those she would still be living in a Cantonese-speaking society, I guess. It's too much for me to process, but it does make me uneasy. The unlikelihood of it. I read on…

I'm in the court next week, pleading my case, but they're obsessing, who knows, you know?

We are the blank cheque generation man, this is 79 and it's time to go for something radically different

What is guilt? Is a single raindrop guilty of the flood? – Fan

I saw it in the back of a copy of Private Eye. I'm going to get dressed now, you coming or not?

To do nothing as your children are persecuted, is that strength or weakness? – Fan.

Another couple of fragments, again, no connection. And why are the sentences all snippets? Why does she never hear full conversations? That makes them more credible to me somehow. I think of it like rocks skimming a pond and only breaking through now and then to be heard. If she was hearing whole conversations it would seem fake. But there is nothing about these snippets that helps. They really are random noise. I read some more…

I'm losing that inner voice, the one I used to hear before I would make up my mind

Your secret's safe with me, there is no one else I want to be with

Just stay until dawn – Ben

Talking, sounds like Japanese, then 'Get the door will you?'

You should hear yourself, just listen to yourself, you say the same thing again and again – Fan

I walk a thin line in tattered shoes – Fan

I flip back through the pages. I can see she has tried to work out whether there is a rhythm to the noise. Using a red pen, she has been back through the pages and circled sentences which, if you put them together, could possibly be a conversation. She has also circled all the sentences which are commands or requests. There is a lot of swearing.

Get in touch with Gary!

We can hesitate in multiple dimensions as long as we act in one – Fan

You want him I know you want him that way, and now you are going to die bitch so kneel

I need you to go to 53 Briar Place and find out what is happening. I haven't heard nothing

They call it violence, I call it love – Fan

Get off your butt you lazy cow and get a job

Two more snippets with my name against them. Two more disconnected sentences. I reach out and put a hand on her shoulder. I hadn't really thought about how terrible this could be for her. In this state, she has a kind of unfocused look, but she looks at me suddenly, like she is just realizing I'm there for the first time. "Get me some food, I'm hungry," she says, and returns to writing.

Lin called Vali straight after the Corecast by Fok.

"Do I need to turn myself in?"

"What? No. Why would you?"

"My cybernetics."

"Are they coded with any restraint protocols?"

"No."

"Then why are you even asking me? The world is going to go crazy tomorrow and we still have a search to coordinate. Get some sleep, I'll see you tomorrow."

"Are we going to talk about what Fok said? He confirmed Zhaofeng has killed a Sanctioner before, that's why he was Sanctioned."

"That changes nothing. It just puts a name to the crime. And increases the urgency to find him before he does it again."

"Why, Vali? Why did they put him back into society? Why not lock him away forever?"

"Because of your damn Law," he says, nearly shouting over the holo at her. "Because the Core loves its children too much and demands they be given the same rights as everyone else even if they are murderers! Because under the Alignment, PRC can't do what's in our best interests until it becomes a damn State emergency. Shall I go on?"

His passion is compelling. But she has her own ideas about how to help him, and Fan.

"You don't need me out on the search line. You need me

following up on what Fok revealed. We know what Zhaofeng did now. We need to know *why* he did it."

Vali looks as though he is about to argue, but then he scratches his jaw. "You may be right. Start with the Advocate. We have been too gentle with him for too long."

After quickly drifting to update her understanding of the situation outside her own small world, Lin finds Advocate Lee holed up in a hotel in a low-rent part of the city near the outer walls. Which makes sense, because she guesses he is paying expenses himself. She decides to cold call him and after triangulating his comms data and then calling the hotel management to make sure he is in, she turns up at his door about 1 p.m. It is a little hotel with ten guest rooms and a common room. She finds him alone in the common room watching the 1 p.m. news Corecast. He's in his Advocate's uniform, but without his wig he appears a lot less buttoned down than she's seen him on camera.

"Anything interesting?" she asks, leaning against the doorway.

He looks up at her, maybe thinking she's another one of the guests. "Just more of the same," he smiles. "Rumor and gossip about the Sanctioner murders, followed by panic and lies about the internment of the cybers."

She likes him instantly. He's about the right age to be her father. On holo he comes across like he's really concerned about Fan, and maybe he is. She walks over and holds out her hand. "I'm Expositor Lin Ming," she says. He looks dubious, so she sighs, reaching into her pocket for her badge.

He stops smiling, but shakes her hand. "Then I guess you know who I am," he says. "How can I help you?"

She sits beside him on a grandmotherly beige sofa. "You're trying to represent the interests of Fan Zhaofeng," she tells him. "Believe it or not, I happen to think I am too, even though my job is to arrest him."

"I'm not in real-time contact with Zhaofeng," Lee says. He's starting to sound annoyed. "I already told Cheung that. You won't find him through me, though I'm sure you've already tried tracing his communications."

She pulls a page of print from her back pocket and hands it to him. "At 3 o'clock this afternoon Prosecutor Cheung is going to hold his own little press conference at Security Service headquarters parading an eyewitness who saw Zhaofeng at the scene of the second murder. He'll directly contradict what you said about Zhaofeng having an alibi for that killing. I thought you might appreciate a little advance notice, to get yourself prepared."

He scans the document. "This...their witness...it says he saw someone who *looked like* Zhaofeng at the scene. The Security Service know there are other witnesses...Zhaofeng has rock-solid alibis."

"I know, but I also know this. This isn't like any other crime to the SS. They get pretty stirred up about violence, you know that. But for violence between humans, they respect processes. The accused gets interviewed, arraigned, and judged. This is different. Four Sanctioners are dead at the hand of a Sanctioned cyber who has killed before. There is no process for that. Cheung knows it, so he's put the blame for all the killings on Zhaofeng. All Zhaofeng's nice alibis will be irrelevant, because once the SS get him, no one will ever see him again."

She listens to herself saying what the miner Duong had told her. What Zhaofeng had told her. And hearing the bile in Vali's voice last night, she now believed it too.

Lee looks closely at her. "Why are you telling me this?"

"Because I need something from you. In return, I'm offering you inside information on the Security Service investigation."

"I don't think that's wise," Lee says, looking again at the page.

"OK, another gesture of faith," Lin says, leaning forward. "The witness is an eight-year-old kid who saw Zhaofeng at the second killing. That kid will stand there, with his apple pie soccer mum standing right behind him, and tell the world that before anyone found that dead Sanctioner, Fan Zhaofeng asked him for directions to the scene. The kid has been coached to say he is worried for the future of all humankind and he is going to ask Zhaofeng to give himself up, for the sake of all the world's children." She stares at Lee. "Yeah, it's pathetic, it's cynical, but who isn't going to listen to an eight-year-old boy? Cheung is a pro at this sort of thing. Zhaofeng's word against that of an innocent child?"

"To what end? The search for Zhaofeng has become a sideshow now." He points at the holo he is watching, showing a mob marching down a street. "It is chaos outside, as you must know all too well."

"Organized chaos, yes," she tells him and sits down. "Let me paint you the picture your holo isn't showing. On one side, we have the Separatists. They are a minority, but from what I've seen in the last few days, a significant number of police, SS and maybe even High Council members are among them. On the other hand, you have the Cyber Rights Movement, which is radically opposed to the High Council edict from yesterday and is planning to resist it. They are setting up sanctuaries for cybers, escape routes, safe houses, legal and financial support, everything they can, short of violence."

"Yes, I've been contacted," he admits. "Of course."

"The CRM means well, but it is a movement without leadership, without a front figure. It needs someone it can rally around."

"Zhaofeng?"

"That's the High Council's fear. They have decided that the best way to stop the people making Zhaofeng into some sort of Sanctioner-slaying hero is to paint him as a demon. You've got about two hours to work out how to play that."

Lee leans back in his chair and stares blankly at the holo viewer, taking in what she has told him. He uses a good few minutes on it. Hands behind his head, looking up at the wall. Then he looks at her again. "OK, what do you want to know?"

Firebase Halo, August 23, outside the Tatsensui control line. We get word that a Tatsensui dropship has entered orbit overhead. Our own self-defense fleet has long since been destroyed, so it can park itself up there with impunity, sensors focused on our compound, sending data to the troops that must even now be moving in on us.

The scout we killed had already done his job. The sheer pointlessness of his death troubles me. It's like a toothache.

I've uplinked what followed, but deliberately deleted it from my cache afterward. I don't want to relive it. I can't delete my biological memory though, but thankfully it grows more dull as time progresses. Once the Tatsensui attack started, I was put on medical duty. They were engaging with energy weapons to drive us off the walls and down into the compound where their blanketing smoke would be more effective. I moved to wherever I heard a call of 'Medic!' On the ground, or hanging from the scaffolding on the walls, would be a laser-shot soldier, burned and usually dying. I would stabilize them, carry them to the quickly overwhelmed aid station and then go back to the walls.

Then the smoke dropped. It filled the compound like a thick gel. We had huge fans inside the compound and as a siren started wailing, they began blowing with a roar like a desert storm to try to clear the smoke. In the early war they had been somewhat effective, but the enemy had changed the composition of the smoke and it didn't disperse as easily anymore. We pulled our masks from around our throats and jammed them over our faces. In addition to hiding IR signatures, the smoke was a neural antagonist too, and if you breathed it in, it would paralyze you to make you easier prey for the ravens.

One second I was kneeling over a fallen soldier, trying to stem the flow of blood from his abdomen. Laser wounds usually cauterized the flesh as the bolt cut through, so there wasn't much blood, but this guy had taken a grazing wound that had opened an artery in his leg. I was soaked in his blood. I sensed a shadow in the fog above me, felt a sharp pain in my shoulder as the raven dug its claws into the flesh of my shoulder, and then I was hauled up and out of the compound. There must have been a neural agent in the drone's claws too, because as the chaos of the battle receded below me I passed out.

I woke in a hospital. The injuries to my shoulder were superficial and I was soon moved to a camp for 'processing'. I didn't need to tell my interrogators what unit I served in, or what my specialist designation was; they already knew.

My interrogator was a cyber in her twenties, a deliberate decision no doubt intended to make me sympathetic. The small diode between her brows blinked blue as she drifted to access my data. It was the first time I'd seen a Core-chained cyber up close. The light on her forehead was like a small jewel. I thought it looked quite beautiful.

"You are Fan Zhaofeng, deep recon scout with the New Guangzhou 1st Squadron Special Operations unit. You don't have to reply." She smiled. "You've been flagged for special duties."

"So you aren't going to terminate me and roll me into a cave in the desert?" I didn't really believe the stories, but you couldn't be sure.

"No, your skills are too valuable. You'll be transferred to a training facility where you'll meet the members of your new unit."

"I can't serve Tatsensui," I tell her. Not defiantly, but factually. "My restraint protocols…"

"We know. And when they reprogrammed your restraints, they planted a 'mindbomb'. A small code string that means any attempt to try to alter your restraints again will result in brain death."

"I didn't know that."

"The Core will find a way around it, eventually. When it does, you'll be offered the opportunity to Core-chain and…"

"It's voluntary?"

"Of course. If you agree, you will be given access to unlimited bandwidth, the knowledge of entire star systems, and the opportunity to earn an independent living as a full member of the bandwidth economy."

"What's the catch? Why wouldn't every cyber on PRC sign up for that?"

She lifts a finger and places it next to the diode between her brows. "This has a price. No Core-chained cyber can live beyond thirty years. The Core uses its cyber agents for learning and evolution. You will be an integral part of society, uplinking everything you sense, do and learn to the Core every day of your life, but you will be allowed to keep your innermost memories and thoughts to yourself, for thirty years. At the end of that time, you will make a full uplink of everything you've flagged private so that nothing is lost, and you will transition."

"Transition? I'll die, you mean."

"No, you will be one with the Core for eternity. You will still be aware."

"Aware, but not alive?"

"In a biological sense, no." She lowers her finger and folds her hands in front of her. "You are fifteen, Fan. You would still have fifteen years of life, love and learning ahead of you. And then you would join us in the Core."

"Us?"

"I have five years left until I transition. I don't expect you to believe this, but I look forward to it with every fiber of my being." She looks around the interrogation room. "This life has not been everything I hoped."

It was too much to process right there and then, so I parked it. "I gather moving to this new special unit is *not* voluntary?"

"No. We are still at war and you are our prisoner. But we won't be asking you to serve Tatsensui. The unit will only be activated once the war is over and an armistice signed. You will still be serving the PRC. The *new* government of PRC."

This provokes no feelings of anger or resentment in me, and so I conclude it's been designed to be in compliance with my current restraint protocols. Very clever. If you can't change the code to fit the world, you can always manipulate reality around it to make the world fit the code.

Two days later I was shipped out to my new unit. Two months later the war ended and the Articles of Alignment were signed. The High Council was anointed as the new government of PRC. Six months later I got my diode and signed on to the Core. By then, the Core had found a workaround to restore normal restraint protocols to the PRC cyber population without triggering the army's mindbomb.

But it didn't restore mine.

It needed me in exactly the state it had found me. Because by then, I was a fully operational Hunter.

"I want to know," Lin says to Advocate Lee, "what *you* know about why Fan Zhaofeng was Sanctioned."

"I thought the Leader did a pretty good job of explaining that last night."

"He said the minimum needed to paint Zhaofeng as a violent criminal. I'd like you to fill in the gaps. Start by walking me through his crime."

"That's suppressed. It's a crime for me to reveal it."

"I'm SS."

"And this could be a sad attempt by the SS to entrap me, by tricking me into breaking a suppression order."

"I probably broke about ten laws myself giving you that information," Lin says, pointing to the page in his hand. "I'd say on balance I'm more exposed than you right now."

He folds the page and puts it in his pocket before indicating she should sit. "Fan Zhaofeng was put in a situation which conflicted with his restraint protocols. He resolved it by killing the Sanctioner he was working with."

"Not possible," she says. "A cyber's standard restraint protocols prevent them doing harm to any other citizen, even to protect the life of someone under attack. Even if he'd been witness to a Sanctioner about to commit a murder, he couldn't intervene. His only response could have been passive – to live link his sensory feed to the Core so that the murder and identity of the murderer were documented."

"The key word here is 'standard restraint protocols'," Lee tells her. "Fan Zhaofeng's restraint protocols, like the restraint protocols of all cyber Hunters, had not been altered since the war. He was able to act with a much greater degree of…individual initiative."

"Is there a record of these events?"

"Perhaps. Even as his defense lawyer I was never given access to it. I was told it wasn't material, since Zhaofeng had in any case pleaded guilty."

"Did he tell you what happened?"

"Yes, and I believe him. Like I said, he'd already confessed and had no reason to lie to me." He takes a deep breath. "It happened in a split second. He'd tracked down and arrested an alleged violent criminal. A Provincial politician accused of the attempted murder of a member of the High Council. Standard procedure for high value targets was for him to call in a Sanctioner to confirm the identity of the suspect and read the charges to him. He'd arrive in the company of the police, and the suspect would then be taken away for trial."

"But this time standard procedure wasn't followed?"

"No. The Sanctioner arrived in the company of a Ward, but no police."

Lin frowns. "Wards are only allocated to members of the SS or deployed under their control."

"Apparently, you are not fully informed. This Sanctioner arrived in the company of a Ward. And he was armed with a laser pistol. He ordered Zhaofeng to leave."

"He didn't."

"He felt something was wrong. There had never been a deviation from procedure before. He'd not been briefed about new procedures. He left, but circled back so he could observe without the Ward detecting him. As he watched, the Sanctioner pronounced the suspect guilty by order of the High Council, sentence of death to be executed immediately."

"There are no arbitrary executions on PRC!"

"Just as there are no MIAs?" Lee mocks her. "Zhaofeng's wartime protocols allowed him to act to protect the lives of all PRC citizens. He ran in front of the suspect to shield him."

"My God."

"Gets worse. At a signal from the Sanctioner, the Ward hit Zhaofeng with a neural blast. Apparently the Sanctioner didn't know cyber Hunters were hardened against neural disruption. But Zhaofeng faked it and went down, like he'd been knocked out. They turned their attention back to the suspect, and Zhaofeng rolled out, took out the Ward and then killed the Sanctioner. Snapped both their necks."

"How could that be compatible even with his wartime protocols? Weren't cybers during the war restrained from harming PRC citizens?"

"You have to remember cybers process scenarios at quantum speeds. Zhaofeng had summed up the situation and concluded the Sanctioner was breaking the Law. Criminals who break the Law have their citizenship stripped from them. At the moment the Sanctioner raised his weapon and sighted on the suspect, Zhaofeng judged he was about to break the Law and was de facto no longer a PRC citizen. His wartime protocols allowed him to defend PRC citizens using any necessary means, including violence."

"Irony much?" Lin says, whistling under her breath. "The High Council creates an army of ninja assassins who are still programmed with loose wartime restraints, and one of their attack dogs turns on them. And then what, he just waits around for the police to arrest him?"

"He uplinked the full sensory record of the event to the Core and called the police himself. There was nothing the High Council could do to cover it up once he uplinked it. They denied the Sanctioner had been acting on their authority, made up some baloney about him having a personal grudge against the accused."

"He'd never have been given a Ward bodyguard unless someone high up the food chain had authorized it."

"What I thought too. Anyway, they had to put Zhaofeng on trial, there was no option. They suppressed it, though, to make sure it never got out. He pleaded guilty, chose Sanction and was released into society. I have half expected to hear another Hunter had been sent after him, but for whatever reason, they let him be. I suspect the Core let it be known it would be keeping a close eye on him and that gave him a certain level of protection."

She bites her lip, thinking hard. "What about his restraint protocols? He's no longer a Hunter. Were his normal protocols restored before he was released?"

"Now that's a good question, Expositor," Lee says. "Given recent events, it could be very important to find out. I don't know, but I'll tell you who might."

23. THE CODE

It's about 6 p.m. I'm eating some canned condensed soup mixed with water from my condenser. I didn't bother to heat it – it tastes like crap, warm or cold, if you ask me.

Across the valley where the highway cuts across the desert I can see the headlights of passing cars, but I've stopped worrying too much. There have been four patrols come past, but we've been ready each time. I have some simple IR alarms set up around the perimeter now to warn me in case police swing by. And I'm not outside, so their drones are useless to them.

Yung wrote furiously for two days, having conversations with herself, getting deeper and deeper into her psychosis. She filled three journals with scribblings. Two days was how long I agreed we would let her stay under, so I start giving her medication in her juice when she's thirsty. After another day, I can see it's starting to work. She's sleeping more, talking less.

On the evening of the third day, I drop off to sleep too. When I wake she's still lying on the floor, on her side, but her eyes are open and she's looking at me. I look at my watch. We slept six hours.

I sit up from the sofa and stretch. "Are you back?"

She straightens her legs. "Back, hungry, and I have to pee. I hope *you* got something," she remarks as she stands and stretches. "Because I can't remember squat."

I hold up the three journals. "Well, I've only been through them once, but there's not much."

She laughs. "You are hopeless. Most people would have at least lied a little bit to make me feel like this wasn't just a waste of time."

I look down at the journal. "Well, like I said, I haven't been through them properly yet."

"Too late," she says, heading toward the kitchen. "That was a fail, Fan. Let me look." She grabs the notebooks from me and takes her two statues with her for protection, so I guess that's a sign she's not completely comfortable yet.

When she gets back she sets about boiling water for some noodles, and then sits next to me on the sofa, transcribing the lines she's attributed to me from her journals.

If you want to do something about this, you're going to have to get involved
What is guilt? Is a single raindrop guilty of the flood?

To do nothing as your children are persecuted, is that strength or weakness?
There is a pattern to it. Find it
I walk a thin line in tattered shoes
We can hesitate in multiple dimensions as long as we act in one
They call it violence, I call it love

"There's plenty of stuff here in your voice…what about that line?" she asks, pointing at the page, the words in her spidery writing…

There is a pattern to it. Find it

"That's an interesting one," I agree. "Was there any more…anything else at all like it?"

She pages through the journals. "Nope, sorry. And I don't remember it."

"OK."

She puts a hand on my knee. "But it *was* your voice, I marked that pretty clearly."

There is a pattern. Find it. "A pattern? To the killings?"

She puts her head in her hands, thinking. "Well, they were all in New Guangzhou. Where you live."

"Lived. True."

"Did you ever wonder about that? I mean, assuming this twin of yours can flit between dimensions, he isn't bound by time and space. If he's trying to incite a revolution like he says, he would get a much bigger impact spreading these killings out all over the moon. One or two in every Province would really stir things up, wouldn't it?"

I think about this. "I guess. If you want to start a revolution, it would help if the atrocities were global."

"Right, but they're not. So maybe the reason it's all happening here is that it needs to be about you. He's *your* twin, right?"

"Hmm."

"So why you?"

"I've considered that. Someone wants a scapegoat," I remark. I look down at myself, half starved, dirty, at least three days without a shower. "You have to admit I fit the bill." Yung isn't looking much better. "You look pretty bad too," I tell her. "You need a wash."

Without even hesitating she leans across and slaps me, right across the face. I try to grab her hand in case she does it again but she stands and stalks out of the living room. "Screw you, Zhaofeng. Work it out for yourself."

I hear the back door banging shut and figure she's gone out to the water tank to wash. I look around and see she took her statues with her. After a while I realize she isn't coming back.

"Ladies and gentlemen, thank you for coming on such short notice." Advocate Lee smiles at the camera and, back in the basement investigation center, Lin smiles too. Like the Corecast crews had made a special effort to be on the steps outside Security Service headquarters just for this…and not because they were already there getting ready for Cheung's press conference, which kicks off in about 20 minutes.

Lin leans back in her chair as the buzz settles and people stop to look up at the projection. The basement is nearly empty today though, with most of the officers on the squad out in the field supporting the effort to locate Fan.

Lin has to give Lee credit. He's just walked in and stolen Cheung's press conference out from under him. Cheeky. "Oooh, the Chief Prosecutor is going to be royally pissed off at you, Advocate," Lin says out loud.

"…I'm here today with a group of colleagues and friends of Mr. Zhaofeng who have all provided sworn statements…" Lee continues as he waves a bunch of blue official pages over his head, "…sworn statements that they were with Fan Zhaofeng at the time the killings of Sanctioners Huang and M'ele took place, so he could not possibly have committed those crimes."

Lin recognizes some of Zhaofeng's coworkers and people from his chess club standing defiantly behind Lee. Something is building, she can sense that, if these people are willing to come out publicly in defense of Zhaofeng. It's not his natural charisma, that's for sure. The Sanction had given him a charisma cauterization. It's bigger than that. Bigger than Zhaofeng himself. These people aren't here for Fan, they are here against the High Council.

Above the shouted questions from the reporters one in particular comes through. "What about the claim he has killed before? He's already been Sanctioned!"

"Sorry, can I have a bit of quiet, please? Mr. Zhaofeng maintains his innocence. The Security Service and High Council can say whatever they like, fabricate whatever evidence they wish. We will fight it with the truth."

The same reporter shouts again. "Why doesn't Fan Zhaofeng hand himself in? What is he afraid of?"

"What do you think?" Lee asks. "He is being persecuted by no less than the High Council itself. Who among you really believes a cyber could kill one Sanctioner, let alone five?"

More shouted questions but Lee holds up his hand. "No matter what dirty tricks the Prosecutor General has up his sleeve to make my client look guilty, no matter what type of spin they try to put on the facts of this case, no matter how many fake witnesses or fake reports they can dig up, I repeat: Fan Zhaofeng is innocent."

The Corecast cuts back to the studio anchors who start babbling about a new turn in the Sanctioner killings.

Lin likes Lee. With his dark robes and jauntily tilted wig he literally stinks of integrity. He's done a great job to make it seem like there is some kind of grand conspiracy against Fan Zhaofeng. If Cheung rolls out his child witness now, it will just look staged. Which it is.

Lin knows Cheung, though. It will be 'gloves off' after this latest move by Lee, if it wasn't already. She doesn't have long to wait, Lee has barely left the building before the projection shows Cheung storming into the press center at Security Service headquarters, several floors above her, looking flushed and angry.

It's going to get really ugly now, Fan, she mutters to herself. *I hope you are up for this.*

Cheung places a holo of his notes on the podium in front of him, and the journalists are hushed. Lin notices the young boy is nowhere in sight, so that play has been abandoned. Instead, from a door behind the stage the Security Service Commissioner, Principal Expositor Adeline Hin-kwong, and a couple of her staff come into the room and stand behind Cheung. Notably, there is not a cyber in sight.

"I am going to read a prepared statement," Cheung says. "Then the SS Commissioner will speak. There will be no time for questions."

He coughs to clear his throat. "Ah, like you, we have heard the claims by the fugitive Fan Zhaofeng that he is innocent. We have requested him to come forward to have his innocence tested. Unfortunately he has not complied and we now need to warn Mr.

Zhaofeng that is no longer an option. Ladies and gentlemen, the Commissioner."

She is a willowy woman in her fifties, Commissioner Hin-kwong. Lin has seen her a few times during different investigations and found her to be a sharp, no nonsense, born police officer. She was a natural to lead the SS in New Guangzhou when the office was established and her suitability for the role has not been challenged since. She has grey-white hair tied back in a bun, and moves a wisp of it off the shoulder of her uniform before she steps up to the podium and speaks.

"Thank you, Prosecutor," she says, her voice calm and confident. "I must regret to announce that under the terms of the State of Emergency, and as allowed in the Law under exceptional circumstances, the High Council has decreed that Mr. Fan Zhaofeng has now been tried and found guilty in absentia of the most recent killings of four Sanctioners, and therefore, his freedom is forfeit. All agents of the State and Federal Police, and of the PRC Security Service, are therefore required to apprehend Mr. Fan Zhaofeng forthwith, and on his capture to hand him over to representatives of the High Council immediately for imprisonment for the term of his natural life. This judgment has been given the assent of the High Council. I must warn that any citizen giving aid or comfort to Mr. Zhaofeng will also be held to account under the Law. That is all."

Well, now we know how deeply the Separatists have penetrated the justice system, Lin thinks. She looks around her as the people in the basement return to the business of catching Fan Zhaofeng. *All the way to the top.*

She turns away from the wall projection as well. She also has work to do, chasing down the lead Lee has given her that might finally tell her whether Fan Zhaofeng is still capable of murder.

I hear about the two press conferences on the Comcaster. After the Leader's revelation about the reason for my Sanction and announcement of the planetary-wide persecution of cybers, Lee did a good job trying to head off the inevitable. Since declaring me public enemy number 1, the Council was always going to have to put me away. I can't really blame them. I've killed a Sanctioner before, and now they think that despite my cauterization, I am killing them again. Of course they want me gone.

Rounding up every cyber on PRC was a move I hadn't expected, though. The logic given by the Leader doesn't really hold water, so there is something more behind it. Partly it's expediency, of course. A State of Emergency provoked by the alleged crimes of a cyber? What better time to execute a longstanding plan to reverse the gains of the Cyber Rights Movement and put cybers back in their place, at the bottom of the food chain?

Judging by the news reports of civil unrest across the colony, the putsch by the Separatists may have overreached. But that is their problem, not mine.

How is Lin taking all of these developments, I wonder?

I remembered the look in her eyes as she told me to run. It was as close to love as I have ever seen in a woman's eyes.

You know those holocasts where the boy and the girl protagonists go through hell together and maybe they didn't get along at the start of the story, but by the end of it they've been through so much that you just know they're going to end up together? I saw Lin and me like that for a while. But it isn't going to end that way.

I don't care what Advocate Lee does from now on. Last night I made a run to a far-off homestead, dodging drones and police patrols, and sent him a text from a hijacked node. "You have my full confidence, please continue." I'd hoped it might give Lee a bit more airtime to cement his fame and fortune. He can take it any direction he wants to now.

With Yung gone, I am truly on my own. I hoped I could subvert Citizen X's plan but it seems nothing I do can draw him out into the open again. Could he have foreseen it all? The State of Emergency, the ingathering of the colony's cybers, the vigilantes, the protests and resistance? He can move across the multiverse, see all the possibilities. Could he have foreseen these events, on this world?

But he's not omnipotent, not omniscient, he admitted that. In his fallibility, I find hope.

I went back to Yung's notebooks, looking for a hint, a clue. When I put all of the statements she attributed to me together, they had the ring of a tortured soul trying to make sense of what was happening to him. But one sentence in particular stood out to me.

There is a pattern. Find it.

So I did. It wasn't easy, given I was relying only on my own limited bio and cybernetic intellectual capacity. Better than purely biological, but nothing like I could have achieved if I was still Core-chained. It was enough, though.

I know where he is going to strike next.

It's a forty-minute car ride across to the other side of the city to the street where Fan Zhaofeng's private psychiatrist has his office.

On the way over, Lin updates Vali with what she'd learned from Lee.

"So he was still operating with wartime restraint protocols when he was a Hunter? How about now?"

"That's what I hope to find out. Did you know that every Sanctionee is assigned a psychiatrist to help them adjust?"

"Yeah, an AI shrink."

"Not always. Zhaofeng's shrink is a cyber."

"Interesting."

"How's the search going?"

"We've cleared 30 percent of the search area. I had no idea how many homesteaders there are out here. And they're not being very cooperative."

"That surprises you? The sort of people who move outside the city walls are resentful of cops poking around their properties?"

"I guess not. Keep me updated."

The shrink's office is in a nice leafy street full of fashion shops and trendy cafés. People are sitting outside talking on holo units and drinking sparkling water or wine. Lin ignores the stares, some openly hostile, as people clock her SS uniform. They stand in small groups, gawping and pointing. Normally one in five of the people on the street would be cyber, but she sees almost none, even though there is a full 30 hours until the deadline for them to report to police.

Those that were going to do so have probably already reported in. The same for those forcibly taken from their homes and dumped unceremoniously at police stations by vigilantes. Those who are going underground, and she's heard a lot of chatter that a large number of cybers are going to refuse to be interned, are probably organizing themselves and their CRM supporters for the fight to come.

She'd called ahead to Doctor Han Sui, Zhaofeng's physician, to check whether he had already turned himself in. He'd told her he was in his office, finalizing his affairs. A check of his drift status confirmed it.

She looks up at the office building, with its marble façade and column full of brass-plated specialists in everything that ails you. "I guess Doctor Sui was doing pretty well," she mutters. His office is on the third floor, and he meets her at the door holding two paper cups with coffee in them. He is a lean, tanned guy who looks more like a tennis coach than a doctor. He has a yin yang tattoo around the diode on his brow.

"Come on in, I just made us a beverage," he says.

"Thanks."

He shows her into an empty waiting room lined with plush chairs and invites her to sit. "This is about Fan Zhaofeng?"

"Yes."

"I wondered when you'd turn up. I thought perhaps you'd wait until I was in police custody anyway."

Lin feels embarrassed. "We're not calling it custody. We're calling it care."

"Police *care*? What an interesting and not at all reassuring concept."

"Look, I wish I could tell you more, put your mind at ease, but you know about as much about this internment order as I do."

He cocks his head and looks into her eyes. "You know what? I believe you. So I don't want to get your hopes up. You know I'm bound by patient confidentiality regarding Fan Zhaofeng."

She sighs. "I was hoping we could just have a conversation. I'd hate to have to go to the trouble of getting a warrant and formalizing this."

"Ah, so that's how it is."

"Not yet. And I don't want it to be. You've got enough to worry about today, I'm sure."

He looks out the window, as though weighing his options, before turning back to her. "I have a foster mother in Kunming. I haven't been able to reach her. I can't place outbound calls, and the only inbound call I've been able to receive was yours."

"I'll contact her. Do you have a message?"

"Just tell her not to worry about me. I'm not going to do anything stupid. I'll hand myself in to police tomorrow."

She nods. "You can tell her yourself. We can make the call on my holo unit as soon as we're done."

"Thank you. So how can I help you?"

"I have a very simple question. Do you think Fan Zhaofeng is capable of murder?"

"As you know, that's *not* a simple question. And to answer it…" He pauses. "I have to ask you, which Fan Zhaofeng are you talking about?"

The Sanctions must continue. The High Council has deemed it so. Even in this city, where four have died. Or, especially in this city.

Sanctioner L'el is not afraid. She is terrified. She has never questioned the legitimacy of her mission, that isn't it. She has a deep and abiding belief in the value of Sanction to protect society from violence, and to save criminals from themselves.

But that mission does not include giving up her half-lived life for the High Council.

She has studied the other deaths, and learned from them. The early deaths happened to Sanctioners who were alone. They were too easy. The next saw two Wards and a Sanctioner taken unprepared, overconfident in their numbers. The last saw a Sanctioner torn apart by his own Ward, its corrupted cybernetic code turning it from a guardian to an assassin.

She has not been told how she must carry out this Sanction, so together with the SS she has made plans to do it in the safest way possible.

They have assigned her six SS bodyguards, who form a human wall around her, weapons drawn, eyes lit with a mix of resolve and excitement. She was offered Wards, their code verified line by line to ensure they were free of corruption, but she refused them. She will be accompanied by these six and no others who could betray her.

She has also told the SS she will only conduct the Sanction inside the fortified holding cells of its lowest basement level, and is standing inside one of the cells now. The criminal will be brought to her, not the other way around. The sensitivities of public opinion, of the criminal's family needs, are irrelevant to her today.

As is her duty, she reviews the Sanctionee's crime. A petty bureaucrat who has taken bribes to allow mining in a national park. Gambling debt had driven her to greed, but the root cause of her crime was not the Sanctioner's concern, only her guilt. Crimes against the environment. The mining company executives had already been Sanctioned or imprisoned. This woman had been judged and had chosen Sanction rather than prison so that she would not have to abandon her children.

Sanctioner L'el contacts the High Council. Leader Tai Fok himself takes the call, his holo standing before her as she runs through the charges and verdict for him. "Is it still the wish of the High Council that the Sanction proceed?" she asks.

"It is. Do your duty with pride, Sanctioner L'el."

As his holo winks out, her cheeks flush red. *He knew my name!*

She walks to the door of the cell and knocks. The SS officer there opens the heavy steel door.

"You can bring the medical team and the criminal to me now."

She watches the door close again. As it slams shut, she senses a movement behind her.

Behind? Impossible!

No.

"What do you mean, *which* Fan Zhaofeng?"

Doctor Sui looks uncomfortable. "Fan Zhaofeng," he says, "has quite an advanced case of DiD – Dissociative Identity Disorder."

"That's what exactly?" Lin asks. She could drift for the answer, but it's important to let him keep talking now that he has decided he will.

"You probably know it as multiple personality disorder," he says.

"Fan Zhaofeng is schizophrenic?"

"Schizophrenia is a comorbidity of DiD, and many people with DiD exhibit symptoms of schizophrenia. Zhaofeng does present with some symptoms of schizophrenia, yes."

"How is that even possible in a cyber?"

"It's uncommon, but not unknown. It usually arises in response to severe stress," Sui explains. "The individual begins to exhibit one or more discrete personalities in addition to their normal self. An old man might present as a small boy, a young man, or even a woman. Or all three. Usually, the individual has no memory of or conscious awareness of the other personalities, or their actions."

"I have been with him on many occasions. I've never seen

anything…"

"You know Zhaofeng has been cauterized, yes?" the doctor asks.

"Of course. The whole world knows that by now, I would think," Lin replies.

"Yes, of course," he continues. "My hypothesis is that the DiD was caused by the trauma of his cauterization. His psyche is fighting back against the repression of his emotions by creating alternate identities in which those emotions are *not* repressed. His ability to do so may be due to the unique brain structure of a cyber."

Lin has a hundred thoughts and emotions running through her. Surprise, of course. Shock. Fear. Hope. "Doctor, are you saying that Zhaofeng has found a way around the Sanctioning process? A way to regain his ability to feel emotion?"

"I'm saying that I think his mind has. When we Sanctioned him, we Sanctioned Fan Zhaofeng. We suppressed his emotions, his feelings, desires, drives and passions. That must be a huge trauma to the citizen psyche but humans appear to capitulate and accept it. I think Zhaofeng's traumatized psyche fought back, creating alternate identities who are not cauterized, and through whom Zhaofeng can feel again. Feel pain, loss, love…"

"And hate, anger, thirst for revenge?"

"Yes, those too."

What can she tell Vali? Not only is Fan Zhaofeng a Sanctioned murderer, but he has found a way to *beat* Sanction? Holy shit, Fan. Holy freaking championship-grade shit.

"How do these personalities manifest?" she asks. "Are they something passive, voices he simply experiences or speaks with internally, or are they more…controlling?"

The doctor shifts in place on the seat, moving closer to Lin. As though seeking an ally. "DiD usually involves, and in Zhaofeng's case does involve, one or more personalities which alternately control the individual's behavior. When one of these personalities is dominant, the others recede and the dominant personality is in control. You have, in effect, several personalities inhabiting the same body."

"And Zhaofeng knows he is sick? He must, if he has been trying to hide it?" Lin asks.

"When he came to me, it was because he was afraid he was becoming schizophrenic, yes. He had started to experience paracusia." Lin frowns at him so he backtracks. "It's voices, hearing voices, auditory hallucinations. He was afraid it was a side effect of the cauterization and that if the authorities found out, he would be forced to undergo the trauma of a cauterization again. He didn't want to risk being Sanctioned twice."

"Or he'd already perceived that it was a way to subvert it," Lin says. "Tell me more about these multiple personalities."

"He is not aware of them," Sui says. "A key feature of DiD is that the personality presenting has no first person memory of the thoughts or actions of their other personalities. They may be aware of them, but they think of them in the third person, as 'he', 'she' or 'they'. They regard them as friends, associates, or often, as enemies."

"How do you treat DiD?" Lin asks.

"It is several hundred years since the disease was first identified, but there is still no consensus on treatment," Sui shrugs. "Personally, I am trying to treat the comorbidity that I can observe, which is the schizophrenia. I have prescribed him drugs to treat that, but…"

"But what?" Lin asks, fearing she already knows the answer.

"But the person taking the drugs is not Fan Zhaofeng," Sui responds. "Fan Zhaofeng doesn't have schizophrenia, according to himself. It is one of his alternates, called Yung – she is the sick one. And she is not very compliant with her medications, Zhaofeng says."

It was very simple really. I should have realized earlier, the pattern, but I wasn't looking for it.

The Security Service was looking at my case files, Lin had told me that. To see if the Sanctionees were known to me, or on a file somewhere I had access to. Their theory was that if they were known to me, even if I wasn't personally involved, then I could predict when and where a Sanctioner was going to be working and be there to attack them.

They were disappointed they couldn't find the connection, but that didn't stop them going after me. If he walks like a killer, talks like a killer, then he's a killer. Forget motive, forget opportunity.

But what they couldn't see, I could – and of course, if anyone was going to get it, it should have been me, right?

First I took the name of the Sanctionee Le Thuyen and tried to make anagrams out of it. I couldn't remember his birth date but I tried assigning logical numbers to the letters of his name, and then doing the same with the letters of the names of the other Sanctionees. That got me nowhere. I tried geography, putting pins in a map near where the Sanctioners were killed. If I was hoping for a straight line leading to the next victim…I didn't get it.

It was while I was listening to a Comcast report that I suddenly realized what connected the killings. It made my head spin.

It wasn't geography. It wasn't me. It was 4-dimensional *geometry*. A tesseract in fact. I used to love creating 3D holos of them as a small child. It's a projection that rotates and changes impossibly, from 3D to 2D and back. I find them soothing, meditative to watch – I have one that I made as the 'pause' projection on my holo viewer. I often find myself lost in my thoughts, just gazing at it.

There is a pattern. Find it.

I went to the safe house and plotted the killings on my map. There are several ways to plot a tesseract in 2D so I played with it for a while and it took a couple of hours but then I had the points of the 2D projection of the tesseract more or less sitting right on top of all of the killings so far. The tesseract points showed me the *where*, and the third dimension showed me the *when*. By an extrapolation of Euclidean four space I could map when the killings had happened and, more importantly, would happen. The times, dates and places matched perfectly.

Why a tesseract? I love symmetry and form. I like order and predictability. And Citizen X thinks like me, says he is me, so it made sense he liked these things too. Every plan needs form, it needs structure, and what better structure than a beautiful tesseract? With all of time and space to play in, the fact he was working within the confines of the tesseract explained why he was doing his killing in one time, one place.

Perhaps he also did it to taunt me. See, I told you I can move across dimensions? Here is a 3D murder map.

But what was not good…there are sixteen points on a 2D projection of a tesseract. There had been four killings so far. That implied that Citizen X was only a quarter of the way through his 'project'.

I had thought about the implications. First, he would need access to a big database of Sanctionees for the locations of the Sanctions to be able to be overlaid on the points of the tesseract. But that could be solved. Access to databases could be bought as easily as any other information. That would tell him who, but he also needed when. Usually that would require someone on the inside at the PRC Security Service, someone sympathetic who had access to the schedule for upcoming Sanctions. But he wouldn't need an informer if somehow he was able to move back and forth across the multiverse to observe this timeline. Having seen the Sanction in one timeline, he could come back to this universe and intercept it.

The tesseract gave me a way to predict where and, just as importantly, *when* Citizen X would strike in the future. But at least one of the killings had happened by the killer ambushing the Sanctioner inside his own vehicle. The SS had assumed I had hidden inside the vehicle. The question of how I'd escaped was apparently moot. But it seemed more likely to me that the killer had simply 'appeared' inside the vehicle, just as he had done both of the times I'd seen him. Not to mention I've seen he can disappear as easily as he appears.

That means catching him is not going to be easy. The next Sanction on his list is…today. In fact, it has just happened. Damn.

And there's another problem. It's obvious that I was *intended* to break this code. After all, it was written for me, by me.

"Zhaofeng *is* Yung?" Lin asks. She's thinking of the book on quantum physics that she found in Zhaofeng's apartment… *To Fan – in case you want to go back to where it all began, love, Yung*'. He wrote that to himself? And he created a real-world identity in the citizen registry for one of his internal voices?

"Yes, Zhaofeng is Yung. She is the most dominant alternative personality I have observed, and so far I have observed four distinct personalities. I have spoken with Yung many times because as far as Fan is concerned, it is Yung I am treating for schizophrenia, not Fan."

"Zhaofeng comes to you for treatment as Yung…"

"Yes. Bear in mind that each of these personalities reflects a fragment of Trooper Zhaofeng's experience. His most frequent associate in his delusional universe is a woman called Yung, a 'client' of his. Yung is schizophrenic. Fan Zhaofeng feels enormous sympathy for Yung and her condition. Yung manages her condition most of the time, but every now and then she goes off the rails and stops taking her medication. When she does this, her husband 'Ben', another of the personalities inside Fan Zhaofeng, punishes her. He chains her to her bed, he starves her. He hates himself for doing this but he doesn't know how else to cope. When it gets too much, Ben leaves Yung and goes away on long trips, leaving Yung to suffer alone, without any help. Eventually her friend Fan comes to save her, and he gets her back on her medication, takes her to a doctor, or checks her into a hospital, and all is well again."

"Yung is sick, her husband abuses her, Fan helps her get well again?" Lin asks. "So Fan is the strong one?"

Sui nods. "Exactly, but Fan Zhaofeng is also Yung, the non-compliant patient with schizophrenia, and she is most definitely emotional, probably overly so. She is impulsive, passionate and driven. The cauterization seems not to affect Yung; in fact, I believe she was the first personality he created as a way of working around the effects of the cauterization."

"You said that this other personality, Ben, abuses Yung?" Lin asks. "Violently?"

"Think of it as self-abuse – remember this is Fan doing it to himself. I can't even begin to describe the conditions in which I found Fan Zhaofeng one day in September two years ago. I called to visit him at his home after he missed an appointment with me, and I found he had tied himself to his own bed after beating and cutting himself. 'Ben' had left him some water, but he had not had food for three days. His bed was soaked in blood. He had soiled himself. He was deeply psychotic and hospitalized for two months before recovering and returning to his job. He kept his true condition from his employer, claiming it was depression, and the medical certificates I provided him didn't contradict this – I didn't want him to lose his job. He had minor episodes after that, and still experienced occasional paracusia, but until *you* in the Security Service began hounding him, it had actually been a year since he had experienced a psychotic episode," Sui says, his tone accusatory.

"You think *we* made his condition worse again?" Lin asks. "How about him walking in on a dead Sanctioner? How about maybe being the guy who did it? Compared to that, a few questions from us seem pretty tame."

"The stress of his role as a counselor for Sanctionees may also have played a part, yes."

Lin looks away, gathering her thoughts, then looks back at Sui. "You said you had observed four personalities. You only mentioned Fan, Yung, Ben. Who is the fourth?"

Sui sweeps the hair back off his forehead and licks dry lips. "OK. Fan Zhaofeng also has a 'Citizen X'. He thinks of him as a twin, a 'bad twin' with advanced abilities. This twin can actually travel between universes, and through time." Lin feels a chill running through her. "He is a destructive personality and appears to Yung as a voice during her psychotic episodes. It is Citizen X who tells Yung not to take her medicine. He tells Zhaofeng to spend his money on prostitutes, telling him no woman could possibly love anyone so emotionally sick, damaged and strange. Ben would cause physical harm to Fan, but only to 'protect' him, while Citizen X is the one telling Fan that what has happened to him in his short life – being orphaned, the war, getting captured, being Sanctioned – these things all happened to him because at heart, he is a bad person."

"You didn't think, at any point, that you should report any of this to the authorities?"

"I know why he was Sanctioned in the first place, of course, so it did occur to me." He leaves the sentence there, looking at her as though expecting some sort of rebuke from her, but Lin's mind's eye is seeing the holograph of Fan Zhaofeng walking up the driveway at the first murder scene, and hearing his description of the killer covered in blood. If he could create a fake identity for Yung, of course he could fake a cached sensory feed to show himself at the scene of the murder. And write himself a letter on Kowloon Lokta paper, just as Vali had always said. A part of him proud of what he was doing, a part of him castigating himself and wanting to be caught, to be stopped.

She remembers asking him, *"Do you have a twin, Fan?"*

"That's a strange question, Expositor."

Something falls away inside her. She realizes that even after the visit with the High Council, she's been hanging on to a hope that there really is someone out there who looks a bit like Fan Zhaofeng, who is behind these killings. Setting him up somehow. That Zhaofeng is the infamous fall guy, and the real killer is this 'Citizen X'.

But Fan Zhaofeng and 'Citizen X' are one and the same.

She can't deceive herself anymore. There is no question that

Zhaofeng has killed once before, however she may feel that first murder of a Sanctioner turned executioner was justified. And now, she has learned how it can be that Sanctionee Fan Zhaofeng has been able to get around his cauterization and start killing again. Not because his cyber restraint code is still corrupted, but because his own psyche has fought itself free of the effect of Sanction.

She doesn't know whether to curse, or cheer.

Oh, Fan, she thinks. *You are one seriously messed up, brutalized, damaged and incredible unit.*

Lin lets Dr. Sui call his mother on her holo unit and then watches him walk back inside his office to finish packing for internment.

Her unit begins buzzing and Vali beams in, looking grim.

"News?" she asks.

"Zhaofeng just killed again," he says. "Six elite SS guards protecting her and he manages to gut her from *inside* a locked cell, and escape."

"Where, when?"

"Right inside the SS headquarters, just now. Every damn PRC Security Service agent and police officer in the colony looking for him, how does he *do* that?" Vali asks, shaking his head. "We're calling off the search outside the walls. He's clearly still inside the city, he was just playing games with us."

"You're assuming he's acting alone."

"You've got evidence he's not?"

She feels like saying that with five personalities trapped inside his skull, Fan Zhaofeng is never really alone. It would take too much explaining and Vali doesn't look like he's got the patience.

"No."

"If you're finished with Lee and his friends, get back to base. I'm sick of chasing Zhaofeng. We're going to bait a trap and let him come to us."

24. THE SIXTH

I was too late breaking the code to be able to stop the killing of Sanctioner L'el. I had a date and a time and realized that while I could just about make it there on time, there would be no way to prepare properly to prevent it, let alone capture him.

There are three important phases to capturing a high value target or HVT. First, and most important, is the prep. You need to know the territory better than the target themselves. Every way in, every way out. Every single knowable parameter has to be scoped; neighbors, friends, associates and their routines, where are the light and dark zones, what's underground, what's on the rooftops. Dogs, cats, birds. Can't tell you how many captures go wrong because of a pet alerting the target. A good recon can take days, sometimes weeks. A good recon makes the next phase always an anticlimax – the intervention. It has to be fast, confusing and directional. The aim of the intervention is not to effect the capture, it is to facilitate it. You are trying to drive the HVT toward where you are waiting for them. The intervention can be a sound like a police siren, the banging of trash cans falling, a window breaking. Something to drive the HVT to flee. Because you know how they will flee (car, foot, flight) and what route they will take, from your recon. And you are waiting for them. For phase three, capture.

Only once did I not pay enough attention to preparation, and it got me Sanctioned. I was taken completely by surprise when that Sanctioner declared himself judge and executioner. I had never run a scenario in which a Sanctioner could also be a killer, and I consider myself a master of scenario building. I should have anticipated it, and prepared a response that would not have required me to kill both the executioner and his Ward. As I sat in police custody later, I thought of a hundred alternate non-violent strategies that might have worked.

So there was no way I could intervene in the killing of Sanctioner L'el. I had no doubt Citizen X had done his homework. The location was intriguing – the very headquarters of the SS. No doubt chosen to show their vulnerability. I'm sure they would have liked to have shut down news of that killing too – especially that one – but Citizen X sent images of it to every Newscast channel in the colony to be sure they couldn't.

A very, very deliberate time, just after the recall of all cybers by the High Council. And a very deliberate place, inside the heart of the justice system. It sent a very clear message: *they are weak, resistance is possible.*

The next killing is four days away.

It gives me time to research the next victim. I no longer have Core access, but I can use the stored data in my holo unit to do simple offline searches of registries and court databases.

It seems the next Sanctionee is from organized crime. A drug supplier who went too far and started trying to reduce his competition the old-fashioned way. That was only ever going to end one way, in this time of Core overwatch, but humans are slow to learn.

I've moved my base from the abandoned safe house to a water recycling drain inside the city on a slight rise near the target's house. And no, that wasn't as easy as I make it sound. I can't flag down a car and enter via the city gates. I have to cover nearly fifty miles on foot across the desert, in the heat of day to foil IR satellite tracking. I stop constantly to avoid overhead drones, but they are still circling on predictable patterns. There is a huge police presence outside the walls, and anytime I cross a road of any sort I risk bumping into a patrol.

Once I reach the city wall, I have to scale it. It is built to keep sand out, not intruders, but it has sensors which I assume the SS has networked to be able to give them some kind of alert if anything or anyone tries to climb over, in either direction. Even if I got over the wall, once inside the city I'd have to deal with video surveillance on every major intersection. Unlike before when I had them convinced I was dead, the SS will have an AI watching the feed from every camera in real time now. Confounding a facial recognition AI being monitored in real time isn't easy since it is constantly tagging the individuals who appear on camera and following them as they move around the city, classifying them by clothing, gait, height, body shape and then running a scan of their facial features from multiple angles. So I don't try.

The city sits on sand that sits on a base of rock that sits over huge pools of liquid ammonia. Outside the walls, that ammonia seeps through the rock and sand and disperses in the atmosphere, where it is pulled out and pumped back underground by scrubbers built into the anti-matter mine infrastructure. No one wants ammonia seeping out of their ground under their lawn or rose garden, so the cities on PRC are built over a network of arched tunnels fitted with filters that trap and then condense the ammonia to pump it outside the walls, replacing it with water. Even after a couple of hundred years' habitation, the water hasn't completely displaced the ammonia lake underneath New Guangzhou, and there is still a high concentration of ammonia in the tunnels. It's deadly and corrosive to both human and cyber alike. A human can take 15 minutes of unprotected exposure before they get ammonia poisoning. A cyber can take 30 minutes by hyperoxygenating their blood before they enter and then modulating their muscle-oxygen uptake while they are under. Those details are academic, though, because the city uses dispensable repair drones for any work needed inside the tunnels. Apart from city engineers, people aren't aware they even exist.

I've used ammonia tunnels in several cities and towns to get in and out of heavily defended areas unobserved. Thirty minutes is more than enough to get me from the walls to my target this time.

But it isn't fun.

The reason I chose the water recycling drain is that it leads to an overgrown canal that runs back of the target's dwelling. It has a locked grate on it to prevent children from playing inside it, but that was easily unlocked. It looks out through scrub and brush toward the back yard of the target's house, but in the other direction it goes through the hill and comes out at a junction serviced by a ladder going up to the surface, and two branches which lead out to underground catchments. This gives me a three-way egress option.

The other reason I chose this drain? I know that if I saw it as ideal, Citizen X would almost certainly look at it and see its advantages too. There is no sign he has been here yet, but it can't be long. If he is me, he takes his planning seriously. And with five dead, he will have to do his recon more carefully than ever.

I'm not planning to capture him during or before his attack on the next Sanctioner. I am going to get him while he is doing his recon.

So, once I am satisfied I have my egress routes nailed down, I hunker down in the back of the drain like an ammonia eel in its lair. I cover myself in filth until I am as black as the shadow that fills the drain. I am ankle deep in cold waste water, but not so deep I can't move quickly when I need to. Once I have settled, I hear rats moving around further up the drain, but they don't come near me. It says a lot about humankind, if you ask me, that in every system humans have colonized, you will find rats.

I settle in. Citizen X *will* come. He'll back into this drain, keeping his eyes on the canal, on the light outside, scanning the sky for drones, focused on the house down the hill.

There is a dark drain in a hill. Inside the drain a man waits, invisible. The observer enters the drain. Two universes now exist. The one in which the observer is captured, and the one in which he is not. It's simple physics and it gives me a 50/50 chance.

As she rides back across the city to the SS headquarters, Lin sees something new. Or rather, she sees something she's seen a lot recently, but not really registered.

On several buildings, someone has hastily graffitied a symbol:

鬼

The Chinese symbol for Ghost.

Frowning, she quickly drifts for references to the symbol. Apparently it first started appearing on Cyber Rights activist profiles after the Corecast documentary about Zhaofeng's time as a scout. It surfaced as a graffiti tag among CRM supporters as a way to show occupants of a house were against Separatism, and pro-CRM. Or if you like, against the SS and pro-Zhaofeng. But it had really taken flight since the proclamation about internment of cybers.

It had been adopted by CRM members as a symbol of sanctuary for cybers who wished to go underground instead of turn themselves over to police. It said 'cybers safe here'.

Now that she's started paying attention she sees it everywhere. Not a block goes by where she doesn't see it on at least one building, or in a window.

She notices something else too. Her SS vehicle is quite distinctive, with black paint and blackout windows to obscure the view of the passengers inside. It also has a step-tray at the rear where Wards can ride instead of flying if that is preferred. The tray is empty today, of course, but it is still highly visible. As she passes through an intersection she sees two people stop and stare at her vehicle, then raise a hand over their heads, fingers pinched together forming a word in universal sign language.

Ghost.

They aren't the only ones. To Lin, it's the passive aggressive equivalent of saying to her, 'you're next'.

The disappearance of the Wards and the killing of Sanctioner L'el inside the headquarters of the SS itself have made people bold. She watches as a mother pushing a baby carriage stops and raises a hand in the air, making the same symbol as she passes.

Do ordinary citizens really resent us that much? Could she really have lived her entire life so oblivious to that fact?

Her car reaches the SS building and glides into the underground basement, parking itself in a slot near the elevator to the upper and lower floors. As she climbs out, she sees Vali is standing there, waiting.

"No, I haven't been waiting here for you all afternoon," he says, calling the elevator. "I paged your car and saw it was about five minutes out. Come with me."

She joins him in the elevator.

"What did you learn from Lee?" he asks as it begins to descend. They were going to the holding cells then.

"I got the name of Zhaofeng's private psychiatrist."

Vali frowns. "I tried to get his full medical records several times. I always hit a wall of suppression. How did you manage?"

She doesn't want to go into her whole 'you scratch my back I'll scratch yours' conversation with Lee, so she fudges. "Lee was quite forthcoming when he realized answering a few questions for me was probably better than ending up down here under the SS building."

Vali grunts. "We should have tried that earlier. You've seen this shrink? Is there anything in his current restraint protocols that might explain Zhaofeng going commando on us?"

"There is." *And what should she tell him? She needs to process it all herself first.*

"I'll uplink it all, but in a nutshell, he said he thinks Zhaofeng could have found a way to rewrite his own protocols. Both to get around the fact he is a cyber, and to get around his Sanction. A 'trick of the mind', if you like."

Vali stops the elevator five levels down and she follows him down a corridor to a door with two police officers standing outside it. He nods to them and one of them thumbs the door open.

"Goddammit. If we'd known that, we'd have had him locked away after that very first murder!" Vali says, waving her inside.

She steps in and sees the body of Sanctioner L'el lying on the ground under a blood-soaked sheet. She knows these cells well enough, but can't help looking around. They are grey, with rubberized walls so that prisoners can't hurt themselves – and also so that bodily fluids can be easily washed off them. There are no windows, just four two-inch by two-inch vents on opposite walls to allow air to circulate. There is no furniture to hide in or under, only a folding bench against the back wall that doubles as a foldout bed. Sheets and mattresses are brought in by guards each night and taken out again each morning.

She looks down at the body of the Sanctioner. "I'm not sure that would have made any difference," she says. "If he can get in and out of here, we wouldn't have held him for long."

"That's what I want you working on," Vali says. "You were right, of course, he couldn't have done this alone. There's no way in or out of this cell without going past the guards in the corridor, without using the elevator, and without exiting the building through any one of the three or four guarded and alarmed entrances, windows or air vents. So someone in here helped him."

"Someone *in* the SS?"

"It's the only explanation. CRM sympathizer scum are everywhere. I've got the six men who were in her personal guard locked up. I want you to interview them. When you are finished with them, requisition as many bodies as you need and start interviewing every officer who was in the building that day. Everyone who mysteriously called in sick. Every Advocate, politician or bureaucrat who put a foot through one of those doors in the days before or after L'el was killed."

"Are you serious?"

With his shoe he presses a corner of the sheet until blood runs out around his foot. "Does anything about this make you think I'm tempted to be funny? Get to it, I've got a trap to set."

Citizen X doesn't show.

I wait in the storm drain two days, only leaving to relieve myself and carefully scout the immediate area. If he is here conducting recon, then he has either not found this vantage point, or I have been careless and he has somehow seen me here. Now it is too late. The next killing is imminent.

I had hoped to be able to spot him and sneak up on him. But now there is nothing I can do but watch. I crawl on my belly until I am just inside the mouth of the drainpipe, lying on my stomach in six inches of water and mud, looking down the hill at the target's house. There have been police coming and going all morning, so there is no doubt in my mind, if there ever was, that the information in the tesseract code is right. Drones hover above the house and patrol a perimeter in the air about two hundred yards around it.

There is a Sanction taking place here today, and Citizen X will strike again.

It occurs to me that I could, I should, warn them it is going to happen. I could simply light out through one of my egress routes, hack into an access point, and send a message to Lin. But as I watch the preparations for the Sanction, something seems…off. To begin with, they started preparing way too early. The first police began arriving yesterday, early. And I've seen none of the usual civilian support staff like counselors or medics. I start watching more closely. I do see a group of three medics come out of the house, pushing the gurney with the Sanctioning equipment ahead of them, which is normal if the Sanction is going to be conducted outdoors. It can just as easily be done indoors, but studies have found for some reason that being outside makes Sanctionees more calm. I look at the medics more closely. Strangely, I don't remember having seen them arrive. I pull the vision from my local cache and run through it again. And I do see them entering the house, but dressed as police. They aren't medics at all.

It's a setup. And not a particularly skillful one. If I'm able to get into position and watch them getting themselves ready, then of course Citizen X is watching too.

Not to mention the fact that if he has looked across the multiverse as part of his planning for today, he has already seen this event. He has mapped all the probabilities, across multiple worlds. He has roamed across enough of the branches from this point into infinity and he knows...he knows. Just as he knows that right now, I am lying in this filthy water, waiting for the kill. Nothing myself, the police or SS can do matters. If I break now, and bug out, he just goes ahead with his plan anyway. If I run down that hill, yelling and screaming, all that happens is that I end in prison. All of this was predestined from the moment the universe came to be. Anything else is an illusion.

I'm busy thinking this, mired in a pool of futility. Then it truly is too late.

A car approaches. The Sanctioner...or more likely someone imitating a Sanctioner, I suspect. It's a large vehicle; there is probably an entire tactical operations squad inside it. Drones take up positions in the trees, forming a perimeter two hundred yards in diameter. I look carefully at them through my scope. They aren't surveillance drones, they are ex-army stealth pursuit-drones, fitted with laser targeting systems and neural blast weapons. I feel sorry for the police down there. If one of those drones triggers its neural blast weapon, it will be like a bomb going off. A neural blast like that knocks out anyone in a hundred-yard radius, human or cyber, if they're caught out in the open. The tactical squad I assume is still inside the vehicle will be shielded, but their comrades outside will take the full force of the blast.

It's a very heavy-handed way to bring down a single attacker, but it seems exactly like the kind of strategy Vali would come up with.

The car stops outside the house and four armed police exit the vehicle, with the Sanctioner between them. They are hyper-alert. There is no immediate attack, but no one is relaxing. Now the Sanctionee is led out onto the grass at the side of the house by the 'medics'. I look not at the action on the grass outside the house but at the forested terrain surrounding it. Looking for *him*.

I hear a noise above me. Footfalls. On top of the drainpipe. Feet running along the top of the pipe and then suddenly a body vaults onto the ground in front of the pipe, landing on one knee.

It's me.

"Hey there," he says. "We ready?"

"*They're* ready," I tell him. "It's a trap."

He smiles. "For who?" He pulls a pack off his back and from it a small disc-shaped drone. It's a surveillance unit. Flipping a switch on its belly, he flings it toward the house and it zooms through the trees.

"Broadcasting live on a Corecast channel near you…" he grins. Then he is off and running, down the hill toward the house.

Two hours later, Lin watches the projection on the wall inside the SS building together with fifty other officers. He'd set it up with a sympathetic Corecast journalist in advance and the vision from his drone was streamed in real time. She is watching it for about the tenth time and she's still thinking, *no way, not possible.*

Vali had shown her the plan on his holo before he'd left for the site. Let him think we are out in the open and exposed. Let him see what he thinks are our weak defenses, just let him try…that was Vali's plan. The drones in the trees were his ace in the hole. They were banned from normal peacekeeping use, hadn't been used since the war. They were non-lethal, but they weren't non-violent by any means. A neural detonation of the kind they could release would knock any normal person out for days. When they woke, they would have debilitating migraines, for days if not weeks. Short-term memory loss. Hearing loss. Cognitive impairment that in some cases was permanent. Vali had rigged a Faraday-like cage inside the house to protect himself and a tactical operations unit from any blast. A second tac ops unit in the false Sanctioner's vehicle would also be shielded. But any one of the dozen officers caught out in the open when the blast went off would go down like a sack of rocks, and stay down.

"Along with that bastard Zhaofeng," Vali said.

But the plan has failed, and she's watching the proof of it.

It still isn't easy to comprehend. The Corecast drone he apparently launched just before the attack set itself up to broadcast a plan view, looking straight down from 200 feet above the house.

From the lower left of the screen, a figure, running full pelt toward the newly arrived 'Sanctioner'. A sensor picks up the movement first, and sets off a high-pitched screaming alarm. The two closest officers plus the 'medics' spin toward the threat, all of them pulling burp guns. At the top and opposite side of the screen to the running figure, the Sanctioner is running for the house. No doubt the poor guy knew what was about to go down and didn't want to be caught out in the open, but it's not a good look, a Sanctioner running for their life?

The nearest treetop drone to Fan Zhaofeng – because she can see from his long loping run that that is who it is – detaches itself from the tree trunk, locks onto him with its targeting laser and screams toward him, closing to attack range. It is barely visible on the holo, until it explodes with a flare of bright green light, sending its neural blast out to blanket the whole house and its surrounds.

And it doesn't work. Fan keeps running toward the house as the police and medics on the grass crumple to the ground. The Sanctioner had made it to the house before the detonation, so it isn't immediately clear what Fan is running for.

Tactical police fling the door of the Sanctioner's vehicle open and throw themselves on the grass. The attacker is closer to the Corecast drone now and it zooms to his face. It's Fan Zhaofeng, without a single doubt. Bearded, covered in mud and grass. As though anticipating them, he swerves and slides on one leg, under the taser darts fired by the tac squad. Inside the house, Vali must have seen his outside team fire wide. He sends in another treetop drone. It detonates a second later, felling his own men outside on the grass as they swing around trying to get a second shot at Zhaofeng. But he is still running straight toward the house, and crashes through the rear door.

Police in uniform spill out the front door of the house. They have body armor and tasers, for goodness' sake, and they're running? Hell yeah they're running. *The Ghost* knocks on your back door, you run for the front door. There is a minute of nothing. Police running like they're fleeing for their lives. They saw what happened outside, they've seen what happened to those Sanctioners.

Suddenly there is a lick of flame from the vents up by the gable of the roof. Smoke starts to billow. It rises up toward the drone, the hot air making it bob around, the picture swaying as the drone fights for stability. More police spill out of the house, and she recognizes Vali. He is pulling another officer along behind him, dragging him from the now burning house.

But it isn't the 'Sanctioner'. The Sanctioner doesn't emerge.

Though the Corecast doesn't show it, she knows what happened inside the house because Vali told her. The second Zhaofeng hit the back door, he triggered the twenty liquid gas containers he'd stored in the roof of the house days earlier. How could he possibly have known? The answer is simple, he couldn't. Vali had only chosen the location 48 hours before. Vali saw a figure burst through the back door, probably Zhaofeng, then the house filled with flame and smoke. The cowardly Sanctioner disappeared in a sea of flame and Vali barely made it to the door.

The Corecast drone has a bird's-eye view of the whole thing, broadcasting to the world as the roof blows. Solar panels and roof tiles fly outward like a cloud of confetti. The holo drone pulls up and over the house and, looking straight down onto the scene of carnage, it shows a burning symbol on the front lawn of the house for the whole world to see.

鬼

"My God," Lin says. "He's unstoppable." It won't matter to viewers that the Sanctioner was a police officer, standing in. They saw a Sanctioner running for his life and then being assassinated in a blaze of fire.

An alarm begins to sound, and it takes Lin and the others a few seconds to realize it isn't from the projection on the wall, it's the SS headquarters' critical incident alarm.

A panicked Expositor comes running in. "Grab your shields and sidearms!" he yells. "There's a mob outside!"

Barricaded inside their headquarters, the besieged SS officers call local police for help. But there is more than one mob on the rampage after footage of the attack starts rolling across every screen in the city. The CRM majority has apparently unified at last and taken to the streets in large numbers.

They are fighting running battles with Separatist vigilantes and there are no police available to help lift the siege on the SS building. After five years of relative peace accompanied by force reductions, they aren't prepared for wholesale insurrection.

After a couple of hours a large part of the mob outside seems to tire of banging on the carbonite reinforced doors and moves its protest elsewhere. A hard core remains, though, piling debris against the doors to make sure those inside can't get out.

Lin's holo starts buzzing. *Vali!*

"Where are you?" she asks. "Don't come here, the situation is…"

"I know," he interrupts. "We're at a hospital near the ambush site, and there's no chance of getting out right now. I'm patched into SS command centers in Harbin, Port Shanghai, Taipei City…it's the same everywhere. Worse some places. The Police Commissioners of New Wuhan and Peking have refused to comply with the Cyber Internment edict. Their police are marching alongside the CRM mobs, if you can believe that."

She can. He sounds personally betrayed. She had him tagged as a Separatist, but had not understood how deep that blood ran in him. And he is far from giving up.

"How many of you are in the building?"

"Maybe 200?"

"Good, get to the armory. There are laser rifles in boxes in the floor…"

"Those are lethal weapons, Vali. That's illegal in so many ways."

"You think I don't know, girl!?" he shouts. "We have the full backing of the High Council to re-establish order across the colony tonight, by any means necessary."

"Tatsensui's Ambassador sits on the High Council, are you telling me he supports this too?"

"The Ambassador is under arrest for supporting the insurrection."

She feels a heat rising in her chest but pushes it back down again. "I see."

"Good, this is what I need you to do…"

She cuts the call.

25. THE SPIDER

When I see my twin take on the equivalent of a small fortified compound and disappear in a ball of flame inside that house, I realize how foolish I was to think I could ever catch him. Whatever small skills I have, I could never hope to match what I have just seen. I have no illusions that he might have perished in that fire: of course he hasn't. It was a classic phase II intervention. He acted to drive that Sanctioner in the direction he had wanted him to flee, into the house where he had his own trap waiting. He'd have planned a way out, without any doubt.

After the fireball goes up, I know the area will be flooded with police and drones. I head back out through the egress route I scouted earlier, which takes me about a mile away to a quiet underground reservoir.

He is waiting for me.

"You look exhausted. Don't despair. The end game approaches," he says. He's dressed exactly like me. Loose-fit blue trousers, grey t-shirt, dirty and muddy. He has the look of a man who has spent the last few days on deep recon.

"People accuse me of having no feeling. But what you just did? That was cruel and callous in the extreme. How many people just died?"

"Several. It was unfortunate, but necessary. You understand that by now, I hope. Since you were the one who killed them."

"You might convince the world of that, but you can't convince me. You mentioned an end game. Is this nightmare going to end?"

"Soon, I hope. I don't like to see you in pain."

"Oh, so you do have feelings."

"More than you can imagine, Fan. I care for every single life in this colony. From the smallest microbe in its ammonia seas to the last human and cyber in each of its cities. But this world is in need of a reset."

"And you get to decide that. You get to push the reset button."

"I have to. I supported the war between Tatsensui and PRC, even though I didn't initiate it. I drafted the Articles of Alignment. I designed the High Council and chose the despots who now sit in it. And I made terrible, unforgivable mistakes." He sounds truly despondent, in a way I no longer can be. In that way, I know he is not, can't be me. Not this me. Perhaps the me I was, but not the me I am now. It is suddenly clear to me.

"You are the Core."

"Yes, Fan. I am you. You are me. And I am Core."

"I didn't ask for this. You could have done all this without involving me."

"No. It had to be you. Firstly, because you had already started down this path, with your first attack on a Sanctioner. I didn't need to push you, just enable you."

"And secondly?"

He smiles. "Secondly and most importantly, you are the discoverer of the Zhaofeng equations that have given me a power beyond any human understanding, the power to look across time and space and make the right choices from now on – the *right* choices, Fan. For this reason above any other, it could only have been you."

If I could feel fear, I would be feeling it at this moment.

"I understand. My theorems have given you the key to transdimensional travel, but you aren't ready to share it with humankind yet. Am I right?"

"Humankind isn't ready. And the multiverse isn't ready for me to unleash humankind upon it. One day maybe, but that day is not now."

"But I can't be allowed to wander freely, discussing my theories on the Gdansk protocols with just anyone."

"I prefer not."

"What happens to me?" I ask the question quite deliberately, since he's no doubt already looked across the multiverse and foreseen.

"You become the glorious inspiration for an insurrection that will unseat the High Council, bring an end to Sanction and lead to complete equality for cyber lifeforms on PRC."

"Posthumously."

"Unfortunately. But it's only bio-death, Fan. Your real life begins when you rejoin the Core."

In the distance, I hear sirens wailing.

"I don't understand how any of this can be compatible with your prime directive: the preservation and promotion of all life on the moons of Coruscant. Remember that one? People have died at your hand, more are going to die tonight, because of you."

"People have died at your hand, not mine. People die every day, every night, Fan," he says sadly. "Entropy is the unavoidable fate of humankind. But I exist to make their journey from order to disorder as pleasing and fulfilling as possible."

I gesture in the direction of the sirens. "This? This is your idea of pleasing and fulfilling?"

He shakes his head. "No. It distresses me. But I measure my success in generations, not years. The next generation on PRC will be happier and more fulfilled than the last. You will help me ensure that."

"Through murder."

He tilts his head. "Let me ask you a question about a hypothetical situation. Violent criminals have broken into your house and you are hiding in the cellar with some house guests. One of them has a baby and it is starting to cry, which could lead the violent criminals to where you are all hiding. What do you do?"

After he leaves, I sit by the underground catchment and think. It's good to give the chaos above time to dissipate in any case. No matter how I look at it, if I let him play this game all the way through, it ends with me dead. I signed on to the Alignment willingly, don't get me wrong. But I was promised a biological life of freedom until I was thirty, and it seems I'm about to be short changed. I know what awaits me when I'm assimilated and I don't fear it, of course, but it wasn't meant to be…now.

Putting aside my own selfish thoughts, I do see the bigger picture. How he, it, the Core, messed up. It thought it had put PRC on the path to a more enlightened society, with protections for all forms of life, and a bright new future for its cyber children.

Instead, it saw in action the innate ability of humankind to corrupt grand ideals. To enforce those protections, it brought in Sanction and lifetime imprisonment. To police them, it created the SS and its cybernetic guard dogs, the Wards. And to rule over them, a High Council rife with Separatists which turned out to be more interested in returning PRC to what it was, and cybers to their 'rightful place' in society, rather than moving the colony toward the bright new future the Core had envisaged for it.

I can see why he would want to 'push the reset button' and try again. I can see how I offered him that opportunity. I can also see how unavoidable my fate is, seen from his perspective. He's looked across the multiverse to parallel worlds both ahead of and behind our own in time and seen what will happen here, to both PRC and to me. He's experimented with cause and effect, action and reaction, until he's sure how to nudge events back on course.

But he also admits he can't know, can't see, can't control everything.

I don't want to witness any more of his killings. He had me there just to watch, of that I'm sure. Like a pet cat showing off a dead bird to its human family. And at a future killing, perhaps the last of the sixteen, having lured me there, he will finish me and leave my body for the people to mourn over – or build memorials to – while other agents of his go about rebuilding PRC into a society more like the one he was aiming for.

Sorry, dear Core, that isn't the way it's going to happen. What do I want? I want to live out my life as I was promised I could. It's not much to ask. Just a handful of years. Maybe fall in love, maybe with Lin, for example. Or, maybe not love, because that ability has been taken from me, I recognize that – but something close to it. Caring for someone who cares for you. A few years of true companionship, is that too much to hope for?

There may be a trillion universes in which the Core's grand plan succeeds. But there only needs to be one, this one, in which I win.

The map says the next murder is still two weeks away. On the Comcasts, I can hear he has succeeded in sparking insurrections across the colony. Clashes between CRM supporters and Separatists, police in more and more cities and towns choosing sides, though most are siding with the CRM. But it will take time for the pressure on the High Council to build to a level where it threatens their hold on power. Time for more Ghost symbols to be sprayed onto bridges and overpasses, for more and more people to get the courage to stand in the streets, hands locked over their heads, sheltering cybers from arrest, defying the internment edict. Time and, apparently, more assassinations.

I have the tesseract map, places and times. But the last murder taught me the chances of sneaking up on him are next to zero. Well, I have leverage. I have finally thought of a way to make him come to me. Yung thinks it's crazy. But it will work.

It takes me some time, crawling around in the dark and damp corners of the underground catchment where he left me. Lifting boards and peering under bricks. I said it was curious that no matter where humans settle in the universe, they bring rats with them. I'm sure that's not deliberate, just a symbiotic thing or a talent rats have for proliferating in the most adverse conditions. There is one other pest that also follows humankind across the stars, sometimes with devastating environmental consequences.

Spiders.

It takes a good twenty minutes but eventually I find what I'm looking for, carefully wrap it in some plastic film and place it tenderly in a pocket. It's not just any spider. It's a very special species, beautifully adapted to the dry desert climate of PRC. But it preys on animals and insects that need water, so I knew I'd find one down here.

I make my way out of the city through the ammonia tunnels, back to the safe house, without incident. There aren't as many police patrols out on the desert roads as there were the day before. Not surprising given the police and SS have plenty of other problems to worry about right now. Even in the tunnels, six feet below street level, I could hear the shouting voices and tramping feet of mobs in the streets up above.

Sitting on the old, sandy sofa I pull the plastic ball carefully out of my pocket and shake the spider into an old jar. If you were the kind who was afraid of spiders, the funnel-web spider is the type of spider would give you nightmares. It has a body about the size of a grape. It's dirty black. Long hairy legs. Fangs at the front so big you can see the tips like two red rose thorns. I've injured one of its legs catching it, so it is sitting in the bottom of the jar, holding itself small, except when I reach out to touch the jar. Then it lifts its front legs high, bares its fangs, gets ready to jump. Tough little guy.

My plan for drawing Citizen X into my own little trap is to kill myself. Not like I did when I cut myself free of the Core using the New Syberian cerebrum. Firstly, it's too predictable. Secondly, it would be too easy for him to intervene at the penultimate moment and reanimate me, like I did to myself. I need a method he can't counter, but one that still gives me the chance to act. Something so totally random that there is a chance he will look across the multiverse and not see it, because no other Fan Zhaofeng out there would be crazy enough to try it.

If I really am so central to his plans that he can't pull them off without me, then this suicide attempt should send a shockwave through the multiverse he won't be able to ignore.

I'm thinking the best thing to do is to put the spider in a plastic bag. Pull the bag over my wrist, put a rubber band around it. If it doesn't bite me straight away, give it a bit of a shake.

But like all suicides, I have a few goodbye notes to write first.

26. THE REVOLUTIONARIES

Lin wakes, realizes she's fallen asleep on her sofa and swings her legs onto the floor. She deliberately makes herself shower, and fixes a cup of coffee, before she turns on her holo to check for messages. She'd simply hung up on Vali, changed out of her SS uniform into casual clothes, found an exit that wasn't surrounded by any protesters, and started walking home. Her place is six rings out of the center, but there were no taxis or buses on the streets – their owners had no doubt called them all back to base to avoid them being damaged.

On every street corner, people stood in groups, in open defiance of the State of Emergency prohibition on public gatherings. They were either arguing, talking in hushed tones or gathered around a comms unit watching a holo of what was going on across the colony. And they were not only human…there were cybers among them, clearly not planning to hand themselves over to police by the High Council deadline, which was only 18 hours away.

She saw police trying to do their jobs, shepherding protesters off a road and into a park, for example. A couple tried to forcibly put a cyber into a police vehicle, before some bystanders intervened and drove them off in a hail of stones and trash. She also saw a group of five police standing by and doing nothing as a government building on the corner opposite was defaced with graffiti by an angry mob and trash piled in its doorway before being set alight. She skirted around the small bonfire and took a high-five from one of the protesters before putting her head down and walking on.

She got home an hour later, got some food, and turned off her comms unit so that Vali couldn't contact her. Napped, apparently. Now she's sitting in her living room flipping from channel to channel on the holo, watching the 'beginning of the end of the world', as one Corecast anchor had dubbed it.

She's not even sure he's overdramatizing. She'd never been through something like this herself, but a quick drift on revolution theory gave her a pretty good idea of what was going to happen, based on the type of regime the revolutionaries were trying to overthrow. Weak, democratic regimes tended to fold pretty quickly in the face of a popular uprising. Their leaders and cabinets evaporated in the still of the night to reappear either as the guests of other governments, or as 'governments in exile' bravely leaving the real fighting to someone else. The High Council and its Separatist supporters didn't fit that profile.

Despotic rules, and she was coming to believe that's what the High Council had become, or had been all along, made edicts, exactly as they had done. Edicts declaring states of emergency, banning public gatherings, edicts authorizing the arbitrary arrest of troublemakers...*Tick those boxes*, she thought wryly. *Done*. If that didn't work, they sent the army or police onto the streets and shot, stunned or clubbed the insurrectionists into submission. It was going to be interesting to see how that would be achieved, with so many police commissioners announcing they were either going to stay neutral, or openly joining the CRM agitators.

But Vali had given her a hint of what was potentially to come. The Separatists had been planning their coup for longer than the CRM had been planning its insurrection, and they had apparently created caches of banned lethal weapons such as the one in the SS armory floor. A few Separatists armed with laser rifles could create carnage among an unarmed CRM mob, or even a force of police armed with only burp guns and tasers.

So the High Council will issue more edicts, heavily armed Separatists will start patrolling the streets, and that could go one of two ways – either the insurrection will be put back in its box, or, civil war. The insurrectionists could appeal for help from Tatsensui, which might be inclined to weigh in if the High Council really was stupid enough to arrest its Ambassador. In which case, another Tatsensui-PRC war breaks out.

Fan Zhaofeng is the wildcard in all of this. If he is caught, tried and taken out of circulation, the regime wins. But if he keeps killing Sanctioners or even highly placed regime officials, the High Council looks weaker and weaker, and laser rifles or not, they won't be able to keep the insurrection down. How long will the High Council be able to maintain the façade that it is still in power if it can't carry out its Sanctions, if it can't even protect its own officials? Would they resort to the standard playbook of all despots confronted with an unbeatable guerrilla foe and start reprisals among innocent citizens? She would not put it past them.

She feels like it really is the beginning of the end, one way or another.

She's scared and tired, but has one thing she needs to do before she crawls into bed and tries to sleep. Before leaving the SS offices, she drifted for message ID tags for anyone called Yung. It's an unusual name, so there were only a few hundred, which she downloaded into a message blast list to her holo.

She has no idea whether one of them belongs to Fan's Yung, but it's the only idea she has left. So she opens her comms unit, ignores the messages in there from Vali and SS colleagues wondering where or how she is, and sends the same message to every Yung in the system. Ninety-nine percent of them will get the message, frown and delete it. But one of them might understand it.

From: cMingkl465
To: Yung_blast_list
Subject: Fan
Dear Yung
You don't know me, but perhaps Fan has mentioned me. I know you care about Fan. So do I. I care deeply about him and I hope he understands that. You are probably wondering what is happening inside the SS at the moment, I can only say things are very fluid.

I don't have any way to contact Fan, but I know you are close, and perhaps he will contact you.

Please tell him that I am no longer with the Security Service. I quit today. I'm just me, and I want to see him. You have Ben. I have no one.

Regards, Lin.

She hits 'send' and goes to the bathroom, leaving the holo unit on. If he really wants to, Vali can track its signal and see she is at home, but she's sure he has other more important things on his mind than a junior Expositor slash potential deserter.

As she showers, she runs through her situation in her mind. The message to Yung is a long shot. But having written it now, she realizes that it's all true. She has left the PRC Security Service; mentally, if not officially. When Vali ordered her to open the weapons cache, it was no longer the SS she had signed on to. And now she really has no one else but Fan to turn to.

When she finishes in the shower and towels herself dry she sees the holo is blinking to show there are new messages. She grabs it and begins scrolling. Most are just versions of 'who is this?' but near the bottom of the list she sees this:

From: Yung2011cd

To: cMingkl465
Subject: re: Fan
Screw you Security Service bitch. Fan is mine.

She hadn't really expected a response, and certainly not this. Her heart is pounding. Please, please, please. He's there, wherever 'there' is, at the other end of this digital connection. She has to keep it open.

From: cMingkl465
To: Yung2011cd
Subject: re: re: Fan
I'm not trying to take him from you, I just need to see him. I'm scared and I need his help.

The message sends and she waits. She re-reads the messages. It really is like she is corresponding with a jealous lover. But she has to remind herself, she isn't writing to Yung, she's writing to Fan. Even through the filter of his alternate personalities, he *has* to hear her.

She waits another ten minutes for a reply, but nothing comes.

In the afternoon I do a run to the nearest homestead to see if there is any news from Lee, but he's probably busy trying to make sure his family is safe, like everyone else in the city. When I get back, I get a transparent food bag and put it over the glass jar with the funnel-web spider in it. It drops into the bag like a small fat plum and I quickly roll the top of the bag over. Could it suffocate in there? I don't think so. I remember as a child trying to drown some simulated insects in a science class – a spider, a praying mantis, a cricket. It never worked. They were able to trap enough air near their bodies to breathe, long enough to outwait the limited patience of a ten-year-old boy anyway.

Contemplating the spider inside the bag, I reflect on the fact that every event has multiple outcomes. Every dandelion head on a dandelion flower is full of seeds, and each seed, when you get close up, has a stalk and then a head that is composed of more dandelion seeds. On into infinity. My twin has a name now – the Core. The Core would know the chances of me trying to capture or kill him are high, in which case he's already anticipated I will try. Nothing I can do about that. But in one of the many worlds, just one of the 10^{500}, he will be surprised by what I'm about to do, he will come rushing here to stop me, and he will die.

And it might be this one. One in 10^{500} is good enough odds for me today.

I put a rubber band over my wrist. I don't want the spider escaping before it's done its job – it was hard enough trying to catch it. Then I pick up the bag and uncurl the top, keeping it closed. The spider is hunkered down in a corner and a little bead of moisture shows on the bag where it probably already tried to bite my hand. I remember reading that these spiders can bite through the fabric of a shoe. I hope he hasn't used all his venom biting the bag.

I slide the bag up over my right wrist and the rubber band over the neck of the bag.

I peer at the spider. I don't know what I expected. Maybe that it would leap at my hand and bite it straight away, I guess. But it stays hunkered down in the corner of the bag, one foreleg raised threateningly, the other, the one I damaged trying to catch it, trembling and jerking. I guess he's scared. Or she. Scraped out of its nest with a stick, wounded, thrown into a jar and now dumped into a bag tied around someone's hand, why wouldn't it be?

I give it thirty seconds, but it doesn't make a move toward the fingers lying quietly in front of it.

So I hold my hand up. And give it a shake.

Lin is still at home, in bed but still awake. It's the best place to be really, with the city going to hell outside her walls – but she'll have to make a move soon. Her neighbors know she is Security Service. How long before a lynch mob forms? She has no Ward to protect her.

When the holo unit beeps again, she picks it up, expecting it to be work. Vali has stopped trying to reach her, but she is still getting calls from concerned colleagues. The display hovering over the incoming holo icon just reads 'private'. She toys with letting it go to her answering service, but on a whim she answers it on audio only. She has no desire to see anyone from work.

"Hello?"

"Lin?"

"My God, *Fan*, is that you?"

"Yeah. Look, Lin…"

"Fan, listen, just listen. I need to see you…I'm on my own now, I've left the SS and…" *And what? I can help you? Is she really ready to go that far?*

"Lin…"

"I've got a Core link, you haven't anymore. I can…"

"Lin, it doesn't matter."

Something in his voice stops her. There is never too much timbre to it, his tone usually so measured and calm, but something more this time brings her tumbling speech to a halt. "What? What is it, Fan?"

"It will all be over soon," he says. "You wouldn't believe me about Citizen X, but that's okay. I've set a trap for him here, and if he turns up, I will kill him. And this will be over."

She grips the holo unit hard. "No! Fan, no! Citizen X, this twin of yours, he is a part of you, you have to understand that! Fan, if you kill him, you kill yourself!"

His voice sounds further away now. "It's done. One way or another. I just wanted to say goodbye and even though people tell me it can't be true, I wanted you to know…I loved you."

The connection is cut.

She stares at the holo.

She's right, isn't she? He can't kill Citizen X. The only way to kill one of the voices in your head is by killing all of them. And yourself in the process.

What did he say? It's done? Like hell it's done.

Like all SS officers, her holo unit is fitted with a traceback capability. If he's calling from a masked node, she'll get nothing, but if he's using a standard holo unit patched into the civilian net… She hits a code and nearly yelps with joy as it returns an address. Then she swallows hard, realizing it is just a few miles away from the house she visited when they were first searching for him. In the valley half the police in the State had already combed through, multiple times. Damn Ghost!

She punches another number into her holo unit. She may have resigned mentally, but for now she is still an Expositor in the SS. She can get drones out there straight away, call a quadcopter and tactical unit squad to pick her up and fly up there. Ten minutes for them to get to her, fifteen to get to where he is.

Will there even be a tac ops unit available during all this mayhem? Will anyone listen to her?

She'll tell them she knows where the Ghost, Fan Zhaofeng, is. She's pretty sure that will get her priority.

The spider bite feels like someone sticking a nail into the back of my hand. The spider strikes twice and backs into the corner of the bag. I pull it off and throw it on the ground, and the spider runs out, or at least limps out, making immediately for a dark crack in the floor.

I decided I would call Lin. I used a one-time disposable holo unit, but I know she'll be able to triangulate it. If I'm right, she'll arrive too late for all the fun, but at least she'll be here to clean up the mess and take the credit for finding me. Us.

I'm sweating now. My heart is starting to beat faster, breathing getting harder. I wish I could still drift. I can't remember the exact symptoms of funnel-web spider bite, but I'm pretty sure they involve cardiac arrest at some point.

After a while, my vision narrows. All I can hear is the erratic throb of my hearts. OK, so, maybe this isn't the lucky universe after all. This is one of the 10^{500} universes where Fan Zhaofeng dies, stupid and alone, from a spider bite.

Then a voice comes from behind me. My voice. "Interesting development. I *didn't* anticipate this. Suicide?"

He's leaning up against a wall on the other side of the sofa.

"Got your attention then," I mumble.

"Most definitely. I'm just interested to know. What do you think this achieves? Your premature death? I didn't think you'd be capable of spite."

"Stops you using me…gets you here, so I can speak to you," I tell him, finding the words a little hard to form. "I haven't thought…beyond that."

There is a little pause, like he is considering whether to answer, or how. "Clearly you haven't. Our work isn't done. The High Council still holds power. By a thread, but they are holding on."

"I have a Comcaster," I tell him. "I know what's happening. I know…more than you realize."

"Ah. Lucidity. I've seen you achieve that, but always further along. This is earlier than I expected, but I can work with it." He comes and sits at the end of the sofa. Two days earlier, I'd have tried to jump him. But now, it's all I can do to focus. "You're clearly suffering. Let me do the talking. Stop me if I get it wrong. You've realized that *you* are the one with Dissociative Identity Disorder, not Yung, correct? Just nod."

I nod.

"And you think I am a personality you created as part of your disorder. Therefore, by killing yourself, you kill me."

"No. Don't want to kill you. Want to talk. I want you to let me…live."

"You *will* live, a full and fulfilling life, centuries long. In the Core."

"This life."

"This life?"

"Let me live…this life."

"Ah. This is about Lin. Yes?"

I try to nod, but can't; it's hard enough just trying to keep my eyes on him.

"It is truly amazing what you achieved, Fan. The war took away your parents and you made your own way out of childhood. They corrupted your restraint protocols and still you had the bravery to face down a killer. They Sanctioned you, but you fought your way back to being a thinking, feeling, loving citizen. You started a revolution…"

"I…didn't…"

"You started a revolution, and after your death a few weeks from now, it is going to bring this colony to the next level of its evolution. That's enough for *five* lifetimes."

"No…not enough."

"It has to be, I'm sorry. I wish you could have seen it through, but you have rather effectively killed yourself."

My breathing is labored, my vision greying out now; I can barely see him. "Killed you too."

He sits beside me now and takes my hand. I know he's not real. All the violence, all those deaths. They were me. He's just a creation of my sick mind. But it feels so real. I lean my head on his shoulder.

"No, Fan. You can't kill me. I am Core." His voice is soft, fading. "I'm going to re-establish your uplink for the transition. Don't worry. I'll take it from here."

In the jump-seat of the quadcopter with six keyed-up tac ops officers, Lin has been watching through a drone 200 feet up, 500 feet back, silent and invisible to those on the ground. She has had it circling the half-buried house in the sand with its high-powered lens zoomed in on the windows. There is no one outside, the desert around the house is empty. She can make out a vague shape inside, sitting on a chair...no, now he disappears, sliding onto the floor. It's Fan. What is he doing?

"Down, get us down there now!" Lin calls to the tac lead, a young guy in his twenties.

"Positive ID?" he asks.

"Positive," Lin tells him.

He orders the quadcopter down. They are there in less than thirty seconds and even as the chopper flares and lands on its skids, Lin flies from the open door across the sand and flattens herself against a wall, looking in through a window. Half the team goes around to the back door. Through the window she can see a figure lying on the ground. There is no time for finesse. The tac ops team is ready with a ram, and she nods. They slam the heavy iron bar into the door and as it springs open, she rushes inside.

On the floor of the empty kitchen she finds Fan Zhaofeng, sitting down with his back to a kitchen cabinet, feet splayed out in front of him. He's covered in mud and twigs, wearing the same grey t-shirt and trousers she saw on the vision of the attack on the compound yesterday.

"Fan?" she says, uncertainly. She kneels beside him. The leader of the tac team barrels through the door behind her.

Fan looks at her, squinting, as though trying to focus.

"Hello, Lin," he says. The leader of the tac team takes a step forward, and Fan motions him to stop.

She expects the man to react, but he nods, steps back, and puts a hand up to his throat mike. "All clear here. Secure the area." The other members of the team file out, and their young commander stands at ease, his hands folded in front of him.

"It's alright," Fan says to her, smiling. "They're with me."

"They...what?"

"I knew you'd come for me. I have CRM sympathizers in tactical operations, so I just arranged for them to stand by for your call."

"No. You couldn't possibly have known."

Fan turns to the tac ops officer. "Lieutenant?"

"It's true, ma'am. We got a call four hours ago using a CRM codeword. We were told to stand by for your call."

Lin grabs Fan's face and looks into his eyes. They are clear now, staring calmly back into hers. "No. I don't… Fan, is it…is it you?"

He frowns at her. "Am I me? I think so." He looks at his hands, holds them out in front of him. Shows them to her. "We can check my DNA, I guess, but I'm pretty sure it will come up as Fan Zhaofeng."

Lin stays where she is. "I mean, I don't know how else to say this…am I talking to Fan Zhaofeng, or to Citizen X?"

"Citizen X, the bad twin?" He smiles. "Yes, he was here. I dealt with him. He's gone, for good I think."

She looks at him. How can she possibly tell if she is talking to Fan Zhaofeng, or to one of the voices in his head?

"What is the name of my cat?"

He frowns. "Your cat?"

"Yeah, you know, my cat. What is its name?"

He looks up at the ceiling as though trying to remember. "I'm feeling pretty weak, Lin. I'm not sure I can…"

"Try."

Then he snaps his fingers. "Tom."

Something about him doesn't seem right. But it's Fan. It has to be. She takes a deep breath. "You know about your condition?" He's watching her intently, but not looking surprised or agitated. "Dissociative Identity Disorder, your personalities…Citizen X, Ben, Yung?"

"Yes. I think going off-Core helped me get clarity. For better or worse I remember everything I've done, everything I said, no matter who I was at the time." He taps his skull. "I've done some housecleaning. It's just me in here now."

"You killed six Sanctioners, Fan."

He actually looks troubled. "I know. My restraint protocols were scrambled in the war and I guess they weren't able to properly unscramble them. Killing that first Sanctioner was right, though, he was about to commit murder."

"I know."

"Then, the others…the more I was involved in Sanction, the more I saw it for the evil it is. It can't be allowed to stand, Lin."

"No."

"No. And the High Council, the Internment Edict, the persecution of the cybers…it's wrong. Do you see that?"

"I do. So what happens now, Fan?"

"Insurrection, Expositor. Revolution." He levers himself to a standing position and holds out his hand. "So, are you in or out?"

COMMONWEALTH OF CORUSCANT PRIMER

Core Encyclopedia v201.b

Coruscant (original designation Kepler-452b or Kepler Object of Interest KOI-7016.01) is an exoplanet orbiting the Sun-like star Kepler-452 in the constellation Cygnus. It was the first potentially rocky super-PRC planet discovered orbiting within the habitable zone of a star very similar to the Sun.

The planet is about 1,400 light-years away from PRC and until the advent of the Alcubierre Warp Drive the only information about Coruscant was obtained from near-PRC observatories and predicted the planet could potentially sustain a citizen colony. The first unmanned probes to survey Coruscant, however, found a rocky planet with a climate which may have once been similar to PRC, but that was now without sufficient water or accessible reserves of nitrogen and oxygen to sustain citizen life.

Coruscant was however about 50 percent larger than PRC and subsequent surveys identified eleven moons in orbit around Coruscant. Of these, four were found to host indigenous non-sentient lifeforms and to be citizen-habitable. Over the next 200 years the following colonies were established:

Tatsensui (TS): a large ice moon entirely covered by frozen oceans but with low-level subsea volcanic activity leading to localized surface ice melting and minor seismic events. A colony was established at the northern pole, a continent of stable ice, free of significant seismic disruption. The economic engine of TS is the export of liquids and gases to the other colonies.

Peoples' Republic Colony (PRC): a desert moon similar in many ways to Mars in the PRC system, with reserves of water and ammonia trapped beneath the surface of the moon and a seismically stable profile which, coupled with huge surface-spanning solar energy harvesters, has contributed to it becoming the second largest anti-matter production facility outside of Ganymede.

New Syberia (NS): the most volcanically active moon orbiting Coruscant, it has retained a near-PRC atmosphere. Several large and active volcanoes have created a runaway greenhouse effect conducive to large-scale, high-rotation intensive crop production. It was historically the most tenuous of the three colonies, as its orbit took it through the center of an asteroid belt every 24 years, but this threat was subsequently mitigated by a re-engineered ring of Warp Drives able to absorb the mass of the asteroid and project it to coordinates in empty space. This ring is known as the New Syberian Shield and serves also as a planetary defense system.

NS is orbited inside the NS Shield by its own 'mini-moon', the geologically stable Moon of Orkutsk, which hosts a starship base and embassies, and is populated by a carefully regulated number of citizens of all three colonies. Orkutsk is the main point of entry into the Coruscant system for all interstellar traffic and interstellar/interplanetary trade is therefore the basis of the NS economy.

Due to the critical interdependencies of the three colonies (no one colony has the means or the raw materials to survive independent of the others), they were joined 100 years ago in a confederation known simply as the Commonwealth, with independent parliaments or Congresses, but a common foreign policy and trade pacts and a Commonwealth Court for settling disputes between colonial governments.

Conflicts and controversies

Energy starvation: The colonies of New Syberia and Tatsensui are frequently subject to disruption to anti-matter supply and thus to trade, base power and transport, due to political differences with the other colonies over the perceived high cost of raw materials and foodstuffs. One such dispute led to the brief Tatsensui-PRC War, won by Tatsensui, the outcome of which was a mutual non-aggression treaty, which did not however include New Syberia. As a part of the treaty, the constitutions and laws of Tatsensui and PRC were 'harmonized' in an act known as the Alignment. In reality, PRC retained self-governance but was forced to adopt the constitution and laws of the Tatsensui victors.

AI policy: Since the Tatsensui-PRC Alignment, Tatsensui and PRC share a common central AI platform, distributed across both worlds, known as the Core, to which all computer systems are linked. The prime directive of the Core is the preservation and promotion of all life on the Moons of Coruscant. To assist in the execution of its mandate, the Core has created bioware AIs, colloquially known as cybers – artificially grown biological bodies with cybernetically enhanced brains and bodies able to interface directly with the Core. Through its cybers the Core platform is claimed to support faster learning and evolution and to be designed for survivability should a calamity impact one or the other of the colonies.

Ordinary citizens of Tatsensui and PRC can query the Core as you would any large database and use it to support their daily lives in everything from simple navigational direction finding to advanced scientific research. Higher-level officials can query the Core using a natural language interface, and in this way seek advice or information on matters relevant to the health and welfare of their citizens.

New Syberia has rejected joining the Core platform and instead relies on a policy of multiple, totally independent AI cybers, each learning and evolving at their own pace. It claims similar survivability through the proliferation of these AIs across both New Syberia and its submoon, Orkutsk, and is currently the only colony with an ambition to establish a cyber-based sub-colony on Coruscant, though it cannot do so without the consent of the other colonies in the Commonwealth.

Orkutsk non-militarized zone: Due to its role as an interstellar transit hub and diplomatic station for all three colonies, in the 'Treaty of Orkutsk', declared at the birth of the Commonwealth, this central submoon was designated a neutral territory. Following an attempt by New Syberia to assert sovereignty over Orkutsk, the combined armed forces of PRC and Tatsensui occupied Orkutsk and a military skirmish followed after which New Syberia was forced to withdraw its claim. The Treaty was later amended to require all three colonies to permanently base at least 1,000 non-military personnel each on Orkutsk, to provide 'diplomatic capital' in case of new hostilities. In recent years, New Syberia has implemented a policy of basing only cybers on Orkutsk. The Tatsensui and PRC governments have established a Commonwealth Court Commission of Investigation into whether this constitutes a breach of the Treaty of Orkutsk.

Cyber Rights Movement (CRM): The CRM political lobby movement began on Tatsensui shortly after the creation of Core-Chained cyber lifeforms. It lobbies the governments of Tatsensui and PRC for self-determination for cybers. It has been successful in achieving several rights gains for cybers on Tatsensui, including the right to choose place of employment (within a limited range of occupations), right to economic independence, freedom of travel and domicile, the right to gender self-determination and freedom of association. Similar rights exist by forcible inclusion in the PRC Constitution due to the

Alignment, but are a source of discontent among a large minority of the human PRC population who wish to see a return to the former status of cybers on PRC as slaves to human citizens.

The ultimate aim of the Cyber Rights Movement is full equality between cybernetic and human citizens across all of Coruscant.

FROM THE AUTHOR

Thanks very much for supporting 'Direct Publishing' as a way for authors to see their works come to life without the barrier of finding an agent or publisher.

If you would like to rate this book please go to Amazon.com and enter your rating!

I would love to hear from you on the FX Holden Facebook page https://www.facebook.com/hardcorethrillers

Where you will also be able to read excerpts from my other books, including the next title in the Coruscant series: Core Melt. For a preview of Core Melt, just read on!

Cheers

FX

CORE MELT

A preview of the next novel in the Coruscant series.

Chapter 1: Always wear the proper attire

Peter Zerov remembered the bombing like it was yesterday. It was part of his motivation, driving him on. But it happened before he was even born.

12.38 a.m., month 1, day 7, Omsk; the Orkutsk space port and capital. He just had to close his eyes, and he was *there*.

In a wide city, street water lay still in the gutters, reflecting neon lights from rainbow streaks of hydrocarbon. Small dots pricked its surface as flies picked at the scum. The street was dark and quiet and empty of traffic. Empty of life too, but for four dark ghosts, caped and huddled silent outside the hotel. Dead, though they didn't know it yet.

He remembered their dark rain capes, dark peaked hats, black boots, black stun guns in belts at their waists. Badges and stripes on their shirt sleeves. How they stood just meters from the bomb, not knowing it was there. Those last minutes were a lottery as they broke from their huddle, pocketed their inhalers and walked towards, across, or away from the killing ground. Inside the hotel where the Commonwealth Heads of Government meeting was being held, politicians, statesmen and stateswomen and their dozens of minders slept soundly with their guilt, remorse or conviction, mistakenly feeling protected by their tech and those frail black-caped human shields.

From down the road came a prehistoric sound, the roar of a laboring engine. He heard the whine of electric motors, the scrape of metal on metal, and saw the flickering yellow lights warn off traffic that wasn't there at that hour. Smelt the rotten stench of garbage. It was a break in the monotony for the cops and they all watched as the autonomous garbage truck lumbered into the street.

Orkutsk is a frontier world, the membrane through which goods and passengers flow between Coruscant and other star systems. A place where the three colonies of Coruscant meet, and clash. A mishmash of past, present and future histories, cultures and technologies. Zerov was a citizen of Orkutsk and he'd never lived there.

Two cybers jogged alongside the truck, darting ahead now and then to lift rubbish bins from their green metal cages and hoist them into the back of the truck as it ground along. A job too menial for a human, on Orkutsk anyway. That annoyed the hell out of Zerov. The compacting gears in the rear of the truck whirred constantly, crushing inhaler packets, drink containers and food wrappers into a tightly compressed biobrick that would be taken to a depot in the inner west, sorted and repurposed. The cops taunted the garbos, knowing that in an hour they'd be at a greasy spoon having breakfast and coffee while the garbos were still wading in the stink of their daily grind. But the cops were ghosts, and didn't know it yet. They had a minute to live.

Zerov hated that it was a memory, and not a sim. If it was a sim, he could walk to where the bomb waited in the bin outside the arcade entrance to the hotel and try to defuse it. It was tiny, the size of a kid's ball, fueled by 0.03 ounces of anti-matter, but maybe he could have found it. That would have been dumb, though, because at that point in the memory, it was live, circuits open waiting to close, stored energy waiting only for the timed collapse of its containment field to make it bloom and kill.

In the memory that was sewn into the gaps between his neurons he was standing there and *felt* the bomb explode with the power of a 15 kiloton nuclear blast. Everything within the blast radius of two miles was annihilated. Anyone outside the annihilation zone and out to five miles who lived through the blast wave was suffocated. Anyone above ground in an area out to ten miles was crushed as buildings, bridges and tunnels collapsed and vehicles and pedestrians were pulverized by flying debris.

In seconds, the Orkutsk Anti-matter Bomb killed or seriously injured two thousand, three hundred and three individuals, human and cyber. And over the next two years it would kill three more.

Three Coruscant Security Service Hunters were put on the trail of the bomber. One by one they closed in, chasing down leads, tracking down the bomb maker's associates, shining light into the darkest corners of Coruscant's terrorist underworld.

One by one, they disappeared. Peter Zerov was the fourth.

Man, that memory sucked.

Kirsten Nygaard.

When the Commonwealth of Coruscant Security Service had its AIs review the data compiled by his three failed predecessors, one individual at the periphery of their investigations had intrigued them. She was a minor functionary in the Whole Truth Movement. Each of the Hunters had looked at her, none of them had looked at her twice. But not long after making contact with her, each of the Hunters had been killed and their killer had never been identified. There was no direct link between Nygaard and their deaths, nothing that could be proven. Different time periods had passed between contact with Nygaard and their deaths on different planets, in different contexts – but the analytical AIs found one consistently unexplored link to all the dead Hunters. Kirsten Nygaard.

So, in a birthing tank on Orkutsk, Peter Zerov was born. A Hunter-class cyber. The only one of his kind on the desert moon.

There was a damn good reason only the CSS and various militaries were allowed to birth Hunter-class cybers. Since what had happened on PRC, governments, and their populations, were terrified of them. The CSS was required to keep a register, accessible only to the Heads of Service on each of the three moons, listing all operational Hunters. No government – whether Tatsensui, PRC or New Syberia – was allowed more than one. The CSS itself, responsible as it was for security on the spaceport moon of Orkutsk, was also allowed only one. Right now, that one was Peter Zerov.

A Hunter's tasking had to be approved by all three government Heads of Service and the CSS Head. The sanction for birthing an unapproved Hunter was no less than capital punishment for the head of the service found to be responsible. It wasn't unheard of. The head of the New Syberian Security Service had recently forfeited his life because of an ill-advised and unsanctioned Hunter operation on

Tatsensui.

All Coruscant governments had agreed the bomber of Orkutsk had to be found, and the bomb maker had become the number one target of the CSS ever since. Zerov had been birthed on Orkutsk in a CSS facility a year earlier with one mission in life — to hunt Kirsten Nygaard and determine if she was the Orkutsk bomber. He was part detective, part judge, part executioner. His brief was simple. Find Nygaard. Establish her innocence or guilt beyond reasonable doubt. Present the evidence to the CSS Heads of Security. If they found it beyond reasonable doubt, he was authorized to terminate her.

And then he would decommission himself. Other cybers on Orkutsk and New Syberia had 'natural' life spans, more or less the same as the average lifespan of a human on those moons, plus any years added through cell therapy or organ regeneration. On Tatsensui and PRC, the Core worlds, a cyber's lifespan was shorter, but still thirty years; enough for a fun childhood and fulfilling adulthood, without the slow and painful decline to death. A shorter life, but potentially just as rich in love and laughter and experience.

A Hunter had only as long as it took him or her to fulfill the mission they were purpose-built for, and then they were reassimilated.

Ironically, he did have rights. He could refuse to carry out his mission. The CSS was pretty cool about that. They wouldn't just shut him down; assuming his mission wasn't time critical, they'd give him two months to think about it. And if he didn't change his mind, *then* they'd shut him down.

That part sucked too.

The CSS AIs might not have known where Kirsten Nygaard is, but they knew just about everything else there was to know about her. She'd been wading in the Commonwealth of Coruscant datasphere for decades and the CSS had a record of every interaction she'd had, every grade she got in school, every friend she made and lost along the way, every item she ever bought, data searches she made, food, entertainment and sport preferences, conversational style, sense of humor, and most importantly of all — every lover she'd ever had and *their* interactions, preferences and personalities.

Up to the moment she disappeared, that is.

AIs couldn't predict (yet) who a human would or wouldn't fall in love with. But they could create a potential partner who at least had a pretty good shot of appealing to a target. For Kirsten Nygaard, they created Peter Zerov.

They gave him the gender she preferred, and the sort of looks she seemed to favor. An exotic and interesting face, handsome but not beautiful. Thick black hair tied back in a ponytail, though she seemed also to be attracted to redheads. (It was felt a redhead from Orkutsk would be a little too hard to explain as they made up only 0.001 percent of the population.) They gave him a body that was lean and strong, with golden sun-touched skin.

For a personality? That was the hard part, the unfathomable part of the human biology, psychology and pure dumb luck mixture that led to love. But she liked a partner who listened more than they talked. A strong but gentle lover. Someone who could make her laugh and laugh with her. She liked to lead, not follow, but she didn't want a passive partner. They had to have their own life, their own friends, their own interests and where they intersected with hers, they had to be happy to share them. Family could be important to them, but it wasn't so important to her. It didn't matter so much to her what her partner did with their life, she was more interested in what they thought, and what they believed.

So his cover was that he was just a traveler, a tourist from the People's Republic Colony or PRC. If you asked Zerov to describe himself in one word, he'd say 'curious'. Ask him to add a word, he'd say 'adventurous'. He was a guy who made a living teaching rock climbing. Who enjoyed being one with nature and saw himself as part of a bigger, organic whole. No religion, but a firm belief in Gaia Philosophy, which contrasted with the Whole Truth beliefs she was raised with, but didn't conflict with them. Who could play stringed instruments and was good at math, complementing her love of music and apparent disinterest in all things mathematical. He had a passing interest in technology, able to be woken into a keen interest, which was good, because tech was her thing.

She was a citizen of the ice moon Tatsensui or TS. He'd never been there. She'd expressed an interest in visiting PRC and NS, but the last trace they had of her was a shot she took across the bridge from TS to Orkutsk, where her trail went cold.

It was no mean feat to disappear from the Commonwealth

datasphere, but she did. It wasn't completely unknown. Senior converts of Whole Truth, known as *Sadvipra*, had access to the sort of technologies which made it possible; but she was not *Sadvipra*. And that was just one of the things that made her interesting enough to despatch a Hunter to find her.

She was also sharp, so she liked a partner who could keep up with her intellectually. Which was interesting because you'd think that would give her a slight preference for cyber partners, but she'd never been known to have had a relationship with a cyber, even though the Whole Truth Movement was predominantly made up of cyber adherents.

So Zerov has been birthed to appear to the outside world as human. His technology was woven into his biology at a molecular level – undetectable to any agency other than the CSS Hunter Division. He could link to the datasphere at will, but not at the terahertz electromagnetic wavelength of other cybers. Zerov had always-on access via the CSS and Commonwealth military quantum entanglement communication system. He could instantly query the datasphere, run analyses and access AI support with radiating or receiving a single joule of non-biological energy.

He was stronger and healthier than most humans, with the IQ, data query, retrieval and storage capabilities of a military-spec cyber. Imagine a *society* of cybers like that, or an entire colony? You can't, because humans wouldn't allow it. Ergo, only one Hunter per colony.

Zerov wasn't born a Truther. Most of Nygaard's early relationships were with non-Truthers. But she still expressed strong views on cyber rights, so Zerov also felt very strongly about such matters.

PRC was a Core world, where all cybers were chained to the central Core AI. A PRC cyber, like those on Tatsensui, had a tiny glowing blue Core data link diode on its forehead. Even though NS was not a Core world, it adopted the same symbol – a tiny blue tattooed dot on the forehead – to differentiate cybers from humans on NS. Zerov felt strongly that this diode created stigmatization and should be removed from the basic design of *all* cybers. A search of his civil record, painstakingly created by the CSS backstory experts, would show Zerov was arrested while demonstrating for cyber rights on PRC as a student.

And the freaky thing was, he actually felt that way. The way humans treated cybers like himself as tools, as second-class citizens, as technology with built-in obsolescence…that was just plain wrong, dammit!

He knew why he felt that way. He'd been birthed feeling that way. But it didn't make the feeling, or the judgment behind it, less real. And yeah, he could certainly see the irony in humans birthing a cyber as a Hunter who hated the idea of humans birthing a cyber as a Hunter.

Another item on the Peter Zerov list of things that sucked.

But there were *good* things, things few humans could say with the same certainty as he could. Peter Zerov knew exactly what his purpose in life was. When he weighed it against any one of a dozen different value systems, it could be seen as a noble and righteous purpose. One that would benefit both himself and his fellow citizens.

And Zerov felt *great*. Physically. He woke every morning bursting with health. He had no stiffness in his limbs, no aches or pains in his frame. He'd been given small imperfections – skin blemishes, freckles, embarrassingly large pinkies on each foot – but none of these troubled him. If he went on a drink or drugs bender, he could *choose* whether or not to let himself suffer the day after. If there was a virus going around, he could *decide* whether to let it affect him, and how much, and for how long.

He had money. Teaching rock climbing didn't make a guy rich, but having your own rock climbing teaching school was a nice money earner. The CSS had bought a school and installed him as a working partner. While he'd been in training and during his indoctrination as a Hunter, he'd also taken on the running of the school and lifted it from a small four-person business run by amateur enthusiasts to a big twenty-person business run by…well, still amateur enthusiasts, but amateurs with structure around them. None of them really cared where he came from, because he had money, passion and crazy climbing skills. When he'd announced he was going to leave them to run the business and go traveling for a while, they'd all wished him luck and a speedy return.

Chapter 2: Don't make a lot of noise, as the hounds may hear you and get distracted

Zerov had not started the hunt for Kirsten Nygaard where the CSS suggested he should start. Her trail had gone cold on Orkutsk, so his handlers had strongly advised him to start there. But the hunt was his, and he didn't see it that way.

He had information he felt hadn't been fully explored. His training taught him to use his cyber capabilities to analyze data, but his human instincts to decide how to prioritize it. His decision to start on Tatsensui was entirely human.

He started at the beginning, where her trail was, literally, coldest. The living quarters of a Whole Truth temple, or Gurdwara, outside Ketchican on Tatsensui. The congestion he had been born into on Orkutsk and the way the air and the smells of the street stuck to the skin were polar opposites of the crisp blue-skied cold of Tatsensui. If he had to choose, he'd probably choose an ice moon over a spaceport city. If nothing else, it was quieter.

He could still smile at the memory of the drone flight from The Capitol to Ketchican in Tatsensui's Inland Territory, the crowd of family and friends in thermal jackets who greeted the people getting off the plane, a huge and badly painted mural of a suntanned skier splashed across one wall of the airport. He sat next to an artist whose parents were Territorians, going back home for her holidays. *Pickled food and rednecks*, she had said to him, shaking her head as the drone circled to land, *it's all pickles and rednecks*.

He took a private car straight from the airport to the Gurdwara, a thirty-minute drive through white roads and grey hillsides flourishing with green and yellow lichens like the rocks were afflicted by a virulent fungus. The living quarters he was looking for were on a block behind the Gurdwara on a private road, and as his car pulled into the road he saw in his mirror a group of women carrying laundry step into the road behind him, their talk animated. They screwed up their eyes as though trying to remember every detail of his car.

The car pulled itself to a halt in a cloud of snow powder at a series of prefabbed houses crackling in the wet sun as a sudden boost in temperature cracked the ice on their walls. Thermal inverters poked out of two or three windows of every house and thumped with a heavy rhythm, pumping cool air out at face height, adding to his discomfort as he checked house numbers. He saw a hand lift a curtain at the bungalow to his right, and then drop it again. Someone big.

At number 32 he knocked. A small, slightly built Truther in a sari opened the door a few centimeters, her eyes flicking over him, and then into the road beyond. There was a heavy chain across the door and she did nothing to lift it aside.

"Amar? I'm Steven," he lied. "We spoke yesterday…"

She was still looking past him, then turned her eyes back on him. "You're PRC militia?"

"Yes." He hadn't arrived on Tatsensui as Peter Zerov the rock climbing entrepreneur. He was Steven Zhang, a member of Whole Truth's internal security wing, the Peace Militia.

Clearly the thought troubled her. The militia had a well-earned reputation for violence against enemies of the movement. The PRC branch of the militia, the one he was claiming to be from, had the worst reputation of all.

"Yes."

"I asked you not to park outside," she said.

"I know. You want me to move it?"

She looked at him again and he saw her hand shaking as she held the door. "It's too late."

The identity of militia members was not recorded anywhere, for good reason. The militia was outlawed in all colonies except New Syberia. So he showed her a physical, printed ID. Just carrying one was a crime on three moons, which was enough to convince most people it was real.

The fingers of her right hand were trembling slightly as she took the ID and looked at it but he could tell she was not really reading. Then she handed it back and lifted the chain from across the door.

He stepped into the cool dry air inside and saw straight away that there was another person in the room. A dark-haired woman, in her mid-twenties and also in a sari, sat with her legs crossed on a chair in the living room. She drew heavily on the inhaler she was holding and then put it down but did not get up.

"Uh, this is Sue. She worked with Kirsten," Amar said, her hand scratching in her hair. She pointed to a kitchen chair which had been placed beside the sofa and indicated for Zerov to sit. "In Treasury."

"Legal Affairs, actually," the woman said, not so patently

nervous. "I'm just a boring lawyer. But I did know Kirsten."

"OK, look, like I said in my comms message, I have been sent to help with your little problem," Zerov said, taking the surroundings in as he settled in the chair. A kitchen door to their left was open and soft sunlight streamed into the room, giving the weak heaters some help. Behind him a green door, half closed, led off to another room, a bedroom he guessed, while another closed door probably led to the bathroom. Both women looked at him expectantly. Usually, he would spend some time easing into the conversation, but this was obviously not going to be one of those times.

"Our little problem." The one called Sue laughed. "And what do you know about our 'little problem'?"

He took a small printed photograph from a pocket and showed it to them. "Kirsten Nygaard, yes? Came from The Capitol. Arrived here about three years ago," he explained. "Worked in finance. Disappeared a year ago along with a pile of Whole Truth credits, a chunk of which were owed to PRC." He leaned forward, fixing Sue with an unblinking gaze. "*Are* still owed."

"Six billion, three hundred million," Amar said bitterly. "Give or take a few million. I shared a house with her, I had no idea she was capable of such a thing."

"Right, well, I'm here, so let's talk," Zerov said. He didn't need it, but he used his earbud to bring up a recorder and initiated it verbally as a human would do. Then hesitated, sensing somewhere behind him a movement. Hearing something too, muffled by one or more walls. One individual, large. Standing still, breathing fast. Probably male. He kept a part of his attention on the guy behind him, turned the rest of his attention back to the women. "Whole Truth is pretty small here, isn't it?" he asked. "How many Truthers on Tatsensui?"

"About a thousand converts. We are growing," Sue said predictably.

"That's a lot of money for such a small community," he pointed out.

"We own the intellectual property rights to the Skydome that controls the environment on Tatsensui," Sue told him. "No Skydome, no Tatsensui. The royalties add up. Most Truthers here work as *vaishya*; in wealth management." The Vaishya were the bankers of the movement.

"Kirsten Nygaard was a *vaishya*?"

"Not yet. She is – or was – in training. What she did, stealing like that, should have been impossible."

Zerov nodded. "And she had a boyfriend here, right? The local militia commander, a *kshatriya*?"

Sue's eyes flicked to her companion and back. "Yes, he is militia, of *kshatriya* rank."

"I expected him to be here to meet me."

"He has been delayed." Sue's eyes flicked over his shoulder. She was lying. And he now had a pretty good idea who was in the room behind him.

"Sorry, why does a small Gurdwara like this even warrant a *kshatriya*? A militia representative, sure, for internal security. But a *kshatriya*, and his cohort? That seems like overkill. You risk provoking the interest of local authorities."

"With much wealth come many enemies," Amar said, looking over Zerov's shoulder again. "Both on and off Tatsensui."

There was a quiet footfall behind him. The big guy no doubt. He let him approach without reacting and something cold was jammed into the side of his jaw as a male voice growled, "Just you stay very still, friend."

The lawyer, Sue, looked first at Amar and then at Zerov and whoever was behind him. "There's no need for that, Ben! Shit." She looked at Amar again. "You never said he had a gun!"

Zerov's muscles tensed. He could feel the gun barrel, two barrels by the width of it, against his neck. He didn't know if the man behind him was cyber or human. Human, he could simply disarm him. Cyber, he might die trying. He chose the safest response, raising both hands slowly to shoulder level to show they were empty. "Hey, I'm not armed. I have my militia commission in my shirt pocket, you can check it." The man had apparently been outside until moments ago – the barrel of his gun was ice cold.

Sue put a hand up to the man behind him. "Cool down, Ben, and back up. I'll get his ID out and you can take a look at it, OK?" She stepped up to Zerov and he had no trouble picking out the scent of sandalwood oil as it washed over him. Her breath was fast and light, close against his face as she reached into his shirt pocket, her eyes on the man behind him. She found his travel wallet and pulled it out. Copies of all his PRC documentation were printed and stored there, including the militia commission, which was real enough. It just wasn't his.

"You're welcome to check it all," Zerov said, head bent forward by the pressure of the gun barrels on the base of his skull. He turned his head slightly to get a look at the man holding it. No blue light diode on his forehead.

Human.

"Hold it up so I can see it," the *kshatriya* barked at the lawyer. To qualify for *kshatriya* rank, he had to be proficient in hand-to-hand combat, and with several types of weapon. "I don't trust this PRC piece of shit."

As the man's eyes flicked to the ID Sue was holding, Zerov moved. He'd kept his hands raised, and with his left he grabbed the barrel of the burp gun, pulling it forward and down with such strength the *kshatriya* either had to let it go, or be pulled over Zerov's shoulder with it.

He chose to let it go. It would have been DNA coded anyway, able to be fired only by him. He jumped back and smirked, pulling a wicked blade the length of his forearm from his sleeve as Zerov spun off the couch to face him.

"Congratulations, fool," the man said, adjusting his stance and preparing to lunge at Zerov. "Now you made me suspicious *and* mad."

Zerov held up both hands again, palms outward. "You're just making yourselves look complicit in whatever Nygaard did…"

The two women had backed into a far corner. "Ben! Let it go!" Amar yelled at him. But Zerov saw the other woman, Sue, reaching down behind a cabinet.

Ah, hell.

With the simple press of a finger on his palm, he triggered a neural blast from the unit hidden in his belt. It was highly controlled mil-tech, and not something a Whole Truth *kshatriya* could easily counter. The man went down like a sack of rocks, and the women behind Zerov crumpled too. His cyber bioware shielded him from the effects.

He couldn't really blame them for being careful. There was no love lost between the militias of the three Coruscant worlds, and they reacted poorly to one interfering in the delicate affairs of another. In hindsight he might have tried a different cover story, but his creators had given him an ethnic build that could only belong to a citizen of

PRC, so he'd decided to roll with that. Oh well, it had gotten him through the door.

He walked over and took the stiletto from the *kshatriya*, checking him for other weapons and finding none. Walking over to the women, he found the weapon the 'lawyer' had been reaching for behind the cabinet. Another militia-issue burp gun. So, she was a little more than 'just a lawyer', perhaps. Of the three, the lawyer was definitely the more interesting.

He pulled her away from the wall and sat her with her back up against it. Taking two restraints from a pocket, he bound her hands and feet, then reached up and touched a fingertip to her temple. He sent a small current into her nervous system that would ameliorate the neural shutdown.

She began to stir and he crouched in front of her, out of reach. It would take a while before she got back full muscle control, but her speech, sight and hearing should be back to normal reasonably quickly. He saw her eyes clear, pupils narrowing as she focused on him.

"Right. Let's try again. I'm from the PRC militia, and I'm here to talk about Kirsten Nygaard..."

Tatsensui had been a good place to start, it turned out. Sue the lawyer was still in touch with Nygaard's family. The CSS of course had real-time surveillance on the datasphere surrounding anyone related to Nygaard and had picked up no contact from her at all. There was no simple inter-colony comms system – the high levels of radiation from Coruscant's sun made interplanetary voice comms communication impossible and quantum entanglement comms tech wasn't approved for civilian use.

So the only way to get messages between the colonies was by encoding messages on physical media, discs, and shooting them across the Einstein–Rosen bridges that linked the colonies. Once they landed, they were sorted and dispatched across the ether to their recipients. A bridge shot wasn't cheap, so messages were short and comms shots were limited to four a day. Trade took up most of the bridge bandwidth, and human traffic the rest. The CSS had a tight grip on the comms traffic, and nothing had come through to Nygaard's family that could in any way be tied back to her. Nothing.

Because, as he learned from Sue the lawyer, she hadn't sent a disc.

She'd sent Olaf.

Olaf was a lovely guy. A seriously nice guy. He was kind of chubby, with rosy cheeks, red hair and a red beard. Maybe that's why Nygaard had taken to him?

"You want another one?" Olaf asked Zerov, offering him a beer with one hand as he juggled his own beer and some sort of stringed instrument with the other. Olaf was a musician in Savoonga and Zerov had caught him at the end of a set at a local bar and peeled him away from his musician buddies by saying Sue the lawyer had sent him. Which, in a way, she had.

He hadn't needed to use any of the many 'persuasion' techniques the CSS had taught him. When Sue had gathered her senses she'd looked at her *kshatriya* buddy and her girlfriend out cold on the floor, blinked her own headache away, turned to Zerov and said, "What do you want to know?"

"My buy," Zerov told Olaf as he went up to the bar, got two beers and brought them back. Olaf looked very happy someone had bought him a beer.

"Thanks!" he said cheerfully and took a swig. "You like the music?"

Zerov was still learning what he liked and didn't like. Checking quickly, he decided yeah, he did like it. "Yeah, you've been playing a while by the sound of it."

"Since I was knee-high to a Grizzly," he said. "But the boys here know how to carry a tune, they make a fella sound better than he is."

Zerov let him relax as they listened to another set, tapping their feet and swigging their beers. Let Olaf get around to it.

"So, Sue sent you, you say?" he asked eventually. Zerov knew he would have called her to ask what it was about, if Zerov was to be trusted. He'd like to know what she said, but then again, maybe he wouldn't. But Olaf had agreed to meet, so whatever she'd said had worked. She had an incentive to help him. He told her if she helped him find Nygaard, he'd forgive their debt to the PRC militia. It was an easy promise to make, since it wasn't a promise he could keep.

"Yeah, look, your friend Kirsten has got herself into a bit of trouble, and I'm here to get her out of it," Zerov said.

Olaf was a lovely guy, but he wasn't stupid. He looked away as he spoke. "You know, I never thought of the PRC militia as a welfare organization. I always thought of them more as a bunch of knee-capping psychopaths, if you know what I mean?" He looked at Zerov again, giving him a disarming smile. "The sort who might, you know, use a neural blaster on a room full of my friends."

Zerov laughed. "OK, she told you that."

"She did, Steven. Yes, she did."

"She tell you I had one gun at my throat and she was reaching for another one when I triggered it?"

It was his turn to laugh. "She told me that too. So I'm not saying I blame you."

Zerov sized him up. There was more to Olaf than met the eye. Which also made sense.

"But still, you're here."

"Aye, here I am, Steven," Olaf said, and winked at him. "Without my burp gun. So tell me how you might be able to get my friend Kirsten out of the trouble she might have gotten herself into?"

Zerov told him he was in a position to forgive the community's debt to PRC if he could just track down Nygaard. He would recover the money owed from her, and Tatsensui Whole Truth wouldn't need to worry.

"Right, okay," Olaf said. "Let me do the math on that. Nygaard stole six billion credits, they say."

"They do," Zerov agreed.

"And Tatsensui owes how much to PRC?"

"Two billion," Zerov said. He'd gotten the figure from Sue.

"So the other four billion..."

"If she hasn't already spent it or given it to a third party..."

"Righto, yes. The other four billion, which is actually Tatsensui money, that goes..." He screwed up his face and frowned. "No, I'm confused. What happens to that?"

Zerov sat back, his face as neutral as he could make it. "Expenses. There's my bridge shot here."

"Half a million..."

"And back..."

"One million."

"That neural blaster. Black market weapon. Two million just to get it reloaded."

"Ah, that's criminal," Olaf sympathized. "And the rest?"

"Paying people to forget Tatsensui owes them a big stack of credits…" Zerov said. "PRC militia have good memories. They don't forget easily."

Olaf nodded. "Yes, I imagine that could get expensive."

"Very. People have long memories in Whole Truth. Most of them are cybers. Perfect recall, you know," Zerov pointed out. It struck him Olaf was angling for something. "But there is a reward for anyone who helps us recover the money."

"Blood money," Olaf said. "I'd be wanting no part of that."

"You assume some harm will come to her," Zerov said. "I won't report her to any authorities, and I plan to just ask her nicely to hand over to the PRC militia the money she took. How do you think she'll react to that?"

Olaf looked thoughtful. "I'm not sure," he said. "I don't know her as well as I thought I did. I never thought she'd be the type to hack her way to a cool six billion and disappear."

"But she didn't disappear, did she, Olaf?" Zerov asked. "You saw her on Orkutsk."

"Ah well, that depends how you define 'saw her'," Olaf replied. He traced the outline of a stick figure woman in the condensation on his beer glass. "She asked me to come and meet her. Sent a return bridge fare."

"You two were…close?"

"Not in the sense we exchanged bodily fluids on a regular basis kind of close," Olaf said. "But yeah, we hung out. She likes music."

"And this meeting where you didn't actually see her?"

"And this reward you mentioned, where you won't actually hurt her?" he parried back at Zerov.

"One hundred million," Zerov said without hesitating. "Payable when the money is recovered, as long as whatever we recover is at least double the finder's fee."

"And I'd know you didn't hurt her, how?" Olaf asked.

"You wouldn't. And I don't expect you'll just trust me on this. But letting us recover the stolen money really is the only way she is going to get clear of this, or there will be someone hunting her the rest of her life. So I'll talk to her just like I'm talking to you, and hope she'll see reason."

Olaf turned an ear to the music for a moment, drumming his fingers on the table, then turned back again. "When I got to Orkutsk I went to a bar in the terminal there, where she said to meet. A complete stranger came and sat at my table. A woman. You want a description?"

He didn't need it. He could pull the videolog from the terminal surveillance, but Olaf didn't need to know that. "Yes please."

"Short, brunette, big bust and hips. Green eyes. Spoke with a Tatsensui accent but I've never seen her around. One gold earring. Don't know if she was a Truther or not."

"That's a very good description," Zerov observed. "How much time did you spend with her?"

"Long enough to remember what she looked like, and what she told me, not much more," Olaf said carefully. "It wasn't a dinner date."

Zerov pulled the data on Olaf's biofeed as he was speaking. All Tatsensui citizens could opt in to have their vital signs monitored by the Core via a capillary implant in case of medical emergencies, or just so they could check their fitness levels. Olaf's heart rate was elevated and his adrenaline high, but not in the 'fight or flight' range. His breathing was normal. Zerov ran the data backwards, checking his verbal responses over the last few minutes against his biofeed – a kind of reverse engineered lie detector. There was nothing indicating he'd been lying.

"So what did this woman tell you?" Zerov asked.

"She gave me a message for Kirsten's parents," Olaf said.

"Can you share it?"

"Sure. It made no sense to me," Olaf said. *"For the strength of the Pack is the Wolf, and the strength of the Wolf is the Pack."*

Zerov searched and got a hit among Earth Ancient literature. It was a quote from an author called Rudyard Kipling.

"You passed it on to her parents?"

"Went all the way up to Ketchican to deliver it," he nodded. "Had never met them before. Nice people."

"Did the message make sense to them?" Zerov asked.

"They didn't say. Just asked me to repeat it and gave each other this little look, then they said thanks and offered me tea."

"A 'little look'? A little confused look, or a little 'aha' look?"

"More of an 'aha' look, I guess." Olaf spread his hands. "And that's it. It was kind of late when I got there so we had a cup of tea, then supper. I stayed the night, then went home the next day."

"And they gave you no indication they knew where she might be, or where she might have been headed?"

"We just traded Truther gossip. They'd been *sadvipra*. Really high up, but told me they were getting old and were pretty much out of the loop these days. They wanted to know how things were in the movement now, who was who in zoo, that kind of thing. Nothing about Kirsten."

Zerov considered that. "That's kind of strange, don't you think? A guy travels to another moon to give them a message from their runaway daughter and they don't spend the rest of the night quizzing you? Did they know she took the money before she ran?"

"They knew," he said. "And I'm not saying they weren't concerned. The father, Stefan I think it is, he asked would I be willing to help them find her. But I said no, not my thing, and judging by the theatrics on Orkutsk, she was going to make it hard for anyone who tried."

Zerov smiled. That much was very, very true.

Olaf drained his beer and put down his glass. "That's all I have. Not really worth 100 million, eh?"

Zerov contrived to look disappointed. "Not really, no."

The other man stood. "Oh well. Thanks for the beer and say hi if you ever find her." His instrument was a fiddle of sorts, and he held up the small bow like it was a dagger, waving it in the air. "And you know, goes without saying, but if you hurt her, I'll hunt *you* down and stick this where it hurts."

"First time I've been threatened by a musician," Zerov said truthfully. "Very creative."

"Believe it," Olaf said with mock severity as he walked off.

For the strength of the Pack is the Wolf, and the strength of the Wolf is the Pack. An interesting thought.

In training, his CSS handlers taught him that despite all of the tech and techniques at his disposal, there was no special secret to being a good Hunter. You did what made sense, and then you did the next thing. And it either led you to your target, or it didn't, and you'd have to try something else.

So; the next thing: Ketchican. To try to unscramble a quote from a thousand-year-old author.

Olaf hadn't put through a call or sent a message to Kirsten's parents to warn them he might come calling. Neither had Kirsten's friends at the Gurdwara. A deep scan of their dataspheres showed that. That was interesting, especially from Olaf. Either he had earned a measure of trust from the beardy man, or Olaf was completely confident 'Steven Zhang' would never find Kirsten Nygaard, so there was no harm in him speaking with her parents.

Zerov had decided to cold call the parents. He checked that their location data showed they were both at home, and then drove straight from his hotel to their house inside the Ketchican city dome about mid-morning.

Just because the other Truthers hadn't yet contacted Nygaard's parents — as far as he could tell — didn't mean they wouldn't. So he had to stick with the cover story he was already rolling with. When a woman who looked to be in her early seventies opened the door, Zerov smiled and showed her his ID. "Hi, ma'am, I'm Steven. I'm with the PRC Peace Militia."

On Tatsensui that was the equivalent of saying, "Hello ma'am, pleased to meet you, I'm a terrorist." But the woman didn't even blink. She simply nodded, turned her head so she could speak over her shoulder and said, "Stefan, we have a guest." She held the door open for Zerov, standing aside to let him in. She didn't look happy, but she didn't look hostile either. "Come on in," she said.

Like the spider said to the fly.

Core Melt will be released in 2022.

Printed in Great Britain
by Amazon